PRAISE FOR
Brotherhood of the Mamluks
Book One
Chains of Nobility

"The text abounds with evocative portrayals... Excitingly illuminates an ancient class of warriors."

—*Kirkus Reviews*

"Graft nimbly inserts the reader into the world and mindset of the medieval jihadi. From the Russian steppe to inside the citadel walls, he takes us where Mamluks are made and loyalty between comrades is sealed."

—Steven Pressfield, bestselling author of *The Legend of Bagger Vance*, *The Warrior Ethos*, and *Gates of Fire*

"*Chains of Nobility* is a harrowing tale of comradeship and combat, providing an in-the-saddle look at the process of creating Mamluks—early Islam's military elite. A great piece of work."

—Nathaniel Fick, former Marine officer and *New York Times* bestselling author of *One Bullet Away: The Making of a Marine Officer*

"A gripping saga of brotherhood and devotion, *Chains of Nobility* is a must-read for military history buffs. Author Brad Graft enlightens us on the little-known reason behind Medieval Islam's triumphs during the Middle Ages: nomadic youth enslaved by the descendants of Saladin and sharpened into the spear tip of Muslim armies."

—Michael Franzak
Former Marine pilot and author of *A Nightmare's Prayer*,
winner of the 2012 Colby Award

"In *Chains of Nobility*, Graft displays an exceptional writing style that captures the emotions, and often the harsh environment, in which the action is occurring. An enjoyable read."

— Ron Christmas, Lieutenant General, U.S. Marine Corps
and past President/CEO, Marine Corps Heritage Foundation

"An exacting, dramatic and absorbing look at a world most readers have never encountered, not in books, movies or history class: military slavery in the Middle East in the 13th Century."

—Mardi Link, award-winning author and freelance
writer, *Traverse City Record Eagle*

Book I of the *Brotherhood of the Mamluks* trilogy,
Chains of Nobility, was a finalist for the 2019 Colby Award
for first-time fiction that has made "a major contribution
to the understanding of military history, intelligence
operations, or international affairs."

Chains of Nobility was awarded a silver medal by the Military
Writers Society of America: "The author has created an
intriguing and believable world from ancient ideas, settings and
characters, a masterful job of both history and fiction."

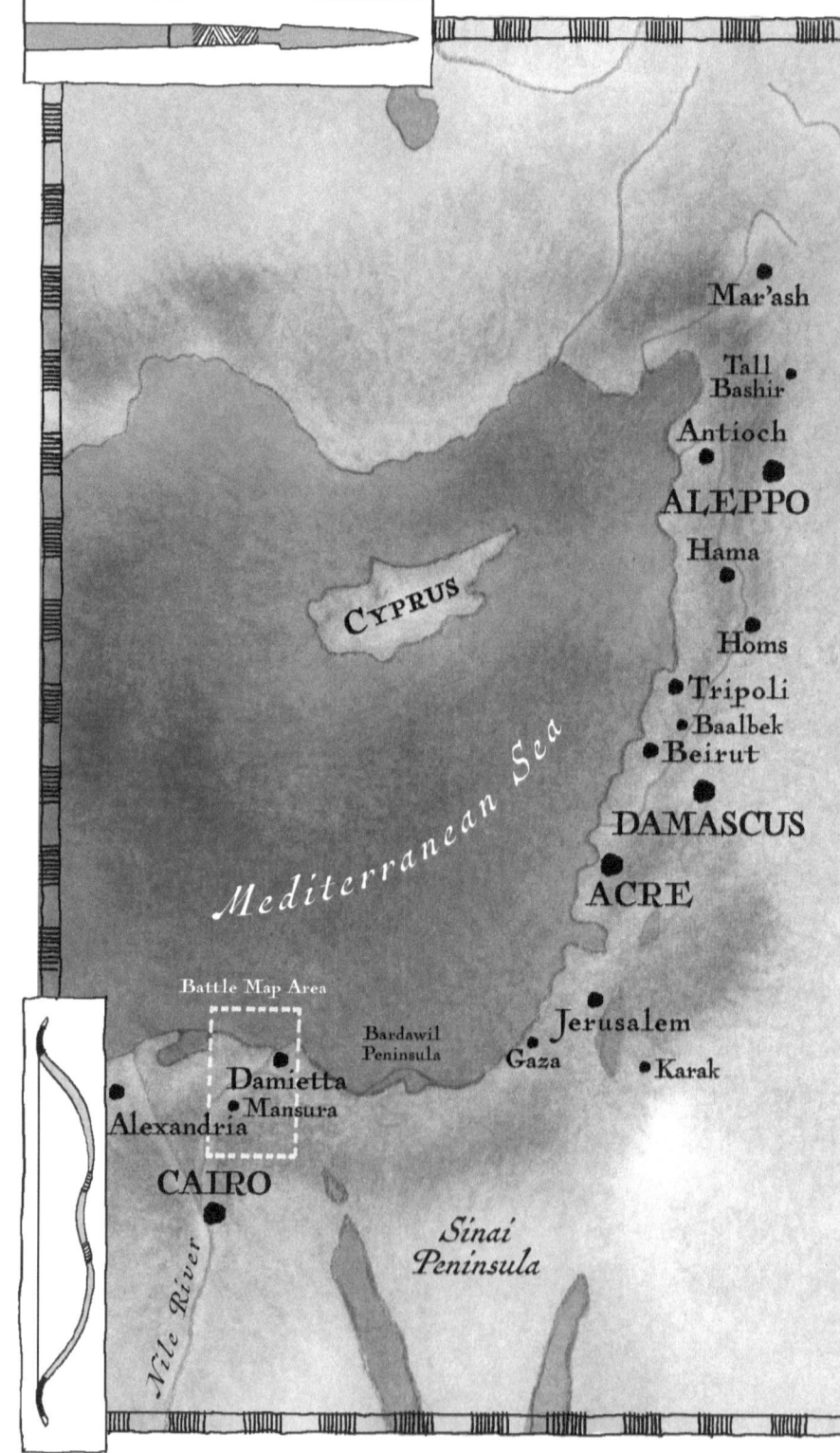

Mar'ash

Tall
Bashir

Antioch

ALEPPO

Hama

Homs

Tripoli

Baalbek

Beirut

DAMASCUS

ACRE

CYPRUS

Mediterranean Sea

Jerusalem

Gaza

Karak

Battle Map Area

Bardawil
Peninsula

Damietta

Mansura

Alexandria

CAIRO

Nile River

Sinai
Peninsula

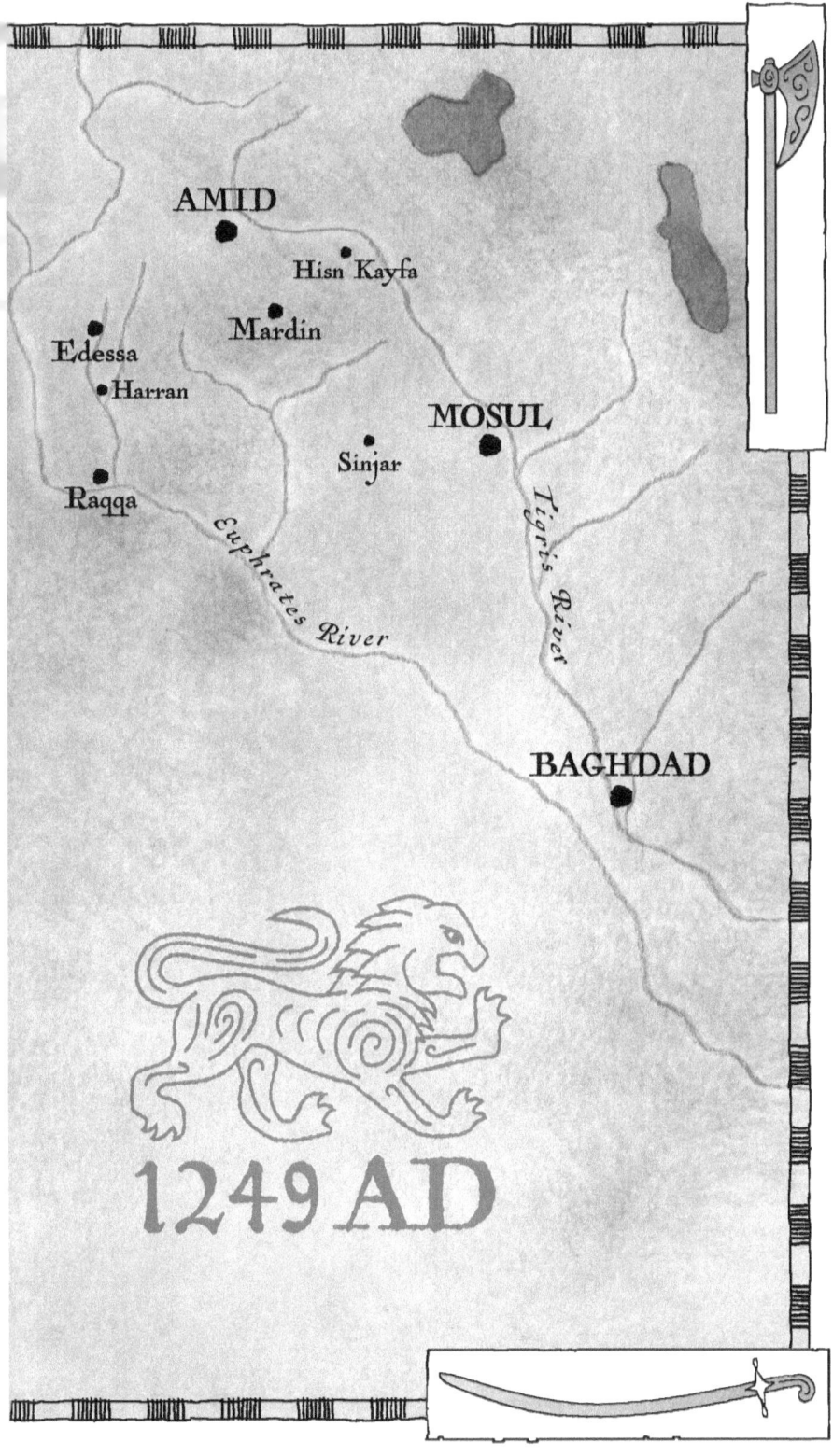

AMID

Hisn Kayfa

Mardin

Edessa

Harran

MOSUL

Sinjar

Raqqa

Euphrates River

Tigris River

BAGHDAD

1249 AD

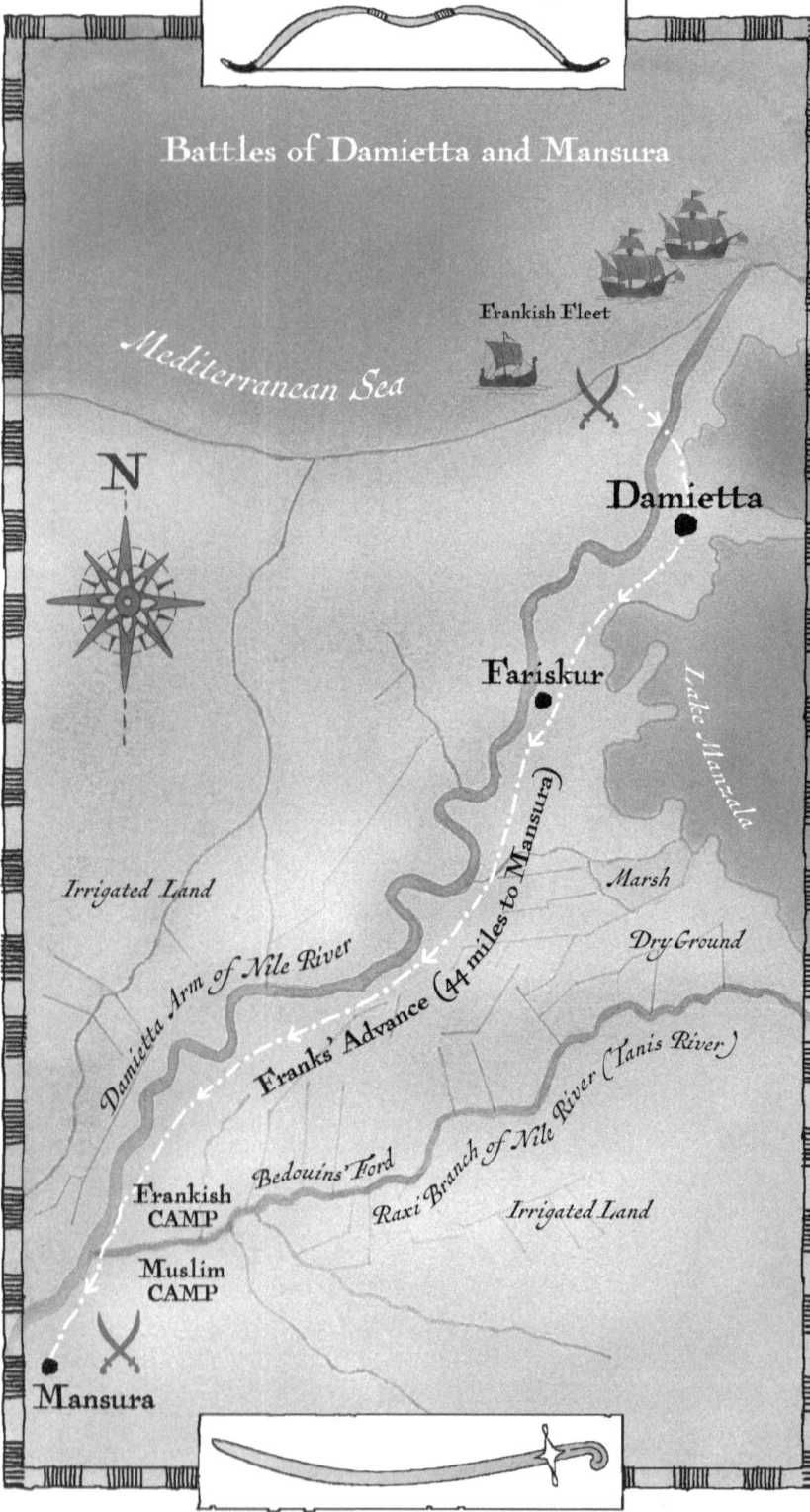

Battles of Damietta and Mansura

BROTHERHOOD OF THE MAMLUKS

BOOK TWO
A LION'S SHARE

A Novel

Cover illustration and design by IP Chernysheva Viktoria Sergeevna
Cover design by Siori Kitajima for SF AppWorks LLC
Maps by Jenifer Thomas of Draw Big Design
Interior Design by Siori Kitajima for SF AppWorks LLC

Cataloging-in-Publication data for this book is available from the Library of Congress.
ISBN-13: 978-1-950154-05-0
ISBN-10: 1-950154-05-X

Published by The Sager Group LLC
www.TheSagerGroup.Net

BROTHERHOOD OF THE MAMLUKS

BOOK TWO
A LION'S SHARE

A Novel

BRAD GRAFT

THE SAGER GROUP

Artifex Te Adiuva

LIST OF CHARACTERS

Mamluks of Amirate Three

- *Leander* (lion): nicknamed "Papa Frank"
- *Duyal* (perceptive person): Amirate Commander
- *Sedat* (just): Amirate Leader
- *Timur* (iron): Leander's squad leader
- *"Slap"*: Leander's friend
- *"Binny,"* nickname for *"Bilgin"* (scholar): Leander's friend

Cenk's Family

- *Cenk* (combat): advisor to Sultan Aybeg, former amir in the *Jamdariyya*, the sultan's personal bodyguard
- *Fidan* (young plant): Cenk's wife
- *Inci* (pearl): Cenk's daughter
- *Turkmani*: Cenk's first patron, an amir killed near Aleppo

Mamluks from Ox's Amirate

- *"Ox,"* nickname for *Balaban* (robust): eventual amir in the *Jamdariyya*
- *Efe* (older brother, brave): Ox's first Amirate Commander, dies at Damietta
- *Isa* (Jesus): Ox's new Amirate Commander
- *Taavi* (adored): Ox's new Amirate Leader

Others of the Bahri

- *Amir Fakhr al-Din*: Mamluk Commander in Chief
- *Aqtay*: Amir of One Hundred, eventual leader of the *Bahri*, governor of Alexandria
- *"Singer,"* nickname for *Halis* (pure, clear, real): Amir Duyal's old friend

Others of the Salihi

- *Aybeg*: Amir of One Hundred turned Sultan of Egypt
- *Qutuz*: advisor to Aybeg turned Vicegerent of Egypt
- *Jacinta* (hyacinth flower): nurse at the infirmary

Ayyubid Royalty

Dates refer to reigns

- *Salah ad-Din*, or *Saladin*: Sultan of Egypt (1169-1193), founder of Ayyubid dynasty
- *al-Kamil*: Sultan of Egypt (1218-1238), nephew of Saladin, father of al-Salih
- *al-Salih*: Sultan of Egypt (1240-1249), son of Sultan al-Kamil
- *al-Adil II*: Sultan of Egypt (1238-1240), son of Sultan al-Kamil, younger brother of al-Salih
- *Turanshah*: Sultan of Egypt (1250), son of al-Salih
- *Shajarat al-Durr*: Sultana of Egypt (1250), wife of the Sultan al-Salih, turned ruler
- al-Malik: six-year-old boy deemed Sultan (1251) by the Bahri, grandson of Sultan al-Kamil
- *al Nasir Yusuf*: Governor of Aleppo (1236-1260) and Damscus (1250-1260), great-grandson of Saladin.
- *al-Mansur Muhammad II*: Governor of Hama (1244-1284), the great-grandson of Saladin's brother, Nur ad-Din Shahanshah

- *al-Mughith Umar*: Governor of Karak/Transjordan (1250–1263), son of Sultan al-Adil II, Sultan of Egypt, nephew of al-Salih
- *al-Salih Ismail*: Governor of Damascus (1237) and (1239-1245), son of Sultan al-Adil I, great-uncle of Sultan al-Salih
- *al-Ashraf Musa*: Prince of Homs (1246-1248), Prince of Tall Bashir (1248-1260), son of Sultan al-Adil I
- *Nursat al-Din:* one of the last living sons of Saladin

French Command
Dates refer to reigns
- *King Louis IX of France*: (1226-1270), leader of Seventh Crusade
- *Lord Erard of Brienne-Ramerupt*: Lord served by Leander's father during Fifth Crusade
- *Lord Erard of Brienne*: Son of Lord Erard of Brienne-Ramerupt, fought in Mansura
- *Lord Henri of Brienne*: Son of Lord Erard of Brienne-Ramerupt, fought in Mansura
- *Walter IV of Brienne*: Count of Jaffa and Ascalon in the Kingdom of Jerusalem (1221-1246), count served by Leander before Battle of La Forbie

Roman Leader
- *Emperor Frederick II*: Holy Roman Emperor, King of Italy (1220-1250)

He held his liege lord so dear That he went with to avenge God's shame, beyond the sea.

—Rutebeuf, French poet

CHAPTER

1

Leander
The hippodrome, al-Rawda Citadel, Cairo, Egypt
June 1, 1249

Riding at a full gallop, a curved sword in either hand, Leander raises the weapons high, appearing as a shimmering metal bird of prey spreading its lethal wings, ready to swoop. He eyes a final pair of arrow shafts anchored in the dirt ahead.

Across the hand-raked grounds about him, the clangs and thuds from dozens of like men plying weapons of their trade echo against the tiered seating of the hippodrome, their giant training arena. Snaps of bowstrings, whiffs and thumps of arrowheads entering straw targets, clanks of steel-on-steel, hollow smacks of sword blades into clay, and the click of bamboo lance shafts all mash into the collective din of proficiency.

Leander adjusts the course of his thundering Arabian with a slight nudge of his right calf, centering himself between the arrows. Leaning down until his chin rests atop his horse's mane, the wavy hair from his beard entwines with that of his beloved mare. Sensing the bottom of her gait, he swings forward vigorously.

The simultaneous ticks of severed wood reverberate through the ivory handle in each hand. The arrow crests flip heavenward, the feathered vanes catching the air, spinning the shafts to gentle landings. Again straight in the saddle, he flips the curved blades across the top of his wrists, twirling them to rest pointing backward.

To his rear, scattered pairs of sheared fletchings lay in his wake at sixteen-pace intervals across the course, evidence of his competence. He grimaces, noticing a single arrow shaft cut higher than required. He returns at a canter to the nine other men in his squad, one of four like units which comprise the Mamluk "amirate."

"Our Papa Frank. I told you the old man's back begins to give. Can't get down on those arrows like he used to," Binny says to his mates, the lanky man failing to hide the educated tone in his speech.

A chorus of deep laughter from the other Mamluks who are fellow slave soldiers and have seen Leander—Papa Frank—run this course to perfection repeatedly for many moons.

Leander shakes his head, tugs his lamellar armor back into place. He pulls down a sleeve from under his mail shirt and runs the strong of his primary blade across the silk, buffing out a smudge before stowing it in his saddle scabbard. He leans to his horse's ear, complimenting his girl, rubbing his cheek against the bristly hair, relishing the smell of horse and straw and the wooden beams of her stall.

His mount is a feisty gray named "Luna," Latin for moon. She is precious to him. Over fourteen hands high, she is one of three animals gifted to him less than a year ago upon graduation— the completion of his initial training—by his patron, the Sultan of Egypt and father figure to his troops, al-Salih Najm al-Din Ayyub. A donkey and baggage camel occupy the other two stalls allotted to him.

Sedat, his Amirate Leader, nudges his horse forward. "Oh, laugh. One shaft cut too high by the sword is no different than an arrow shot out of the target's black—an enemy almost killed," Sedat says, flashing a scowl at Leander.

Leander falls in behind his mates, nodding in agreement to Sedat's remark. He must do better, must remedy his error in his next run through the course.

Slap circles behind him and pats Leander on the back with the flat of his blade. "Good work, brother," his thick-chested friend says in a raspy voice, returning to his signature rocking motion in the saddle, the intensity of the man's swaying typically an indication of his state of mind.

"Our next encounter won't be another 'almost battle' like our trip to Homs—soon there'll be no room for error," Sedat says.

Leander's Amirate Leader is right. Just three moons ago, al-Salih deployed nearly his entire regiment of five hundred men, as the Prince of Aleppo—al-Nasir Yusuf—had seized Homs, one of the sultan's key Syrian possessions. There, Leander's first test in combat against al-Nasir's forces had been cut short. Even though stones from the siege craft—the mangonels dragged in from Damascus—had softened the enemy, the storming of the fortress was called off, as their patron became ill and they concurrently learned of the Franks' intent to assault Egypt.

Making a hasty peace—for the time being—with al-Nasir, al-Salih headed back to Egypt with his full army and began taking measures to protect Egypt from imminent attack by the newly-reinforced crusading King Louis IX of France. The worst of it: by the time they made it back to Cairo, al-Salih's health was so poor that he was being carried in a litter. To the constant worry of his troops, their fatherly sultan's health remains imperiled, his coughing at times uncontrollable. Since they returned home, weapons, foodstuffs, barrels of water, fodder for the horses, and all other things of the army were staged near the beachheads where the Crusaders are anticipated to land.

As always, al-Salih's army trains for war—yet as this campaign looms, the command extends the *Bahri's* sessions in the arena. The Sultan's elite regiment, the *Bahriyya*, is named after the Nile River, *Bahr al-Nil*, but known within the army as the Bahri and renowned by its enemies as the "River Island Regiment."

Surely running through the minds of all is the coming day when the felt guards will be pulled from lance tips and the targets down range will be cross-bearing Franks rather than straw-filled hide.

Binny flips his sword and pokes Slap in the shoulder with the grip. "That 'almost battle' was kinda like the 'almost wife' you almost took last year, eh?"

Snickers from those nearest, some groans.

"Just leave it," Slap growls through an upturned lip.

Binny is rarely able to stop if his banters retrieve even a single chuckle. "Maybe we'll have a chance to get into the baggage train of the Crusaders soon. Maybe we'll find you a new 'almost girlfriend'—a fine infidel to be converted. A soon-to-be widow of the mothering type."

Slap increases the pace and span of his sway, small beads of perspiration surfacing on his brow, an involuntary spasm twitching the raised-fleshed scars crossing his cheeks. "Keep working your jaw and I'll pull your skinny ass from that flea-bitten runt and give you an 'almost broken' nose."

Snickers from several men. Binny comes alongside his friend. "Now, now. Save that aggression for the invaders. Save that fighting spirit for the Franj." He winks at Leander.

The Franj. The Franks. When Leander was first brought into the fortress during his initial training, the prison guards called him "The Frank," since Leander was the only French man those guards had ever seen. Later, the younger troopers transformed the name into "Papa Frank," as he was three to four years older than most of the other novices in his training unit, or *tulb*. Of course, the tag even now designates him as the "grandpa" of the unit. Despite his junior rank, only Duyal, their "Amir of Forty" or *Amir Tablkhana*, and the amir's assistant, Sedat, are senior to Leander's twenty-one years of age.

But he figures as his years in the citadel passed, less and less meaning was attached to the second word in his nickname. He doubts if many in the amirate even see him as a Frank anymore. But he is indeed from France. There, he was given his profession of mounted crossbowman and his name, Leander—meaning "lion" to those people.

His trade he came by honestly, as his father, too, carried the crossbow, serving Lord Erard of Brienne-Ramerupt some thirty years past. Both he and his father were born of modest means, raised in the same tiny cottage in northern France. There was never a question that Leander was to become a soldier, it was just what form of soldier he would be.

Certainly, Leander no longer considers himself a Frank. Early in his training, he thought the Mamluks would assign him the Turkish version of his name, "Aslan," as was customary—yet they never did. Regardless, he no longer sees much nobility in the Frenchmen's code of chivalry, no longer embraces their religion. He is thankful to be more than just a crossbowman, more than a warrior. He is a Muslim, a Mamluk, serving in the Bahri.

His path to this calling could not be called typical. In fact, he knows of only one other former Crusader in the ranks of al-Salih's two elite regiments of Mamluks; there may be only a half dozen Franks in the entire Egyptian army. Nearly all of al-Salih's Mamluks are of Kipchak descent, taken as adolescents from the vast steppe north and east of the Black Sea, traded on the slave block and trained for several years in the *tibaq*—the sultan's barrack schools—to be masters of the bow, lance and sword.

Leander, too, shared in this training, this screening of recruits—the sole Frank, older and strange amid the Kipchak lads in his training unit. A young man among boys. For the first few days, none of the Kipchaks spoke to him, just stared at him in silent wonder. Yet during those early weeks at the tibaq, Leander willingly converted to Islam with his fellow *Muta'allim*,

Mamluk novices under training. And for four years more in the west side of this great stone house, he earned the title of Bahri beside them.

Within these very stone walls, their instructors revealed the basic skills of the *Furusiyya*, or the Mamluks' cavalry principles. As there are six Pillars of Islam, there are also six skills of the faris: mounting the horse, employing the lance, use of the sword, holding the shield, shooting the bow, and the game of polo.

None of it came easy to him. On horseback and especially in the skills required with the recurved bow, Leander would have been considered superior among the Franj, yet he was close to the weakest among the Kipchaks. And this was understandable. For his fellow novices, these competencies seemed innate to the boys of the steppe. A nomad's life depended on his ability to track and kill enemy and game, especially the predators that tirelessly trailed and ambushed their herds of sheep and goats. Though wielding the sword had been new to the enslaved Kipchaks, shooting the bow was second nature to them, their archery skills developed concurrently with learning to walk.

But despite this huge Kipchak advantage, Leander realized quickly that he still had an edge over most of them. Long before his younger mates, Leander recognized one important thing: how very fortunate he was to be in this place. They were all blessed to be enduring the difficult training, the screaming and harsh beatings from their *Mu'allim*, or Furusiyya instructor.

Almost straightaway, Leander knew he had found a home. Conversely, many of the young Kipchaks experienced a painful adjustment to their new lives, their biological families having been slain or at best, left behind.

They lived now without the comfort of their pagan Gods and their nomadic existence in movable and felt-swathed shelters, surrounded by the endless rolling hills of grass and high mountains cleaved by clear-flowing rivers. In its place, they faced a new life in a dusty city, their new residence a gigantic stone house set in a stark desertscape.

Along with Leander's immediate gratitude for being one of al-Salih's military slaves came a natural, unconquerable endurance for pain and abuse—one soon and easily mirrored by his fellow novices, as nearly all Kipchaks were accustomed to the miseries of hunger, cold, and pain on their steppe homelands. Miseries... the tibaq... Leander grins.

Sedat moves his horse closer to the pair of young slaves— *ghilman*—scrambling across the groomed surface, his presence quickening their pace. One yanks spent arrows from the bamboo tubes dug into the dirt floor, replacing them with fresh shafts from a packed pouch that hangs down to his ankles. The other boy zigzags, gathering the scraps of fletching from the ground.

Before the pair can finish, Sedat squares his broad shoulders to the squad. "Let's go. Next rider."

CHAPTER

2

Leander
The hippodrome, al-Rawda Citadel, Cairo, Egypt
June 2, 1249

Leander cradles the bamboo shaft of his weapon in his armpit, absently waiting his turn among the ten Mamluks in his squad. He takes a deep breath and grins, the air thick with the flavor of the River Nile.

The morning sun warms the cream-colored blocks of the arena, accentuating the moist patches in the dark clay floor. Across the hippodrome, three other squads from their unit of forty are assembled in pairs, executing drills that make up the *Bunud*, or lance exercises of the Furusiyya, their war manual.

These forty of al-Salih's best sit atop Arabians, many colored in chestnut—some splotched in white—and others on grays and muted roans. These Mamluks wear the lighter summer uniform of the Bahri, long coats of brilliant white wool, covering their heavy chain mail hauberks. Atop each of their coats lies a *jawshan*—the new iron lamellar cuirass appearing as overlapping fish scales made of tortoise shell. Their trousers are unique to the

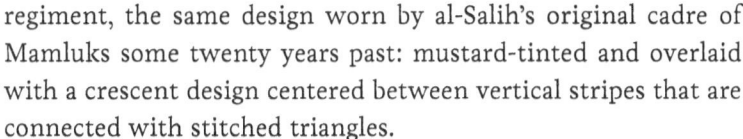

regiment, the same design worn by al-Salih's original cadre of Mamluks some twenty years past: mustard-tinted and overlaid with a crescent design centered between vertical stripes that are connected with stitched triangles.

A warmth fills his chest. He loves this place, loves al-Salih, the man who equipped them, the man who built this new citadel for them. By Allah—long live the sultan. Leander feels he must reciprocate the honor shown by his patron; he must conduct himself more competently in the coming battle than he had in the exercises yesterday. He must continue to measure up to the uniform he wears, the title he carries.

As a sign of his devotion to the Bahriyya, al-Salih built not only this arena, but also the quarters for this hand-selected outfit and his adjacent, elaborate palace. Located on the island of al-Rawda, the barracks allow the Bahri to reside purposely separate from the Fortress of the Mountain. That giant citadel was constructed by Saladin some sixty years past, where the remainder of the sultan's Mamluks, the *Salihiyya*—or *Salihi*—and several other units dwell.

On first glance from the muddy, blue river, the fortress at Rawda Island might resemble an elegant retreat opposite the shoreline of Cairo. Adjacent to the Royal Mamluks' billeting, stone-columned *manzirs*, or arched belvederes, face the river with numerous porches. In the cooler evenings, white-coated men take dinner in the open air on yellow-clothed tables or lean on the carved-stone railings in conversation, overlooking the lazy flow of the wide river. Yet the steep-faced towers at the structure's corners, manned with helmeted archers, plainly signal that this place is more than a sanctuary of the privileged.

On a tactical level, al-Salih's preoccupation to segregate the Bahri on one of the largest islands on the Nile seems to cloud the sultan's good sense. While in theory, the river could protect the Island Citadel and isolate the regiment, the landmass is actually too low for adequate defense and several bridges add to its vulnerability. Yet no Mamluk inside the walls cares. Let any attacker try to wrest this citadel, their patron's gift, from the Bahri.

For Leander, the island fortress is more than a reward, more than al-Salih's symbolic offering to his most talented; the structure and location characterize the sultan. When al-Salih was just a prince, far north in the Jazira, ruling the towns of Amid and Hisn Kayfa, he was already paranoid, sequestering his Mamluks in that hilltop bastion, away from the evils and scheming of the local population.

Here in Cairo, al-Salih takes his obsession a step further, using the broad river and its strong current as yet another obstacle to keep even his regular army and regiment of *Salihi*— nine thousand strong—from spoiling the loyalty and hardiness of his most valuable five hundred Royal Mamluks. With a deep-rooted suspicion—almost an alienation from his relatives ruling in the adjacent provinces of the empire—al-Salih feels safe here, detached from the cunning Ayyubid princes.

But the sultan's distrust is not some personality flaw, some mental defect. Leander sees his master's action as logical, a condition born of experience. For many years, al-Salih was too often double-crossed by his uncle, brothers, and cousins—too many times left on a far-off battlefield by his regular army with only his slave soldiers by his side.

As a result, the sultan purchased more Mamluks than any previous Ayyubid ruler and was adamant that these Kipchaks be the core of his Egyptian Army. To the astonishment of his kin, he did the inconceivable with those in the Bahri, assigning the most capable among them key positions in the state and surrounding himself and his family with these fine men.

Movement catches Leander's eye in the arena's seating. Amir Duyal, the amirate's commander, salutes his senior, Amir Aqtay. Before the pair depart, Aqtay grabs Duyal by the elbow, the men share parting words and a nod of mutual respect. Duyal again salutes Aqtay and proceeds down the steep stairs, tapping each step in a thoughtless dexterity, his armor unmoving upon his body.

Leander grins, as he often does upon seeing his idol. While Duyal's grade of Amir Tablkhana entitles him to have drums, timbals, trumpets, and flutes played in front of his house every evening after prayer as well as prior to battle, he detests the privilege. The man is void of anything smacking of glimmer and ambition. Only through skill and reputation has Duyal risen to Amir of Forty, the second-highest tactical grade allowed by al-Salih.

Duyal moves sideways through an open gate without altering his pace. Now out into the arena, he strides purposefully across the raked dirt with head down. One hundred paces away, Leander can make out Duyal's scrunched brow, his pursed lips. Leander already knows the gist of what his mentor will utter. Sedat does, too, whistling twice. The other three squads stop their exercises, turn their horses and give heels.

By the time Duyal reaches Sedat, his amirate has formed a semi-circle to greet him. Leander enters a crease, where the smell of polished leather and seasoned wool and the ripeness of sweating men diffuses. Duyal steps into the center of them and looks up for the first time. A horse snorts. Two others paw the ground.

"As expected, the Franj come. The sultan's emissary unit has verified that in only days the Crusaders will leave Cyprus for Alexandria," Duyal says.

Leander feels an unexpected pang in his stomach. For his mates, the coming enemy will be nameless, faceless foes—infidels to be exterminated. At a level incomprehensible to most present, he understands fully the many reasons why the Franks come: ambition, riches, land, promotion, obligation to their God and pressure from kin and lords alike.

Unlike the Muslim army met at Homs, which he did not know, Leander understands the approaching French opponent too well. He is certain that he will even know some of the enemy leaders and troops by name.

About seven years past, he had even traveled the same route that many of these Crusaders had taken to Auxonne, where the foot journey ended and their boat voyage to the holy land began. Memories of his old homeland, of that first leg in his journey to the Levant, fill his head.

Leander left the road and sat upon a large rock, setting his hat beside him. He put his foot across his knee and dug his fingernails into the raw pad, pulling out a thorn long set.

Down the road he had come, more of those like him followed, dressed in "Pilgrim's weeds" identical to his own, their gray robes signed with the cross, topped with round felted hats, bearing staffs and scripts. They were a scattered file of ragged sheep, easily persuaded, loosely tethered by their hatred for the Saracens and the infidels' occupation of the Holy Land and firmly bound by their common intent to avenge their Lord Jesus Christ. Shaggy pilgrims of slaughter.

Leander recognized some of their faces under heavy woolen hoods, knew their gaits: lords of vast lands next to squires, mounted sergeants abreast of infantry crossbowmen, counts walking beside the unfree serf knights who had pledged their titles and bits of property in return for silver to cover the cost of going on Crusade.

Franj whose rich fathers paid their ways walked next to bannerets who were leaders of knights, privileged men with access to the holy money, and somehow connected with the heads of the Church. A temporary solidarity existed between them all. Their egos and bold personal agendas were set aside during this walk for their God.

A young girl's voice peeped behind him. Pale blue eyes and soft blond hair. He smiled at the petite thing and rested his elbows on his knees to make himself smaller for her, more approachable.

"Please for you. God bless, God bless," she said, with a dripping ladle extended from her little bucket of water. She turned back to her mother, the elder beaming, surely tickled that her daughter was doing her part to aid the effort of these Crusaders—men, who as Lord Erard had said, "heighten the merit and efficacy of their good deed by taking this long walk unsupported."

In that pilgrimage before his insertion into the Holy Land, Leander left his home in Ramerupt and walked ten days, stopping only to pray in candle-lit churches and visit the religious relics in Saint Urbans and Blechicourt. Along the way, lines of villagers occasionally cheered them. Farm hands, bony men who dropped their tools to walk over and nod their respect to Leander and the other barefooted soldiers as they trod the dusty path. Old women with bits of their family dinners heaped into their head cloths, who thrust the goods into the Frenchmen's hands, saying, "Dieu soit avec vous" ("God be with you").

When the Crusaders neared Auxonne, the road became full of them, men filtering in from the east and west, swelling the holy flock, pushing south, pushing south. On the tenth day, Leander caught up with his horse and baggage in the city, and the Crusaders all boarded boats on the River Saone, floating down from Auxonne to Lyons, where they met more warriors. There, they were loaded on to larger boats which took them down the Rhone's big water, all the way to the northern shore of the Mediterranean, where the tall ships were docked at Marseilles. Without looking back, he embarked at the Rock of Marseilles.

By the time the fleet reached Cyprus, half the men on his ship were seasick, most never having been on the open water. How glad they were to see the white outline of Kyrenia Castle on the north shore of the island. Cyprus. The last stepping stone to the Levant.

Leander feels eyes upon him from within the hasty formation of Mamluks. He looks up.

Sedat studies Leander with squinted eyes. It is as if the Amirate Leader can read his face, read his mind, can see the cross that he once palmed and the shoeless pilgrim and Christian that he used to be.

Duyal digs his thumbs under the thick shoulder straps of his iron-scaled cuirass and continues to address them all, his eyes riveted on the closest about him. "After our meal, you'll grab your kit and wait with our other gear. We've orders to head for Alexandria in the cool of evening with the lead element. Those living in town, go now to your wives and families. Let them know we'll leave before sundown. Tell them you'll make them proud, Amirate Three serving Allah and our Sultan. Tell them we go to push the infidels back into the sea."

"Err!" the men blurt.

"Carry on," Duyal orders.

Sedat approaches Leander. "Soon the former Crusader will be tested—forced to clash with his own kind." He raises his bushy eyebrows and slightly nods his head.

Leander looks at him blankly, a year-old, overheard argument between Sedat and Amir Duyal from the day Leander first joined the unit now ringing in his ears.

> "If the Frank is so valuable, then why has he not been pulled directly into the service of the sultan? Surely such a well-read man, a man knowing so many languages, would fit well into the staff of the Grand Chamberlin, or even with some of the other Men of the Pen?" Sedat shrugged.
>
> "Last moon we were begging for men to fill our shortfalls. Now you suddenly become picky? He's plenty skilled. You watched him in the tibaq," Duyal countered.
>
> "Truly, my amir. Such a fine gift shouldn't be wasted on our meager amirate." Sedat set his jaw. "What a shame to have him beside us simple men tasked with slinging arrows and hacking flesh."

Binny and Slap move up on either side of Leander, pulling him away from his recollection. Sedat grins, taking a last look over his shoulder at the Frank before riding away.

"Tsst." Slap puts a hand on Leander's shoulder, shakes his head. "Don't listen to him. We're the ones you'll be fighting beside in Alexandria, and you don't see us stewing about the Papa Frank and any shortage of fire burning in his belly."

Binny nods. "Yeah, what does Sedat know? He was never forced to spar against you during those years in the tibaq." He chuckles. "We were. A Frankish tornado of spit and steel. I almost feel sorry for old King Louis and his merry band of raiders."

Slap grins.

Leander looks down. He appreciates the support but knows full well that if not for his previous skills on lance and sword—abilities drilled into him as a boy in Lord Erard's castle back in France—the Mamluk command might well have ousted him during his early years in the citadel.

Leander figures that it was not really his seniority in years or the fact that he had already been a French soldier that had gained him both admission to the Mamluk brotherhood and the respect of his peers. Nor were his incumbent skills with bladed weapons what preserved his status until graduation.

He reckons that during those years in the tibaq, both his fellow novices and the instructors saw in him an inextinguishable blaze, an aptitude to brawl that never waned. In Leander's heart was the brashness and scrap of his namesake, the lion. With no real vanity attached, he is simply grateful for being blessed with the single trait of fortitude, the possession of which seemed to make his other technical deficiencies more bearable to the command.

Perhaps it is little wonder that the terms "grit" and "resilience" were repeatedly used by his peers to describe him when peer evaluations, or "spears" as the novices called them, were released. His father had never pampered him; his mother and sister had not been around long enough to soften him. As a youngster, he was often left alone, hunting, fishing, and exploring the hills from dawn till dusk. Even his French instructors, years ago in Ramerupt, had given him little quarter.

The fight. He had been born with the mentality to embrace it. His father and his before were warriors, nothing more. Leander never doubted that he was placed on this earth to clash. Slashing steel and strikes of wood and metal against his body and helmet in no way deterred him and seemed to only further stoke this inferno of martial energy in his core.

He loved to spar. Even when losing, whether in France or here in Egypt, he pulled himself up off the dusty ground and praised his victorious opponent after the match, often hugging him—so happy he was to see the other lad's progression, so content to be among such capable fighters. His was not some false motivation. His Kipchak mates were at first dumbfounded by his response but eventually embraced his sincerity.

His instructors' angry, belittling words—those, too, shed from him like rain from an oiled skin. He accepted his instructors' crude punishments and whippings silently, willingly. These were often deserved and only made him stronger, he believed. He simply refused to quit and forbade himself from being defeated mentally. In time, so did those who remained of his fellow novices, their tulb of over eighty teenagers, whittled down to thirty-nine at graduation four years later, many of them with him now in Duyal's amirate.

Leander smiles. "Well, my brothers. How about a feed? Sounds like we have a long ride ahead of us tonight."

CHAPTER

3

Leander
Damietta, Egypt
June 5, 1249

Leander crests the dune. "Look, there," he says, pointing at the six tips of sail, barely visible, breaching the Mediterranean's skyline.

"By Allah," Slap says, dropping the cask in his hands with a thump upon the sand. "Only our luck would have the invaders landing here," he says with a sigh.

Leander nods and looks back to the road behind him. Hundreds of the sultan's men unload carts and stage supplies hastily brought up from the towns of Damietta and Alexandria. "We best alert Amir Duyal that we've spotted the French ships."

Slap grimaces. "I'll go." He steps off to find their leader.

Leander closes his eyes and puts his nose to the wind, taking in the briny scent of the surf. Yesterday, fierce gales tossed most of the king's two-hundred ships up and down the eastern coast of the Mediterranean, scattering them. Last night they drifted in a soft breeze, out of formation, barely organized. Only now do some of the vessels rejoin the king's formation.

All aboard the Franj ships must have seen yesterday's winds as a bad sign. To the Mamluks ashore, the tempest was the blessed breath of Allah, God signaling that providence is against the Franks and their invasion. Allah blew the enemy ships askew, seeking to preserve Egypt and uphold Islam.

Leander imagines what must have taken place on the deck of the command ship earlier today. The French King, Louis IX, had likely gathered his leaders about him to confer. Most of their fleet had been strewn up and down the coast and would take days to regroup.

Leander pictures how the counts and lords likely argued—Crusaders' egos, conflicting goals, and selfish aims all surfacing. Surely aboard the King's ship was the infighting and indecisiveness that Leander's father had recalled from the Fifth Crusade—that which caused King John of Brienne at one point to relinquish his role as overall commander and return to Palestine. King Louis would have hidden his frustration and been forced to act in order to appear decisive to his barons and what Crusaders called the "heathen enemy" waiting onshore.

Al-Salih knew the Franks were coming, knew they had arrived in Cyprus this past September, and so had placed his spies among them. Through his light-skinned emissaries in influential places, the sultan knew about the quarrels between the French lords. He knew about the squabbling between the Genoese, Venetians, and Pisans over who would provide additional transport and at what price, and over who would build the smaller vessels—the "lighters"—for landing and river travel.

For eight moons, the French King had collected ships and outfitted them for war with supplies, wine and food. Everything was overpriced, as gold often had a way of outweighing the religious convictions of Christian merchants and shipmen.

Patiently observing the delays and turmoil on Cyprus, al-Salih's skilled infiltrators had sent word when the Franj departed and were sure the aggressors would soon land west in Alexandria. In response, the still-bedridden al-Salih sent the bulk of his forces there to meet them. Only the storm and not any calculated brilliance by the Franks, now put the Crusaders in a position to land on this less-defended beach.

Leander sets his eyes farther across the teal blue water of the Mediterranean. His face hardens, taking in the surreal view of more ships appearing closer now on the horizon. Dozens bobbing in the surf, all bearing upon their highest masts the blue background and abundant gold lilies—the fleur-de-lis—symbolizing the Kingdom of France. France, his previous homeland. He had not seen the place in nearly seven years. It may as well be seventy. His former existence as a Crusader seems like another lifetime ago. So much has happened since then. The rolling green hills of the north country feel so far away from where he stands now, on the beach of Damietta, only a two-and-a-half day ride north of mother Cairo.

Soon hundreds of men on those ships, holy warriors from the land of his birth, will attempt to put ashore. "Chivalrous men" answering the call to crusade from Pope Innocent IV, to replenish manpower at the coastal fortifications, to "take up the cross" and reclaim territorial losses in the Holy Land. The Franj seek to avenge the grave defeat they suffered, the devastating losses experienced during that vicious battle now called "Harbiyya" by the Muslims, "La Forbie" by the Franks.

La Forbie. October 17, 1244. A twinge runs down his spine. That was the place, just northeast of Gaza, where Leander ceased being a Frenchman.

Staring into the distant cobalt, the depths haze over into images of that October day five years ago, those memories rolling back into his mind like swells from a distant sea. That crisp fall afternoon at La Forbie, when he walked away from France and from every item and idea of the place, save his crossbows and the name Leander. That day will forever be the defining one in his life, a rebirth of sorts. He was but sixteen years old and serving as a translator in the service of Walter IV of Brienne,

Count of Jaffa and Ascalon, in the Kingdom of Jerusalem. Just two months before the battle, Jerusalem had been captured from the Franks by al-Salih's allies, the Khwarezmians and the Kurdish *Qaymariyya*. Rootless and driven always by their quest for booty, the Khwarezmians killed hundreds and ravaged the Holy City, destroying religious relics and filling their saddlebags with plunder. Muslims and Christians alike mourned.

The sacking of Jerusalem so troubled the Ayyubid princes of Homs, Karak and Damascus that the three allied themselves with the Franks—those Crusaders of Walter's in Jerusalem, plus the Templars, Hospitallers, Teutonic Knights, and the Order of St. Lazarus. Their opposition: the forces of the Egyptian Sultanate and the allied Khwarezmians, the latter's willingness to assist the sultan being in direct proportion to the quantity of additional spoils they anticipated. The two large armies assembled. The stage for a major battle had been set.

The battle, the outcome, all of it—fate. If not for his interest with cultures other than his own and his natural ability to quickly pick up the languages of most in the Levant, he wonders where he would be at this moment. Probably six feet under.

During his first two years on the Mediterranean coast, he had spent much time speaking with his fellow French and with the English he met, and also with the Arab merchants, Bedu herdsmen and Turkish vendors. The Egyptian farmers, the peasants, the women at the river. He was enchanted by their languages and lives. He chatted with them all, absorbing the prominent strain of their Coptic vocabulary, one conversation at a time.

It was from these contacts with the "enemy," these varied interactions with the "infidel," that he grasped not only the nouns and verbs of their languages, but also the values and souls of the Muslim people. When he greeted the locals in their own tongue, he felt a tepid acceptance. Secretly, he found himself gradually drawn to the people of most regions he traveled through, looking forward to his conversations with them.

Muslim children, realizing he knew their words, surrounded him, bombarding him with questions, joking, harassing him for sweets and dried fruit, asking permission to touch the blade in his scabbard. Some invited him to their homes to share a meal. Leander gracefully declining, knowing that most of the families could not afford another mouth to feed.

Because of his rare competency in Arabic, Coptic Egyptian, French, English, Turkish—and even a few Kurdish strains— Leander was often pulled from his combat unit to facilitate trade with the Muslim merchants and work deals with allies and enemies both. And while he enjoyed the company of the locals, by 1244 he had also developed a great respect for all of al-Salih's Royal Mamluks, the Salihiyya—their skills upon horseback with lance, bow and sword unrivaled in the Levant, their loyalty to the sultan, al-Salih, unwavering.

Once, on a translation mission for his former lord, he had been allowed into the hippodrome at the Cairo Citadel—the Fortress of the Mountain. There he watched a demonstration of the Salihi's skills. His head spun. Men stood atop their narrow saddles, galloping their horses in synchronized columns, passing only inches from each other in opposite directions. They twirled a sword in each hand, spun flaming lances in unison, flipped arrows from finger to bow, and shot upon horseback at a speed and accuracy that sent shivers down his spine. After the presentation, he spoke with some of the troopers, appreciated their candor.

Like an awestruck child, he marveled at these abilities and admired the fair-skinned men atop their splendid Arabians. These Mamluks. As if it were the forbidden apple, he began to yearn for what he could not have, what he could not be.

Being one of only a handful of Franks who knew the varied tongues of the Muslim enemy, on October 14, 1244—a few days before La Forbie—he was asked by the Frankish command to help facilitate a tactical plan between the Crusaders and their Muslim prince allies. Once again, Leander, the simple mounted crossbowman, the unlikely attendee of such an important gathering, was put into a room filled with counts, princes, and Muslim amirs, due to his linguistic capacity, the Franks' distrust of the local translators, and the fact that he and Walter shared the same hometown.

The meeting was held in a simple house outside Gaza. As the pre-battle plan was formulated, he witnessed what was all too familiar—each group of Crusaders argued over not only the plan but endless petty concerns, such as whose pennant should be located where and who earned the honor of being the first to enter the Holy City, once they retook Jerusalem. He translated when his skill was needed, then retreated to the farthest corner of the house to brood about human vanity.

The only level head in the room that day was the Muslim prince of Homs, al Mansur. He calmly discouraged an attack, encouraging the allies to take the defensive and wait. "The Khwarezmians are greedy. They've little discipline, no patience. Let them sit idle long enough and they'll depart Jerusalem and leave al-Salih's forces undermanned," al-Mansur had said. Walter, the overall commander of the Franks, dismissed this sound advice. He thought his allied forces of nearly twelve thousand were advantage enough and ordered an immediate attack.

On October 17th, Leander and two other translators were sent to the gates of La Forbie to demand that the enemy surrender, a gesture considered gracious by the Crusaders and aimed at preventing needless shedding of Muslim blood. In the Mamluks' eyes, Leander saw a steely resolve to defend their homeland, and respected the unwavering unity in their response. Then something snapped inside him.

He recalls that unexpected but determined voice inside telling him the time had come.

> "The allied forces of Walter IV, Count of Brienne, demand your immediate surrender," the Hospitaller at his side had said in broken Turkish, standing arrogantly with foot forward, palm on the hilt of his sword.

The Mamluk commander looked this Franj translator slowly up and down and responded sternly, "Words will not win you victory this day. If you want our lives, if you want the holy places, you'll have to take them from us."

Leander smiled. With no contemplation, he took two steps back and chucked his broadsword back toward the Crusader line. End over end the blade spun, like a wounded goose hit midflight, twirling to its inevitable death. He took the dagger from his belt and stuck it deep into the soil. He faced the Mamluk amir and spoke fluently in their Turkish dialect, "I wish to join the ranks of the Salihiyya, I wish to enroll with the Bahri." He ducked under the strap that secured the bag on his back, surrendering both crossbows inside it to the Mamluk in charge.

Holding the bag in bewilderment, the amir looked him in the eye. Then he turned to the fellow Royal Mamluk beside him and laughed. This young Crusader must be jesting, or crazy. His chuckling did not end once he realized that Leander was serious. The Mamluk commander shrewdly eyed the pair of beleaguered translators accompanying Leander and awaited their response to this most unexpected development.

The Hospitaller turned to Leander and erupted. "Traitor! You'll spurn our God, insult your motherland and family. You'll burn in hell!" He spat in Leander's face. "I'd kill you now if not for the disturbance it would cause, if not for our duty at hand."

Three Mamluk guards approached their new detainee, one eyeing the plump count. The count appeared visibly worried, likely for his own well-being. He snarled at Leander and then said to the Mamluks, "You'll get no resistance from me. Take him. He's obviously no use to us."

Leander wiped the spittle from his face, not humiliated by it, but rather refreshed—a reverse baptism, a freeing of the fanatical bonds of these Crusaders' version of Christianity.

Thinking him mad or a spy or both, the Mamluks quickly whisked Leander to the rear. Days later in the citadel dungeon,

Leander learned of the Egyptian victory, of the nearly five thousand dead Crusaders, of the annihilation of the Frank's Muslim allies, of Lord Walter's capture. At the Battle of La Forbie, the Franks suffered their worst defeat since Saladin decimated the Crusaders in 1187 at the Horns of Hattin. While not Leander's intent, surrendering before that battle had surely spared his life.

Shortly afterward, thick-armed guards took him up a flight of winding stairs to a room with bloodstained floors. He was pushed down upon a three-legged stool and made to face a throng of iron-faced amirs. One by one, they interrogated him, each seeming to probe not only his mind but his heart, as well. The last interview was with the sultan himself.

Al-Salih inched forward in his chair, his eyes narrowing. "How is it you could possibly forsake your own God and your fellow soldiers, and instead wish to serve me and the book of Islam?"

He had anticipated the question. Leander nodded and looked directly into al-Salih's dark eyes. "Perhaps the Sultan will find this sad, or maybe unbelievable, but in my few years of dealings with your people and your forces, I've found that I have a greater respect, a deeper fondness, and even more in common with those who my people call the enemy, than with my own people. I'm not sure Jesus himself would've blessed the Frankish invasions. I wish to join a united force that only craves to defend its own lands and the holy places, not conquer them. I feel suited to serve with your most elite."

The sultan scowled. "Did you know Lord Walter was somehow disadvantaged, that he was destined to lose the battle at Harbiyya? Did you desert just to save your own hide?"

Leander shook his head. "I knew nothing more than their hasty plans. I had no idea whether the Franj would win or lose that day."

Al-Salih stared at him for a long while, possibly hoping to detect a lie, or sort out an inconsistency in Leander's story, differing from that told his amirs earlier. "Christian turned Jihadi. Crusader gone Bahri. It just doesn't happen," Al-Salih said, leaning back and placing his hands peacefully across his lap. "Even if I were to bring you into my army, why would I allow your admission into the Bahri—my very finest—when I have proven Mamluks in the sister regiment—the Salihi—men who would slit throats to gain a post in the River Island Regiment?"

Al-Salih looked over to his white-coated guard, yet the burly man only shifted his long ax into the other hand and continued glaring at the renegade, Leander.

"I've seen the Salihi in action and can attest to their superior skill level with all weapons," Leander said. "But nearly all of these men, plus those in the Bahri, speak only Turkish. I speak many languages, that of your enemies and allies. Being a capable fighter with this expertise—plus having an intimate understanding of your Frankish enemy—I would be a unique resource for the sultan's best regiment."

Al-Salih smiled for a moment and then shook his head. "But your brothers-in-arms. How could you turn on your own kind?"

Leander nodded. "Sultan. I understand your hesitancy. If I were you, I'd be suspicious of me, too. But I no longer feel like they're my 'own kind.' I'm not a spy. I'm not interested in betraying my people. I'm interested in embracing yours. I've seen too many Frankish units come to the Holy Land with their only intention being to slay Muslims wherever they find them, innocent or not, and acquire riches. Your men's mission is to shield a long-standing empire. I admire the harmony within your forces, the select nature of the Bahri, the steadfast devotion shown to you by all of your Royal Mamluks. I can't help if the Bahri feel like the right fit for me."

The sultan sighed. He looked Leander up and down, his eyes staying on the yellow-lioned heraldry of the Brienne's upon his chest. "You say that you feel Jesus would not have blessed the Franks' invasions. So you do not reject your God, you merely despise the leaders of your religion. That does not sound to me like a man who wishes to embrace Allah. As you know, one must become a Muslim before becoming a Mamluk."

Leander licked his dry lips. "I have no trouble with either God. Seems to me it's not God, but the 'men of God' who too often *make a mess of things."*

The sultan looked at him sideways, then scoffed.

"*The heads of Christianity chose the holy sites as the objectives of their many campaigns, but from my eyes, only used these aims to justify invading another's homeland and snatching the most fertile of this ground for the enrichment of their barons. This has not felt so holy to me.*" Leander said, meeting the sultan's eyes. "*I, too, have Muslim friends who have lost land, and sisters and fathers to the Franj.*"

Al-Salih seemed to soften.

"*Respectfully, Sultan, this may not be the response you desire, but ultimately, I will not lay my life down for either God. Yours or mine. But I would sacrifice it in pursuit of a just cause and for warriors about me who deserve such.*"

Leander leaned toward the sultan. "*And this may sound as shameless flattery, jabbered to save my own life, but I know that when a Mamluk finishes his initiation at the tibaq, then he's manumitted, freed to leave if he wishes. Yet nearly all of your Mamluks remain in your citadels, gladly serving you. And when you assign senior amirs a promotion in cities far from Cairo—even good stations like Homs, or Damascus, or Aleppo—your amirs are known to grow depressed, feeling an assignment away from you akin to banishment. They adore you like a father. Men such as I have met in the Bahri and Salihi would only respond this way for an honorable man, a fine leader.*" Leander nods slowly. "*I wish to serve you, too.*"

Al-Salih appeared unmoved by the adulation. "*So you'd become a Muslim, would renounce your Christianity?*"

Leander straightened. "*I won't pretend to have totally embraced Islam, or rejected Christianity.*" He shrugged. "*But the Bahri is made up mostly of former Kipchaks. Had any of these nomads you purchased from the steppe already forsaken their pagan gods when you pulled them from the slave block? Surely I'm as likely a convert as most of them.*"

Al-Salih chuckled. "*I can see why the Franj made you a*

translator. A man of words. You surely know how to cleverly use them."

Leander again locked on the sultan's eyes. "I've seen the comfort that Islam has given your people. This seems reason enough for me to listen to your Imams."

Al-Salih seemed to ponder all that was said. A sadness fell upon his face. "But how could you be anything but a traitor or a spy? How could a military leader ever trust a man like you?"

"Sultan. I can't deny that I'm a defector, but I'm no traitor. I feel there's a difference. Through my work as a translator, I was able to observe events in the Levant—at levels both high and low—long enough for the unsavory actions of my people to peck away at my soul."

Leander put his hand over his heart. "I won't lie and say I have this all figured out. But just before LaForbie, I could feel God summoning me, prodding me to make a change. And I heeded his call."

The sultan looked him over carefully. Eventually, he set his tired eyes hard upon Leander's. "A swift execution would be yours if I suspected even a speck of infidelity."

"I understand."

"You'd serve me loyally?"

"Yes. Of course. Until the end."

Al-Salih stared at the Crusader's face for a long while, slowly combing his beard with slender fingers, before finally looking up to his guard. "You can take him away."

The next day Leander was put upon a camel's back, joining a caravan destined for Cairo. He was taken to the west side of the island citadel at al-Rawda and placed into the tibaq to begin the years-long process of being schooled in the weapons of the *faris*, the Muslim cavalryman.

CHAPTER

4

Leander
Damietta, Egypt
June 5, 1249

They sit their horses. Three thousand horsemen, three and four ranks deep and spread across the shoreline. Two hundred from the Bahri hold the place of prominence on the right flank, leather-armored *faris* from the Turkmen auxiliaries take the center, and a small detachment of shielded Egyptian infantry occupy the left. All stare at the sea in silence.

Gray smoke curls from the wreckage of three Egyptian scouting vessels. Another small Egyptian galley lurches its way toward shore. In its side, a hole just above the waterline is plugged with a wadded sail. Seared wood adorns its gunwale. Two men bail water over the sides. A few sailors flounder in the waves, pawing at the oars. They are beaten away, those on board knowing their craft is unfit to hold additional passengers.

Leander shakes his head. Just after sunrise today, these four scouting boats were sent by Fakhr al-Din—the Muslims' Commander in Chief, or *Atabak al-Asakir*—to inquire about the intent of the foreign ships that had been sitting for days offshore. The Franks shot fire darts into the sides of the Muslim vessels and launched glowing flasks of quicklime across the decks, first adding one part water to three parts white powder to activate the devilish substance. These incendiaries, along with stones from the French mangonels, made short work of the tiny Muslim fleet.

Most of those Egyptian crews must be dead, Leander thinks. Any sailors hoisted topside the French command ship were likely tortured into disclosing what they knew of the strength and disposition of the sultan's forces. The Crusaders will now know that the amirs expected the Franks to land in Alexandria, a three-day ride west, and that the beach here in Damietta is only lightly defended. The Franks will know that Fakhr al-Din commands little more than a harassing force here, not a sizable one that could effectively defend this beach, much less the town.

To the front of Amirate Three, an Egyptian sailor swims his way toward the beach, his arms plunking the sea in wearied strokes. A wave crashes across him, yet he forges on, the weakness in his kicks causing his lower torso to sink in the water.

Leander anticipates a signal from his Amirate Commander, knowing Duyal will want the man saved and will pick a Mamluk who best speaks the language of the locals to do the saving. Amir Duyal moves forward to ask permission of the commander. On his way back, he finds Leander's eyes in the formation. He points at the struggling man and nods Leander the assignment.

Leander dismounts, tosses his reins to a mate, and wades into the sea, the soft waves lapping his thighs. Farther out now, the warm water up to his armpits, he takes an angle to intercept the struggling sailor. He grasps the man's shoulder, turning him to his back.

"Don't strike me, infidel!" the man groans in his Egyptian dialect, out of breath, looking up blankly with charred face, his left eye scorched white.

Leander turns away, surprised at the gore. "I'm no infidel, friend. Settle down, I'll get you ashore."

"Oh, thank God. Thanks be to Allah," the sailor says, seemingly relieved to hear the words of his native tongue.

Leander drags him in by a fistful of tunic. Once he trudges into the shallow water, several camp followers help him. With his legs now dragging on the bottom, the sailor crawls, then staggers, to his feet. Reaching dry land, the man again drops to his knees and weeps.

Leander watches him for a moment, feels sorry for him. He turns, knowing that he can do no more. Wiping the saltwater from his face, he feels the sting from the white powder that he picked up off the man's tunic, squints the substance from his eyes. He leaves him to the women and remounts, the soaked leather and wool making him feel twice his weight.

Across the beach, a pair of sandpipers scamper away from an incoming wave, one dipping its beak to feed in the backwash. A gull glides overhead. Leander finds peace in their presence. These birds rarely fight and don't understand the hatred between men or the revulsion between competing religions. He wonders how it is that man has the audacity to call himself the superior life form.

Dripping from beard and behind, he waits with the others, the sun creeping above a bank of clouds on the eastern horizon. A larger wave tumbles in. Three more like it. So many times just east of this place he and his mates had swum, riding the lazy rollers like children, the squeals from the young local boys and soldiers becoming indiscernible. He sighs, smiles.

Luna tosses her head, paws at the sand. Leander whispers her some calming words. In the past year, he has not once heard his four-year-old nicker—the skilled Bedouin, or "Bedu," trainers having broken all of the citadel's Arabians of this nature long before arriving in Cairo. No Bahri worries whether or not his horse might communicate with the enemy's in any battle, giving away the owner's location. No rider in the Bahri sits atop a stallion. Mares are lighter and often show greater agility, so both the Mamluks and the Bedu breeders are adamant that females are more practical than males in the desert climate. And on the beach today.

The heat of the late morning bakes the sand beneath them, forming a salty film upon his armor and coat, concentric rings crusting about his knees and elbows. He tightens the lion-shaped belt buckle at his waist, his tunic still damp, the silk gone itchy beneath the wool from his earlier wade into the sea. He rubs the rope of scar tissue at the base of his biceps. He tightens his lips recalling this self-inflicted laceration made years ago near graduation when he and his brothers in the tibaq sanctified the end of their training during the Mamluk ritual. Bloody arm hinged in bloody arm, they stood silently in the circular formation, the novices' merged lifeblood dripping from elbows, each man eyeing his *ikhwa*, his blood brothers, about him. Their years of initial training had finished, but their *Khushdash*—the lifelong allegiance among brothers in common slavery and manumission—had just begun.

He fixes his gaze back on the horizon. The white canvases of the thirty French *magne naves*—great ships—billow against the background of turquoise water and clear sky, propelling the ships shoreward and away from over one hundred supply vessels left in the darker water. The advancing ships are each more than one hundred feet in length and hold most of the French fighters plus their mounts. Leander picks out the twenty constructed by the shipbuilders of Marseilles, forecastles and mizzenmasts distinguishing those ships from the other three-decked vessels made in Genoa.

Leander takes a deep breath. Soon the Franj will attempt a landing. The time of trial is here. He tries to calm himself. God has a plan for him. And if it now includes confronting those of his own blood on the field of battle, then so be it.

He will prove to his Bahri brothers, and Allah, too, that he is worthy of having been spared by the sultan at La Forbie. He must prove his faithfulness to the core of Islam, the Sixth Pillar, Jihad of the Sword, the military struggle on behalf of God. He trained for it. Now he must do it. Now he must employ holy weapons to protect Islam and mother Egypt. It had taken nearly five years for the Franj to recover from the manpower losses suffered a LaForbie. Only now have the Crusaders recovered enough to remedy their setbacks in the Holy Land by way of this Seventh Crusade. And right here it begins, on the beaches of Damietta. Allah help us.

Leander's own father had once stood on this very beach as a young man, thirty years earlier during the Fifth Crusade. Only days away from going home with his Lord Erard of Brienne-Ramerupt, his father had been abruptly ordered to stay in Egypt to guard goods promised to his lord.

He was pulled into the Battle of Damietta at the last minute by King John of Brienne and put aboard an adapted fortress ship with the Frisians. Just south of the beach where Leander sits, his father had once shot countless bolts from the small castle atop the ship's masthead. His target had been the formidable Chain Tower, constructed on an island opposite the city walls. His ship had been overcome by a barrage of Muslim Greek fire and peppered with javelins launched from both the Chain Tower and the city's high walls. "The bravest men I ever saw," was all his father ever said of his time in Damietta, describing the Frisians he had fought beside.

His father had carried home from the battle a giant link of chain, and hung it from a spike above their mantle. It was a piece of the obstacle the locals had strung across the Nile from city rampart to island tower to block the Franks. What his father did not bring back to France was his left arm. This was the injury that ended his military career.

Leander never asked his father about the rusty iron's significance. Leander learned that story in Erard's castle and later from the older Egyptians. As a boy, Leander knew only that the chain link on the wall represented what ended his father's only real passion—the crossbow that hung right beside it.

Leander wonders what his father would say now if he could

see his own son on the same shore, serving the spawn of the very sultan that he had once opposed, his son fighting against the French sons of his father's beloved Lord Erard. Leander hopes his father has not lived long enough to actually find out.

Fakhr al-Din signals to the keepers of the carrier pigeons. The cage doors flop open. A flutter of black-bordered wings and a burst of white, heavenward. They carry the identical message for the sultan that the infidels will soon land and ask for al-Salih's final orders. The birds bank right toward Cairo, the eyes of the entire force following them until they are but flecks on the southern horizon. A red-lioned pennant from the center of the Muslim formation snaps erect from its horizontal resting position. Leander nods. Fakhr al-Din will give the Crusaders something to think about on their approach.

From behind the formation of Muslim warriors, the kettle drums sound, their rumble deep, almost deafening. Angrily, the Turks pound on the leather heads, the hides stretched taut across the tarnished brass kettles. Tremors from the percussion resonate through Leander's horse's legs and up into his own chest in a competing second heartbeat. The four-noted whine of the Arabian horns interjects and the Turkmen's ivory-horned olifants declare their own hollow tune of impending death.

The largest of the two-masted ships can come in no farther. The Franj tack into the wind, the helmsmen not wishing to ground themselves. The enemy is close now.

A roar from the Muslims, as Crusader anchors plunge into the sea, the Franks' smaller landing craft descending in erratic jerks soon afterward. Franj drop over the sides of their ships en masse, upsetting the lighters on impact. Some soldiers wearing cross-embossed uniforms hang from the rails by one hand and one foot, and then fall heavily like iron snowflakes, sprawling, weapon-splayed crystals plunging from the sky.

Port-side doors on the large round ships slam open. While these hatches are meant to be used at traditional port facilities—not on defended beachheads—the sailors improvise, lowering horses rigged in heavy-clothed slings into the landing boats. These beasts rock into the sides of the ships and gawk at the waves and the crowded decks below them.

Aboard the Franj lighters, arms wave and fingers point, as the Crusaders push each other into the tight holds of their boats. Several Franj clamber out of the smaller landing craft, climbing into the portholes of the larger ships still joined by lines, or up over the rails via ropes tossed by mates.

"By Allah, what are the pig-eaters doing?" Binny whispers, turning to Leander with a scrunched brow.

"The Franj overfill the landing boats. Those climbing up look like sailors, probably refusing to take the soldiers ashore," Leander says quietly.

"How is this?"

Leander shrugs his shoulders. "How? Well, whatever plan they might've had for coming ashore—and I doubt they all ever agreed to one—was likely just tossed to the wind. The Franj are ravenous, dumb with their hunger to spill Muslim blood. Some likely ignore their king and commanders."

"Incredible," Binny says, tilting his head in contemplation, as if a complex math problem were just set before him.

Well-spoken, skinny-armed, and tall, Binny's nickname sprang from "Bilgin," his given name, meaning "scholar." Close your eyes and listen to him speak, thought Leander, and you'd swear the man talking was an educator. In appearance alone, Binny looks more like a young merchant than a gifted cavalryman.

His Kipchak mother had fought to save his life at birth. When Binny exited the womb with a deformed left hand—possessing only a thumb and tiny pinky finger—the maidens at his mother's side wrapped Binny in a blanket to hide his defect from his mother. Wordlessly, they carried him toward the ger flap to rid the weary mother of the curse beset her. Binny's mother would have none of it. "You'll not kill him. Bring him back!" she screamed in her delirium. She named him "Cahit," meaning "hardworking" in Turkish.

The daughter of a khan, she could read and write and taught her son both skills at a young age. She imagined that his disfigurement would dictate a life in which his mind, not his body, would be of use to the tribe. Her son learned so quickly that when he was four, his mother changed his name to Bilgin, anticipating that he was destined to be an academic. She saved her coins for his eventual travel west to the schools of the Rus.

Yet Binny wanted nothing of that chosen path, excelling at the games of youth, especially those employing the simple bow. For boys without a deformed hand, the u-shaped cradle between the webbing of the left thumbs and forefingers introduced inaccuracy into their shots, but Binny's two-fingered claw was perfectly spaced to snuggly seat a bow grip. It was as if his left hand had been made for nothing else.

Even the sword and the butt of the lance rested securely in what the Mamluks called his "falcon's talon." His bookish speech, his birth defect and gangly appearance were quickly forgotten as soon as the lanky man employed a blade or the Mamluk *qaws*, the heavy recurved bows used by the Bahri in battle. Then Binny became forbidding, as lethal as they come.

With the heel of his claw now resting on the pommel, Binny analyzes the Franj. His eyes to the aqua blue water, he watches knights who had flung themselves into the smaller galleys climb back up the rope ladders now hanging from the ships' sides. Other sailors climb back down, while rowers from the first-launched galleys dip their oars, putting some distance from the ships.

"What a gaggle," Binny says, shaking his head.

The thump of lance shafts on Turkmen shields fills the air as more Franj leap down to boats already half-filled with horses. The Crusaders' beasts snort and ram the hulls and each other, some straining their necks toward the shore, the whites of their eyes peeled wide and restless.

Atop one galley, Leander spots the yellow lion against blue background—the standard of the Briennes. In this boat must be one of Lord Erard's sons, Henri or Erard, Jr., the male offspring from the lord that Leander's father once served. Both of Erard's sons had supervised Leander's training in France; Leander had even sparred once against Henri. The last pang of homesickness stirs within Leander. The sight of the rounded turrets and the castle's dark-shingled roofs after making the last bend of road, the clang of swords, the tail-wagging hounds, the beat of hoof inside the courtyard arena.

A splash. A roar of laughter from the Turkish ranks as one of the Brienne's knights jumps awkwardly down from his ship, bounces off the smaller vessel's rail, and falls into the sea. Coated in heavy iron mail and with a broadsword strapped to his waist, the man quickly sinks.

A sudden twinge in Leander's stomach. He pictures the man struggling to free himself from his belt and pull the heavy chainmail over his head, while slipping lower and lower in the deep water. The Frank has little chance. Leander wonders if he knew this man, perhaps as a lad, or maybe knew his brothers— the knight was certainly from near Ramerupt, like Leander. He stares at the water around the boat, hoping to see him pop up.

Several moments pass and the knight never surfaces. Leander scorns himself for the pity he feels. Fool. Hoping for the survival of the enemy?

Duyal signals for Amirate Three to make bows ready. Leander's mates remove strung recurveds from their saddles. Wiping the sweat from their hands, they methodically stage arrows between fingers on both bow and draw hands.

Leander unfastens his crossbow. He depresses the trigger and shifts the roller nut backward into firing position. The nut spring clicks into place. He thumbs the nut to confirm it is locked, while placing the ball of his foot through the single stirrup at the weapon's tip. With knee braced outside the tiller, he grabs the thick hemp on either side of it and pulls back, the beeswax coating sticky in his hands from the heat. After hooking the string up and over the top of the roller nut, he carefully slides his right hand along the strock, leaving it underneath the trigger assembly to act as a safety.

His eyes flip back to the enemy and hold there, his fingertips delicately searching through the thirty short bolts in his quiver, neatly arranged by type of deadly tip—a wide assortment of crescents and squares and points. Intending to avoid a glancing shot off shield or armor, he settles on a square-faced head with one point protruding from each corner. Leander loads the bolt, admiring the weapon that his father taught him to adore: her stout elm butt; her worn "tickler" trigger system, the steel rubbed shiny smooth; the composite bow staves of wood and sinew and yellowed horn, bonded by fish glue, only a little different from his father's weapon that hung above the mantle back home.

Leander calls this bow Galina, Rus for "woman of serenity." She has a twin sister, Gamila, Arabic for "gorgeous woman." His father had given him both weapons in 1239, when Leander was but ten years old, just before the boy was sent away to serve as an *armiger* to the knights of his former lord, Erard of Brienne-Ramerupt. Both weapons were made in Genoa and purchased in Damascus in 1238. This was fortunate for Leander, as the treaty signed between the Franks and Saracens expired the following year, quashing such trade.

Slap and Binny call Gamila "the mistress," joking with Leander that he is a louse each time he chooses the gorgeous woman over their favorite, Galina. His friends' allegations have no basis, as the bows are nearly identical. His mates rib just for the sake of ribbing. Facing an enemy with the same French blood pumping through their veins as his, Leander decided his girl, "serenity," was the best choice this day.

Two knights onboard a landing craft begin punching one another. The Franj in their boat lean to the hulls, making a space for the pair to settle their differences. Soon each has the other by the hair.

More merriment from the Turk horsemen on the beach.

"I hope all of them are nothing but buffoons," Slap grunts.

Leander nods, as he watches what appears to be the Franj lord making amends between the two. The Frenchmen are made to kiss, bringing more chuckles from the shore. A blush falls on Leander's face, a sense of shame knowing that he was once part of them, that his comrades may still somehow associate him with the feuding brutes.

Soon this lighter comes alongside a larger galley, where a giant, helmeted man holds its standard in the bow.

"Whose banner would that be?" Binny asks, pointing to the brilliant red flag depicting a giant yellow sun with rays dispersed all the way down to the thin points of the pennant.

"'Tis the Banner of St. Denis, another strain of the Franj," Leander says.

These two craft now join the king's galley, their oars plying the water in unison. A fourth galley comes on line, this one packed with roughly three hundred knights belonging to the Count of Jaffa. In time with each dip of the oars, the colorful escutcheons emblazoned on the hull—the *cross gules patee*—rise and fall above and below the waterline. The warriors' shields of matching scarlet and gold are secured to the rails, their red streamers clapping noisily in the breeze.

In reply, another Muslim pennant raises. Heavy-shouldered Turks stationed on either side of a dozen camels employ their felt-tipped sticks to pairs of giant kettledrums mounted over the backs of the beasts, the thick-handled devices resembling the largest of the maces carried by the infantry.

The deep tone feels as if it quakes the sand beneath his horse's hooves, as if the throbbing gongs might suck both horse and rider under. The Muslim horns grow louder, more of them whining. Luna grows anxious, her ears swiveling, a stomp from a front hoof. He pats her neck, speaks into her ear. "Soon time for work, girl." He kisses Galina on the tiller.

Men in the king's galley begin to shout angrily at the two craft near them.

"Why are they fighting now?" Binny shouts.

"I'm guessing because the Count of Jaffa's boat and the other look to land before the king's," Leander says.

Binny shakes his head.

The Franj now pour over the sides of their lighters, the enemy wading ashore, their shields hanging from necks, their weapons slung over shoulders. Fakhr al-Din sends part of the Turkmen—three Amirates of Forty—to greet them. The Turks spur off, shrieking.

Anticipating them, the Crusaders come online and ram the points of their shields into the beach, nearly touching one another. They do the same with their long lances, securing the staves in the sand so that across their front is a wall of angled points and armor. The Franj crouch behind their hastily constructed fortification.

A flurry of projectiles sizzle the air but the Turkmen arrows thud harmlessly into the Crusaders' shields. Seeing that the infidels will not come out from behind their barrier, the Turks rein in. Some turn back, hoping the Crusaders will follow and make themselves into better targets for the others. Yet the enemy does not budge.

A second wave of Crusader landing craft arrive well short of the beach, their deeper keels digging into the sand, several of the boats tilting sideways. Frenchmen leap over the sides, some landing in waist-deep water, others up to their armpits and higher. These men become targets for the Turcomen archers. A half-dozen chain-mailed Franj fall into the surf, arrows jutting from chests and shoulders and heads. Their mates drag them ashore and scurry to higher ground, dropping quickly behind their kite-shaped shields.

To the Muslim left, knights carrying the Banner of St. Dennis find breaks of dark water and navigate it to the tumbling surf, abandoning their boats in shin-deep water. This time, Fakhr al-Din signals for two more amirates of Turkmen and two from the Bahri. Finally, Amirate Three will get its chance.

Duyal raises his right arm and Amirate Three moves forward, the four-columned formation transforming quickly into a single line of Jihadis across their amir's front. Horses snort. Men make final adjustments to their gear. When they are set, Duyal drops his arm. Amirate Three gives heels to its mounts, taking a position left of the Turkmen who have already departed, these auxiliaries, too, anxious to keep their own formation tight or balanced.

Leander gives Luna some calf and she quickly comes up to the gallop with the others. He props the weight of the crossbow on his thigh. Midway to the Crusaders, his horse leaves the harder-packed soil and sinks into the soft sand. He lifts her head to keep her from stumbling.

On signal, Duyal halts the formation. The Bahri let loose a flurry of arrows, some catching Franj shoulders and heads that peek around the tall shields. Wails from the injured Franks. Leander flips up his sight, raises his crossbow, and takes aims at the intersection of the cross upon one shield. He slowly squeezes the trigger, loosing a bolt. His projectile goes clean through the pavise, its effect unknown to him.

To his right, more of the Turkmen return to the main body, unwilling to crash through the Crusaders' barricade. One of these Turkmen reins in and sits his horse alone mid-field. He looks heavenward and then turns back to the enemy. He charges back to the Crusaders' line at the gallop.

The man's intent is obvious: he wishes to meet Allah this day. Crashing through a small gap in the line, the Turk swings his sword at the first Crusader he sees, cleaving a man's shoulder. A Frenchman gets a lance point under the Turk's arm, nearly removing him from the saddle. The Turk veers left. Another Franj rushes with a broadsword. A hack to the Turk's leg. A scream from his horse. Soon the Muslim is engulfed by a throng wearing a mix of Crusader tunics—the man smothered, then cut to shreds by those in the sun-dappled yellow, joined by those in the red crosses.

Amir Duyal sees a gap in the Crusaders' front. He calmly

motions for his men to exploit it. Leander dumps his lance, stows his crossbow across the back of his saddle and pulls his sword from its scabbard. The Bahri pour through the opening, fanning left and right behind the Crusaders' line, by unit. Leander peels right behind Binny and his squad leader.

He spots a Crusader with back turned and closes. The man turns to face him. The enemy puts his second hand to the grip of his heavy sword, inviting Leander. A fury rises within Leander, an almost comfortable inferno. A smoke seems to swirl in his head, clouding his peripheral vision. Seeing only through smaller circles, the edges of his vision blackened, he focuses solely on the broadsword bisecting the red cross on the man's chest.

A flash of blue. He looks down and right. From seemingly nowhere, a squire in the yellow lion of his former lord peers up with scared eyes, sword at his side. Leander gapes at the boy in the oversized chainmail hood. He sees himself as a lad ten years prior—fetching water for Erard's knights, brushing horses, cleaning lances from his ax-hewn stool. He is this very boy standing before him. Time slows.

Slay your past. You must slay your past. Leander raises his blade, yet his mind becomes muddled, preventing him from finishing the stroke.

Instinct, or perhaps self-preservation, brings him back to the present, his arm extending to parry the young squire's swing. The clang of steel on steel. A sting across his calf. A slash through his gaiter. Trickles travel down into his boot.

Whoosh. Another's blade comes across the squire's neck, detaching the boy's head. It rolls twice and stops, resting upon its right ear. The sideways head gawks at Leander, the chap's eyes blinking twice, his brow furled, the boy seeming disgusted that he will not finish off the mounted Saracen.

Leander can only stare as a sadness seems to fall upon the lad's face, the boy appearing just now to fully comprehend that his head is detached from body, that his dome has but seconds to see. The boy dies with a scowl.

Leander eyes the Mamluk who holds the bloody blade. Sedat. His Amirate Leader smirks.

Leander turns to locate the Crusader in the red-crossed tunic that he had targeted previously. Two Mamluks have already finished him off. One removes his foot from his stirrup and presses it to the Christian's chest to retract his lance from the man's torso.

A dampness in his boot. Leander looks down. A steady stream of crimson seeps from the red lion on his gaiter. He shakes his head in disgust.

CHAPTER

5

Ox
Cairo Citadel
June 9, 1249

Hunched over the table with his forearm wrapped around his plate, Ox scoops a wad of hummus atop his *aish* and shovels the mounded pocket bread into his mouth. He grunts while munching, sounding like a muffled version of the crated boar they saw floated ashore by the Crusaders in Damietta some three days past. He closes his eyes, savoring the hint of sesame, the aroma of the fine meat about him. "Mmm." He snatches a skewer and pulls three of the five spiced meatballs from it in one tug.

Along the length of the table, his fellow Mamluks pick at their meals, most chomping glumly, their manner signaling minds adrift. Others sit silently; some share hushed conversations with long faces and tight brows.

Understandably, they mourn. Efe, their amirate commander, is dead, an unlikely Crusader bolt fired from afar driven deep into the center of his chest. A fluke shot. Bad luck. For him.

They had all felt their commander indestructible, yet there he lay on that beach in Damietta, both hands grasping the wooden shaft, the spiraled parchment of the projectile's flights between his fingers, his helmet slid over his face, channels of blood pulsing over his jawshan, soaking the tips of his blond beard.

Efe's name translated as "older brother," or "brave," and he had lived up to both interpretations. There may be a more respected Amir of Forty in the regiment, but Ox cannot pick the man's name offhand.

Ox had liked him enough—their amir had always treated him, his senior squad leader, respectfully. Ox will miss him, no doubt. But he is lying to himself if he does not admit to feeling a hint of excitement inside. Soon the command will announce Efe's replacement, and Ox is primed for the promotion. Of course, this is not the way he wishes to win his new position; he would have been keen to lead another amirate. But Allah decides these things, not he.

The other troopers do not say as much, but all know that with an expected long campaign against the Franj to come, the senior amirs will want to keep continuity in this amirate by promoting from within. Being the most senior man among them, Ox surely will become the Amirate Commander. But with the second in command—the Amirate Leader position— also currently vacant, he wonders who will be chosen as his assistant. Chomping slowly on the wad of meat, he looks down the tables at the other squad leaders, assessing the strengths and weaknesses of each.

He daydreams, seeing himself standing in front of his new residence, Efe's tidy house, which he would take over, the one adjacent to those of the other amirs in Cairo. The trumpets and drums and wind instruments sounding his greatness after evening prayer, while those passersby on the cobbled path out front look up in awe of him. He huffs. No longer would he have to live among the younger troopers, as he has for so many years.

He has never been the most popular cavalryman in the amirate, and his fellows speak to him even less often since Efe's death. No real surprise. They know what is coming. They will have to get used to the professional distance that is necessary between men and their commander. It is supposed to be lonesome at the top, and he will get used to it.

He takes the last of his aish and mops his plate, revealing the curly-tailed lion heraldry of their sultan upon the porcelain, flanked in wide stripes of blues and golds and fat-petaled blooms. He belches, appreciating the dish's opulent look.

A Mamluk sitting across from him stares vacantly around the room, sadness written on his face. His plate is untouched.

"If you're not hungry, I'll take that *Kefta*," Ox says, through a mouthful of food.

The Mamluk looks up coldly and pushes his entire plate across the table. Ox snatches it midway and grabs the half-charred stick. He pulls the first meatball off the tip with his front teeth. "Shame to waste 'em," he grunts with a full mouth.

His given name is Balaban, meaning "husky person" in his native Kipchak land, yet only his mother had called him by it. All others called him "Ox" for as long as he could remember. Having always been two heads taller than his peers and blessed with a strapping build, Ox picked up his nickname early, as his father was tossing his three-year-old son the hand-me-downs from a chap more than twice his age. While merely a boy on the steppe in the lower Dnieper country, he was doing the work of men— shearing sheep, scything grass, tending the ewes at birthing—all tasks requiring the long and muscular arms of an adult.

He had hated it: the work, the sheep, the goats. Sure, he had some decent friends in his tower—what the Kipchaks call their tribe—yet he had not kept track of a single one of them. He was elated some thirteen years ago when their khan had called his name from a list of adolescents who would be taken by the encroaching Mongols and sold on the block to the Ayyubid royalty in return for lenient treatment for his people. So happy he had been, certain his future life in military slavery was to become his best chance at freedom from the herder's life, a chance at riches and an escape from the tower that had never quite embraced him.

Thirteen years. He cannot believe that much time has slipped by since he left his people. And as promised by those instructors in red, once graduated from the tibaq and manumitted, he and his fellow Kipchak graduates have done little else other than beat down al-Salih's opponents as they appeared, most of the adversaries being the sultan's Ayyubid relatives. In the process, nearly a third of those in his initial training tulb had been killed, those brothers of his Khushdash—men sharing both the unbreakable bond of those long years of training in Hisn Kayfa, and the same theoretical release from slavery.

That old citadel in Hisn Kayfa: the huge beige blocks; the steep stairs dug into the pocked stone, zigzagging down to the Tigris; the endless layers of sword-hacked felt; the archery targets, moved farther back each week; the brutal lance and sword sparring; the frail or incapable of them being chucked out of the gate. Buckets of sweat and constant pain—all part of the Mamluk progression, all component requisites to earn the title of Salihiyyah Mamluk. And Cenk, his tulb leader. Surely that instructor was insane.

A sadness fills him as he thinks of Ilker and Demir, his two best friends back then—men who, years ago, died not gloriously in battle but miserably of the fever in that filthy cell they all shared in Karak. He has resigned himself to the fact that he will never again have friends like they were.

Grimacing, he clenches his giant mitt into a fist and stews on those circumstances ten years earlier that put him, his mates, and master into captivity. Hundreds of allied soldiers—even the Egyptian regulars—abandoned their prince near Nablus before battle, leaving al-Salih with Ox and only seventy other Mamluks. Outnumbered by the enemy, their prince was forced to flee and seek asylum in Karak with al-Salih's cousin, al-Nasir Da'ud. Then his master was betrayed by his host, the prick al-Nasir chucking al-Salih's men into the dungeon for fourteen moons. And there, the illness took too many of his friends, one by one. A hollowness swells inside him. These were the men he loved most, men now gone or spread to other units in Damascus and Aleppo.

Back then, it was not a foregone conclusion that the former Prince al-Salih would become the ruler of the empire. Ox reckons 1240 was the pivotal year, the year when the stars aligned, when destiny showed itself. April of that year, al-Salih's brother, al-Adil II—sultan at the time—broke his promise to provide military support for al-Nasir's conquest of Damascus. Fortunately, al-Nasir was furious, soon releasing al-Salih and his surviving Mamluks from the Karak fortress. Ox knew then that al-Salih, his prince and patron, was blessed, or at least very lucky.

Once the subsequent maneuvering by the Ayyubid powerbrokers was complete, al-Salih and al-Nasir eventually came to the agreement that al-Salih should become the Sultan of Egypt and al-Nasir should have the lordship of Syria. Together, the two allies advanced to Gaza, yet no battle was to be fought, as al-Adil II's own Mamluks, fed up with the Sultan's excesses and debaucheries, revolted and dethroned their own patron. The conspirators offered the empire to al-Adil II's brother, al-Salih Ayyub. Ox's patron, his father figure, became sultan.

While al-Salih could never completely rely on the alliances he forged in the following years, the one constant al-Salih could count on was unquestioning support of his policies from his professional corps of Mamluks. Since manumission, Ox has been a faithful dog to his sultan, with al-Salih every step of the way since his patron was an outcast prince stuck in Hisn Kayfa, on hand at every battlefield that al-Salih fielded to win and maintain his sultanate.

Ox has done his duty, and soon it will be time for his reward: the prestige and silver and respect that comes with promotion and command.

Things tend to work out with patience, he reckons. He feels grateful to be part of the original Salihi—the sultan's own personal Mamluks—and fortunate to have been purchased by the right prince all those years ago. Destiny had placed him in the right hands. Al-Salih's appointed governors now rule all lands south of Baalbek, aside from the coastal strip north of Jaffa and a few other Crusader strongholds in Galilee and south Lebanon.

The sultan has organized the empire into three broad regions with generally autonomous governors responsible to the sultan in Cairo: Palestine, with the towns of Nablus, Jerusalem, Gaza and Bayt Jabril; Transjordan, governed from al-Karak; and Damascus, comprising Harran, Biqa and Mt. Hermon.

Ox picks his teeth with the long skewer, smacking his lips as would an old man. He again looks down the table at the blond and red-haired youths in brilliant white coats. As each year goes by, more and more of the men look like mere boys, not a hint of gray in their beards, hardly a wrinkle on their bronzed faces. Shit, among his fellows, he is the elder in every way possible— age, body deterioration, experience.

Conversations drop off. Heads swivel toward the arched entranceway. Ox turns.

Aybeg, the Amir of One Hundred, struts in. Ox smiles. But who are that beanpole and the squat-assed troll behind him? Respectfully deferring to Aybeg's seniority, both the skinny one and short man shift to Aybeg's left side. Ox's heart seems to stop beating, his blood seeming to drain into his boots. And then Ox sees it—the jewel-studded belt and the new purse on the young Mamluk's thin waist, designating the man's status.

The stick falls from Ox's mouth. This can't be.

"All rise!"

Ox is the last to his feet. He locks his body, a slight slump in his stance.

"At ease," Aybeg says. He turns to his left. "I want to introduce you all to your new Commander, Amir Isa—and his next in command, Amirate Leader, Taavi." Ox's eyes glaze over. A gurgle in his belly. He takes a deep breath to keep from puking. All of the blood from his boots feels as if it is now rising to a boil in his head. The pressure in his skull intensifies. He averts his eyes, setting them high up on the gray blocks of the opposing wall, a steady thump coursing over his temple. He looks down, staring at the chickpea paste remnants on both plates, his gaze fixed on the smeared emblems, both lions upside down and facing each other.

Isa steps forward, his chin held high. "I know I replace a great man," he screeches. A few mouths hang agape along the tables; several men conceal their snickers. "But it will be my honor to lead this amirate. Both Taavi and I look forward to meeting you all. Please, carry on, finish your meals."

Ox cringes at the pitch of the man's voice. "By Allah," he groans.

He plops down, snaps the skewer between his fingers. He bends it over and snaps it again. And again. Unbelievable. He pushes the bread away from him. Isa? They would give *his* amirate to this skinny-armed, squeaky-voiced fuck? Allah help us! And worse, he was not even considered to be the outsider's next in command—who is this Taavi?

He burps, slowly blowing out a putrid gas, a scowl setting upon his face.

CHAPTER

6

Leander
The infirmary, al-Rawda Citadel, Cairo, Egypt
June 16, 1249

The clink of shears on pottery. The chatter of women's voices. Leander rolls over, the faint smell of piss from the nearby pans reminding him of his whereabouts. He opens one eye. The women in light blue make their way down the aisle, each carrying two stacked basins filled with bandages and implements protruding between. Small vessels of water already sit at the foot of some cots. He struggles to his elbow and pushes the pillow beneath his armpit. Two newcomers have arrived during his nap and there are still more empty beds than occupied ones.

Why wouldn't there be? They had not given the Crusaders a proper fight eleven days ago on that beach in Damietta. To the sultan's great disappointment, they had lost the town, the occupation of which all Crusaders view as the key to taking Egypt.

What had taken the Crusaders of his father's era a year and a half to accomplish during the Fifth Crusade, King Louis's men had accomplished in just a day-and-a-half with minimal casualties.

Disgraceful. The Egyptian forces departed with "Te Deum"—the Christian hymn of praise—in their ears, the Frenchmen being in fine spirits as they erected their tent camps. War with the Saracens would be easy business, they surely thought.

Leander sighs. Slightly outnumbered and having no return message from the pigeons as to al-Salih's wishes, Fakhr al-Din withdrew from Damietta, unwilling to sacrifice his precious cavalrymen. The Egyptian forces set fire to their own bazaar, destroying all the food and merchandise stores organized by al-Salih. This had only made their ailing sultan angrier.

Several beds away, his assigned nurse sets down her stacked containers. Unlike the others, she has her supplies arranged neatly, the bandages in one container tightly rolled, the squared-shaped dressings in another laid flat, their corners aligned. Neither the Muslim *hijab* which covers her head, nor the *niqab* which conceals her face can completely mask her beauty. With some clear, olive skin exposed at the fringes of her veil and black hair pinned to the back of her head, he can tell she is stunning. Her body is firm, her motions fluid.

He finds himself watching her often, imagines what she might look like with that shining dark hair free about her shoulders. For days, he tries to imagine an animal that characterizes her efficient ways and controlled movements, yet he is unable to do so. Perhaps a leopard or maybe a gazelle.

Her name is Jacinta. It means "hyacinth," and that flower may well describe what she is: something beautiful to be seen and appreciated by the wounded men who are fortunate enough to receive her care. Twice daily she freshens his dressing. In between changes, he thinks of questions to ask her and looks forward to their interactions. Their conversations the past eleven days have been short, but from the start, mostly void of shallow content. He likes her and senses that she enjoys his company, as well, but that may be because he is the only one among the wounded here who fluently speaks her Coptic dialect. Nonetheless, he does not know why, but feels he can trust her.

She grasps the vessel and walks the passage between the bed rows, her eyes locked forward, the water in her jug not sloshing but remaining as placid as her demeanor. Leopard, not gazelle. Stopping at the first bed, she touches the wounded Turk's shoulder.

Leander's heart sinks. He wished there were a connection between them, but he is probably mistaken. She is most likely just a nice person, pleasant to everyone. Geniality is merely part of her job here. What would she want with a renegade Frenchman? Hell, what would a girl like her want with any soldier? She surely deserves better. He rolls to his backside, ignoring the twinge of pain remaining in his calf from where the young Crusader's sword bit him. He stares at the arched beams in the vaulted ceiling until they blur.

He wakes to a hand on his arm and the smell of her perfumed oil. He looks up to dark lashes and deep brown eyes. These eyes squint, Leander quite sure that a faint smile on tiny lips hides behind the required veil. He melts. A tingle radiates to his fingertips.

"I'm sorry, each time I seem to waken you. We must change your bandage," Jacinta says, averting her eyes and setting out of his view the basin half filled with bloody dressings.

"Oh, no problem," he says, tossing aside his sheet and propping his foot underneath the bad leg to expose the bound gash. "There's no reason for not getting plenty of sleep around here." He smiles.

She unwinds his binding resolutely, slowing only as she arrives at the wraps closest to the wound. Exposure to the air stings the dripping slash.

"How does it feel?" she asks.

"It's fine, fine. You think they'll let me get back to my unit soon?"

She carefully twists his leg so that she can see the laceration in its entirety. "You're lucky—the wound wasn't too deep. You heal quickly. But these things take time."

He sighs, looks up to the crinkled brow above her niqab.

She looks down to her blood-speckled smock. "I've tended others in the Bahri before and they, too, were in a hurry to get back into harm's way. It always concerns me."

He shrugs his shoulders.

"Your wound has yet to heal up into the center. We don't want it to break open. I fear there'll be plenty of fighting to come, so there's no need to rush it. I'm sure you've already done much for the sultan."

"No, I haven't done enough," he snaps.

She looks at him, startled.

He closes his eyes. "I didn't mean to nip. It's just that I was injured due to my hesitation, my inability to strike the killing blow when I had it. A moment of weakness." He shakes his head. "I got myself hurt and am now no use to my brothers."

Her eyes signal a soft understanding. She likely grins again behind the veil. She looks over her shoulder to where the lead nurse roams and then meets his eyes. "Weakness ... you belong to the sultan's most elite unit. The weak don't dwell with the Bahri, Leander. If I asked your comrades, I'm thinking they'd say that you didn't fail them."

"At least one would. Sedat, my amirate leader. He killed the Crusader that I should have. He saw that I vacillated, knows that I could've put my brothers in danger. It's not good."

"I'm no soldier," she says, looking down the row of beds. "But don't these things happen? Don't the actions in battle occur quickly—and sometimes the hand isn't as fast as the eye?"

"I suppose," he says politely, refusing to be rude again but unwilling to accept her rationalization.

"Being faced with killing your own people—it must be difficult."

He shakes his head. "It shouldn't be. They aren't really my people anymore."

"No?"

He heaves a sigh. "I think Sedat has always doubted me, has always seen me as an outsider. Doesn't trust that I have it in me to slay the Franj. What I did in Damietta now gives him proof of his hunch. I worry my entire amirate may have lost some faith in me."

She nods. "This Sedat. He's but one man. You confronted the enemy of Islam and were wounded in the process. Allah may actually look more favorably upon you now than he did last moon. Your Bahri brothers, too."

He looks down with pursed lips, embarrassed that he has confided such serious concerns to a woman he has only known for a few days.

"The Bahri. You're pleased to be with them, right?" she asks.

"Yes, of course."

"Do you have confidence in the men you serve beside and the sultan who leads you?"

Leander grins. "Who wouldn't? I doubt a better fighting outfit exits." His smile widens. "And al-Salih. He's like a second father to me."

"And you now see Egypt as your home—something worth defending."

"Without a doubt." He shakes his head, shamed by his whining and the sensibility in her reasoning. "I snivel like a child. You've a job to do, other men to take care of."

She sits on the edge of the bed. "Until you heal, you won't be of any help to anyone. There's no sense torturing yourself. Soon enough you'll have the opportunity to show your sultan and friends that you're willing and able to kill the infidels." She lowers her eyes, then flashes another unseen smile up at him. "Cairo needs men like you fit and well."

He admires the curves and dark skin about her eyes. Lovely. She is so very lovely. He laments, wondering if he will be able to kill those whose blood he shares the next time the two armies meet.

She seems to read his mind. "Do your part in fighting them

so that they leave our homeland. And then your problem and Egypt's problem are solved."

He grins. It is that simple.

She spreads the salve.

He appreciates her calming voice and simple logic. He cannot help but stare at her. She is right. The sultan and amirs have invested much in him—in time, animals, equipment, and drill—and have faith that he is worthy to be one of them. He has skilled mates who rely upon him. Amir Duyal counts on him. Leander has only one solution going forward: heal up, get back to his amirate, embrace his training and carry out his duty when he again faces the Franj.

She looks up from dressing his wound. "It must be difficult for you to face your old people. Does anyone else in your unit face this burden?"

He shakes his head.

She nods. "When were you last in France?"

"Closing in on seven years ago."

"That's a long time. Did you live in that big city ... Paris?"

"No, no. I'm from just a tiny hamlet in the north—Ramerupt."

She looks at him blankly, understandably having never heard of the place. "Do you have brothers, family that came overseas with you?"

"No. Two sisters. One older, one younger. The older sister married a Templar, after he came back from service in Ascalon."

"I see ... Your mother, does she know you're still here?"

"Ah, no. My mother died of the fever when I was nine. A year later, my father sent me to a castle, serving the knights of his lord. It is the way of Franj, the way of soldiering families."

She scowls. "And what could these lords have wanted from boys so young?"

He grins. "To groom them for future use in battle, naturally."

"It must've been dreadful—so young to be away from family."

He shrugs his shoulders. "Maybe at first, but there was some good in it—I was able to spend much time with my lord's dogs." He smiles.

She chuckles.

"And the stag and fox hunting was quite good." He grins. "I learned falconry and became quite good at chess. But it was mostly religious instruction—and, of course, cleaning, oiling blades, mucking stalls, feeding out the horses and other chores."

"I see. But your family. Did this lord ever let you go home to see them?"

"Sometimes. To visit. But it was inevitable that I would grow apart from my father and sisters. And I did."

"So, then it was easier for you to leave when you came to the Levant. But how was it that you even came here?"

He looks down sheepishly. "Basically, once a squire, my father paid my way."

"He's a rich man?"

Leander laughs. "No, no. My father was but a simple *sergeant*, an infantry crossbowman. He couldn't afford the financial obligations of knighthood. Even his equipment was provided by his lord."

She squints. "It's widely thought among the people of Cairo that even the vassals of the Crusader kings are men of great wealth."

Leander nods and sighs. "Some, not many. When not on campaign, my father was often toiling on his tiny plot with the peasants. It was from these labors that he paid to get me into Erard's castle. And it was because of his prior service to this same man that this lord gave him the silver that ultimately paid for my gear and transport to the Holy Land."

"I suppose it's no different than here. The sultan, the senior amirs, the rich merchants—they control everything."

Leander frowns. "Right. Lord Erard was quite old when he gave my father that silver—likely Erard's gratitude for my father's years of loyalty, or maybe just a dying man's guilt. Maybe pity for causing my father so much pain and grief. Seems to me that in old age and especially at the end, a wealthy man is nothing but a poor man with silver."

Jacinta looks up.

"You see, my father lost his left arm in battle, and he came home to the sorrow of losing most of his friends, as Erard had waged and lost the War of Succession—for a territory in France called Champagne, while my father was away. Once home, my father had his children, but he was empty inside—few friends and the end of his soldiering. When my mother died, then, well ..."

"How sad."

He nods his head. "You're very good at leading me into babble. I haven't told half of these things to anyone else. Yet you're not so good at talking of yourself. Do you—"

She looks to the entranceway.

"Uh-oh," he says.

"See—some of the Bahri. Here to visit their friend. I see your fellows haven't forgotten you and don't find you unworthy." She raises her eyebrows while getting to her feet.

The pair of Mamluks stroll down the line of beds, the bull-necked Slap and gangly Binny, looking out of place as they weave through the nurses, looking for their comrade's bed. Finally spotting him, they beam.

Leander groans.

"By Allah, do the benefits of flopping in battle never end?" Binny asks, looking first at Leander and then straight at Jacinta.

Slap elbows his friend. "Not so loud—and a woman present," he says in earnest, yet unable to withhold his deep chuckle.

"Ah, sorry," Binny says, bowing to Jacinta, tucking his claw of a left hand behind him. "But our Papa Frank, he'll be ducking out on the inspection tomorrow, and he gets to lounge and look at this all day," he says, nodding at the girl. He pulls from his case a tattered book and tosses it on Leander's bed.

"Ah, thanks," Leander says, recognizing the copy of al-Tabari's *History of the Prophets and Kings* that was borrowed from an amir and left sitting on his shelf, half-read. He appreciates their thoughtfulness, yet wishes they had brought three more books, as he will devour this one by tomorrow.

Jacinta looks away from his mates. "Please excuse me, I must finish my work." She stoops to pick up her kit.

All three watch her as she walks away.

"Slap, quickly now, slash me a good one with your dagger—a training injury. I want to be here in bed next to Papa Frank," Binny says.

Slap pulls out a dagger hidden in his boot and moves to Binny's right arm.

Binny cuffs him. "No, no, my left arm, goon."

All three laugh.

"You two leave that nice nurse alone," Leander says.

"Why? You aren't," Slap says.

More chortles.

"How's everyone?" Leander asks with inquisitive eyes.

"As well as we could expect. The army may have lost over four hundred men. Our regiment is just waiting to see what the next move will be. All are anxious to kick the Franj off our beach," Binny says.

Leander nods. "Our patron. He must be disappointed with us."

Slap looks over his shoulder. "Word from the guards was that upon hearing of the news, al-Salih called in every senior amir and dealt them a tongue lashing, as severe as they'd ever heard."

Leander shakes his head solemnly. "Not typical of the sultan."

Binny shakes his head. "Worse—he delivered it from his bed. His heath declines."

Slap crosses left arm over right and begins to rock slowly in place.

CHAPTER

7

Cenk
Cairo
October 14, 1249

As they near where the path forks north along the wide river, Cenk moves to the side closest the water, putting himself between it and his daughter—an action of habit, not necessity, since his girl is old enough now to know danger. He clutches her little left hand in his right, so that she does not have to feel the stub of finger on his left, although she pretends the nub does not bother her.

"Oh look, Papa, sailboats," Inci says, pointing at a pair of felucca boats plying the water, their pointed lanteen sails bulging in the northern breeze.

"They like this wind today, eh?" he asks.

"Yes. You think one day we'll be able to ride on one—on a windy day, just like this?"

"Hmm. Yes, I think that one day we'll sail on a boat like that. Maybe one day soon—you and me and mother, too. You'd like that?"

"Oh, yes, yes. I can't wait!" she says, latching on to his two sausage-sized fingers. She swings his hand to and fro, her cheerful steps now further elevated into a half skip. She looks up at him and smiles the grin inherited from her mother, her high cheeks flushed a pleasant rose.

Looking down, he feels a familiar warmth spreading, the deepest of affections that originates from his very soul. He needs to honor these promises. His daughter is four years old now—no longer a baby. Inci will remember these things, will be disappointed if he does not follow through.

Scanning the ridgetop, he tries to pick out the red coats through the narrow arrow slits in the rounded towers that anchor the outer curtainwall of their citadel. His guards. There they are—the red forms centered between the cross-shaped shooting stations. His eyes move up and inward to the fortress proper—to the battlements, where even at this distance his men appear straight and alert above the rectangular cutouts in the walls. Good.

Enough. Stop working. Inci. Enjoy this stroll with her.

He grips her hand tighter. He needs to be done with the corps. It is the only way. Yes, his career has played out brilliantly. What better way to end his duty than as an amir in the *Jamdariyya*, the sultan's personal bodyguard? He never would have dreamed.

Only by slipping from the knots of endless responsibilities will he have more time to spend with his daughter, before her entire childhood is behind them. He knows the transition out of soldiering will be hell—it is all he has ever known. But it is time. It's time.

He grins. Soldiering. There is just not much room in it for old men, anyhow. To formulate strategy and lead the army en masse, the regiment requires senior amirs, but only a few. And the entire corps knew he was not cut out for the politics and bootlicking that men in those grades were forced to tolerate.

A man of thirty-nine years, Cenk knows he is physically unable to meet the rigorous standards required of younger troops and that mentally he is losing his competitive edge. He notices his own gradual slippage, even if most Mamluks probably perceive no difference in him. In his twenties, he was fearless— forever certain the enemy's blade and arrows would find the other man. Now he knows such thoughts are foolish.

Perhaps he will tell the command he is done. Maybe soon. Maybe once they have driven the Crusaders off Cairo's doorstep, once he feels confident of the safety of his family and all of Egypt. Yes, then he will tell them.

"Why does the river always go that way, Papa?" She points north.

"Well, all rivers eventually end in the sea. That's what they do. And our big one is almost there."

"If I were a river, I think I'd sometimes go the other way, just so that I could see things in the other direction."

Cenk laughs. "Yes, of course you would. It's good to get out and see new things." He pauses, drops to a knee and gives her a hug. "And if I were a river, I think I would do like you do."

Her little arms wrap around his neck. Tighter now. Again, the warmth fills him.

He stands. "Should we go a little farther? Sometimes there are more sails on the backside of the island."

She smiles, takes his two fingers and resumes her skipping. "All right."

Oh, how lucky he is to have her in his life. She was so close to not existing at all. He had almost destroyed everything. He would not have blamed her mother, Fidan, for leaving him eight years ago. She is a saint. A saint. He was unbearable back then. Violent, miserable. Fidan is an angel for having remained with him. And because she did, they have this godsend walking beside him. Oh, my Fidan! I did not know it was possible you could present me with a gift as sweet as this!

Fortunately, he no longer resembles the man he was, the man who struggled for years coming to terms with that patrol, that terrible ambush on the route between Aleppo and Hisn Kayfa, when his amirate bumped into the blood-thirsty Khwarazmians. He knows that this one fight, that single ambush, changed him forever.

In that barren canyon, on that cold, sleeting day, Cenk lost his patron, Amir Turkmani. Thought of his name sends a stab of pain to his core. Time has taken away the details of his patron's face, but Cenk can picture those blocky shoulders, bull neck and soft eyes. The man was more than his commander, more than a patron—he was a father to him, closer family than any kin from his native Bashkir forest. "If they were all like you, Cenk, I'd have little to worry about, eh, my son?" Turkmani said numerous times. Cenk fights off the tears that well in his eyes.

In that canyon, in that Khwarazmian trap, he had his closest comrades torn from him, most killed or severely wounded. Afterward, al-Salih, still a prince then, disbanded Turkmani's Amirate of Forty. He spread the remaining souls from Cenk's Khushdash across the realm to various amirs. Only Cenk and a few others were blessed to join al-Salih's personal Mamluks in the Jazira. The luck.

For years, this attack tormented him, in nightmares and bouts of anger directed at his young wife and the unfortunate novices he trained. Most nights, he drank himself numb, trying to deaden the pain of his losses. He still wonders how the *koumis*— the fermented mare's milk he bought in the back alleys—and the wine did not kill him, how his drunken furies and relentless quest to cull the weak from the training ranks did not end in his own banishment. How and why his battered Kipchak wife did not sneak away in the night. Surely she came close to it.

Oh, how he regrets his conduct back then. He hopes his God has some sympathy for a man who went astray but changed his ways. Cenk mended his relationship with his wife, abstained from alcohol for a decade, and harnessed his anger into a proper ambition to mold Mamluks into competent warriors. Allah must have forgiven him by now. It has been at least four or five years since he has had one of his dreaded nightmares. If Allah has not forgiven him, the Holy One at least spares him the bad dreams.

Cenk and his daughter stroll farther along the dirt path, past the fish vendors in their rickety hooches, through the remnants of mudbrick homes washed away by the floods years ago. He waves to a neighbor, passing those huts higher up the bank, made with two brick layers, the straw and papyrus reed ends protruding from their walls like a lazy man's whiskers. On the crown of the short ridges, they see sturdier homes made of bricks and limestone blocks.

"Did you have a river like this of your own when you were growing up?"

He smiles. "Well, we had a river, but it was much faster, narrower. And shallow, filled with many round rocks."

"Big rocks?"

His mind swirls to the snow-topped peaks north of his tower's summer camp, the scraggy mountain routes that he rode as a boy, high up in the Ural Mountain Range. Endless woods, ample game. The majestic place that he loved, but where he was not loved—or at least never felt loved. Not uncommon among his people, his Bashkir father regularly employed the switch for little reason, while his mother looked on with haggard eyes and thin lips drawn tight, as frightened of the burly man as was her only son.

He had grown up hard, hunting and—once the raging river settled in mid-summer—fishing. He preferred the solitude of the wilderness to the company of his tribe, his self-worth derived from his success on the hunt. The only times he recalled his father showing affection—usually in the form of a pat on the shoulder—was when Cenk had a marmot across his back, a string of trout in his hand, or a deer tied upon the rump of his pony.

When he was sent to the slave block as a thirteen year old, there were no sobbing women, no sniffles of anguish from his extended family. Only his father speaking with the Mongol Khan, making sure his payment in flesh was adequate to keep their small Bashkir clan safe from the Mongol bows for another two seasons.

"Some rocks in that river were very big, the size of our shed." He stoops and pulls her hand up to his mouth and kisses her tiny thumb. "And some only the size of your thumbnail," he says, holding it up for her to see.

He refuses to subject his daughter to anything resembling the upbringing he had. He is thankful to Fidan for chiseling away most of the ice that once surrounded his heart, for stepping in to provide emotional support for his daughter, whenever Cenk was incapable.

"You were lucky to grow up with such big rocks!"

"And the small ones." He grins.

He wants to go on more walks with Inci. That boat. He needs to find the owner and find a way onto that boat. His eyes grow tearful. If only those poor novices in his training tulbs could see their instructor now. Most would laugh—the harsh man gone docile, the devil gone semi-soft. Departure from the service. He feels the tug inside, maybe a sign from Allah telling him that his parting from his beloved corps is near. Somehow even the sultan could sense that Cenk was not long for the game. His patron had made the kindest of gestures to him last moon, even with so much on his father's mind and his health failing.

> He entered the sultan's chamber as requested, the air stuffy, almost stale. Thoughts of his grandfather's ger were in his head, when as a kid his mother made him go say his final goodbye to his old, shivering kin. Al-Salih sat on his favorite chair, appearing as if he had just been propped up in place.
>
> "Cenk, how's my fine amir of the guard?" His smooth voice gone hoarse.
>
> "Well, well, my father. The more important question is, how are you?"
>
> "The mind still clicking, even if the body is rebelling." He coughed hard into the crook of his elbow. "I called on you because

I wanted you to know that I have just made arrangements to increase your iqta. With the extra land, you should easily pull another ten dinars per month from its crops."

Tears filled Cenk's eyes. He bit his quivering lip. His voice cracked. "But my father, that was unnecessary. I have enough. I assume you use that land to feed the treasury and equip our forces."

The sultan waved off his comments. "Of course you would. That's why I did it." He forces a smile. "The Grand Treasurer already has the scrolls together. You must go to him and make your sign on them."

Cenk bit harder on his lip, embarrassed at the tear running against the bridge of his nose, disturbed that his father was preparing for his own death. "But ... I, I could only wish the money to be spent making you as comfortable as possible. I ..."

Again a wave from the sultan's hand. A half-hearted grin. More coughing, this round harder.

"We all must fight on. It's what Allah directs. What else is there, my son?" With this, the sultan rose, raised a hand in farewell, and shuffled in the direction of his bed, his raspy coughs and tick of cane tracing his slow progress down the stone corridor.

Inci sees the tears in his eyes. "Papa, why are you crying? I hoped you were enjoying our walk."

He picks her up under her arms and swings her around, her little legs splaying out.

"Sometimes the tears, they don't come from sadness but joy." He pecks her twice on the cheek. "How could I be happier than when I'm with you?"

She looks again to his eyes, unconvinced, the pout gradually leaving her face.

He needs to remove all doubt from her little head. If he left the service upon the death of the sultan, he would have his small pension. This, combined with the income from his fief, would be enough to sustain him and his family into old age. They would have to rein in their spending, but Fidan was suited for this. His little family would not require much, but at some point, there would be a marriage to pay for; he would also need spare coin for the unexpected.

"There they are—just as you said they'd be," Inci points to the boats skirting the north side of the island.

"Ah, that nearest one. Isn't it pretty?" Cenk asks.

CHAPTER

8

Ox
East Bank of the Nile, Mansura
December 29, 1249

B ehind the hand-dug berm, Ox reaches into a pocket for his last chunk of dried goat and stuffs the entire piece into his mouth. He leans on his bow, listening, the tip of the upper limb buried into the tongue of his boot.

A hollow click of hefty gears breaks the evening silence, followed by metallic clanks along the Muslim line—bars applied and removed from the bolts, right hand turns loading collections of magonels. Among the ticking winch wheels, alternating groans of oak on torsion bundles sing out in varying tones, as ropes twist tighter upon each of the sixteen catapult machines.

In the pale light, two *ghilman*—slave boys wearing thick-cottoned coats and trousers, the heavy-leathered gaiters atop their boots riddled with black marks and burn holes—waddle over to the nearest catapult. With gloved hands clinched upon the carrying handles, they tote their steaming cask of naft in step. They count three and raise the sloshing liquid into the bucket on the far end of the weapon's arm. Warily, they remove their handles, backing away from the powerful machine as would a young child from his angry mother.

Muffled orders from another magonel crew upstream, as the first engine is prepared for launch. A young Turk walks from the machine with rope in hand, stopping after removing the slack in his line, the far end attached to a metal restraining lever. He hunches, moving his head as far from the contraption as possible.

"Prepare to loose." He turns to his mates behind him and then checks again around the device one last time.

"Loose."

He pulls hard on his rope.

Wham! Whoosh! The stout arm slams to an immediate stop against its frame with great force, launching the scalding naft towards the Crusader towers. Delighted in its newfound freedom, the projectile roars as it devours the air, like thunder overhead, a globe of fire hurtling through the sky, trailing a hissing streak of orange behind it.

The fire orb soars over the western tower. A chorus of growls and mumbles and shaking heads down the line. A man in the Egyptian crew goes to the hook on the launching arm and turns it several times to adjust the weapon's range.

Wham! Whoosh! A cask from a different machine is sent.

Wham! Whoosh! And another.

Spheres of fire arch in the half-dark sky, casting auburn ripples on the Raxi branch of the Nile across their front and also the larger Damietta Arm of the river behind the Crusader positions. The glow highlights the earthen causeway and twin towers built by the Franj to protect their sappers who labor and casts shadows on the half-buried stones that dot the opposite bank, remnants of the weeks-long bombardment from the Egyptian siegecraft.

At various times during the past several moons, the Mamluks and Turk allies had employed only the smallest pieces in their arsenal, the wagon-towed *arrada* and the even smaller *ballista*. Both machines had wreaked hell on the Frankish forces—the beam-sling arrada having been especially effective, easily able to hit targets with both stone and naft at three hundred paces.

A collective cheer from the Egyptian forces fills the air, as a shot splatters the eastern-most tower. Flames leap across the wooden planking, brightening the sky.

"Magic, by Allah. Magic," Ox says, over the growing crackle of flames. In the last of the daylight, he spots a Crusader helmet bouncing behind their wall, worn by one of the enemy's fire crew tasked with attempting to extinguish the blaze that now begins to take full hold. "Come out from your tower, Frankish devils, so Ox, the infidel, can stick your ass."

As if responding to his plea, two Crusaders rush to the top with buckets, exposing themselves.

"Thank you," Ox says matter-of-factly. With gloved hand on bow grip, he nocks an arrow, pushing the fletchings toward him through the copper tube on his bow, the pipe mounted to shield both him and weapon. With just the arrow's felted tip extending out the far end of the cylinder, he dips the felt into the smoldering pot at his feet, letting the naft soak into the wool and the excess goop drip back into the clay container. He faces the enemy and reacquires his target.

He draws his bow using the ivory thumb ring given to him personally by the sultan, taking in a deep breath as the heat intensifies, the smoldering arrowhead moving closer and closer to his face, putrid fumes curling from the end of the tube. He blows away the wisp of black smoke drifting across his nose.

He raises his aim a touch, accounting for distance. Emptying his lungs, he places his bottom aiming bead on the chest of the bigger Franj. Steady. Steady. He winces from the heat on his face, the pain in his right shoulder, the joint worn from too many years of pulling back the stiff composite bows and training with the other weapons of the Salihi. He eases away his thumb, until the string releases with a "thunk."

He smiles as the naft-soaked head rises skyward, hissing its way in an elegant arch of gold toward the targeted Franj. "Eat dung, mongrels," he mutters. His projectile lodges harmlessly into the planks with a "thud," only three feet from the Crusaders.

"Shit."

Six more arrows sizzle across the Raxi on high from Mamluk bows. One Crusader catches a fire dart in the thigh and drops the bucket in his hand. A roar from the Muslim line. The other Crusader dives to the deck and crawls to his mate, pressing himself upon his friend to douse the flame, all the while enduring Turkish insults flung at them from the far bank.

"You! Turn your virgin eyes." Ox says to the baby-faced ghulam who walks behind them. The boy freezes, unsure if the ogre is serious. Ox's faux scowl switches to a laugh, as he turns back to the Crusaders. "He's mounted him—another pair of sweet French lovers!"

"Yeah," a Mamluk beside him says with a chuckle. "Getting what they deserve. Who'd be dumb enough to trap themselves at high water when they had every chance to move south moons ago when the river was down?"

Whoosh. Ox fires another flaming arrow and turns to the man. "The same who'd be dumb enough to rebuild those towers after we'd already torched the first set. The same that spends a month rebuilding that dam, when they already saw we can undo their work in a day by digging hollows on this side of the stream."

"Amir Isa said the Crusaders put themselves on that exact piece of ground, got themselves in a similar fix thirty years ago, during their Fifth Crusade."

Ox scowls upon hearing their new Amirate Commander's name.

"I'm thinking their head engineer might be a Muslim."

Ox does not follow. He turns to see the smirk forming on his friend's face and then smiles. "Yeah, maybe one of the sultan's moles over there doing some damn fine work for us."

His comrade points to the Crusader tower, crude and painstakingly built upon the opposite bank. "Some of that wood they used—see the paint? Almost looks like it came from their landing craft."

Ox nods. "Good. The invaders will have a harder time getting away with their boats torn to pieces. Whoever survives our arrows can try swimming home."

The Mamluk chuckles.

The Franks were indeed foolish to ensnare themselves on the sliver of land between the two flooded branches of river. Since June, they have been a food source for the flies and sand fleas, the Franj suffering the most four moons past, during the worst of the summer heat.

Ox remembers the look on the Senior Amirs' faces when they left the sultan's tent in Ushum Tannah, east of Damietta, this past June—moping, like a mob of herders' children, after being scolded and beaten for losing a sheep on their watch. His friends in the Jamdariyya, the sultan's personal bodyguard, had never heard the sultan so angry as he was raging about his sons giving up the west bank of the Nile and Damietta to the Crusaders, providing the enemy a foothold from which to press south toward Cairo.

Yet only Allah himself could have been the one to cloud the French King's mind, causing Louis IX to wait almost four moons to consolidate his forces. During this time, the Franj kept busy doing what infidels do. Almost immediately, the Crusaders' entourage hired booths from which to hawk their wares at ridiculous prices. Soon after, Egyptian whores filtered into the French camp, spending many nights in orgies with the men who bore crosses on their chests—holy soldiers believing that the only good Saracens were dead, but making an exception when it came to plowing this land's brown-skinned women. All of this within a stone's throw of the king's tent and the shelters of the fat barons, who gorged nightly on the lean Crusader stores.

Ox snickers to himself. No discipline on the battlefield makes for an easily conquered enemy. Will the foe's lack of personal restraint during their down time transfer to tactics and personal conduct on the battlefield, when the real battle comes? There is a difference; the two behaviors do not always parallel each other.

He does not blame the Crusaders for wanting to stick the Egyptian women—many were gorgeous. Hell, the Franj are only men. The Crusaders are not the first soldiers to sample the local girls on foreign shores.

He grinds his molars. He had been a good boy for nearly a decade, following the sultan's wishes, staying away from the merchants' daughters, bending knee at the mosque, avoiding those same luscious, dark-skinned tramps across the river that now tempt the Franj, and remaining "married to the regiment." All the things that make one a good man, a good Muslim, a good Mamluk. What has his loyalty to the corps and abstinence gotten him? A half-empty purse, too many dead friends, and the same rank that he held five years ago.

He sighs. He should have plowed all those women. Every chance he had. He tries to block the memories of missed opportunities over the years, squeezes his temples to squash the thoughts of their succulent breasts and dark skin. Ah, my.

Greed, lust, gluttony. While the pious Muslims hate the devilish Crusaders for possessing these traits, Ox refuses to fool himself that he is morally superior to those he shoots at today. He simply does his duty. He follows orders. In the end, he just wants to make sure the Franj don't take his sultan's lands and treasure and wants his share of whatever coin Louis brought.

The King of France. Despite the insults thrown at Louis by the Salihi, the French monarch is not all buffoon. After Damietta, Louis was obviously holding tight until the rest of his forces arrived so that he could conduct a major attack with better odds of success. It was not until late October that the king's brother, the Count of Poitiers, appeared on the horizon with reinforcements.

The colors flown by the king's brother bore close resemblance to the sultan's own—a single red lion, dead center. Ox grins. They should have left that banner at home, as its similarity to al-Salih's acted to further stoke the Mamluks' wrath. Once the count arrived, the silly Franj waited on their sandy spit for two more moons, enduring rain and insects. Truly stupid.

The sun rises. Movement across the river catches his attention. A pair of Bedouin slink down the steep bank, hidden from Crusader view. One Bedu has a grisly head slung over each shoulder, the nomad's fists wrapped in the sandy-brown locks of the French. The other Bedu lugs a gourd sack, surely crammed with more skulls, likely Templars, the "brothers" wearing their hair so short that the Bedu have learned to bring their women's bags with them on their grave-robbing ventures. Crimson-stained water from both the bag and the cleaved necks drips down their sheepskin tunics.

"The Bedu are not dumb, eh?" Ox says, pointing at the two, who creep into the high scrub of the river bottom and disappear.

"No. At least not when it comes to coin and plunder—and slicing throats at night."

Ox nods. Fairly talented with long lance on camel and an enemy's nightmare in the evenings with their blades and leather choke straps, the Bedu had been quite useful earlier in the campaign. The Bedu listened for gaps in the jingle of tack from the king's mounted patrols, then crept into the Crusader camp to behead sleeping men or nodding sentries.

For a while, it was common for the Crusaders to wake up to headless mates in the cot next to them, or to relieve decapitated watchmen, whom the Bedu had "re-armed" with longswords lashed on to their palms. The Bedu's motivation was the king's reward—two hundred dirhams, or silver coins, for every Crusader's dome brought to the stairs of his palace—than by any real desire to oust the infidels.

Ox sighs. "Of course. But did you see where those two Bedouin came from?"

"Yeah. The graves. They've been going there ever since the Franj tightened up their security and it got harder to pick off the live ones. Grave robbing's nothing new for the Bedu. Only here, it's for infidel grapes instead of jewelry." He nods across the river. "The bold no longer care if it's dark or not."

"Yeah, I know. But those two came from the far left, from the freshly dug burials."

"So?"

"So, didn't you see those heads? Still fresh. And the Bedu had given those heathens their last bath in the Nile."

The Mamluk yawns.

"Al-Salih's probably on to them, must've adjusted his old offer, after seeing too many rotten heads, too many with dirt mashed into the ears. No more paying for the sick and rotted, only the freshly-slain Crusaders."

"So the Bedu found a new skill—a knack for spotting freshly dug soil in the dark."

"Where the new skulls are." Ox grins. "The Bedu. If Louis was smart, he'd offer the Bedu coins for our heads, too. The French, Kipchaks, Turks, English—hell, we're all foreigners, to them."

His mate sneers, looks behind him once, and lowers his voice. "Maybe if we were paid by the head, we'd have already cleared out the invaders."

"Oh, no, no. Careful now. Don't you know we're above bounties? We're killing infidels for God and Cairo." Ox points up to heaven.

"Oh, yeah. I forget."

The pair of Bedu reappear on the near bank. They pull reeds from their little boat hidden riverside and chuck their human merchandise into the bottom with a clunk.

"Clever bastards."

Ox nocks an arrow and looks down to his jar of naft. Empty. "Ghulam!" he shouts. The slave boys ignore him.

Ox shrugs his shoulders. He eases himself to the bottom of the trench, leans his head against the dirt wall. "Damn hips," he mumbles. "You know, it's just not that complicated. If I were the Frankish king, I would've pushed forward moons ago, when he had us on our heels. Swooped south and taken all of Egypt."

The Mamluk smiles. "Maybe. Or taken Alexandria—another base, another bargaining chip. And on the sea for easy resupply. But we're just Amirs of Ten. Those are decisions for sultans and kings."

"Tsst." Ox wonders how is it that he has more sense than a king, yet he sits here in the mud, unqualified in the eyes of his superiors to lead more than a mere squad.

CHAPTER

9

Ox
East Bank of the Nile, Mansura
December 29, 1249

The wind shifts, sending the reek of resin and sulphur to Ox's nostrils, awakening him. He shivers, looks up to the sun's position in the sky, realizing that he has snoozed for only minutes. He pulls a filthy blanket off the bottom of the trench and covers himself. Tired of the smell, he covers his nose and from over the lip of the trench, watches the ghilman work behind the line.

Several of these slaves sit with their backs against rocks and a bundle of arrows across their laps, as they wrap felt just below the arrow tips and secure the mound with hemp. Under the watch of an amir, another lot of them tends the fires and mixes a batch of liquid hell, stirring it until the brew is ready to burn. Six more boys ladle the concoction from the big pot into earthenware jars, while eight weary lads bring back the archers' nearly empty containers, dumping their minimal contents back into the big pot to be reheated. More of them run the readied vessels up to the archers, sling men and catapult crews.

"I'm growing tired of this shit," Ox says to the Mamluk beside him.

His mate looks around. "What shit?"

"All of it."

"Don't worry, won't be long and they'll be pulling us back to defend Mansura. Cramped in that tiny citadel, you'll wish you were back in our hole, back in the open air," the Mamluk says.

"Eh. This petty harassment—it's a job for the Turkmen, not us."

"You're too good for this?" he asks.

"Yep," Ox says.

The Mamluk chuckles. "Show me a campaign that wasn't shit. I just hope we can stop the Frankish king, hope he doesn't know how to command his infidel horde."

"We'll whip 'em. I'm not worried about that," Ox says.

Doubt creeps into his head as soon as the words leave his lips, Ox recalling the Frankish sails covering the horizon in Damietta and those bigger ships that stayed back. All the goods and weapons and men within those hulls. And more brought up since the Count of Poitiers' arrival—all of it to be thrown against Mansura. How will Egypt keep the invaders from taking the little fortress, from slinking their way closer to Cairo?

He ponders if Mansura will be his last battle. He feels an inkling of disappointment in himself, a hunch that his legacy is to end here. He loses himself watching the servants mindlessly scooping and mixing the ingredients from the sacks and canisters—ten parts of tar, three parts of resin, one and a half parts each of sandarac and lac, three parts pure sulphur, five parts melted dolphin fat, five parts liquid fat from goat kidneys.

He looks down and across the river. Helmet tops catch the firelight from the burning Crusader tower. Movement in both directions from behind the enemy's freshly dug trenches and glimpses of their dark robes, strike a fear in him for the first time. He thinks of their thick-bladed swords. At the very least, he will take some of the heathens with him into the next world. This he knows.

Maybe Allah will take pity on him. Maybe instead of the whores who the Franj root, he will get the virgins in heaven that the Prophet promises. Seventy-two of them. He smiles. They would certainly be beautiful, Allah being incapable of providing ugly ones.

He pulls up his blanket and yawns, the silky skin and voluptuous figures of his future women morphing back into thoughts of the foe. The bastards. In the end, the Franj are just another enemy of his sultan, just another force trying to pull down his patron and take his possessions, just another army to be crushed. Just another rival.

"I noticed the precious ones from the Bahri and Jamdariyya have not joined us for a shift down here," the Mamluk says.

"They're smart enough to know this work is beneath them. Like the command would risk them slinging fire."

"Yeah, they might burn a hole in their new uniforms." His friend laughs.

He looks down at his own coat and trousers, worn, the folds in his red coat fading into a dark pink. Soon the garment will be deemed unserviceable by the command, yet his *kiswa*, or biannual pay to cover his uniforms, has not been raised in five years. He is not being paid what he is worth. He takes a few deep breaths and tries to push away the negative and exhale the resentment that builds within him.

He sheds the blanket, raises himself to a seat on the edge of the trench. Thankful. Be thankful. Especially for his sultan. By Allah, he still owes his patron everything. The shame and tolerance learned from his indoctrination thirteen years past douses the anger inside him. He must remember that while al-Salih was still a prince, his patron was the one who bought him and gave him his new life in 1236—saving him from that awful life on the steppe, taking him away from the tiresome livestock, ultimately providing his tailored uniforms and the best weapons. Perspective. He could be one of these ghilman. He must keep his wits.

Yet he wonders if al-Salih now regrets bringing in so many Kipchaks, wonders if the sultan had any idea that the more nomads he gathered, the better he trained them, the higher positions he assigned them, the greater the problems they would eventually cause him. Al-Salih. While Ox would never say it aloud, the feeble man was like a nervous old lady with a trinket-collecting fetish. Once the bowing shelves covering her walls became too full, she was forced to build a new room to make a place for only her favorites. For al-Salih, that was the Bahri and the smaller Jamdariyya.

He figures the formation of the Bahri was done logically, almost predictably. As the years passed and the sultan's Kipchak Mamluks multiplied, al-Salih split off his darlings and grouped them into the more prestigious units. Ever since, the animosity between the Bahri and the sultan's other Royal Mamluks, the Salihi, only festered.

Ox knows he has his flaws, but at least he is a realist. He recognizes that the hostility between regiments comes right down to the Salihi's jealousy. They are especially envious of the Bahri—those most-favored five hundred, living in their island citadel next to the sultan—while Ox and the bulk of al-Salih's remaining Mamluks continue to toil from the original citadel on the mainland, the *Qal'at al-Jabal*, the Fortress of the Mountain, what the Bahri now call "the old house on the hill."

Almost symbolically, the deep-blue Nile divides these forces and splits these men. When they meet in town, tempers occasionally flare. The most common infraction he must deal with in his squad is brawling with members of the River Island Regiment.

He cares nothing of the rivalry. Competition is fine, maybe even essential in keeping the entire army strong, yet he would be lying to himself if he said he was not resentful of the Bahri's special treatment. Unlike some of the Salihi, Ox admits he sometimes wishes to be one of the Bahri, if for no other reason than being able to live in the same house as their patron. And, of course, their pay and fiefs are superior to those of the Salihi. Yet the sultan and the amirs never pulled Ox across the river. Perhaps this alone has been the worst wound of his career, a gash that refuses to heal.

A ghulam passes too close to him. No respect. He thinks about sticking out his bow to trip him but does not.

"Where's Amir Isa?" his friend asks.

"How would I know where the squeaky mouse went?" Ox says. "Hope he realizes the slaves are about out of dolphin fat and resin. Hard to fling fire darts without the fire."

Ox would not have let the amirate run short of anything, had he been in charge. Increasingly, he feels as if he has been lost in the shuffle. He senses that Aybeg, their Amir of One Hundred, sees a flaw in Ox, something that keeps Aybeg from giving Ox more than ten men to lead. Twice now, Aybeg has overlooked Ox when promotion seemed likely.

As the flames leap across the Crusader tower, Ox feels his own inferno rise within him. It cracks him. How could it be that Amir Aybeg promoted that scrawny rascal? Isa cannot be even twenty-three years old—just an average squad leader from another amirate in the regiment. But somehow this weakling leads *Ox's* Amirate of Forty. This promotion should have been *his*. Some of the men now show a pathetic sympathy toward him. Ox wants none of their commiseration. Isa. He is nothing but a skinny bootlicker.

The wind shifts. Flakes of ash pass over Ox, fine cinders landing upon his arms and head. He looks up to the sky, a column of gray fumes sprinkling the dawn with charcoal particulate.

He tries to calm himself. Isa will not last. If a Crusader lance or sword does not do him in, perhaps a Mamluk arrow or blade may. These things happen in battle—by mishap—during the din of combat. A dark leer crosses Ox's face.

A flock of collared doves flutter overhead, just leaving their evening roost. He lays his bow across his beefy thighs, works his thumb across the lump of painful bone atop his shoulder.

"Old man's got a bum shoulder to match that limp in his walk," the Mamluk says with a grin.

"Maybe if you'd been on half the campaigns as I, you'd have a few more dings yourself."

The Mamluk snorts. "Always so grouchy. Good chance when I reach twenty-six, I'll feel just like you. But hopefully I won't look like you."

"Don't worry, you're long past your final growth spurt, and I doubt that grizzled face of yours will get any more handsome."

Again a wave of disillusionment passes over him. He needs to find an edge, a way to the power and riches which motivated him toward this profession in the first place. He isn't getting any younger. He needs to remain tolerant and must not become desperate, even though he can feel his career's door of opportunity slowly closing.

He wonders how Duyal—one in his Khushdash—managed to be shifted over to the Bahri years ago. There, he was recently promoted to Amir of Forty, an Amirate Commander. Duyal was plenty competent, yet when it was announced, word was that Duyal acted almost as if he dreaded the promotion, preferring to remain leading his squad of ten.

Currently, Ox's *Jamakiya*, or monthly pay, is just over half of Duyal's seventy-five Dinars. And although Duyal's frame is lean and he eats like a bird, his *lahm*, or daily meat ration, is twice Ox's. More distressing, soon Duyal will receive his *Iqta*, or fief, that comes with being an amir of greater rank, something Ox has dreamed about since manumission.

He spits, tries to push out the envy that works into his mind. That bastard. Duyal—his benchmate on the same slave galley that took them across the Black Sea all those years ago, the friend he rattled along with on the back of the slave master's cart. Another life ago. Ox still loved him with all his heart.

Duyal must be disguising his aspirations, must have had an inside contact, must have made the right connection without knowing. How else could he have snaked into the Bahri? How else could he have been promoted before himself? Even Singer, another of their Khushdash, outright refused command of an amirate, yet is still currently senior to Ox.

Provided the chance, Ox would give anything to leave the Salihi altogether and get across the river and join the Bahri. A fresh start, leading an amirate of the River Island Regiment. From his first days in Hisn Kayfa, he had admired their commander, Amir Aqtay. If given the chance, he would serve Aqtay well, and finish his last years of service near Duyal and Singer, two of the few surviving mates with whom he had started this long journey.

The stiffness worsens in his hips, bringing him awkwardly to his feet. He stands hunched, struggles to straighten himself. He refuses to linger in self-sorrow. Self-pity is the way of the pussy. There are only two ways upward in this army: getting noticed on the field of battle, or riding a senior's coattails aloft. He is willing to do either. He must become more watchful, more bold, more willing to find a way forward on either front. Only this way will he receive his share of the spoils in life that he knows are rightly his.

Flames and black smoke now engulf the Crusader tower. The Franj bucketmen have given up on trying to save her. Some of Ox's fellows continue to shoot the odd arrow at Crusaders foolish enough to expose themselves. Ox takes in the blaze with the others, the spectacle causing most on the line to stand idly.

He reckons a fire looms on the horizon for the Mamluks as well. None speak of it, yet the whole army knows that only a single spark could soon ignite it. One day the sultan will die. And when he does, Ox knows that he and the other lower-ranking Mamluks will be pawned off to some senior amir.

The amirs know this and have a say with the sultan as to who goes where. The maneuvering has already begun. Rumor is that two of the senior amirs—Fakhr al-Din of the Bahri and Jamal al-Din Muhsin of the Jamdariyya—will seek retirement instead of taking on the burden of caring for more men.

Ox feels the power base will then shift down to the mid-level amirs, those handful of Amirs of One Hundred. The talented and ambitious of this lot will have their status elevated and will inherit a spread of the sultan's Mamluks. These men will have their eyes on the best of the Mamluks from all amirates.

It will be days like today that determine one's fate. Ox knows at this stage he cannot be picky. He looks over his shoulder, finding his Amir of One Hundred, Izz al-Din Aybeg. While no longer an admirer of the man, Ox must still take steps to impress him, as Aybeg may become his future patron. At least Aybeg is a man with the ambition that matches Ox's own. Ox must shine in front of them all.

A jar breaks. A scream. A young ghulam writhes in pain and frantically tries to remove his cotton jacket, the burning naft having already reached the slave's arm. Isa rushes over, grabs a blanket, pushes the slave down, and pats frantically to smoother the flame. Ox jeers.

The ghulam, cradling his singed arm, rises with a look of amazement on his face that an amir of such grade would do this for him. He drops to a knee and then into the fetal position, where he begins to moan.

Ox hopes Isa is not another of the stupidly brave, as willing to risk the whole amirate as he is his own safety for a cause unworthy. He turns to his men. Most gawk at the scene unaffected, the Mamluks standing with bows over their shoulders, waiting for their pots to be filled or arrows to be replenished. The rest of the ghilman surround their blackened mate, some fetching water to douse his smoking coat, another rolling a tunic to place under the injured's head.

Ox strolls over to them. "The show's over!" He points to his Mamluks. "Arrows! Fill their pots! We still have work to do!" Returning to his squad's station, he peeks over his shoulder, wondering if any amirs witnessed him taking charge, wondering if Aybeg heard his words.

CHAPTER

10

Leander
Fortress at Mansura
February 9, 1250

With biscuit in hand, Leander winds his way up the stairs, the rock beneath his feet scuffed smooth and black. He heads for the parapet farthest from the lookout stations, the closest thing to a private sanctuary he has found in Mansura's tiny citadel. He follows a jog in the passage, takes a step around the corner and halts. Another man already sits on the bench—a bull-shouldered Mamluk swaying back and forth, the bench creaking in time with his motion.

Recognizing his friend, Leander smiles and strolls to the parapet. "I see my secluded breakfast nook is found."

"No hiding places to speak of in this rathole," Slap says gruffly. He scooches right to make room, his rocking slowing to a shallow bob. He turns to his friend, grins, stretching the deep scars across his cheeks and chin into thin forms less intimidating.

Like Leander's friend Binny, Slap is of Kipchak descent, another enslaved remnant from those towers smashed by the invading Mongols as the Tartars stormed across the steppe lands, between the Black and Caspian Seas. Slap had lived on the Don River, one of the four major river drainages of the old Kipchak confederation.

Binny was passed to the Mongols with other boys as human tribute in return for lenient treatment for his tower of Ural River Kipchaks, but Slap's tower had refused to live under the Mongol yoke. For this they paid a dear price. During a Mongol attack many winters past, nearly every warrior in Slap's tower was slain. Slap and several other boys escaped to the wooded hills, living off deer, marmots, and mice for several moons, before being tracked and captured by the Tartars.

Like many of al-Salih's Mamluks, orphaned at the prime slave age of thirteen or fourteen, Slap and his strain of Don River adolescents were driven south like livestock, forced upon the block at one of the trading hubs on the north shore of the Black Sea. Slap will say little of his time with the Mongols, yet Leander gathers most of the slashes on his friend's face were a result of his uncooperative time with the Tartars. He guesses Slap's self-calming sway was also learned during his distressing stint with the hordes from the east.

"Seems they pack us in this shithole so that even battle is a preferable option," Slap deadpans.

Leander breaks his hard bread in half and hands part to his friend. "Yeah, like an overcrowded cage of rats. I'd take the sandfleas on the Raxi, living in a tent and closer to the action with Fakhr al-Din, rather than staying crammed in this leaking house with you stinky bastards."

"Well, you knew Fakhr al-Din would put himself closest to the thick of it," Slap says, a look of sadness and resignation in his eyes. "The grand one doesn't want to feel the sultan's bite again, doesn't want to disappoint our master twice. Wouldn't be able to live with himself, knowing failure was the sultan's last memory of him."

"That's true." A lump forms in Leander's gut. No one has seen their sultan in weeks. Perhaps the senior command wishes to spare them the misery of seeing their father suffering, as surely the sick man is not long for this earth.

Nevertheless, for nearly two weeks, almost two hundred of the Bahri have been holed up in Mansura's fortress, plus another three hundred from the Salihi, under Amir Aybeg. Fakhr al-Din wishes to position his forces closer to the Crusader enemy, the Franj camped just two miles north and downstream of Mansura. Only a couple of days prior, King Louis dropped a few tents. For a week, his supply requests to the locals have grown, a signal that he may be preparing to move his army.

Fakhr al-Din responded by personally leading six more Amirates of Forty from the River Island Regiment and hundreds of other troops of Egyptian regulars and *Halqa* about two miles north of Mansura's fort to join the Muslim camp on the Raxi Branch of the Nile, directly across from the Crusaders' position. Fakr wishes to be nearly on top of his enemy, ready if Louis manages to spring his men from the high water trap the King has set for himself.

"That leg bother you anymore?" Slap asks.

"Nah, it's fine," Leander says, casting his eyes north across the shining water at the split of the Nile main stream and the Raxi Branch, forking downstream to their east.

"Good. What about that girl? Uh…"

"Jacinta?"

"Yeah."

"We've talked most days after she finishes her work, but they move her around a good bit and keep her pretty busy at the infirmary. I don't want to be a pest. I just saw her a few days back. She's nice—but Egyptian, you know."

"Uh-huh. Amir Duyal and al-Salih—neither would approve. Kipchaks. They want us all marrying those girls dragged down from the steppe. But maybe not you. I saw that little twinkle in Jacinta's eye when she looked at you, Papa Frank," Slap says, looking up from his boots.

Leander looks away. "Well, I don't know about that." He feels the blush coming to his face, looks down to the seam in the tan block at his feet in hopes of changing the topic.

"She's got you hooked a little, doesn't she?" Slap asks.

"Maybe."

"Why is it always the ones we can't have who are the most irresistible?" Slap asks.

Leander smiles. "That seems the way of it."

They sit silently for several moments.

"I'm thinking her father may be a rich man. Even if it came to it, he'd never let me marry her anyhow," Leander says.

Slap slows his rocking to a more introspective swing. "Yeah, so you have obstacles on both ends of the affair. Might be different if you were a senior amir with a little brown in that face, eh?"

"You mean instead of being a pale-skinned former Christian."

"A pale-skinned former Crusader with no damn rank," Slap adds with a wink.

They both chuckle.

"Yeah, if it were easy or made sense, I probably wouldn't be interested, eh?" Leander says.

They sit, crunching their bread, watching the river and horizon from on high.

Slap shakes his head as if to change the self-talk inside. "I wish Amir Aqtay were here."

Leander glances rearward. "Yeah, we'd be better off. You can tell Duyal's worried."

Leander figures all in their amirate feel the same, frustrated that Aqtay, their Amir of One Hundred, has been whisked away far to the north on special duty, and Duyal's amirate has been subsequently attached to another man of the same grade.

Slap's sways deepen. "Yeah, Amir Aybeg, he'd have every reason to spare his own and send only the Bahri into worse of the shit. Amazing how some guys, some leaders seem to draw men in, while others just rub you wrong."

Leander does not get a good feeling about Aybeg either. Perhaps it is less this amir's harshness and more the commander's zeal for personal gain that irks him. Maybe it is just the contention that seems to be growing between the two leaders and their respective regiments.

Leander smiles. "It's just the nature of things, the nature of people, eh? Aqtay is charismatic, while Aybeg ... you might call him a man of opportunity."

Slap grins. "Yeah, that's one thing you might call him. Both being of the old Salihiyya, you'd think they'd be more similar in thought and nature."

"You'd think."

"All they seem to share is the same patron."

Leander raises his eyebrows and nods.

"Weren't both Aybeg and Aqtay in al-Salih's original line of Mamluks?"

"No—just Aqtay. I think Aybeg had been purchased by Amir Turkmani and then picked up by our sultan after Turkmani's death on that patrol."

"That slaughter near Aleppo?"

Leander nods, chewing his biscuit. "Pretty damn bold by al-Salih, back then."

Slap smiles. "You mean the young al-Salih, digging into Cairo's treasury to buy all those Mamluks when his father was away? That must have been—what, fifteen years ago?"

"I think more than twenty. From what I've picked up, I think Aybeg's jealousy of Aqtay might have started a few years afterward, when al-Salih placed Aqtay in charge of the tibaq in Hisn Kayfa."

Leander struggles to picture their sultan as a younger man, when al-Salih was merely a prince, pushed to the outer reaches of the empire by his Sultan father, al-Kamil, to rule the upper Tigris valley, the northern fringes of the Ayyubid Empire.

During that time, al-Salih had just begun to grow his army of Mamluks. With great confidence, he had positioned Aqtay in charge of the training citadel, where hundreds from Amir Duyal's line of Mamluks had germinated. When they graduated, Amir Aqtay's tour of duty at the training citadel also concluded;

he has since commanded many of Duyal's second generation of warriors.

Slap's rocking has transformed into a thoughtful bobbing of his head. "That sounds right. Hopefully Aybeg doesn't let his hate of the Bahri and his spat with Aqtay affect his leadership of us when we finally do face the enemy."

Leander nods, setting his eyes to the vast skyline over the top of the parapet wall, the lush vegetation near the river forks fading gradually on both sides to the dull tan of the boundless desertscape. In the distance, a wisp of dust rises up from the brown plain, a faux lake, the fleeting haze lifting above the shimmering radiant heat. He cups a hand to block the rising sun. "Here comes one."

Slap stands. "That's a rider just right of the river, isn't it?"

"Yeah."

An opaque figure emerges from the wavy gleam. A subtle fluff of dust is nearer now. Soon, the dark form materializes into horse and rider, his dust cloud trailing sideways behind him. "Farther back, there's at least three more. Hopefully, they're ours."

The eastern watchman belts out the two-toned warning call from his Arabian horn.

"We better get back down there," Slap says.

CHAPTER

11

Leander
Fortress at Mansura
February 9, 1250

L eander and Slap thump their way down the narrow stairs, circling toward the belly of Mansura's citadel. Leander reminds himself that there is no reason to rush. They are prepared. Amir Duyal issued their tulb's operations order earlier in the week. Each man knows his job. For days, they rehearsed their plan in the cordoned section of town, away from eyes that might be sympathetic to the Crusaders.

Exiting the stairwell, they cross the courtyard, weaving through Mamluks, who pull chain mail over tunics and strap swords onto hips. Saddles lie, loaded with their complements of weapons, dried meat stuffed into saddlebags, and flasks topped with water. He feels the tingle in his extremities, a twinge in his gut. The impending encounter. Some stroll toward the gathering of men, waiting to hear words from the first rider. The gate swings open. A trooper in the scarlet and gold sharbush hat of the Halqa Regiment reins in.

Clad in yellow trousers, yellow coat, and the same style of lamellar cuirass that Leander wears, the Halqa are second in status only to al-Salih's Royal Mamluks. Their ranks are largely filled with freemen, often the sons of Mamluks. These are men born and bred in the lands of Islam, many of pure Kipchak stock, yet because they were never enslaved nor born on the steppe, the sultan deems them unqualified for acceptance into the one-generation nobility of the Royal Mamluks. Unlike their fathers who kept their Turkish names, most in the Halqa bear Arabic titles and weapons of slightly less quality than those adorning the saddles of both the Bahri and Salihi.

Leander has made no friends among them. He reckons it is purely due to most of the Halqa seeing his sliding into the Royal Mamluks as an injustice, since he was born nowhere near the steppe. He does not blame them for their disgust in the double standard. Al-Salih shuns the Halqa because of the perceived softness and poor habits that sons of his Royal Mamluks may have picked up from the local population, yet their patron made an exception for a Crusader's son—a simple crossbowman, no less.

More than anything, Leander pities them. He sees the Halqa filling a rather uncomfortable function, a somewhat midway role between the Mamluk aristocracy and Cairo's civil population. Many are capable warriors in every regard, yet because of al-Salih's directive, these men are destined to be yet another strain of bastard children within Egypt's elite ranks. They are warriors of great lineage, yet unable to fully capitalize on their Kipchak bloodline. The Halqa often receive a fief from the sultan, but are prohibited to rise above the rank of Amir of Forty. These cavalrymen are Egyptian citizens, assimilated into the Cairo population, yet their white skin and high-ranking fathers keep them from completely meshing with the locals.

The rider's eyes dart among the men, looking for a familiar face, or perhaps for a Mamluk with a purse on his belt, identifying him as an amir. Finding one, the Halqa trooper dismounts and bows. "My amir, Fakhr al-Din sent me—the Crusaders crossed the Raxi at first light. They found a ford upstream of our camp, and I fear they caught us by surprise. Our commander said only to execute the plan. Execute the plan."

On this, the remaning Mamluks disperse to their gear. Those fully dressed head for the stables. Slap and Leander stride to their berthing area. When they arrive, Amir Duyal is at the head of their line of cots with his arms crossed, watching the men as they gather their staged kits. Sedat stands on his Amirate Commander's left side, his white-knuckled fists crossed and mashed into his lower back.

As Leander passes, Sedat says quietly, "A fine morning to kill the fucking Franj, eh, Leander?"

Leander continues walking and looks back to his Amirate Leader. "Indeed."

Doubt creeps back into him as the words leave his lips. Will he be able to do it this time? Will he be able to slay his own countrymen?

If not for Duyal's presence, Sedat would be stressing them, hurrying them. Why wouldn't a former Mu'allim, a Furusiyya Instructor, resort back to antics perfected on recruits? Especially when a situation becomes a little tense, when his men were soon to be tested? Fortunately, the lanky Duyal is present. As always, he emits a soothing effect. Because of him, Amirate Three is prepared. They have a plan. All that is left to do is accomplish it.

Men in full armor grab their loaded saddlebags and shuffle sideways through the narrow aisle. Others finish dressing, tight-lipped and lost in their individual thoughts of what is to come. Leander goes to his rack. His armor is laid out in the order he must dress. He sits on the edge of his cot and steps his heel into his left gaiter, secures a buckle across his boot, one across mid-calf, another at the top. Embossed in leather at his shin is the lioned heraldry of their master.

Before securing the other gaiter, he reads the Arabic verse written down its leather side: "Fight them, Allah will punish them by your hands and bring them to disgrace." And the verse continued on the right gaiter: "and assist you against them and heal the hearts of the believing people." He nods at the words from the Koran, selected for him by his instructors at the tibaq, words known to be dear to him, words chosen to give him strength at times like these.

After pushing the leather strap through the last buckle, he stands. Grabbing the rear hem of his chain mail hauberk and holding it away from himself, he leans his head forward and draws the mound of tiny woven links over his head. He wiggles to settle the heavy shirt over his silken tunic. He takes a deep breath, finding comfort in the tinny smell of the flexible metal covered in Mamluk scarlet.

The best mail has alternating riveted and punched links, and this is the weave that al-Salih has provided for them, the armor giving him and his mates confidence. He smoothes the thick, rawhide piece that stiffens the collar and then lashes the neckline with the pair of dangling leather ties.

He snatches his cuirass, or jawshan, and raises it above his head. "Make yourself skinny," he thinks, as he brings in his elbows and sucks in his breath. The armor slides down his torso, dropping to a rest on thick shoulder straps. He raps his knuckles twice on the chest plate of rectangular iron "lames" laced together with leather strapping in overlapping rows. Compared to most European varieties, this is light armor, well-designed for mobility and the hot climate of the Levant.

Whispers and creaks of broken-in leather sound from the men about him. He pulls out his sword from its silver scabbard, the mottled blade of imported "wootz" steel, honed razor-sharp and thickened near the tip to power the stroke, the ivory handle fitting perfectly in his palm. He brings the flat of the blade to his lips and kisses it, leaving the scent of oil from his steel lingering at the tip of his nose. "Allah be with us. Allah be with us." He secures the belt and baldric around his waist.

He works the wrinkles from the qayah, or satin skull cap, atop his head, while inspecting the raised lines, or vertical keels which radiate downward in three directions from his helmet's gold-inlaid point.

The heathen merchants from both northern and southern Europe sell Muslims arms—despite the pope's directive otherwise. However, al-Salih allows his merchants to buy helmets from only the Italians, knowing the craftsmen from Genoa and Venice provide headgear with these keels along the fronts and sides of the helmets, giving the one-piece design greater strength and providing better protection for his prized possessions.

Turning his helmet over, Leander spreads the leather chin strap and places the helmet on his head, securing it with a jiggle, seating the inner webbing securely. He works the leather strap around each ear and fastens the buckle under his chin.

He turns to Slap. His friend is fully geared and waiting for him with a length of yellow silk in his hand, brilliant in the color of the Ayyubids. Slap takes one end and flips it along the right side of his helmet, leaving a two-foot tail hanging down his massive neck. He pins the tail to the back of his helmet with his left hand, pressing cloth to the helm of his helmet with right. Leander takes the folded running end from him and begins wrapping the silk band around the gilded bronze strip on the helmet's rim, removing any twists or bunches in the material as he winds. He continues until he has his friend's *imamah* form of turban completed, leaving only the pointed dome of Slap's helmet exposed. He finishes by tucking the end into the tight wrappings, leaving the tail end hanging on Slap's back.

Slap nods and executes this identical process for Leander. Both stoop to run their arms through the grip straps of their *turs* shields. The light wooden construction reaches from waist to knees, the shield's convex face covered in gold-dyed leather, the red lion of al-Salih boldly centered, six rivets holding hide to wood. On the apex of the face is a bronze boss, looking like a miniature version of the helmets they wear. Inside the bowl of every shield, the identical writing resides: "Defender of the faith." In tribute to their patron.

They head for the stables. Passing through the courtyard, they slow as three Arabians prance in through the open gate—a gray, a black and a washed-out bay—none of which Leander recognizes. All are covered with the buffed leather and rich scarlet-and-gold horse armor covers of the Bahri. Strangely, upon their backs sit men in the mail shirts and crude helmet style of Egyptian infantry, men not trained in the art of cavalry, or even permitted to ride the elegant steeds. The fear on the riders' faces draws Leander's eyes back to the horse armor, where splattered blood stains two of the ornate covers. His heart sinks. These infantrymen have escaped the battlefield near Damietta riding the horses of slain Bahri.

He sees no need to make his way closer to the riders, as do some of the others, to hear the soldiers' pathetic stories. They fled the field. That is their account. All the while, al-Salih's Mamluks stayed and died fighting for their Sultan and Egypt. Likely Fakhr al-Din's troops downstream are now outnumbered. Leander fears for what will become of the brave who remain.

This story is not a new one. He shakes his head in disgust. For some of the auxiliaries—those performing military duties on a part-time basis, or civilian volunteers undertaking support functions—it is not their fault. Their training is substandard and they contract mental weakness like a disease from living among the undisciplined locals. This flaw is like poison, tainting the army's thoughts and actions.

But some soldiers in the sultan's force are purely a disgrace to Allah, always present with hands out for al-Salih's silver, yet unwilling to stick when things become tough. He figures the only Mamluks who will pass through this gate will be those who leave seeking the enemy, those who return after having accomplished their mission, or those borne on the backs of their mates' steeds, severely wounded or killed while performing their duty.

Leander climbs back up the stairs to the parapets. He scans the horizon.

Men with wild eyes run toward the fortress, their stowed shields smacking their asses on each stride in deserved self-punishment. He recognizes the green tunics and white turbans of the *Harfush*, or rabble, as they are called—ill-trained infantry auxiliaries. Some of these peasants are limping on injured legs, some holding hastily bandaged wounds, or helping their fellows.

Some appear to have fought for a while. Noting the full quivers and bloodless scabbard lockets, Leander figures most simply bolted, each man for himself. He feels a swell of anger tapered by a tinge of commiseration. He has yet to see a single Mamluk among them, though some Turkmen cavalry filter in, as well. These respected fighters are allowed in the fortress, while the big doors swing closed to the masses. The amirs realize the deserters are too numerous for all to receive shelter.

He turns to the south. The citizens of Mansura smell the situation and recall what happened just north in Damietta eight moons past. That entire town had been sent into panic and was vacated upon the initial Crusader attack. For months, the people of Mansura have feared the same for their own town. Now mothers clad in veil and long dress already take to the south road, bundles on their backs, expecting the worse. Men push carts loaded with food and children toward Cairo, their tiny hands visible grasping the sides.

Leander nods. Good. Their abandonment of Mansura will make it easier for the Mamluks to execute their mission and will limit the collateral damage. He hopes the local men, the civilians tasked with the barricade duty, have kept their nerve and not chosen to join their families in escape.

He recalls the miniature model of the city laid out in the courtyard: pieces of horsehair twine as each major street in Mansura, painted blocks of wood depicting neighborhood buildings and mosques, white cloth designating the bazaar and vendor areas, and chunks of leather strapping representing the barricades, which were to be pulled across the critical arteries in town.

The amirs' plan was as simple as it was brilliant. They divided their forces into three elements. Mamluks and Turkmen, comprising the "rabbit element," head north of town on horseback to make contact with the enemy and then disengage, tempting the infidels into a chase into the city proper through the open outer gates. Once inside, the rabbits will scatter, dispersing the Franks into smaller groups throughout the tight city streets and herding them into preplanned kill zones.

Members of the Egyptian infantry, dressed in peasant garb and merchants' robes and designated the "barricade element," coordinate civilian men in dragging pre-made barricades across the streets, after the Crusaders pass. These pre-staged timbers, many enhanced with waist-high spikes, were already distributed to various sectors of town and hidden in alleys, sheds, and homes.

The "hammer element" units are light cavalry and exclusively Mamluk, both Bahri and Salihi. They hide in the alleys and behind homes throughout the city. Once the barricades are set, they close with and engage the enemy. Leander's squad has been assigned to this group, tasked with occupying a zone in the eastern part of Mansura.

Two short horn blasts from the parapets. Time to assemble. Leander descends the stairway, chiding himself for questioning the nerve of the civilian men in the barricade element and for mentally berating the ancillary forces who ran. What of himself? His conduct before the enemy so far has been nothing to boast about. Despite his squad's training and his nearly healed calf, he has not recovered his full confidence.

During his whole life, in both France and Egypt, he never worried about fighting, never shied from locking horns with the best of his peers. Even when getting his ass kicked, the emotional setbacks had lasted only seconds, the disappointment shedding from his mind like water down the Alps. Yet oddly, none of that past conduct matters. All that matters is now.

He snarls, thinking back to Damietta and his indecision when the fighting became close there. By design, the fighting today will to be hand-to-hand. He will not have the archer's greatest allies this day: time and distance. In fact, his crossbow twin sisters, Galina and Gamila, will remain behind, cased and staged in their quarters. How will he respond when the enemy appears quickly, when he hears his native tongue and sees the insignia again of once-friendly units?

He continues through the crowded courtyard until he reaches the northern corner, where his unit assembles. The ghilman bring up the last of the horses. Men of the Bahri slide hands under girth buckles, checking for proper spacing and verifying the fit of breast and crupper straps.

Three men inspect a stack of lances, turning the yellow bamboo in their fists, their eyes only inches from the rigid wood. Seeing his outfit prepared and making only final tweaks to their gear buoys him. Binny looks up from tightening the cheek strap on his horse's bridle. He nods to Leander, the usual smile gone from Binny's face. Duyal and their new squad leader, Timur, made Binny a team leader within the squad. Binny handled the duties incumbent with promotion easily, not letting the assignment go to his head.

Their Arabians seem to sense that today is not preparation for training. Several paw the dirt with hooves; others flick their ears back and forth, eyes roving about the bustling men. The boldest of the mares shake their heads and elevate their tails in anticipation, causing their slave tenders to shorten the leads.

Gathered in the neighboring corner are the *Jandar* infantry, some of al-Salih's best foot soldiers. Cloaked in leather smocks and dusted in fireproof talc, the men look like assassins. Their leather hoods cover all but the front of their quilted hats and cast sinister shadows across their faces. They are called "grenadiers" and are well-trained in the handling of Greek fire.

Slaves tend to kettles of naft. One soldier carefully pours the concoction into apple-sized clay pots through a metal funnel that is dinged and oblong-bent. Others in the Jandar produce pre-cut fuses and insert them into the empty pots staged along the wall. They hand longer pieces of slower-burning hemp to their fellows, who feed these sections up their left sleeves, leaving a tag to be lit just prior to departure, for use in igniting the short fuses of the grenades. Accustomed to fighting independently, these men will be employed in pairs today, stationing themselves at the barricades of the most prominent roads, where they will create chaos, chucking their ceramic death at trapped Crusaders.

In the courtyard center, Amir Aybeg calls for his amirs, his thumbs locked assuredly behind his jewel-studded belt. One of the sultan's most senior Amirs of One Hundred, Aybeg has held this respectable position for over a decade. Al-Salih requires Aybeg to maintain a Mamluk force of one hundred, funded through Aybeg's *jamakiyah*, or salary, plus the income from his fief holdings. Further, he must be proficient enough tactically to lead up to one thousand men—some of these soldiers often being auxiliaries.

Aybeg signals for all to surround him, his customary scowl fitting on this serious day. "We have a report that an infidel force is making its way to Mansura," he announces. "A sizeable cavalry detachment pushed southward from the Nile ford at the River Tanis."

The throng of Mamluks are silent, taking in his words.

"Remember, the Franj will have struggled to cross the river and then galloped several miles before hitting Mansura. Use their fatigue to our advantage. None will know their way through the city streets." He nods his head assertively. His dark eyes blaze. "All that is left is to carry out our plan."

He looks intently into the eyes of as many as possible, as if to detect any confusion or hesitancy in implementing their scheme. "This is the day we'll send them all back to the devil. Execute. Execute."

Silence.

Leander stares at the metal rectangles across Duyal's steel-clad back, his leader's armor looking almost new. Only the worn neck guard on Duyal's jawshan looks out of place. An affection fills Leander, as he recalls why. His commander removed this piece from the original hardened leather cuirass gifted to him by then Prince al-Salih ten years past and secured it to every jawshan he has worn since. Duyal saved the neck guard, not because of its make or utility, but solely because of the writing upon it and his perceived luck when wearing it. Even Amir Duyal's armor is the stuff of legend.

Etched into the leather is the first part of a Koranic verse, the other two sections adorning the length of each gaiter. Through the scratches, scuffs and black stains, Leander slowly reads the nearly obscured Turkish on the fired-dried slab of thick hide covering his commander's neck: "And be not weak-hearted in the pursuit of the enemy."

Again, a wave of doubt flows through him. Leander grimaces. "Weak-hearted. Don't prove yourself weak-hearted," he murmurs. He must not let down his mates; he must not disappoint Duyal. Or al-Salih. Leander looks heavenward for a moment.

The crease between Aybeg's brows goes deeper, pushing sun-damaged skin to its sides. "At stake is everything. By holding Mansura, we prevent the French King from having a short road to Cairo, the mother of our empire. By holding Cairo, we keep Jerusalem. By protecting Jerusalem, we save Islam. Go now, brothers, and perform our God's will upon the infidels."

The entire group responds with a simultaneous, guttural snort of motivation. "Err!"

CHAPTER
12

Leander
Mansura
February 9, 1250

The hooves of forty-one Arabians clop the hard-packed street. Straight-backed riders in scarlet and gold proceed southward in a column of twos, following Amir Duyal. Approaching the north side of Mansura, the Mamluks from Amirate Three overtake the last groups of civilians—women in fine dress pushing overfilled carts alongside meager families carrying bags and hasty packs, some with human cargo strapped across their shoulders. Wiped from their faces is any shred of optimism that the Crusaders will be stopped before reaching their town.

Farther south, the amirate passes the mudbrick-and-papyrus-reed constructions of the poor, the walls of their homes exposing patches of rotted cane, looking like a mangy dog's coat. Sun-cracked bricks crumble on the structures' south sides, unable to endure the blazing heat.

Horses snort, a clink of their ornate tack sounding with each hoof stomp. A feeding goat pauses his sideways chewing to watch the red-coated men clomp by in a whoosh of dust. Along the road are homes long abandoned. Weeds choke untended gardens and only single rows of stone bricks are still erect, the rest toppled or eroded. Leander wonders if his family's tiny house in France is in similar condition and if his father is still alive and able to maintain his tiny fief in Ramerupt.

Into the heart of Mansura, they move among the white-bricked homes of the rich, abodes with ramped stairs leading to doors four feet off the ground and branches of fruit trees extending above the clean walls of their courtyards. An old woman looks up with tired eyes from a block bench built into her wall—perhaps somebody's mother, unwilling to abandon the family house.

The town is largely empty. Only some of the merchants remain. Those are not men of principle or courage who are unafraid of the impending fight, but those Leander sees as being men of greed: dealers refusing to leave their shops or wares to the hands of heathens, traders adoring their silver perhaps more than their lives, and men with too many goods or not enough carts to transport their merchandise.

Fully aware of the consequences of combat, Leander is keen to be out of their fortress and moving in the open on the back of Luna, rather than staring at those high block walls. Doing, rather than stewing about what might be.

A robed man heaps another load of linen upon his barrow and rests with turbaned head buried in his elbows atop the load. Hearing the horses, he looks up to Duyal. A sweat stain blemishes the fine silk cloth across the man's brow. His lower lip trembles. "Save us, warriors of Allah. Please save us and our homes." The formation passes him without a word.

Duyal takes a road veering left, leading half the amirate toward the northern part of its assigned east sector. He turns back in his saddle only briefly to nod at Sedat as his second-in-command continues southward with the other two squads of ten. Mamluks eye their brothers on diverging paths, Leander and the others wondering how many of their mates will not return.

Closer to the city center, Duyal and his twenty trot past multi-level houses painted white with reed mats covering most of their barred windows. Duyal extends an arm and motions downward with his palm. The men slow their horses, hoof clomps turning to noisy claps on the fire-baked brick, the clatter bouncing between the mud-slathered buildings. Farther down the road, the homes of the wealthy flash their elegance, their walls spread with limestone stucco, some splashed in pastels of orange and green.

Amir Duyal's men move through the remnants of a small bazaar, where flies buzz abandoned fish and scraps of meat left to spoil on the slanted displays. A lettuce head fallen from a cart lies smashed by a wheel. At windows overhanging the streets, brown arms pull shutters closed on shops and houses. A woman wrestling an overburdened cart catches Leander's eye. Hers are wet and swollen. She blurts in broken Turkish, "The Franks are too many—go back, ride away, while you can!"

Leander looks down, speaking to her softly in her own Coptic dialect. "Where's your faith in God, believer? Where's your confidence in those who'll defend you?" He feels the butt of his horse sway slightly back and forth and hears the splat of shit hit the ground, as if Luna wishes to add her contempt to the woman's statement.

He turns in the saddle. The woman lowers her head, her lip pouting. He shrugs off the tenderness, the sympathy that builds in his heart. Many of the locals are too quick to ditch their faith, doubtful of any who protect them, willing to believe ranted exaggerations about the coming enemy.

Clicks from a multitude of shod hooves resonate among the town's taller buildings. Without turning his head, Duyal points left. Three men peel east into the tight side street. He does the same all along a two-mile stretch, distributing more of his twenty men into the smaller streets and even the tight alleyways, where his Mamluks of the "hammer element" will be well concealed.

Again, their commander's finger points. Binny bears left into an alley with Slap and Leander following, while the remainder of the squad rides on with their commander. Leander watches Duyal until his bouncing shoulders round the bend. "Protect him, dear Allah, please protect him."

The trio walk their horses slowly into their station, eyeing several broken crates on the right.

"Behind these, eh?" Leander asks.

"Yeah, let's stack a few of 'em," Binny says.

They push crates into the alley and heft smaller ones atop them until the height of their hasty structure reaches their horses' windpipes. They tie off their mounts behind the heap and sit atop some of the smaller strongboxes, facing each other.

"I hope the Franj are dumb enough to chase our rabbits," Slap says.

"Yeah," Binny says in a whisper.

They wait in silence, Leander at times reaching up to stroke the neck of his horse.

"Both of your girls sit at home together. You know they whine and conspire against you," Binny says.

Leander smiles, knowing his friend speaks of his twin crossbows, Galina and Gamila. "No. They love me."

"How will you function without your mistress along?" Slap asks, mocking a serious tone.

"I already explained to them that we'd be in tight quarters. They were fine with it," Leander says.

"I doubt it—they're women," Slap says.

They laugh.

Binny shakes his head. "The command hasn't asked you to carry a qaw in a year now, my friend. Do you even remember how to shoot one?"

"Can you fault them?" Leander asks with a raised eyebrow. "Surely you wouldn't want me covering your backs with a recurve, after what you saw of me with that weapon in the tibaq. The amirs had to put some sort of projectile weapon in my hands."

Binny grins. "You'd prefer to carry the crossbow, even if you shot the qaw better than your girls, wouldn't you?"

"Given the choice, I prefer the crossbow."

"Why?" Slap asks. "For every bolt through that mistress, you can shoot twenty to thirty arrows with your qaw."

"But that one bolt will travel six hundred paces and go through a Crusader's plated armor."

Slap shrugs. "But it's more than that, isn't it?"

"On the deepest level, I guess I carry it for my father. You remember, he loved the crossbow. It was nearly all we had in common. When he lost his arm and couldn't shoot, I figured I became his other arm. It was then that he taught me everything about the weapon and shooting. My shots were his. My shots are still his."

"Didn't you once say that your father was a little disheartened that you hadn't become a mounted knight in France?" Binny asks.

"That's right."

Leander pushed open the old door of their home, the grain in its vertical planks spread wide and crevassed.

His father looked up from his gruel and smiled. "Look who's home." He rose painfully, pushing his stub atop the table to assist. Shuffling like an old man, he patted his son on the back. "Did you find anything out yet?"

Leander smiled, looked up at his father's most prized possession—the dust-covered weapon sitting on pegs high above the hearth next to the big chain link, the crossbow gifted to him by Lord Erard. As a younger boy, he had loved when his father would bring it down. Its fine finish and composite bowstaves were produced in England by the legendary craftsman, Peter Saraczenus, "The Saracen," snatched from the Muslims by the English during Richard the Lionheart's Crusade.

His father loved this weapon but hated most of the Parisian artisans who made bows. He saw the craftsmen as soft and overpaid, most earning four sous per day, the same as the brave souls firing the weapons in battle. "A dreadful injustice," his father often ranted. But for some reason, his elder made an exception for Saraczenus, whom he had never met, adoring the artillator for the accurate and sturdy crossbows he constructed. None were better.

"My path is chosen. I'm now a mounted crossbowman," Leander said, searching his father's face.

His father looked down at the floor, then up at Leander with a furled brow. "But what about the chevaliers engage? You said they had you targeted to become an enlisted knight."

Leander's heart sank. "In the end, I wished to carry the same weapon that you did. How could I waste all that you'd taught me? I thought you'd be pleased."

A hint of disappointment on his father's face. "Well, yes, yes. Always. But the knights ..."

Leander stiffened. "Just as you, I despise the arrogance of the bannerets. I couldn't force myself to be near them, to be one of them."

His father gave a tight-lipped nod of regret, likely wishing he had held his tongue more often in front of his only son. "I thought you'd be something more than me. Maybe what I hated was my own lack of skill and coin needed to become one of them. But you ... you had the talent. And with Lord Erard's willingness to fund ... "

"No, what you hated was the infantry and crossbowmen doing the dirty work, while the knights galloped in for the glory."

His father looked down, sighed. "Well ... "

"I'm in with talented men and I ride a horse from the same stock as those the knights ride. I receive five sous per day. With it, we'll be able to put a new roof on this house."

His father grinned, yet melancholy still lingered in his eyes. "You're a good son. Let's get you a meal."

Binny looks at Leander sideways, waiting for more. Slap

raises one eyebrow, the rope of scar on his temple bulging.

Leander sighs. "Crossbowmen in France—in all of Europe— they're viewed as second-rate soldiers. The lords used them to protect the flanks of the more valuable infantry, or to engage the enemy before the knights would assault. We were tolerated support elements there."

"Hmm. 'Tolerated support.' Kind of like Slap, as our friend," Binny says with a grin.

"You mean Slap as Leander's friend," the bull-necked one says.

Leander chuckles softly, drawing his hand through his rough beard with a grin. "To the Franks, the crossbow was a weapon for the weak man—maybe one for the injured to tote when a unit was shorthanded, something to put in the twisted hands of an old man, when desperate. A weapon of the peasant. It's the way the European lords look at any guy who fires any missile—javelins, stones..."

"And arrows," Binny says with a sneer. "Just another reason for them to hate us Muslim infidels." He wipes the sweat from his face, the heat of the day up and the lack of shade and breeze in their alley only heightening the conditions.

"Right, many Crusaders see all Saracen archers as the lowest. We're cowards, preferring the bow because we're too scared to engage in close combat."

"Yeah, we'll see about that today," Slap says. "They forget we also carry these." He pats his lance and the sword at his side. He begins to rock contentedly in his saddle.

Binny grunts. "I always found it damn odd how the Church—a supposed institution of peace—not only starts these wars, but is also keen to dictate how men braver than they are should fight."

"The Church throws its weight against anything but close combat," Leander says. "They tried to ban not just crossbows, but even ordinary hand bows in warfare—except for use against 'infidels,' of course."

"Easy for the holy ones to suggest foolish rules in war when they can sit in castled sanctuary, never having to engage in the bloody business themselves," Binny says.

Leander chuckles.

"But why does the Church do this?" Slaps asks.

"I think to suppress any weapon, *any thing* that challenges the existing military order. And remember, there are merchants selling swords and lances who nod their heads at this policy, not wanting their heaps of silver impacted." Leander scoffs.

"Right. War—it always seems to come back to coin," Binny says.

Leander lightens. "Well, anyhow, deep down I think my father was proud of me, carrying on his legacy with the crossbow."

"Carrying on the tradition of being a renegade," Binny says.

"But it wasn't just the Franj attitude toward the crossbow that made you leave them, was it?" Slap asks.

The grin leaves Binny's face. "Yeah, all these moons together and you've managed to sidestep that topic. By Allah, we may not survive the day. You at least owe the two of us a straight answer as to what really made you ditch them at Harbiyya."

Leander nods his head to Binny. "La Forbie ... I never completely said, but think you know already. It wasn't that I didn't love my homeland, or the men I served with. It's just ... well, let me ask you this. Do you love our patron? Would you do anything for him—put aside all of your personal ambitions for his aims and well-being?"

"Of course," Slap says.

"And our unit—you feel the same toward it?"

"Yeah," Binny says.

"And what about the rest of the Bahri, and even the Salihi, and Halqa. All the better units. You feel each would basically answer these questions the same way?" Leander asks.

Binny and Slap exchange glances.

"Yeah, aside from the odd fellow," Binny says.

"Well, from what I saw, such didn't exist with the various

elements of the Franj. At least not from what ... "

They turn their heads simultaneously to where the alley discharges into the street and the sound of distant hooves. All three jump from their crates and untie their horses. The lighter signature of the Arabians approaching from the north is closer now, followed by the heavier pounding of Crusader hooves, this thudding taking Leander back to his former life, the boy affixing the metal horseshoes to Lord Erard's horses, six nails per shoe.

Hearing the sound of those shoes skidding on the slick brick surface just north of them, the trio pull down on their reins, bunching them into a fist below the horses' throats, dipping their horses' heads behind the crates. Each man pats his mount, whispering to keep his animal calm.

Six Mamluks in the "rabbit element" roar past the alley entrance heading southward. Shortly afterward, there's the racket of metal on brick as more than a dozen Crusaders follow, wearing the garb of the Templars. When the sound of hooves dissipate, Leander hears a mumbling of voices and the sound of wood dragging on brick. A screech of metal.

"The civilians set the blocker," Binny says. "I don't trust them. When they're done, let's check it."

They wait, Binny eventually nodding to Leander.

Leander mounts, nudging his horse forward. When reaching the entrance to the side street, he pokes his head out, peering both ways. Nothing.

He rides north a short distance, past a slight curve in the street, and stops. Several hundred feet away, a pair of men struggle to pull another beam across the street. Women add small pieces of furniture and two men carry a large bureau, setting it length-wise in the street. Men push donkey carts. A child sets rocks on either side of the cart wheels. Tables turned so their legs face the enemy are piled onto the growing mass.

Leander returns to his mates in the alley. "It's being done surprisingly well. The Franj won't see the blockage until a bit after our spot."

His friends nod.

They again wait in silence, their horses becoming fidgety.

In time, they hear muffled shouts from the south. The far-off clank of steel. The muted drum of more hooves now spreading about the east sector.

"They're coming back—they're on to the game," Slap says.

"The Franj may never get this far back north," Binny says.

"If they're killed before arriving to us, all the better," Slap says.

Soon the three-beat tap of metal on brick. Two horses moving quickly, one losing its footing, scrabbling to regain it, and then sliding to a stop.

"*Non, cette façon! Cette façon!*" ("No, this way! This way!")

Slap and Binny look to Leander.

Leander nods emphatically. "They're coming," he whispers.

CHAPTER
13

Leander
Mansura
February 9, 1250

A pair of black-skirted stallions gallop by, their riders in the white surcoats of the Templars.

"Let's go," Binny says.

They walk their horses out of the alley and into the street, with Binny in the lead. Turning north, they round the bend, three abreast. The Franj probe the length of the barrier, right up to where it abuts a high wall on either side. Unable to find an out, they turn their horses.

Leander again feels his head go fuzzy as it did in Damietta. He tries to shake it off, runs his fingers along the scar on his leg. "Kill them or they kill you and your brothers," he mutters to himself.

The Templars bunch and approach warily, clad in long-sleeved chain mail hauberks, the signature white mantles, or *habits*, of their brotherhood gone gray from the dust. Leander becomes fixated on the red cross stitched across their hearts, the same cross that adorned his brother-in-law's cloak that hung on a peg in their house in Ramerupt those years past.

> *Leander sat on the far end of the table, listening as his brother-in-law described the training in his brotherhood. Leander's father nodded; Leander yawned.*
>
> *The Templar turned to the young Leander. "You still in Erard's castle?" A smug chuckle and shake of the head. "You know I could put a word in for you, maybe get you a look next year—a chance at becoming one of the best." Leander's sister's eyes brightened, a cheery smile crossing her face.*

A creep of doubt swells within him.

"Don't think the Templars untalented with sword—some of the butchers have the gift," Duyal said.

Likely identifying their foes as Royal Mamluks, the two Templars halt, a harsh exchange of words between them. Binny's team continues forward, stopping thirty paces from the Crusaders.

Old braids of sweat left an interlacing of brown streaks down the Franks' cheeks like remnants of dirty tears. Slivers of the white padded coifs beneath their mail hoods show waxy and black. The rectangles of face not covered by chain weave expose frizzled beards and skin red from dehydration. Dread fills their eyes.

The Templars dip their shoulders, causing the curved shields lashed on their backs to slide forward. In one motion, they slip their left arms through the dual leather straps and square the black-and-white insignia of the order across their bodies. One Crusader has lost his iron-plated "kettle hat;" the other pushes up his brim to better see who opposes him.

"*Nous devons les tuer. Maintenant!*" ("We must kill them. Now!") the near man says.

Leander ignores the threat, his eyes going quickly to the men's hands and saddles to assess any advantage. "Near man's lance sheared," Leander says in a forced calm.

"Near man, mine," Binny says, lowering his lance.

Upon hearing his friend's voice, Leander feels the cloud of uncertainty being sucked out of him, as if a giant bellows has been opened inside his mouth, pulling the feeble air from his lungs.

He remembers that he is not alone, that beside him are not just friends who are merely like him—they *are* him. And he is them. One being. Inside is the same fear, the same pride, the same comfort in knowing that each will protect the other man, each will fight to his last gasp to preserve the others. In this one, ordinary phrase uttered by Binny is a force more powerful than the tides, more comforting than any words of reassurance spoken by his mother when he was just a boy.

Leander gains heart, the fog in his head clearing, as if burned off by the warming sun of Binny's three simple words. He nods to himself. "As you were trained, as you were trained," he says.

Binny charges. The lead Templar, whether delirious or simply careless, raises his broken weapon, seeming to forget that a full three feet of ash and the weapon's iron head are missing. He gives spurs.

Realizing at the last second his error, the Frenchman reins in and attempts to parry the incoming blow with his shattered lance, shifting his shield to protect, yet in the process exposing the left side of his chest. Binny thrusts, running his lance's sharpened head clean through the Crusader's rib cage, driving him into the high rock wall behind him, and lodging Binny's lance tip between a deep gap in the stacked stones.

The Frank's wood-slatted shield falls to the road with a thump. The Crusader grasps the cane with both hands, the whites of his eyes enlarged. His jaw drops in amazement that the shaft is in him. With his feet having somehow slid through his stirrups, the Templar stays affixed to the wall, his torso stretched but twisted, his ass two feet off the saddle. Also wedged against the stone face, the Crusader's horse struggles to free itself, its thrashing growing increasingly frantic.

Unable to remove his lance from the wall, Binny backs off as the Franj's white-hooded stallion rears. The force rips apart the leather cinches on the Frank's belt, violently pulling the iron chausses from the knight's legs in the manner of two squirrels being skinned simultaneously. With the leggings now detached from his rider's feet, his horse runs down the street, the chain mail fronts and backside leather of the leggings wadded partway in the stirrup and dragging on the ground on either side of the horse's belly.

The dead Templar remains impaled against the wall, his feet pulled grotesquely flat, the man ridiculously exposed in his tan breeches, his tongue protruding from his mouth. His mate stares with mouth agape at the peculiar scene.

During the fray, Slap snuck around and behind the remaining Templar, and deploys his lance. Binny falls in behind Leander, who now approaches the lone Crusader. The Crusader spins his horse in a useless attempt to watch all threats. A resigned look of imminent death fills the man's face. He pats the cross emblazoned upon his white mantle, leaving his gloved hand upon his heart. The Templar seems to draw strength from the emblem, authorized by Pope Eugenius III one hundred years past. The insignia's meaning: martyrdom.

The Crusader rips at the leather bindings, securing the ventilator across his chin and mouth. It flops open, revealing a stubbled cleft chin and a fatalistic, white-toothed grin. Leander speculates on the thoughts that must be streaming through the Templar's head.

This man is surely convinced that after dying on the battlefield fighting Muslims, he will win instant entry to heaven. Because of his commitment to the brotherhood, the Templar knows that he is only seconds from meeting his Lord Jesus Christ with his sins already wiped clean. The Templar signals the cross.

"He's fighting to die. Stay disciplined," Leander says to his brothers in their native Turkish.

"*Vous pouvez aller en enfer, c'est pas le ciel, Temple*," ("You'll be going to hell, not heaven, Templar,") Leander says to the Crusader.

The Templar raises a lip, showing his teeth as would a dog before growling. "*Un Français parti aux infidèles. Ne me dites pas qui est lié à l'enfer.*" ("A Frenchman gone to the infidels. Don't tell me who is bound for hell.")

In this man's accent and tone, Leander hears the conceit of his brother-in-law. Leander leers darkly.

The Mamluk trio closes the distance. Slap pokes at the enemy's back to put him off balance, and prods at the man's elbow to unsteady his lance, which the Templar alternately points at both Leander and Binny. Slap quickly transfers his own lance and smacks the man across the back of the neck with the long cane, the jolt pushing the Templar's kettle hat over his face. Spastically, the man forearms the brim of his helmet and it falls to the ground. He drops his lance in the process. His faith cannot overcome his fatigue.

The Franj looks down at his helmet wobbling back and forth in the street, the alternate ticking of each side of its brim against the bricks a signal of the Templar's fate. He grimaces, pulling down the hooded coif behind his neck. His runs a sleeve atop his brow, his hair wet and matted to his head, the youth in his facial features now exposed in full. He pulls his broadsword, determined, motioning them in with his blade hand. "*Viennent maintenant les païens.*" ("Come now, heathens.")

The Templar's head snaps back and forth between Binny and Slap. Each time the Crusader's eyes leave him, Slap plunges his lance into the Crusader's back with just enough force for his tip to penetrate the chain mail but not enough to entangle his blade in the linked armor. When the Crusader turns toward Slap, Leander slashes at the Crusader with his sword. All the while, Slap repeats in broken French the sentence he made Leander teach him earlier. "*Nous allons maintenant vous envoyer en enfer. Nous allons maintenant vous envoyer en enfer.*" ("We'll now send you to hell.")

Growing tired of the words rolling clumsily off his tongue, Slap shortens his chant to just its essential element, stating it each time he thrusts. "*En enfer. En enfer.*" With the back of the

Templar's ivory habit now splotted in crimson, Slap reverts back to his native language, continuing to curse the man as he jabs. "To hell. To hell."

Weakened and out of options, the Templar moves in and takes a wild swing at Binny, who blocks the lazy stroke with his shield, purposely leaving the man's arm up and exposed. Leander, sword already up, comes down with his blade atop the man's bicep, feeling the clunk as his sword cleaves bone. The Templar's arm collapses like a hinge, held on only by the unsevered links of chain mail beneath his arm.

The clang of broadsword on brick.

The Templar hugs his wound, cowers on his saddle, his grunts becoming hisses. Leander has the same unnerving sensation as hearing a wounded fox back in the forests of France, the coy predator screaming, twirling with a crossbow bolt through him. "Put him out of his misery," he mutters.

Slap buries his lance in the Templar's back and spins his own mount away. With a quick backhand stroke across the neck, Binny severs the Crusader's skull. The Frank tips in his saddle and crumbles to the ground, propped up grotesquely by Slap's shredded cane. The Crusader's horse stomps fretfully, its unblinking brown eyes large and fearful, peering through the slits of his white head covering, the red cross on either side of its neck and shoulders obscured by its rider's blood.

The Mamluks make a hole for the beast in the tight street and the horse dashes through the opening, from brisket down, the black section of his covering fluttering in the wind. Evil's transport departing.

With heaving chests, they look about, listen for the sound of more horses, yet hear nothing. Already, Leander feels the shake coming to his hands. He grasps tighter on his reins.

"We're squandered to stay here and wait for possibly nobody," Binny says, licking the dry from his lips. "Duyal said use our best judgment when it came to moving in search of enemy."

"But also to stay in our corridor," Leander says.

"Yeah. But we must keep on them," Slap says.

Leander looks to the mangled lump of chainmail, the French blood seeping between the brick pavers, and then over to the wall, where flies already begin to land on the tongue of the other skewered Templar. "Your choice," he says to Binny, still out of breath. "We'll follow you, regardless."

"South we go," Binny says.

They turn left, walking their horses down the town's main artery, listening and looking both ways, peeking down the side streets and alleys as they ride. They squeeze through a tight path in another barricade, one cleared by the Crusaders. Leander feels the adrenaline draining from him. A weariness sets in.

They continue, passing lances and even crossbows chucked by the Franj in flight, their longer weapons of little use in these cramped spaces, their crossbows only adding weight to the backs of tired mounts. Farther south, the Mamluks slow to crest a bump in the terrain. From the other side, smoke lifts in wispy puffs. They pull their swords and look over the top.

Naft still burns in the street among remnants of shattered clay. Strewn about are blue shields covered with abundant gold lilies. A single, horizontal red stripe adorns the shield's top and three vertical stripes, as if each strip were a red banner hanging down, decorated with three yellow castles apiece.

Three dead men in mantles of the same design lay crumbled, some with their bright colors blackened from the Greek Fire, their straight-banged hair and eyebrows singed.

Thirty paces away, six more men of this prince lie slain, some with heads bashed open, most hacked to death, their shields in varying degrees of splinters. Not a single Mamluk lies among them.

"Who are they, Leander? Is this the king's own heraldry?" Binny asks.

Leander stares at the fleur-de-lis on the shields. Some in France say the fancy symbol represents a lily, others say it is lotus flower, but all agree it means royalty—signifying perfection, light, and life. Yet those carrying the symbol today do not look so perfect.

Legend has it that an angel presented Clovis, the Merovingian King of the Franks, with a golden iris as a symbol of purification upon his conversion to Christianity. Leander's father told him that water lilies showed Clovis where to safely cross a river, helping him earn victory in an ensuing battle, so the king took on the symbol as his own.

Leander shakes his head. "Close—these are Robert of Artois' men." He looks at the cleaved neck of one and then up to Binny. "*Were* knights of the king's own brother."

"Look at their damn chins, some slick as a baby's ass," Slap says, a look of bewilderment on his face.

Binny chuckles. "Not manly enough to keep a beard. By Allah—look at this one, the fuzz on his ... "

A shop door creaks open. A shot of adrenalin through Leander's limbs. He pulls his reins to face the doorway as all three raise their blades to the ready. Two hooded men in scorched leather walk out with palms open. One smiles.

"Friendlies," the older of them says, his arms spreading wider, a curl of smoke rising from the fuse up his left sleeve. "We hid when we heard your hooves, not knowing if more devils were coming back."

Binny smiles, relieved. "Men of the Jandar! Looks like you did a job on these."

"We only helped. Your Bahri made short work of them." The younger flips down his hood, exposing burn holes and pits in his filthy hat, dark smudges about his ears and cheeks.

"We heard more fighting," the older grenadier says, pointing west. "We ought to head where the infidels remain."

"But that's not our sector," Slap says.

The grenadier scowls. "Rarely are men punished for leaving an area of no enemy and heading to assist where there is."

"Actually, it happens regularly. Our amirs call it disobeying orders," Binny says sarcastically.

They all go silent for a while.

"Wasn't the idea to kill them and keep them out of Cairo?" the younger Jandar asks.

The Mamluks look at each other.

"He's right. I'd rather err pursuing the enemy and take a spanking for not following orders than sit on our asses, when others might need the help. How many pots do you have left?" Binny asks, turning back to the Jandars.

The grimy man lifts his arm, exposing a leather pouch, where three of his six leather dividers retain clay containers. "We each have three."

"We'll take you with us," Binny says.

The pair untie their pouches and cautiously hand them to Leander and Binny before being pulled onto the rumps of the Mamluk mounts. The five of them continue farther south, eventually taking a street bearing west.

Midway down it, they find a single Mamluk sitting atop a piece of rubble, petting his toppled horse. Close to him are two dead Mamluks, a horse cover spread over their bodies, only their boots exposed. Nearby is Crusader carnage more gruesome than the sight prior, a blue banner with five yellow lions adorning the casualty's armor. Pools of blood. Faces looking up with the soft expression of dead children.

"Fellow Bahri, you all right?" Binny asks as they near.

The Mamluk does not acknowledge their presence. The grenadiers slide off the backs of the horses.

When only feet from him, Leander notices the purse at the man's belt, sees that he is an Amir of Forty. "Our apologies, my Amir, we weren't aware of your grade."

The brawny man finally looks up from his horse and scans the men before him. "It's all right. What unit are you with?" he asks, with a deep voice over the wheeze of his horse.

"Amir Baybars, we're with Amirate Three," Leander says, in case Binny did not recognize him.

Baybars, at only twenty-one years, is the youngest Amir of Forty in the regiment. A rising star. Leander knows little of the man, except that he is a Kipchak, like most, and has been in charge of Amirate Seven for many moons.

The man nods, his eyes going back to his horse. "She's been my favorite mount for six years. I think this may be it for her."

"I'm sorry," Leander says.

"Amirate Three—Duyal's outfit. You're lucky to be led by such a good man. Very lucky." He looks up to them with a half-smile, his eyes seeking their faces to see if they realize it.

"Yes, my Amir," Binny says.

"This world can be a very small place. Very small." Baybars' eyes go to his dead brothers' uncovered boot toes showing from under the horse armor. He purses his lips. "I knew Duyal's older brother, Gozde, many years ago."

His face goes softer, surely his mind drifting back to that time. "I was just a boy and Gozde took the time to instruct me on his weapons. Drills even. Who could've known that fate would one day place us in the same regiment? Too bad for only a short time, though. Gozde was the best, maybe none better. Allah bless him."

"I had no idea," Leander says.

"Is there a place you wish us to find the enemy, or can we give you a ride back, my Amir?" Binny asks.

"No, I think the enemy that entered Mansura is beaten—I believe there are only a few of our units still mopping up. And the rest of my unit will come for me." He again eyes his mates. "But you can find a cart for this one," he says, pointing wearily at a bloodied Crusader sprawled over his dead horse. The man is a mess—his left foot missing, his right hand gone, still clutching in his remaining paw his sword with a severed tip.

Leander and his mates look at the amir with bewilderment.

"We'll haul him back with ours," Baybars says, somberly. "While I have no love for them, unfortunately there are some brave ones in their ranks." He spits. "The sultan may offer this body back to the Crusaders. As you know, he does have a weak spot for the courageous, even if infidels. I believe this one is the Englishman, William Longsword. Mercifully, the sultan will have no need for me to tell their people of this man's tale, as two of the mongrels managed to escape this tangle." He shrugs. "At least this one goes to our master stiff and lifeless."

They nod.

Baybars looks to Leander with head tilted, one eye half-closed in thought. "Are you the one they call 'the Frank'?"

"Yes, my Amir."

Baybars gives a fast, short smile and then resumes comforting his horse.

CHAPTER

14

Leander
al-Rawda Citadel, Cairo
Feb 17, 1250

With his knees buried into his elbows, Leander daydreams from a riverside bench tucked under an open-air belvedere at the al-Rawda Citadel. The morning sky bleeds swirls of orange and violet into the dark Nile. Midstream, two men standing in a pile of net ply their oars to a papyrus reed boat, its arching hull twisted, its tightly bound reeds splitting at rail and stern, its rotted face splotched in ugly black.

Black. Rotting. He squeezes his forehead, as the images of the slaughter and its aftermath at Mansura come flooding back to him. Last week, Leander's squad gathered a more complete account of the battle from a captured Crusader. Pulling the half-drowned Templar from the Raxi, they pried the French version of the bitter story from the waterlogged man.

Slap pressed the tip of his sword beneath the Templar's exposed throat. He growled. "You best tell it all. I'd be pleased to slit your pipe and chuck you back into the river with your bloated mates."

The man's sodden chest heaved. His eyes fluttered, taking in the Mamluks surrounding him. Taking a deep breath, he nodded remorsefully. Slap eased the blade away.

"The king planned to fight his way to Cairo, knew he had to take Mansura first," the Crusader muttered in passable Turkish. "When he quit our camp on the north bank, the king assigned his brother, Robert of Artois, to march an advanced party of personal knights and us Templars downstream to secure the ford." The Franj snarled, seemingly disgusted to even utter Artois' name.

"But how did the king even know of that crossing?" Leander asked.

The Templar looked him in the eyes. "King Louis had paid a Bedu a few gold pieces to learn of the exact place."

Leander shook his head. "Then?"

The Franj grimaced. "Once across, instead of staying put to guard the far shore, as the king directed, Artois chided us into leaving our station and joining his troops in finding the enemy."

"Before the main army forded?" Leander asked.

The Franj looked down at the red cross emblazoned upon his chest and the mud pressed into his chainmail sleeves. He nodded, picking at the muck that coated his hands. "Artois defied his own brother, disobeyed the king's order."

Leander looked at his friends. Binny raised his eyebrows.

The Templar continued. "Artois led our detachment upstream along the south bank of the Raxi until we came upon the Muslim camp. With most of the Saracens asleep, Artois ordered us to attack."

Slap dove at the seated man, knocking the Crusader to his back. He wedged his massive forearm against the Templar's neck and held it there. "And there you slew every living man, woman, child, and beast!"

Two Mamluks jumped in, each man wrenching one of Slap's beefy arms from the enemy. Slap relented, wriggling to his feet

*while pushing his brothers. He walked away, tears streaming
down his scarred cheeks. "They're fucking butchers!"*

*Leander hovered over the Templar, attempting to control his
own anger, as only days earlier, all in Amirate Three had walked
through Fakhr al-Din's ravaged camp and seen the carnage. "And
filled with confidence—or bloodlust— after your massacring of
hundreds, you decided to continue southward into Mansura."*

*The Crusader rubbed his throat. "Artois argued that we
should exploit our success."*

"Easy as that," Binny chimed.

*"No. My lord, William of Sonnac, reasoned that we should
instead stay and guard the captured siege engines at the camp.
When a messenger rode up with the king's instructions to proceed
no farther, a great argument erupted between Artois' men and
ours. But it was no use. Artois would listen to no one."*

*"And into Mansura you gallantly rode—to your blessed
demise," Binny said, mocking the Frenchman's accent.*

*The Templar buried his hands in his crossed arms, his back
quaking as he sobbed.*

Leander felt no pity for the Templar that day; Amirate Three
had no reason to hear another word. They knew how the rest
of the battle played out. Joined by more Franj and English who
had also forded the river, Artois' Crusaders chased the fleeing
Muslim horsemen and the Turkmen "rabbits" positioned closer
to town. While the Muslims had paid a high price by not properly
guarding their riverside camp, the Mamluk plan of luring the
Franj into the tight city spaces had worked to perfection.

In and around the town of Mansura, the Mamluks and
supporting units slew over five hundred Crusaders. Among them
were men from Leander's hometown of Ramerupt. Slain were
both of Lord Erard's sons—Henri of Brienne and Erard, Jr.

Leander recalls the senior Erard poking about his French
castle with his cane, clearly satisfied with the forces his two
sons were building. Could the old man have ever guessed that

Leander, his young page, would one day fight for the enemy and take part in the downfall of both his sons? And Leander's own father. If still alive, what would the remaining Briennes do to him if they knew his son's role in Mansura? Leander hopes his father has mercifully passed.

Pummeled in the streets of Mansura, hundreds of the Crusaders managed to flee the barricaded traps in town and scurry back north toward their old camp—where the Raxi splits from the Damietta Arm of the Nile—only to drown in their attempts to swim across the Raxi upon the backs of weary horses. The king's brother, Robert of Artois, was among them. On their heels: swarms of men from the entire Egyptian Army.

Driving the disorganized Franj north, the Muslim forces trapped most of the infidels against the south bank of the Raxi. The Muslims pelted the Crusaders with Chinese Arrows and naft canisters chucked from the ends of spears, before sending wave after wave of infantry and cavalry charges, some in the Bahri and Salihi participating. For days the Egyptians pressed their attack, yet the Franj managed to beat back each assault.

Having finished their task of going door-to-door in rooting out the Franj hiding in abandoned homes in town, Leander and his fellow Mamluks from Amirate Three were ordered north to assist. They waited for a day on the south riverbank for orders. None came. Thankfully, the bloodbath ended.

For two days, Leander and his mates curled up, exhausted, in the river scrub opposite the enemy, watching, smelling, listening to the Crusaders. Wafts of breeze drifted the honeyed fragrance of Crusaders blood, as the Franj tended their wounded. With the Crusaders' backs against the Raxi Branch, carts creaked in from the east and the pounding of tent stakes echoed long into the night. The foes reestablished their camp near the Muslim one they had destroyed at the battle's start.

By the time Duyal's amirate packed up and headed south to Cairo, the north wind floated the rancid stench of decomposing bodies and the hisses and burps and farts from the round-bellied corpses that drifted to the river banks.

Technically, the Muslims had been stopped short of Damietta and driven away from the new Crusader camp, yet the Franj could hardly claim that they won what may one day be known as the "Battle of Mansura." Egyptian forces had overwhelmed most of the Frank positions and recaptured the Mamluk siege engines lost earlier in the battle. The French army had been so bloodied, it was a wonder the Franj had not returned to their ships in the Mediterranean. King Louis now owns a crippled force.

Leander rises from his bench, stretches, and leans against an ornate arch. His eyes return to the boat on the wide river. Three goats on its front deck pace nervously. One gives him a sideways glance. Leander sighs. Even the goats sense that all is not well at the island citadel.

And things are not. Al-Salih is dead. The long respiratory illness had finally taken their sultan. His funeral was a spectacle: the royal regiments in scarlet and Ayyubid yellow, flanked by the Halqa and Turkmen and the rest, all witnessing their patron's frail body being placed into the mausoleum, an army of rough men sobbing like young boys.

An indescribable sadness has fallen upon the regiment. Gone is not only the leader of the empire but also an irreplaceable father figure—a relationship that, for some Mamluks, stretched over twenty years. For nearly all of the Bahri, torn from the steppe as adolescents, al-Salih had superseded their natural-born fathers.

Al-Salih had bought them as hungry urchins and transformed them into the noblest knights of Islam. He had provided for them in every way, for many, even picking their Kipchak wives. To the younger Mamluks, their sultan was the wise grandfather with high standards who looked after them. For all, he was the man they never wanted to disappoint. This overwhelming presence in their lives is now departed.

Because of the ceaseless backstabbing from his Ayyubid clan—his brother and cousins and uncles—al-Salih had done the unthinkable over the past decade of his rule in promoting his Mamluks to the highest government positions. His Mamluks responded to this trust with an absolute devotion and widespread gratitude.

Leander, too, is grateful to al-Salih. Put in his place, Leander wonders if he would have been as gracious a sultan. He drops his head. Al-Salih not only accepted Leander into his army, he gave Leander a chance to earn a place in the sacred Bahri. This his patron did for a lad who was not only an infidel but a member of the most despised of his foreign enemies. Leander wipes away a tear.

The sultan had actually died more than two moons past in Mansura, yet, remarkably, the entire army was kept in the dark. Fortunately for Cairo, a level head remained in al-Salih's palace— the sultan's favorite wife, Shajarat al-Durr, or "Spray of Pearls." Initially one of al-Salih's slaves, she caught his eye years ago with not just her dark beauty but also her intelligence. Leander reckons this woman's intellect and her sensible conduct through personal and political crises had likely saved Cairo, and maybe the whole empire, from the Franj and only Allah knows which other cunning enemies who could have rallied their forces and snatched territory during the leadership void.

Queen al-Durr knew her husband's death would not only cause the regiments emotional distress, but also embolden the southward-encroaching Franks. Convinced that Egypt's Mamluks must focus on the enemy, she kept her husband's death a secret to all but two senior commanders, Fakhr al-Din of the Bahri and Jamal al-Din Muhsin of the Jamdariyya, the sultan's close bodyguard. The queen and these two men carried out al-Salih's wishes by sending Leander's Amir of One Hundred, Aqtay, north to Hisn Kayfa to bring back al-Salih's remaining son, al-Mu'azzam Turanshah, the sultan's vicegerent, or second-in-command.

The Mamluks now wait anxiously for this son to arrive any day to provide unity for the realm. Al-Salih's only other son was murdered years ago, allegedly by his uncle. Turanshah will be the next sultan of Egypt. Being led by a trusted blood relative, the seed of their patron, will do wonders for morale. Leander anticipates the youth will be greeted ecstatically.

Leander wrings his hands, depressed that al-Salih was not able to witness his Mamluks' performance in Mansura. While some of the Egyptian army had scattered in panic, al-Salih's chosen ones had held their own and won victory. Their sultan would have been proud.

Instead, he likely died with fresh thoughts of their loss of Damietta in his mind, wondering if Cairo and his entire empire would be swallowed by the French. The sultan knew well that if King Louis could take Egypt—its agricultural and economic centers being the empire's bread and money baskets—then the Franj would possess the critical logistical and military stepping stone that would ease the taking of Jerusalem and further gains into Syria.

By the time the Bahri and Salihi reached the northern outskirts of Cairo, word of their exploits, delivered by pigeon messengers, had preceded the warriors.

> Amirate Three rode their horses at the walk. Fatigue from the long day was finally setting in, their bodies beginning to shut down once their brains told them that the danger was past. Leander heard the populace before he saw them, like the faint roar from a distant waterfall. As they approached Cairo's fringes, people spilled from their mud-bricked homes, cheering and weeping and hugging in the streets. Staggering men passed mugs of beer to the soldiers. Slap pulled an admiring lad upon the rump of his Arabian.
>
> An old woman approached, a loose shawl about her rounded back. Leander drew the dagger from his saddle sheath and pressed it against his thigh, opposite her.
>
> "You protected us and shielded Islam from the devil. You're blessed slaves," the toothless woman said, her lips curling over her gums, smacking as she spoke, her palms together across her breast,

as if she were entering the mosque. She slid a tiny pack from her
shoulders and dug into it. He gripped his dagger. She came up with
a mangled chunk of bread. "Please, you take this. Please."

Leander rose in the saddle, famished. He sheathed his dagger
without her notice, grinned sideways, and lied. "I couldn't think
of it. We'll get to eat soon. I'm much happier to see you feed
yourself, your family."

She smiled, for the first time exposing three brown teeth,
protruding long in her puffy gums. "Of course. Saviors of the
faith. The lions of Islam." She rejoined her friends.

Binny rode up next to Leander. "Easy now, killer. You weren't
going to let another stick you in that same leg, now were you?"

Leander gave a parting wave to the old lady, who smiled
broadly again, pointing him out to the other elders. He nodded
politely toward their group and then turned to Binny. "Hell, no."

The celebration was cut short only by the announcement
of the sultan's death. This was just as well, as Leander worried
that Egypt's victory merriments were inappropriate and surely
a tad premature. While the Crusaders were damaged, they were
not all dead.

Leander descends the belvedere's polished stairs on stiff
legs. Reaching the tidied grounds, he spits. The French king
miscalculated on step one of his plan—the men in Egypt's army
will not roll over, at least not those in the Bahri and Salihi, no
matter how heartbroken they are. And if the sultan's son is even
half the man his father was, what's left of the Crusaders will
soon be tossed back into the Mediterranean.

He sucks in the fresh scent of the river and thinks of Jacinta,
missing her. Too much death, too much killing.

From Amirate Three alone: Hasad is dead, Kismet has
lost an arm, Ata is dead, Evren is dead, Rifat is dying, Najat
may lose a leg, and Can and Emre are unaccounted for, likely
drowned in the river or lying dead somewhere. Men from his
Khushdash. Brothers. Leander feels a guilt and a frustration but

mostly a reluctant acquiescence to fate. If he and his brothers had been anywhere near those who fell to Crusader blades, Leander and his squad might have shielded these comrades from the enemy or shown their loyalty by fighting and dying beside those friends who were overcome by the Franj. There was no doubt of this.

They had all been operating independently, and so far apart, that it was impossible to know who was where and in need of what, much less do anything for his brothers. Because of this, the amirate has only memories now of these dead friends and crippled mates, some fathers, whom the survivors will support with coin as long as they live.

Dozens more from other units are wounded or killed at Mansura. War is a horrible, awful undertaking—all of it. But just as his brothers came to see him when his calf was injured, he will do the same for those wounded and miserable.

He walks the long corridor of the island fortress barracks to the opposite side of the structure. He exits and walks over the bridge leading to a series of large tents that is an outpost to the infirmary, now overstuffed with casualties. Perhaps he will be able to see Jacinta's pretty face and hear her calming words. She may not know that he is still alive. He hopes that she cares.

Reaching the first tent, he peers inside. It is nearly empty, the cots arranged in rows, nurses preparing the area in anticipation of future sufferers. He walks to the second and quickly steps aside to avoid running into an Egyptian boy, the lad struggling out of the flap toting a covered basket, a blackened foot jutting from the top.

A look of alarm befalls the boy when he sees the scarlet coat and mustard-colored trousers of the Bahri. "My forgiveness, I didn't see you coming," the boy says.

"Worry not. You're working and I was in your way."

Swaths of blood smudge the youth's trouser leg and dot the passage. Under a small overhang is the remainder of the boy's work—a line of reed creels tucked against the south wall of the huge tent, undersized pieces of cut oilcloth beneath them, insufficient in keeping the oozing contents from staining the tan rock at their feet.

Leander steps into the tent. Medical men are peeling off their soiled garments. Their servants clean chopping implements with filthy rags. Leander passes them, the faint smell of decomposition and urine becoming stronger with each step he takes into the bowels of the place.

A Mamluk approaches. Seeing his purse and ornate silver, indicating an amir's belt, Leander stiffens. The amir's head is down in thought, the man mumbling to himself, shaking his head.

"Good morning, Amir," Leander says.

The man passes him in silence, too lost in thought or grief to even notice him.

Unable to locate his mates, Leander leaves this tent and enters another. Cots loaded with lumps of bandaged men in loose-fitting silks. Women in crimson-smudged aprons scurry between the beds, wearing sleeplessness in their eyes. The place drones in a buzz of hushed conversations, men enduring their pain in wheezes and low-pitched moans. He is brought back to Damietta and his own doubts and aches, when he wondered if he would ever again be fit enough to fight.

A woman carrying a basin of red-stained water pushes past him. He steps aside to make a pathway for her and another who follows. The stench here is overpowering. Dried flowers soaked in perfume and hung in thin cloth about the cots have almost no effect in combating the reek of shit and infected flesh. A gloominess fills him.

He searches the pus-soaked bandages and matted beards of the men on the lines of cots, looking for the faces of his two mates. Midway down the second line, he senses someone watching him. He turns to the middle of the aisle.

His heart flutters. Jacinta. Her eyes convey a sense of melancholy, mixed with relief. She nods. Her subtle gesture is short, its moderation fitting of this place. He makes his way to her, his eyes not leaving hers.

"Good to see you," she says, hiding her soiled hands in a wad of smock, her dress littered with handprints and creases soaked in miserable red streaks from her work.

"Good to see you," he says, feeling sorry for her, regretful that such a nice woman must be exposed to such carnage.

"I was wondering if you made it." She looks him over. "I am very happy that you survived. And apparently unhurt. The battle. It must've been terrible."

He nods.

"You fought bravely beside your friends, didn't you?" she asks.

Leander looks down. "I did my job."

He detects her shy smile from beneath the veil. "The people of Cairo and Mansura. They now call your Mamluks 'the lions of Islam,'" she says.

"So I've heard."

"I'm sorry, but I can't talk right now." Jacinta looks past him to a man with an arm hacked at the elbow, his hair sticking up, his stump wrapped thick in a soggy dressing.

"No, no. Of course. I distract you from your work. We'll talk later, after your shift?" he looks at her with eyebrows raised.

She sighs, a sadness in her eyes that he has not seen before. "I've been meaning to say something. I ... "

He waits with tilted head, expecting what comes.

"Leander, my father will not allow me to spend any more time with you. He tells me I must go straight home after work now. He ... "

Leander closes his eyes and forces a smile. "It's all right. You needn't explain. I understand. I do."

An older nurse walks past Jacinta, scowling.

"And not only do I get you into trouble at home, I also put you in poor standing here. I best go."

Her shoulders drop. He touches her arm and resumes the search for his wounded friends.

CHAPTER

15

Ox
Bahr al-Mahala, Nile delta
February 28, 1250

Ox raises his hands and delivers the takbir aloud. Bringing his hands to his sides, he and the others recite the Fatiha.

"In the name of God, the Compassionate, the Caring. Praise is to God, the sustaining Lord of all worlds. The Compassionate, the Caring, Master of the day of Judgment. You do we worship and you we ask for help. Guide us on the straight road. The road of those whom you have given on them Not those with anger on them, nor those who have gone astray."

"'Those who have gone astray.'" Ox huffs. As of late, he might fall into that class.

He finishes his short personal prayer with the other soldiers, their collective murmurs lost in the breeze and rattling palm fronds. He completes the prayer cycles, makes another prostration, and then returns to the seated position. He hopes that his prayers to Allah will be answered—that the new sultan will prove to be as wise and brave as the former. Yet, he doubts it.

He struggles to rise with a groan, holding his lower back. Turning away from the direction of Mecca, they trudge to their loads, the afternoon's heat scorching them as they leave the shade of the palms. He attempts to squeeze the throb, the effects of a lingering hangover, from his temples. He spits, his saliva exiting like a puff of cotton.

He somewhat regrets what he has put his body through the past several weeks. Ironically, it was not the fighting in Mansura that took its toll, but what came afterward. Once the deeds of the Turkish Lions in Mansura were made known to the populace, Cairo became a giant festival. Merely walking the street in the red coat of a Mamluk meant that beautiful women hugged him and men offered him jugs of *bouza*, Egyptian beer.

For many in town, the celebration lasted only days, until the sobering word of the sultan's death was shared. The amirs who knew their patron best stayed inside their Cairo homes for days and mourned. He heard that Aqtay was inconsolable. Surely, that is why they sent Aqtay to the Jazira to fetch the sultan's son, Turanshah, rather than allowing him to command valuable men in the fray. Aqtay would have been unable to hide his emotions from his cavalrymen, from Bahri who still had Franj to kill.

"Maybe a bit too mild for an Amir of One Hundred," Ox says to himself, picturing Aqtay of the Bahri sobbing in travel. "But what do I know?"

Once the Muslims had pushed the Crusaders to the south shore of the Raxi branch, the command had halted all operations, leaving the enemy to lick its wounds in camp north of Mansura. Why the amirs checked the Egyptian momentum after they had the Franj reeling remains a mystery to Ox. But with the sultan's funeral and time needed to resupply and reorganize a Muslim army of almost twelve thousand, downtime was inevitable. So, for some in Ox's Salihi, the merriment in Cairo went on for nearly two weeks.

For Ox, the spontaneous celebration was no more than an excuse to drink and hunt the streets for local women. On a deeper level, he figures being drunk was the only way to face the loss of his patron. And he was not the only one. Too often, he saw groups of laughing men with mugs raised only minutes later become whimpering loners. He understands. How he misses al-Salih already and the confidence gained by just the sultan's wink and nod when he recognized Ox among the others. How will the man Ox thought of as his second father ever be replaced? And the sultan truly had been his father, more than any man Ox had ever known.

Fortunately, Ox has no regrets regarding his relationship with the man. He thinks al-Salih must have passed with few negative thoughts of him. And how not? Ever since his patron assumed the sultanate in June of 1240, Ox had been a willing supporter as al-Salih faced the complicated, ever-changing web of alliances against him. By 1244, al-Salih Ismail of Damascus, al-Nasir Da'ud of Karak, al-Mansur Ibrahim of Homs, and the crusading Franks had all militarily opposed Cairo's al-Salih Ayyub. Yet, through a series of messy clashes and an endless chain of broken and repaired alliances, al-Salih had consolidated the empire.

How the assigned governors in each principality will react when Turanshah takes over is anyone's guess. Loyalties among the Ayyubid kin ebb and flow like tides in the sea. Surely, things will change somehow; all seem anxious whenever speaking of Turanshah. But with the Crusaders still on Cairo's doorstep, at least al-Salih's Mamluk regiments have something else to concentrate on.

Ox slogs through the loose sand toward their bizarre loads—two dozen sleds bearing large wooden hulls, papyrus reed boats, mast, oars, and sails. About him are not the men of his amirate, but rather a two-hundred-man detachment, handpicked and organized for their mission. Men assembled not based on some skill set or knowledge they possess, but because they share the strongest of backs, thickest shoulders, and most powerful thighs in their units.

They are Kurds, Egyptian infantry, men from the Halqa Regiment, guards from both the Bahri and Jamdariyya. All of them are stripped of coat and insignia, wearing nearly identical silken tunics. Only from their trousers can one distinguish their parent outfits.

The Ox grumbles to himself. "Soldiers doing the work of beasts. Men of the Salihi and Bahri hitched to loads like teams of oxen in the old country." He spits, recalling words from his Furusiyya Instructor at the tibaq in Hisn Kayfa, twelve years past.

> *Cenk leaned into his face. "I see now why your fellow worms call you Ox—you couldn't hit an ox-sized target from twenty paces. Or is it because they know after your removal from the ranks, you'll be yoked to a cart, hauling arrows and ger poles?"*

He sighs. Today Cenk's old prophesy from the Jazira rings true. How pathetic that the mean bastard's foretelling would occur, not once Ox was expelled from the ranks as a youth for his deficiencies with the bow, but while he is a seasoned veteran in al-Salih's elite corps.

This is drudgery for common slaves, not a mission for the sultan's select. Ox understands that "time is of the essence" and that no amount of whipping could motivate Egypt's thin-armed common slaves into the speed and strength needed for this task. But at this stage of his career, he feels this work is beneath him.

He stops, lifts a flask of water to his lips. This job is bullshit. The amirs allocated every available camel for this chore and also "volunteered" beasts from the merchant class, but most camels in the Nile Delta are away on caravans, or are bringing in the food and materials necessary to continue the fight against the Franj.

So, no surprise, really. If there was shit work, it always seemed to find him.

The men continue to their stations wordlessly, with heads

down. On each step, screeches in the dry sand audibly mark their paths, as if their sore feet yelp in protest. Are the others just tired, or do they, too, worry about their future in the army? The sultan's death and the Frankish enemy camped just south are not the only reasons for the angst and drunkenness that taint the ranks.

When the sultan's deathbed scrolls were unrolled, it was clear that al-Salih had tried to allocate his horsemen evenly between leaders of the two primary regiments—the Bahri and Ox's regiment, the Salihi. The sultan's death inconveniently interrupted the completion of his personnel-shuffling task, so the amirs now tussle with how the remaining troopers will be allotted to their respective ranks. Predictably, Ox is one of the unassigned bastards. And with the new sultan on his way, all of Egypt's Mamluks fret over how their place in the army might shift under al-Salih's son.

A lad from the Halqa, with whom Ox has chatted before, stows his flask across his back. This man's father was slated to be al-Salih's Grand Master of the Armor, the Amir Silah: the official charged with supervising the arsenal, the man who bore the sultan's arms during public appearances. Ox angles toward the lad.

"Soon Amir Aqtay will lead Turanshah to Cairo and then maybe north to us. You be on your best behavior now," Ox says jokingly.

The trooper looks around him and then sneers. "No need. Nothing but opportunity for us in the Halqa, when the son arrives. Hell, I'll be seeing Amir of Forty before you."

"Tsst. You're dreaming," Ox says.

The bearded youth smiles, looking down at Ox's decorative yellow trousers of the Salihi. "Oh. Am I? Al-Salih's Royal Mamluks—you've the farthest to fall, while we of inferior status" —he bows sarcastically to Ox—"we can only rise."

"Just like a campaign, it's all a matter of planning and foresight. A cunning man will attach himself to the right amir,"

Ox says, pointing to his brains.

"Oh, you're a schemer," snorts the youth. "A matter of foresight? Here's some foresight. You in the Salihi will be the ones that Turanshah pushes the farthest away. You're the greatest threat to him and his own Mamluks. Your fiefs will soon be in the hands of the new sultan's guard."

Ox scowls, knowing that history is on the side of this man's prediction. With each succession within the Ayyubid Sultanate, the incoming ruler brought with him his own Mamluks, the *mushtarawat*, the men he purchased, trained, and trusted most. His troops would expect their status to be elevated alongside their prince's.

Will Turanshah want to lay a solid foundation of authority with his own men, while brushing aside his father's personal Mamluks, pushing them into the status of *qaranis*, or purged men? That is the real question. Ox hopes al-Salih's unusually high number of Mamluks will help Turanshah see his father's force as too talented and too numerous to dismiss and not utilize fully.

Ox pretends the soldier's comment has no effect. "Maybe as a whole, but my status is already marginal. I have no iqta to lose, my friend. Much like your lowly ass, I have nowhere to go but up. I'll embrace our new sultan."

"Sorry, Ox—not sure it works that way. You wear the wrong coat, the wrong insignia." He chuckles. "With your fellow Royals, you may go from prestige to peasant, all in the same moon."

"What do you know?" Ox says, pondering the conversations this lad must have had with his father, a man of wealth and prestige, an insider with the former sultan.

The trooper shrugs his shoulders. "Enough. We in the Halqa smell promotion. Your boys reek of approaching demotion."

A camel roars its wretched cry as a heap of sails is reloaded to the poles strapped to the front and rear horns of its saddle. Several more are added until the beast ceases his screams.

"Enough on that one," a gray-bearded Bedouin says to the adolescent beside him, the old camel puller knowing that the

beast will oddly stop its screaming only once the load becomes equal to its strength.

More guttural bawls as the sheepskin-clad Bedu remove the hobbles from the knees of other camels, prodding the beasts up from their leg-folded rest. Ox recognizes the leather hobbles as Egyptian, gear pillaged from the Mamluk camp weeks ago. He scoffs. The Mamluk amirs rarely punish the Bedu for snatching booty, post battle—even if it is Mamluk gear. Scavenging has always been the way of these nomads, and staying in the Bedu's good graces was considered prudent. Ox supposes this policy pays, with the amirs needing Bedu help on this mission.

The Bedu. Ox has little respect for them, despite the fact that as a child he lived a nomadic lifestyle not so different from theirs. These drifters inhabit large swaths of the Ayyubid Empire, living on the milk of their flocks and herds. Those who choose to stay put pay a heavy tribute to the princes of each principality for the rights to graze beasts. The more they roam, the less the Bedu pay. Little wonder so many wander continuously.

Bedu travel in a family unit known as a tent, or *bayt*, which usually includes two or three married pairs, plus their children and other youngsters from the extended families. When resources are plentiful—as they are now— several tents travel together as a *goum*, these groups often linked by some patriarchal lineage.

Two camels grunt. The Bedu hiss in their native tongue, smacking the beasts about their asses and shoulders. The animals strain to get up from their leather-padded knees, like old men roused from their rugs. This outward appearance is misleading. Ox wishes he had the camel's strength and endurance. Loaded with man or baggage, the creature can travel one hundred miles or more in the desert summer without drinking; it can lose nearly half its body weight without harm.

In the winter, he has witnessed camels going weeks without a sip. For most of the forty-five-plus years of a camel's hard life, it will haul heavy loads on scant water for its Bedouin keepers.

Even upon its death, the animal continues to serve, its flesh suitable for consumption by the nomads, its hide used to cover the Bedu's crude shelters.

Here, the Bedouin lead camels unburdened with loads back to the rear of the dual columns, to the sleds bearing the bigger boats and those with wooden hulls. The dark-bearded men shake the sand from pre-rigged loops and slip them over the front pommels of the saddles—three, seven, eight, twelve camels per sled, depending on the weight of each load.

The soldiers, too, find their stations, some grabbing shovels and crude rakes, which lean against the wooden rails of their sleds. Others snatch the running end of ropes, these secured to the sleds carrying the smaller boats and rigging for the large ones.

Ox walks to the front of his sled, scowling at the papyrus reed hull lashed to the runners and crossbeam, anchor rings radiating his team's eight ropes. Reaching his length of weathered hemp, he stoops to flop it over his shoulder. He sighs. Another sip of water.

Four lighter sleds at the front begin to move in lurches, block and tackle from stowed rigging knocking masts in rhythm with the soldiers' tugs. Clunk, clunk, clunk. At the front of each file stands a single camel, loaded with a pair of water bladders, the leather bags attached to both the front and rear saddle horns by holes cut through the hide on each side.

Waiting in line along the sides are a dozen more beasts similarly laden. A Bedouin on either side of these camels sprays water from punctures cut in in the bottom of each giant sack, moistening sand previously raked flat by the infantry. The darkened earth marks the path each sled runner should follow.

The Bedouin apply just the right amount of river water to bind to the grains of sand, stiffening the otherwise loose material, reducing friction on the runners. Shovelers on each side of the sleds remove sand that is pushed in front of the upturned edges of the runners. And more men behind each load work their rakes and shovels to smooth the damp sand in their wake, repacking it for the rig behind them.

Eastward they plow toward the mighty Nile.

Isa, Ox's Amir of Forty, steps forward. Ox looks away. He still cannot stand to look at him.

"By evening we'll be at the river. I'm proud of each man," Isa says.

Ox cringes. By Allah, the man's whiny voice alone should have disqualified him for promotion and made him unfit to lead. Who will follow this weed when things get ugly?

"Ready!" Isa says, watching as the last man shoulders his rope and secures his footing. Now all are squatting and prepared to pull. "Heave!"

Ox leans into the rope with a grunt. His knees rebel; his left hip aches.

"Heave!"

The tendons in his right elbow shoot a zip of pain.

"Heave!"

Ox's mind roams. Isa's high-pitched squawk transforms into the equally annoying cry of the pipe. The hemp in hand becomes the carved grip of an oar, as he and the other Kipchaks plied the windless Black Sea toward their new lives as Mamluks. So many years ago, now.

He grimaced, sitting like a compressed spring, he and Duyal crouched on their bench. The pipe barked. They lowered their spoon into the sea and pushed against the timber at their feet, pulling back against the pine in their grip.

Their submerged oar hardly budged; his lower back screamed. The moan of oar merged with those from the boys. The galley, with its masts of limp canvas above deck, defied their exertions and plowed the water unwillingly, sending only a subtle gurgle along her massive hull.

Forward again, he fixed his arms to use mostly legs on the backward stroke.

Tweet. She started to submit. Forward again they leaned

and a blast of pipe sounded, shorter than the last. A ripple of current against the planks.

Their tempo quickened. A soft draft of air finally moved against his face through the crescent-shaped gap above his oarhole. Air blasted from his lungs in great snorts, in time with the dreaded blare, a useless attempt to drown the sound from his ears, soon substituted only by the piper's high voice.

"Legs and pull." Tweet. "Legs and pull." Tweet. "Together now." Tweet. "Pull now." Tweet. "Ease up on port." Tweet. Tweet. Tweet.

Beside him, Duyal, the thick-legged boy in a bile-splattered tunic, somehow plied his oar despite no water or food for days.

"Heave!"

"Heave!"

A melancholy fills him. Karak. That imprisonment of his old amirate a decade past changed everything. When al-Salih's cousin, al-Nasir Da'ud, betrayed Ox's patron and tossed al-Salih's men into the dungeon for fourteen moons, life seemed to start its plunging trajectory for Ox. Ox lost too many friends in his Khushdash that year. Sure, he still ran into Duyal and others on occasion, but once the regiments were divided into the Salihi and Bahri, it was inevitable that their friendships would fragment. Never again would it be the same as those old days, when the loyalty between mates was highest, when Ox's ambition for rank and riches was far less.

Yet, he still wishes to be with those from his old training tulb who still survive; he wishes he could be attached to the Bahri. If forced to be only an Amir of Ten, allow him to work for Duyal. Maybe a promotion later. Allow him to finish out his career working for a friend.

"Heave!" Grunts from the others.

In several minutes, they are ordered to halt. Ox drops to his ass, panting. "Bullshit," he murmurs to himself.

From the corner of his eye, he sees Amir Aybeg approach. Ox knows he must not look tired, must somehow convey confidence and pride, despite the menial task. With the others seated or lying fatigued on their sides, Ox shifts to one knee, keeping his head down. He hears Aybeg's deep voice among the crew several sleds ahead.

Aybeg will be watching which Mamluks complain or feel this work below their status. The amir will likely scratch those from his mental list of whom he wishes to comprise the *Muizziyya*, Aybeg's personal guard. Ox tells himself he must exude a willingness to take on any assignment with vigor. If landing a spot with the Bahri is fantasy, perhaps Aybeg will still consider Ox for an Amir of Forty slot down the road.

Aybeg strolls up to their sled. Ox pretends not to see him.

"Ah, the Mamluk they call Ox," Aybeg says.

Ox feigns surprise. He jumps to his feet along with the others. "Good afternoon, my Amir. My apology, I didn't see your approach."

"This was supposed to be toil pushed to the young bulls, not those men getting a bit long in the tooth. Have your amirs lost their love for you?" Aybeg winks.

Ox's heart sinks, yet he smiles broadly. "How could they, my Amir? I think they still see a few years left in these bull legs, a little push left in these old shoulders." He pats himself across the chest. "Their only disappointment may be that instead of owning the strength of three young men, I suppose they figure now I'm only equal to two." Ox holds his smile, while inside telling the amir to get fucked.

Aybeg grins. "By Allah! Tough to beat us men of the old corps, eh, Ox?"

Ox rests his hands atop his buttocks. "Yes, my Amir." He ignores the rolling eyes and scowl from the Halqa trooper he had chatted with previously.

Aybeg turns to the rest of the men on the sled, who now stand with their hands locked behind their backs. "Keep heart, my brothers, for each tug on your ropes is equal to the death of an infidel to the south. None in all of Egypt has a more important job than yours today. The Franj have no idea of the trap we now set."

Some of the men smirk.

"Today we received a pigeon message. The honorable Turanshah has arrived in Cairo from Hisn Kayfa and will soon be on his way to Mansura. Shortly afterward, he'll be coming here. Let our new sultan see these boats reassembled, slid into the Nile downstream of the Crusaders and loaded with archers and grenadiers. Let him be impressed with not just our brawn but our brains as well. Let him see our fire darts flinging liquid death at the Franj supply ships that push upriver from Damietta to resupply the Crusaders. And us, sneaking between King Louis and the coast! You'll be the men that cause the Franj to wither on the vine. You'll be Allah's strong hands, strangling the infidels."

"Err!" the men reply in earnest.

Aybeg continues to the next sled, where he will likely repeat a similar message. Ox jeers behind the man's back. He stands no chance with Aybeg. He needs to impress Amir Aqtay when he arrives with the new sultan. The Bahri. He needs to find a way into that unit, where the last of his true mates serve.

CHAPTER
16

Leander
Fariskur
April 6, 1250

A sliver of setting moon hangs over the west bank of the Damietta Arm of the Nile, a screen of clouds obscuring the crescent's light. Dim ripples cast wide upon the river, the moonlight silhouetting a half dozen Crusader galleys, anchored and packed with the king's sickened soldiers: Louis' broken men in a broken attempt to break through the Egyptian blockade that for weeks gave them nothing but complete misery.

Amirate Three stands in loose formation alongside two other amirates of Bahri, these units being held in reserve by Aqtay, their Amir of One Hundred. Slave boys tend their horses a safe distance east. Leander stares west toward the boats and beyond at the far shore, the banks splotched in chalk white, piles of dried canine feces appearing curiously as if they were patches of frost on this warm spring night.

A nip of breeze carries the pale smell of salt air and seaweed across Leander's nose. He gulps it in before the wind swirls, returning the rank of decaying bodies to his nostrils. A squall clatters the palms and sends wisps of surface current dancing across the river.

A hideous cackle from a distant hyena cuts through the gust. A jaw-snapping response from another and the ruckus of a short tussle, as the scavengers compete for the human carrion littering the banks along the Raxi Branch behind them. A chill creeps up Leander's spine.

"This is twice that Allah's breath has spelled disaster for the Crusaders," Slap says.

Binny turns to him. "That's dead right. God loosed the wind both times the Franj needed their boats most." He shakes his head solemnly. "Allah lets us know who is in the right."

"I'd almost have some pity on them but sometimes this all feels like fate," Slap says, looking at Leander.

Leander pulls a wrap of silk tighter across his nose, a nearly useless attempt to deaden the stench. He nods. "Sometimes fate is just a bench on a boat where a man sits riding the current of God's plan with no control, death's hand at the rudder."

With his face likewise covered, Binny exaggerates his lift of eyebrows. "Papa Frank—not just the translator of languages but also the wise philosopher."

Leander puffs a half-hearted chuckle through the cloth. It is not his rumination but rather Slap's reflection that rings most true. The wind had indeed scattered the Frankish fleet when King Louis first landed in Damietta nearly a year ago—a divine signal that spelled the destiny of their folly, a sign ignored by the Frenchmen. And now, during their desperate nighttime escape from the Muslim's naval blockade, the gales again keep the Franj from their goal, pushing them upstream toward Allah's swords.

The blockade. It has worked faster and better than any of the amirs could have hoped. Last moon, Turanshah, the new sultan, arrived north of Mansura to find that his amirs had shown great initiative in lugging overland the Muslims' small navy, dropping their boats into the Damietta Branch of the Nile a full league downstream from the Crusader camp, cutting the

Frank's logistical lifeline from Damietta and the open sea.

Leander's thoughts go to his father. For the Franks, this Seventh Crusade has become nearly a repeat of the events from the Fifth Crusade his father endured. King Louis had either forgotten his predecessor's lessons nearly thirty years past, or was unable to prevent the eerily similar events from repeating.

Regardless, for the past few weeks, the Mamluks and sailors aboard the blocking vessels captured nearly all of the Frankish supply ships that were bold enough to venture upstream from the Mediterranean. In only one moon, the sultan's galleys—with Mamluks throwing glass grenades filled with naft and firing darts through tubes mounted on their bows—captured eighty Crusaders ships. The Muslims burned every Frankish boat and spared no French sailors. Word of this horror spread quickly to the sea, eventually causing those Franj on the bigger ships to balk when ordered to sail south on the smaller cruisers.

Upstream of the blockade at the Crusader camp, the price of food soared. A sheep or pig cost the Franks thirty pounds; a hogshead of wine, ten pounds; a single egg, twelve pence. Soon, King Louis' men had empty purses to match their empty bellies. Starvation set in.

After months of battle, the river filled with rotting corpses and a contagious disease hit the Crusader camp—by mid-March, even the amirs' most dependable spies refused to enter it for worry of catching the deadly plague. Twenty to thirty Franks died each day from pestilence or hunger; those not sick wore white badges in a hapless attempt to ward off the infected.

No man or beast escaped the scourge. Earlier this week, Leander heard evidence of the Crusaders' plight from the Franj camp: heart-wrenching screams sounding like a troupe of women in labor as the barbers cut away engorged sores from the men's mouths so they could eat.

Crusader horses died alongside their riders, once the fodder supplies diminished. An unfortunate dog or cat wandering into the infidel camp immediately became a meal for the desperate

Franj. Rich barons were no better off than the lowliest page. Lords owning vast fiefs in the old country joined a meal of varmint or rotten fish, served by any man.

French morale crumbled. Rumors and facts alike were muttered throughout camp, all of which Leander thought had to make Allah smile: King Louis' silver was depleted, Christians were deserting to the Muslim camp, and the flower of the enemy's army perished in Mansura, those knights loyal to the king's dead brother and the Templars pulled into Artois' folly. Through all of this, the Saracen harassment from land and river never relented, the Turks and Mamluks badgering the Crusaders with Greek Fire, arrows from horseback, and even chucking clods of earth.

Cursed with the sickness himself, King Louis suggested a treaty: the surrender of Damietta in exchange for Jerusalem and some towns on the Syrian coast. The new sultan, aware of the Crusaders' miserable situation, rejected the besieged king's offer. Louis, his ranks and fighting spirit zapped, ordered the camp to evacuate under cover of darkness.

The Crusader plan this evening was to slip through the Muslim blockade on foot along the riverbanks and via smaller galleys snuck upstream from Damietta. The Franj would load their stricken men in the dark and make for the bigger transport ships at sea.

In the Franks' haste to leave, they neglected to follow the king's commands. They failed to cut the ropes that held their pontoon footbridge together over the canal. Leander and several hundred Muslim soldiers crossed the bridge after the Franks and followed the Crusaders westward to Fariskur.

Finding the enemy in the dark was no challenge. The foolish sailors, in an effort to guide the sick Franks toward their lighter vessels dragged riverside, set large fires near each craft. Amir Aqtay directed Duyal's Amirate Three and the other Bahri to wait on the east shore, while Aqtay sent the Turkmen auxiliaries in his charge downstream to attack the Franj, using the Crusader fires as the Turk's objective markers.

A clop of approaching hooves breaks the silence. Leander picks the silhouette of the rider's helmet being that of a fellow Bahri, a messenger returning from downstream. The broad-shouldered rider dismounts, once recognizing Amir Duyal in the faint dawn light.

"Good morning, Amir," the Mamluk booms in a deep voice.

"Morning. What's the situation downstream?" Duyal asks.

"A complete gaggle, my Amir."

Duyal grimaces.

"For the infidels, my Amir," the messenger says, grinning. "Those sick Franj reaching the small galleys were crawling over one another to get into the boats. They nearly swamped some of them. And the Franj assigned to defend the galleys—they fled on foot toward Damietta."

"Good. Good. No surprise," Duyal says.

"It was unbelievable, Amir. When several of their boats rowed downstream for the sea, refusing to wait for their King, the Franj on board had to duck behind the gunwales to keep from being skewered by heavy bolts—fired from their own men on land!" the messenger says, shaking his head.

Duyal crinkles his brow. "Sounds like at least some of the infidels have a little respect for their monarch ... And the Turkmen auxiliaries. Are they showing themselves well?"

The Mamluk smiles. "The Franj never bothered to put out their signal fires. The Turkmen fell upon both the sick Franks crawling into boats and those healthy enough to attempt the trek seaward." The messenger's face goes stern. "By the time I left, I'd guess hundreds of the pig eaters were already killed."

Duyal nods, his lips pursed.

"Amir Aqtay should arrive soon. By your permission, my Amir, I should be off to deliver another message."

"Of course. Thank you," Duyal says, returning the man's salute.

As the Mamluk turns, Binny elbows Leander, "Hopefully the Turkmen had light work with them."

"I doubt our work this day is done," Leander says, his eyes drawn back to the six boats two hundred feet to their front, the rising sun exposing for the first time the men aboard.

"Yeah, I guess these are the 'fortunate Franj', eh?" Binny asks, his eyes also upon the sailors and ailing Franj crews who chose not to—or were not physically able—to make the push to the Mediterranean.

"Yeah."

These Frenchmen survive for now, huddled in their boats midstream, some anchored in the backwater. Their weak-armed crews, unable to overcome the wind in the downstream push toward Damietta, make the best of their poor choices, waiting here in the only safe place left, in hopes of the wind dying down.

Leander shakes his head. Grave choices to be sure. Soon the sun will break the horizon and there will be no hiding for the Franj. To oar downstream and fight the wind means falling into the hands of the Egyptian galleys waiting to hurl their Greek fire and slay the Crusaders on the water. To come ashore puts the Franks at the same risk as those who already tried to make the slog downstream along the bank.

So, the Franks sit in their lighters, wondering not if, but when, death will arrive. Leander feels more than a tinge of sorrow for them and ponders what thoughts fill their minds—loved ones, the rolling green hills of their homelands, the majestic peaks of the Alps? None of which they will ever see again.

From one boat, a strong-voiced Frenchman calls out above the wind, "Then the angel showed me the river of the water of life, bright as crystal, flowing from the throne of God and of the Lamb through the middle of the street of the city." Mutters of prayer respond from this boat and the others anchored nearby.

Through the lifting darkness downstream, the moans from the dying lying along the banks give way to the clank of weapons, armor, and coin. Bedouins slip in to pillage the Crusaders' bodies, pulling rings from fingers not yet stiff and collecting French daggers, swords, belts, and tunics into heavy leather bags.

Farther along the bank, a gangly-legged profile emerges against the purple-black horizon. A camel. Another. A turbaned man flops open a giant saddle bag strapped to his saddle, while Bedu kids drag their smaller bags of booty through the sand to him.

Again, the deep French accent sounds mid-river: "Also, on either side of the river, the tree of life with its twelve kinds of fruit, yielding its fruit each month. The leaves of the tree were for the healing of the nations. No longer will there be anything accursed, but the throne of God and of the Lamb will be in it, and his servants will worship him."

A striped hyena giggles cross stream, as if mocking the Crusaders and their God. Three huffs. Some growling. The beasts move closer from the distant scrub to a clearing near the bank. In the low light, a slope-backed demon materializes from the thicket. With its rear legs shorter than its front pair, the nearly full-grown cub labors at a canter. Bisecting its massive jaws is a severed femur secured between its bared fangs. It lifts the human bone higher to keep from tripping on the rotted flesh that drags through the dirt.

Behind it, a dominant female struts after the young male, her guard hair standing along the length of her back, high and rounded like the horsehair crest on a Spartan's helmet. Two more hyenas pile out of the brush, slinking in behind the female, ready to snatch the bone in case it is dropped during the likely brawl.

It had not taken the hyenas long to discover the food source of decaying men lying along the shore. After the Battle of Mansura, bloat in the guts of the slain acted like filled airbladders in raising the dead from the bottom of the Nile. Bodies soon choked the Raxi Branch from bank to bank. Most of the carcasses were Crusaders, killed or drowned during the Frank's chaotic exit from the town. At first, the French searched for comrades in the gore, but soon gave up. Only the odd coat and insignia could be recognized, as the eels had gorged on the soft cartilage of noses, ears, and flesh, all tenderized after several weeks in the cool Nile.

For weeks, packs of hyenas waited until darkness and then slunk in from their papyrus reed hideouts to feed on the swollen bodies that surfaced from the deep nightly. All night, one could hear the snap of jaws and grind of canine teeth pulverizing the Crusaders' bones.

Last moon, when the bodies rose en masse, the king hired local laborers to unclog the corpses upstream of the Raxi bridge. He had the Muslim bodies pitched downstream, and had the Crusaders pulled out and buried in trenches. When the hyenas' grisly food source became scarce, the persistent scavengers proved themselves competent diggers, pulling the brethren from their shallow burials, sometimes in pieces. The Crusaders were eventually too sick to dig deep holes and too weary to post guards at the mass graves.

Now, only the odd body finds its way into the eddies and only smaller scraps of flesh and bone litter the Nile shore, so the hyenas have begun to defy their nature, some coming in before dark to beat the others to the smaller meals and staying later into the morning to protect their turf.

Cross stream, a man moves tree to tree. One of the Turkmen has slipped behind a palm without the four beasts noticing. He draws on one hyena that offers him a broadside shot. He releases, the arrow landing with a smack a little too far behind the shoulder.

The cub is put into a death spin—whirling, twisting, his lungs filling with blood. Tottering, the animal lumbers a few paces and tips over. His shaggy-coated companion rushes over and tears into the belly of the dying animal.

The Turkman sprints at them, pulling out his dagger on the run. Some of the Mamluks laugh. The trio of hyena scatter into the scrub. Reaching the downed animal, the archer kicks the beast in the ass to confirm its death, looks across the river, and seems to notice the Mamluk formation for the first time.

Undeterred, he drops to his knees and quickly digs out both hyena eyeballs, stuffing them in his open pouch. Wadding the animal's lips into his fist, he cuts off both sides of the male's face in two slashes.

"Look at him stealing your beer money, Slap," Binny says.

A few chuckles from the ranks.

"Those eyeballs alone are worth six beers," Slap says.

Expertly, the Turk overturns the beast and rips his dagger up the animal's gut, pulling up a handful of entrails, carving out the choicest selection. Deeper into the carcass he digs, likely removing the heart. He cinches his pouch, sheaths his dagger and disappears back into the vegetation.

"I could sneak over and buy the heart off him right now. You might be able to use it shortly," Binny says.

More snickers, but mostly groans, as all in the amirate are aware that some of the locals still consider the eyeballs and whiskers of the hyena as magical and keep them as charms. A few Egyptians even believe that eating select organs from the hyena impart strength and bravery.

"Don't worry," Slap scoffs. "I don't think it's going to take much courage today to put the blade to a few skinny-assed, monkey-mouthed heathens. But, Binny, maybe you want to flip the Turk a coin. You could build a little fire, melt a bit of that hyena fat and spread it on your walnut sack like the Persians do. Might be a way to make that little snake of yours perform when you need it next."

More chuckles, this time heartier.

Their Amirate Leader, Sedat, turns with a scowl, "You best be shutting your mutton holes and start thinking of the coming work. I'm doubting any of the Franj will be so kind as to offer up their throats for a quick dispatch to hell."

Again, the chant from the Frank upon his cruiser: "They will see His face, and His name will be on their foreheads. And night will be no more. They will need no light of lamp or sun, for the Lord God will be their light, and they will reign forever and ever."

Slap leans to Leander and whispers, "What words does the infidel deliver?"

"Passages from their Bible, from a book they call Revelations. He tries to comfort his mates with visions of Christian heaven," Leander says.

"They figure they're done."

"Yeah."

Slap nods, patting both hips in an instinctive check of his sword and dagger.

Amir Aqtay appears out of the wine-streaked skyline on horseback. Returning safely from his mission to bring the new sultan from the Jazira to his palace in Cairo, their sober Amir of One Hundred scans his ranks—those whom al-Salih had determined would belong to him after the former sultan's death. Leander is pleased that Aqtay has retained command and that the bonds of this amirate's Khushdash will not be broken during the transition in leadership.

Aqtay signals for Amir Duyal. The two remove themselves from the ears of the troops to confer. Aqtay dismounts, placing his Arabian between himself and the flank of the formation in an attempt at privacy. Yet Leander has a perfect line of sight to Duyal's face.

He watches Duyal's expressions for any cues that may signal what happens next. Duyal seems to sense that some eyes are upon him and he turns his shoulder to them as far as possible, while still being able to face his superior. But Leander can still see.

Duyal listens, attempting to show no emotion. Yet, soon his sunken eyes squint at Aqtay's words, his stare goes hard. Duyal's lips, so often and easily moved to a smile, go tight and inward.

Aqtay stands before him, seemingly awaiting a response. Once Duyal nods his head in confirmation of the assignment, Aqtay steps away. A salute from Duyal, void of its usual snap. Aqtay mounts, and with a squeeze from his calves, his Arabian heads to the adjacent amirate.

A hollowness fills Leander's gut.

CHAPTER

17

Leander
Fariskur
April 6, 1250

With his orders received, Duyal steps in front of his men. He takes a deep breath. "Three of our galleys have taken many captured Franj onboard—enemy whose vessels were seized and burned, or had surrendered before reaching Damietta. These men, plus those cruisers to our front, will be landed here. We'll ensure the boats are dispersed along the bank to prevent the Franj from massing. When they come ashore, you'll disarm them." He hesitates.

Duyal's face goes blank, he seems to detach, assuming the disposition of a man who now mindlessly communicates the provided directives. His eyes focus over their heads, to the waving palms that line the shore. "You'll slay those Franj who resist or appear sick with the fever. To those cooperating and who appear healthy, you'll ask one question: 'Will you abjure?' In French, '*Votre renier?*'"

Duyal looks straight at Leander with tilted head and scrunched brow, looking for support in his pronunciation.

Leander nods twice.

"All of you. Repeat these words—this question—to me three times, now," Duyal says.

The response returns in jumbled form, "*Votre renier? Votre renier? Votre renier?*"

Duyal nods, his eyes returning on high to the chattering palm fronds. "*Votre renier.*" Back to his recitation in monotone. "For those Franj refusing to renounce their Christian faith, you'll put them to the sword. For those who forswear, you'll direct them to a gathering place upstream to be taken as prisoner. Are my words clear?"

Leander's heart sinks. The amirate is ordered to kill sick men. Defenseless men. And men with the balls to stick to their Christian faith. This is not the Mamluk way; this is not in accordance with their corps values, which were endlessly preached to them in the citadel during their initial training. He tries to swallow the swell from his throat, but it only seems to balloon larger in his gut.

In unison they answer, "Yes, my Amir."

For the first time, Duyal meets their eyes, searching faces in the dawn for their willingness to comply. Surely it is assured; they will do anything for him, have always been willing. Noticing some of the men looking downstream, Duyal turns away from them.

The line of Muslim galleys approach, a chain of staggered dots enlarging to three blobs atop the cobalt water. Black hulls with single sails soon emerge. Oars stowed, only one sheet powers each reed and wooden hull up the Nile.

The Frenchmen midstream also see the galleys. Likely thinking the boats to be French, many men cheer, rocking their overcrowded cruisers severely. Once they correctly identify the advancing boats, they return to their seats, mumbling on the water. Arguments erupt on one boat, men pointing bony fingers at one another. Another craft holding mostly sick men again falls into hushed prayer, some burying their heads between their legs.

Turks onboard the approaching galleys stand and ready their bows, aiming at the six smaller craft.

"*Ligne à la rive!*" an amir in the lead boat yells to the Crusaders, commanding the Franj to the shore.

Some of the Franj confer. Men in one boat begin to pull in their anchor.

The Muslims close. Turks in the bow quickly lower and stow the sail. Oars plied in unison place the Muslim galleys in a position broadside the French vessels, giving all Turkish archers clear shots.

"*Ligne à la rive! Ma prochaine commande est pour les flèches pour voler.*" ("My next command is for arrows to fly.")

A Crusader on the lead boat orders his oarsmen to pull back toward the east shore. Another cruiser follows. Mamluks wade into the water to catch the first boat. "Your rope! Throw the rope!"

Duyal whistles and points the second boat to a spot fifty paces downstream. He turns, searching. "Sedat! One boat per squad. Leander, come!"

Leander runs to him. "Yes, my Amir."

"Tell them to stay in their boats, until we say otherwise. All of them," Duyal says.

Leander approaches the boat, pushing his palms downward in signal for those standing to sit, "*Restez dans votre bateau.*" He strides to the other boat. "*Restez dans votre bateau.*"

Sneers from some of the men on the cruiser. Heads rise. A waft of wind crosses the length of their boat. The smell of rot. Skin rotting. Clothes rotting. The reek of rot from their mouths. Narrowed eyes now from the hollow-cheeked men, soldiers recognizing the fluidity of this infidel's French as being homegrown.

Their eyes search his face and locks, some in disbelief that a Frenchman could possibly go infidel, that Leander's thick beard and light-colored hair had grown wild on the Saracen steppe as did those of the enemy. Yet, those convinced of his original birthplace keep their lips upturned.

Once all of the boats have landed, Leander returns to his squad.

Their squad leader, Timur, takes charge, approaching the nearest cruiser. "Out! Get your swine-eating asses out," he says, signaling with his thumb for the Franj to exit over the sides. "Detach your belts and hold them over your heads!"

Some of the Franj stare at him blankly. Others crawl over the gunwales, pulling their broadswords from scabbards.

"No, no!" Timur groans. He removes his belt, holds his scabbard over his head in example. "Like this! Like this!"

Men half-covered in blankets clumsily remove their belts and disembark, some with hardly the strength to hold their weapons above their heads. Their faces are drawn, pale. Each wears a chain mail hauberk, yet only the padded coif covers their heads. No chain mail protects their heads and necks. No helmets.

Leander shakes his head and murmurs to himself, "Too sick to care."

The mishmash of Crusaders struggles over the sides, some of the king's own mixed with the white-coated Templars, even the surviving remnants of the Count of Artois' men, cloaked in the blue and gold-lilied heraldry of their lord. Those falling into the water are grasped by mates and lifted to their feet. Two men carry a friend, an arm over the shoulder of each. Another knight holds his and his comrade's naked swords over his head, his friend's arm locked across his red-crossed chest.

"Drop weapons here. Each man will walk on his own. Over there," Timur says, pointing.

The Crusaders stop and gape at him vacantly.

"Leander!" Timur calls.

"*Pas d'aide de camarades. Marcher à plus là maintenant,*" ("No help from comrades. Walk over there now.") Leander says, pointing first to the growing tangle of swords and belts plopped at the river's edge and then to a stretch of beach that will serve as a staging area. The squad of Mamluks wait in file, swords drawn.

Those Franks helping their mates grudgingly release them, tight lipped or scowling. Some of those abandoned stagger. Others collapse in the sand and begin to crawl. A gap grows between those able to walk on their own and the sickest left behind. Crusaders look dejectedly over their shoulders to their struggling friends, some of the able dropping their heads, others with tears now flowing down their cheeks.

Timur approaches a one-armed Frank, the excess chain mail on his sleeve cut and the frayed links folded and stitched above the elbow. Timur turns to his Mamluks, shaking his head in disgust. "We have our instructions, let's go. None are innocent here." With these words hardly out of his mouth, he turns with a violent backswing, his blade severing the one-armed man's head. The Franj grape lands noiselessly in the soft sand.

Slap strolls over to a crawling Frenchmen and with one downward stroke likewise beheads the man.

A Crusader wearing the king's coat of arms scuttles forward on his elbows and hip, blood dripping from his nose, the sign of pending death in this affliction. He crumbles, unable to slither any further. Seeing the boots at his side, he pushes up to his knees and elbows. He looks up to the faris, the blood now running over his chin and down his neck. Before their eyes meet, two hacks from the curved blade and his head drops to the sand. The Mamluk kicks the melon over to momentarily scrutinize the sand-covered eyes.

Leander walks up to a Templar, who sits on his ass in a stupor, his legs straight. Moldy patches dot his shriveled hands, which sit limply on his knees. Clear liquid dribbles from the man's nose, across his lips, and down to the dried and whisker-stubbled spackle coating his chin. The man licks his lips, his stare remaining forward. Leander walks behind him. "Your duty," Leander mumbles. He tightens his grip with a second hand on the blade and swings. With a thud, the head lands in the man's lap. Leander topples him with a bump from his knee. "No more suffering," he says.

Some of the Franj now appeal for mercy—not the loud, desperate shrieks of cowardly men unprepared to die but rather the wretched pleas of helpless men imploring grace. A raspy voice from a man on his knees, his palms pressed together. "Lord, forgive them for their sins."

Forgiveness. Leander turns the other way, pretending not to see this one.

In seconds, a dozen Franj torsos lay bleeding in the sand, their heads in ghastly orientations. Muted sobs come from the unwell, who await their turn at death, their illness turning the feeble into toddlers. The slosh of blade through flesh, the dull thwack of sharp metal cleaving bone. Leander looks farther downstream to where the Muslim galleys have landed. More of this from the other three squads.

Leander walks up to one of the king's men straggling behind the others, the man looking healthy enough. "*Votre renier?*"

A look of hopelessness sits upon the man's face. He nods and slurs his words. "*Oui bien sûr. Quel choix ai-je?*" ("Yes, of course. What choice do I have?")

Leander pushes out a sigh of relief. Maybe more will save themselves. But as the man speaks, he exposes the swell of dead flesh in his mouth, another sign of the scourge. A deep red patch on his gum line.

Duyal's words buzz in Leander's ears. "You'll slay those Franj who resist or appear sick with the fever." Leander nods to the man and without notice, swings his sword across the man's neck. The head lands with a thump. As the Frank trunk tips, a stream of red pulses from the neck, draining into the thirsty sand.

Leander closes his eyes, the ivory-handled sword held limply at his side. "Allah forgive me. Allah forgive me."

A bead of French blood loosens from the tip of his wootz steel. It drops. A second one, undetectable, is lost in the countless grains at his feet, imperceptible amid the shouts and whimpers and cleaving of pulpy flesh.

"*Votre renier?*" Slap cuffs a Templar across the back of the head. "*Votre renier?!*"

The Crusader refuses to answer and stands terrified, his eyes riveted upon the infidel's scarred face. The high-mounded slashes on Slap's cheeks are inflamed and contorted, the skin seeming to have a life of its own, like a shovel full of worm-filled soil. What the Franj's mother might have told him the face of the devil would appear as. The man presses both palms to the red cross embroidered upon his chest.

Slap shrugs his muscular shoulders, takes a step back, and with a backhand swing beheads the man. "*Nous allons vous envoyer en enfer.*" ("We will now send you to hell.")

Leander scans the beach. His Amirate Commander. Where is he? Does the best of them also partake in executing these dreadful orders? There. Duyal shuffles through the sand from boat to boat, a bloody sword in hand. Feeling the eyes upon him, Duyal turns to Leander, a dejected look on his face. Their eyes meet only momentarily; they both turn back to the slaughter.

"Get it over with," Leander grumbles.

Behind the boat, a group of five Crusaders kneel in a circle. Covering their hauberks are the tattered colors of St. Denis, a yellow sun on their chests, its squiggly rays splayed outward. If their heraldry was meant to represent the optimism of a rising sun, today their sun is setting. Black-splotched hand in black-splotched hand, they pray.

Leander walks to them, the faint whispers of the Bible verse now catching his ear. "*Je leur donne la vie éternelle, et elles ne périront jamais, et personne ne les ravira de ma main.*"

Leander winces. John, Chapter 10, verse 28. His mind flips back nine years to his homeland, on his knees with the others on the cold stone floor of Erard's castle in Ramerupt with the identical verse bouncing off the high walls of their chapel. Warm light flickering atop the thick-stemmed candles. "I give them eternal life, and they will never perish, and no one will snatch them out of my hand."

His mind wanders out the iron-banded door of the chapel and through the courtyard to where the sour-smelling oak logs had been piled high, the place where, for two autumns, he and another page spent weeks splitting and stacking wood, loading the pieces into their packs and lugging them up the winding stairs to each giant fireplace.

Leander stops several paces from the kneeling men. The knights of St. Denis ignore him, their eyes closed, their thoughts on prayer, on the God they will soon meet. Leander does not blink. His vision blurs. Their faces go from a pale gray to the rumpled brown surface of oak bark.

He hacks wildly, the clunk of blade through skull and thump of steel on bone now become the sounds of ax on gnarled oak, some of it splitting stubbornly. Their thin arms held out in defense are now just limbs to be hewn off the trunk.

He redoubles his effort, chopping harder, chips of bone and globs of meat sticking to the iron mesh of chain mail and scales of his cuirass. A bloody mash splatters his coat, dribbles down the slick metal of his helmet, damming at the turban mound on his forehead. He strikes and strikes, the rage burning inside him.

Panting, he finally lowers his sword. He loses sense of time and space.

A poke on his shoulder, not sharp. Still winded, he ignores it, his eyes to the hue of red in the puffy clouds on the eastern horizon. In the same place, a harder nudge.

He turns with bloody sword to face the enemy.

Slap cowers, taking two steps back. He stands for a bit with the oar across his body, a single eyebrow and half lip raised. Binny stands beside him. They stare at him as one would at a wounded wolf or fang-bearing panther, unsure if the bloodied creature might still pounce.

"I think you're done with these fellows, Leander," Binny says.

Leander looks about him, still oblivious to the gore at his feet. Panting, he nods and walks away, nearly tripping on an arm caught between his feet.

He plops down in the sand and lowers his head between his knees. In time, he looks up to the sky, the morning sun half-risen, shining glorious upon the wide river, casting a radiance on the butchery about him. He is beyond tears. "What have we done?" he murmurs to himself. "What have I done?"

In time, Binny sits beside him.

"If Allah is indeed merciful, and we are his agents of war, how is it that he allows us to massacre unarmed men?" Leander asks.

"Don't think so deeply on this one, my friend. This is the culling of infidels from our soil, the slaughter of diseased sheep from a wayward flock—nothing more. Let it go. We just did as ordered."

Leander sighs, licks the metallic taste of Crusader blood from his lips. He sneers, feeling the drying blood growing tight on his face, taut like a shrinking second skin. "As ordered."

Binny spits, wipes the sweat from his face with a grubby hand. "They got what was coming to them. We killed only the infidels and those already cursed to die—they're lucky we didn't kill them all. Shit, in not doing it, we're leaving Franj that we'll probably have to face another day. While it doesn't feel like it now, we actually showed some mercy here."

Leander turns to him. Binny seems to read the look of disbelief on his friend's face.

"Don't even look at me like that. The foes we spare—don't think they won't be back once their ransom is paid and they've regained their health. They'll be happy to return and run their blades through your belly and steal more of the Holy Land. Let's not look for reasons to spare the invader, my friend."

"Mercy," Leander mumbles, staring at his boots, the sand gripping in clumps on the thick blood there.

Leander feels Binny's hand upon his back. "It's done. Just stop thinking."

Near them, one of the older Franj cries out in broken Turkish to a young Mamluk he argues with. "Even the teachings of Saladin said that one ought not slay any man who has laid down his arms or has once tasted your bread and salt."

Sedat overhears this and pushes aside the Mamluk. Sedat faces the Crusader. "Shut up. Saladin also believed in slaying the infidels, who came from across the sea to desecrate the holy places and kill his Islamic brothers. None of your men who died today were good for anything. We've done you heathens a favor here." He tilts his head sideways. "Will you abjure?"

The Crusader looks up at the towering man calmly.

Sedat gets into the Frank's face. "I'll not ask the question twice. Denounce your faith and move over to the staging area with the rest of your kind, or face the consequences."

The old man looks up with tired eyes. "Will you really trust the word of those who abjure under duress, or those whose faith is so weak?"

Sedat scowls. "Trust? Tsst. I don't trust a one of you. You all deserve to die. Oh, scholarly one, perhaps you also know another famous line of Saladin's—'One never met with a good Saracen Christian, or a good Christian Saracen.'"

Sedat grins, his eyes now searching the beach. He turns, delighted in discovering Leander so close. He elbows the Mamluk next to him. "Ah, but look at our Papa Frank, covered in the infidels' blood and bowels. This day he proves even the great Saladin wrong." The big man laughs.

The gray-haired Crusader shakes his head. He stares at Sedat sadly for a moment, then takes a step back, removing the white coif from his head and throwing it to the ground. He tucks the collar of his shirt into his hauberk to better expose his neck. He drops to his hands and knees, keeping his head raised in dignity.

Sedat looks to the Mamluk beside him. "What are you waiting for? Looks like we finally have his answer."

CHAPTER

18

Cenk
Fariskur
April 28, 1250

Cenk sets aside his file and lifts the sword from its wooden block. Resting the grip on his bearded chin, he turns toward the light emitting from the open flap of his guard tent. With left eye closed, he looks down the edge, ensuring he has filed the proper angle along the entire length of the blade. He nods.

He flips the sword over and places it back on the block. Starting near the tip, he pushes the file across the other edge. The grated file teeth bite. One, two, three, four, five. He inches the blade farther down the sharpening block. One, two, three, four, five. He continues all the way down, until he reaches the chappe at the strong of the blade. Again, he looks down the length of the weapon.

Satisfied, he removes his block from the table and replaces it with his coarse whetstone. He adds a dab of oil to the rough surface and begins to run the sword across the stone back and forth along the entire length of the slanted edge, concentrating to keep his angle true. After six uniform strokes, he turns the blade over and repeats the process. To test, he rubs a stubby thumb across the sharp blade.

He snickers. Here he is, an Amir of Forty in the Jamdariyya, the best of the sultan's guardians, doing the work of a common laborer. But hell, he could easily do this for a living—sharpening swords, repairing grips. Perfectly tedious work. Nobody to keep track of, no senior amir's problems to solve. Just the satisfying whisper of steel on stone and maybe the odd visit from his old friends.

More and more, he has thoughts of calling it quits. He knows from experience that a man with these contemplations needs to get out of this occupation soon, before Allah or some unknown god of war destines an enemy arrow or steel blade to finish the decision for him.

He looks up from the sword and stares at the tent wall. Maybe he has just lost some of his stupidity. Maybe he finally realizes that his luck cannot last forever. Maybe the rejuvenated bond with his wife, Fidan, and the joy of their four-year-old daughter, Inci, has changed his outlook, softened him. Maybe this is all right.

Fidan has been his wife for more than a decade. He never took another. Their early years of marriage had been agonizing, with Fidan making a difficult transition to city life from her old ways on the steppe and Cenk battling his drinking and the mental trauma from his action with the Khwarazmians. But things had been stable for most of the last five years. In time, she had calmed him and taken the edge off his personality. She never asked for much, just an orderly house and each other's company. Cenk smiles inside just thinking of her and her pleasant, unassuming smile.

Predictably, their relationship blossomed at about the same time their young daughter, Inci, was born. The child that Allah blessed them with had also helped to decompress him. "I'm pretty sure when I get older that I'll wear a Mamluk's turban like you," she told him last year. He had howled in laughter. Inci had endless questions and comments on topics that so often melted his stone heart, made him feel like a kid, and caused him to think of things other than training recruits and preparing for the next campaign. He had initially dreaded the thought of a baby in the house—especially a girl—yet Inci was his prized one, right from the start.

Retirement. It is not that he has lost his gratitude. He knows that plenty of Mamluks in the regiment would literally kill to take his slot in the Jamdariyya, a leadership role in the elite guard within the sultan's own Mamluks. Or at least they would have done so when their former sultan, al-Salih, was still alive.

A stab of pain returns to Cenk's heart. Just a few weeks ago, he was one of the most trusted Royal Mamluks, one of the few permitted to carry a sword at all times and to wear the dedicatory *tiraz* band on his sleeve. But with the arrival of Turanshah, al-Salih's son, all of the confidence Cenk had built up with his former patron became water under the bridge. It is as if each man in every one of al-Salih's regiments is starting over. Cenk wonders, does he really have the energy to do that again?

Departure from the service. It is logical. And what else does he have left to prove? After all, his twenty-four-year career has already been a hell of a ride. Serving under his first master, Amir Turkmani, for nine years after manumission, he endured three campaigns throughout the Jazira and Anatolia. He took part in the relatively bloodless campaign at Amid and endured the butchery in prying the fortress in Hisn Kayfa away from al-Masud's obstinate garrison there in 1234.

Later that year, he experienced full-scale carnage when the then-sultan—al-Salih's father, al-Kamil—convinced sixteen Ayyubid princes to travel up the Euphrates and snatch territory from the defending Seljuks. Numerous attacks against barriers of stone and wood resulted in the needless death of too many of his friends and training mates, his Khushdashiya.

While that Anatolian campaign was demoralizing, it was inconsequential compared to the grief caused by that brutal ambush along the trade route fourteen years ago, against the Khwarazmians south of Hisn Kayfa.

He elbows aside the abrasive stone and pulls into place one with a finer surface to polish the metal. Once again, he runs the steel back and forth across the worn stone. As he has learned to do, with each push of the blade, he shoves away those memories of the trap outside of Aleppo, of the grizzly death of his first real father-figure, Turkmani, and those of too many of his old friends killed there.

He becomes lost in the blade's hiss. For a while, he works completely from muscle memory on the already-sharp weapon, his mind roaming over the barren desert and battlefields of his past, trying to remember the faces of men he knew, those friends slain by enemy or banished for some slight so many years ago. Always, his mind returns to those days in the citadel in Hisn Kayfa, under al-Salih.

He had served almost fourteen years under this man—the Prince of the Jazira turned sultan, the man who became his new father. Allah rest his soul. During the first half of those years, Cenk graduated two tulbs from the training ranks. The first tulb he had literally tortured, hell-bent on removing any who showed a pinch of weakness.

Some of those graduates—second generation members of the Salihiyyah, the old corps—are still alive and had performed well in the regiment under the stress of combat. Singer and Ox come to mind. One man was even recently promoted to the same grade as Cenk—Duyal, now an Amir of Forty. Cenk figures the misery he put them through back then contributes to their effectiveness now. He finds this satisfying.

In the second seven years with al-Salih, the sultan's corps of Mamluks grew, and the command formed the additional regiments. Cenk survived more battles, stomached a stint in the Karak prison and participated in countless standoffs, most against his patron's own family members. The Ayyubid dominion then, as now, being a perpetually messy affair among the sultan and those conniving princes who share Saladin's bloodline.

While Cenk always performed well in battle, it is not his string of campaigns that earned him his reputation in the army. It is, surprisingly, his impact upon the training ranks while at the citadel in Hisn Kayfa. Among the Mu'allim, instructors who now lead tulbs of novices at both the Qal'at al-Jabal (Fortress of the Mountain), and the Island Citadel at al-Rawda, Cenk is seen as a living legend. Young instructors nod, grin, and point him out to their peers as he passes.

Word of his ageless exploits filtered down into the ranks of the guard he now commands. At thirty-nine years old, with gray streaks in his beard, he can tell that his troops see him as an ancient relic to be adored, regardless of his flaws. They are lucky to have caught him near the end of his career, or they, too, would have hated him as did his novices, years ago.

Cenk refuses to let his fabled status go to his head. He knows his road has been rocky and that he is fortunate to be alive. He is secretly glad that the stories of his time in the Jazira still serve as examples for the young Furusiyya instructors in the tibaq; he is pleased his hard ways of forging Kipchak youth into Mamluks are still being used to create lethal faris, horsemen for the empire, as Cairo faces no shortage of enemies.

Cenk looks down at the stub of an index finger on his left hand and at forearms riddled with a patchwork of scars. For many years, he could assign each wound to a battle—a slash from this desert plain, an arrow from that attack on that castle. Now, specific memories from most of the skirmishes on behalf of his patrons overlap and blend together like the welts and cross-stitched patterns on his arms, looking like the prehistoric tracks of centipedes etched into leather.

All for Turkmani and al-Salih. He would do it all again for them both. Al-Salih. Oh, how he misses the man. Oh, how he wishes his patron were still alive!

He lifts the blade to his eyes and slowly twists his wrist. He detects a subtle burr in the blade and puts that side back to the stone. When finished, he runs a piece of parchment along the blade. The thin skin splits, falling away from the edge, fluttering to his feet. He reaches down to pick up the scraps, yet his lower back rebels. Up. He must get up; he must move.

Before standing, he runs through his routine to ward off the worst of his pains. With both hands, he rubs his knees vigorously, moving down his legs to his ankles. He eases to his feet and works a kink from his shoulder with a hand half-gnarled with inflammation. He moves gingerly toward the light, shuffling in small steps like a grandfather. "Off soon to battle on those legs, old man? Allah help us," he mutters.

He leaves the tent and stands with his hands on his hips to observe progress on the eyesore that dominates the landscape. Two carpenters pound pegs through support beams on the second level of the sultan's tower—flooring for a veranda, which will extend from the main structure. Men on the ground saw timbers; others heft more of the imported lumber with block and tackle. Cenk shakes his head—another place yet higher from which the new sultan can view the river.

Since late February, Turanshah has brought back the carpenters time and time again to make improvements to the four structures in his complex—the river tower, his bathing pavilion, his bedchamber, and now this viewing tower—all built of fir planks and wrapped in blue-dyed cloth, boxed in by a trellised fence adorned with the same cotton fabric. None could view the royal one from the outside.

Cenk sneers. Al-Salih would have worked from a simple tent like the rest of his army and pursued the enemy, instead of engaging in this useless fetish. But not his son. Whether driven by fear for his safety or a desire to elevate himself above all, the spoiled one seems obsessed with construction of this complex, when he should be leading the army and putting the final dagger into the Franj.

By Allah, the Mamluks had utterly destroyed the Crusader enemy earlier this month. Thousands of the infidels had died or been taken prisoner near this very spot. King Louis and his two surviving brothers are in chains. It is said nearly ten thousand infidels are held in the camp outside of Mansura. Yet, there is rumor that al-Salih's boy wishes to negotiate a treaty with the king. Cenk scoffs. Why make peace and return prisoners to an enemy that will only return stronger and better equipped to fight Egypt again? Greed. And stupidity. Turanshah probably can only smell the coin from the ransom he assumes the king will pay for his men's freedom. A wise sultan would put all the prisoners to the sword.

A veiled girl with long eyelashes and a fine robe apprehensively approaches the fort, escorted by one of Turanshah's personal Mamluks. Again, Cenk shakes his head. Many good Muslims died to push the Crusaders back, yet this untested sultan seems content to spend Cairo's time and money on drink and whores and wasteful construction, rather than take the fight to the enemy. Cenk snarls, "The boy idiot—they should have left him in the Jazira."

As he turns to leave, Turanshah stumbles out of the river tower's gate, in apparent drunkenness, his beard untrimmed, his robe looking as if he has slept in it for three nights. The sultan eyes the concubine up and down, flashing a smile to his guard. The three of them talk. Two senior amirs from the Bahri Regiment, men waiting for their turn to see their new ruler, approach respectfully, armed with scrolls and maps. Good. Finally, the Mamluks will continue the fight and deal the Crusaders their final blow.

Yet, within a few short minutes, the concubine enters and both amirs step away from the entrance, one visibly furious and the other with a dumbfounded stare of disbelief on his face. The first mashes his scroll into a fist as he stomps back to his tent.

Turanshah. Cenk will follow the new sultan's directives,

even if the Ayyubid drags his heels. What other option is there? Over the years, he followed others he knew were not up to the tasks of command. But never at this level.

"This is the man who will lead an empire?" He looks skyward. "Oh Allah, what will become of your Egypt? Will you please kick this pathetic man in the ass? Just make him nod his scatter-brained head so that we may leave him to his sin, while we destroy your enemy still holding Damietta."

CHAPTER

19

Cenk
Fariskur
April 28, 1250

Cenk ducks back into the guard tent. Turanshah. How could he be from the blood of al-Salih?

Sight of his outfit's wares put him at ease—the polished axes, the swords blades evenly spaced in their racks, the dress uniforms of the guard hanging on a rod. He takes in a deep breath, savoring the smell of Mamluk wool and oiled steel.

His eye is drawn to the middle sword rack and to a single blade coated with a thin layer of rust with several chinks gone from its edge. He turns his nose. "Did the silly pricks use this one to bust rocks?" He pulls this weapon and takes it back to his bench.

Two knocks on the wood frame of his tent.

"Enter," Cenk says firmly, accustomed to many bringing a myriad of annoyances and questions his way.

Amir Aybeg enters. "Afternoon, Amir."

Cenk scrambles to his feet, his knees screaming. He flips the sword blade up to his shoulder and locks his body at attention.

"Sit down. By Allah, sit down—this is your own hooch."

Cenk relaxes, grins. "My Amir, you pretty well own every hooch around here."

"Maybe before this past February, before our patron's seed arrived," Aybeg says sarcastically. "I'm starting to think I don't command shit around here anymore."

Cenk grins, pulls out a stool for the Amir of One Hundred and grants him a respectful nod. He waits to sit until Aybeg does so.

Aybeg furls his brow. "I saw you stick your head out of the tent. You might want to watch your body language, or our new sultan's guard may read what I did. I'm sure his Mamluks are looking for a reason to separate some of us from our heads," Aybeg says, a smirk stretching his sun-furrowed face.

Cenk sighs. "Yes, my Amir. I didn't know it was that obvious."

Aybeg's smile broadens. Then his weathered brow goes stern. "Remember in Cairo when Turkmani first told us that the sultan, al-Kamil, would send al-Salih to the Jazira? You remember how it was way back then?"

Cenk smiles. "I do, my Amir."

"Al-Salih was shifted to Hisn Kayfa partly to push him as far away from the power center in Cairo as possible," Aybeg says. "Hell, the whole empire knew it."

Cenk nods, a hint of depression and nostalgia hitting him concurrently. "Al-Kamil's most ambitious spawn, he was. The sultan had good reason to sequester our patron to the hinterlands, away from the silver," Cenk says, referring to the common knowledge that the young al-Salih had done a fine job of spending a chunk of his father's treasure on his own personal Mamluks, back when he was left in charge of Cairo for a stint during his father's absence.

Aybeg smiles. "But al-Kamil also knew al-Salih was a son capable of independently governing a vital territory."

Cenk purses his lips in thought.

Both Hisn Kayfa and Amid were just as crucial then as they are now. Both are key ground, trade-wise and strategically, and both sit on the edge of enemy territory as northern buffers to the Seljukids, and now, even to the Mongols. Of course, possession of both towns seals Ayyubid control of the Jazira.

Cenk nods, inviting the amir to make his point.

"You know what I'm saying, Cenk. It was the same duty, the same governorship, yet there was a vast difference in the intent and in the purpose behind the assignments," Aybeg says, matter-of-factly.

Cenk feels a twinge of nervousness. He had always thought that Aybeg liked and trusted him, as Aybeg, too, had once called Amir Turkmani his first patron. They had both once shared the same regiment, but much has changed since those old days. Once al-Salih's Mamluk ranks swelled, Aybeg remained with the sultan's Salihi and Cenk was elevated to the Jamdariyya. While the two were not personal adversaries, their units were.

But all things have changed with al-Salih's death. Could Aybeg be looking for new allies? Or could he somehow be testing Cenk, baiting him into something? Cenk tries to show no expression. "Yes, my Amir, that could well be."

Aybeg shifts his stool to squarely face Cenk. "It's becoming plain to see that unlike his father, Turanshah wasn't sent to the far north to protect the empire's vulnerable flank. He was sent away because the sultan didn't have the stomach to view his son's debaucheries firsthand. Al-Salih shoved Turanshah away because it pained the old man that his son did not have the character necessary to hold the position he was ultimately destined to inherit."

"For our own well-being, my Amir. Please pardon me for just one moment." Cenk slips out of the tent and walks around it, scanning the men about the camp, rubbing his shoulder and moving his arms as he would do if taking a break.

Cenk returns to his seat. "I've thought the same, my Amir.

Al-Salih's remaining son probably reminded al-Salih too much of his own brother, al-Adil II. Our patron was only too aware that this brother's shortfalls and immoralities were the reason al-Salih was offered the sultanate in the first place."

Aybeg nods. "Unfortunately, I think Saladin's blood in Turanshah is too many times removed, too watered down, and the result is what we have now. A petty, deficient man heading the sultanate. I've heard that the treasury in Damascus is empty. Turanshah hadn't been there even a moon and he squandered over three hundred thousand dinars to not only the amirs but to nearly every administrator and office holder there."

Cenk's jaw drops. The oldest of games. "If one isn't talented enough to instill a conviction in his subjects through charisma and sure-handed guidance, then bribe them all into complicity with silver."

Aybeg rises with a grimace. "I fear for the empire if al-Mu'azzam Turanshah continues his course, if he thinks that leading an army means watching his Mamluks fight from the safety of a galley. I hope he comes to his senses soon and realizes that it was his father's army that not only welcomed him warmly but also preserved Cairo so that he had a throne to take. Alienating us, replacing us, is the work of a fool." He turns to leave. "I best go, best heed my own advice, since already one of the scamp's henchmen might have heard my belligerent words."

"My Amir," Cenks says, standing.

Aybeg turns with the tent flap resting on his back.

"Thanks for the visit."

Aybeg smiles. "Once again, everything has changed for us, my friend. We old birds, we old men of the Salihi need to stick together."

Cenks grins as the senior amir leaves. Old men of the Salihi. Hardly. What he and Aybeg had in common back then and even now was *not* being completely accepted by the Salihi—that cadre of men fortunate to call al-Salih their first and only patron. Since he and Aybeg both started out their careers as "Amir's

Mamluks," a standing lower than the Salihi, they were destined to be second-class citizens in the brotherhood.

When their first patron, Amir Turkmani, died more than a decade past, their status dropped further, the two assuming the dreaded title of *sayfiyah*—orphans of the military order. While Al-Salih had snapped them up, rescuing both Cenk and Aybeg, it was the pair's shared trait of tenacity that kept them relevant. Against the odds, both of their careers blossomed. The two had proven themselves survivors.

But now they seem fated to endure yet another form of indignity. Cenk figures he was lucky to have shed the curse of being a sayfiyah, yet at this stage of his career, could he really survive losing his Royal Mamluk status to Turanshah's thugs? Amir Aybeg must be thinking the same.

Cenk sits back for a while, still somewhat stunned by the amir's social call, trying to put into context all that was said. He shakes it off. His words were true but just talk. Just talk.

His guard. He must check on the troops. His senior—Jamal al-Din Muhsin, overall commander of the Jamdariyya—will be back soon. And he must let his men know that he remains vigilant, still motivated despite their predicament.

Morale has sagged since his guard was relegated to perimeter security, Turanshah not trusting even the best in al-Salih's ranks to step inside the fort, or even stand watch at its gates. Cenk was not surprised, but his men should not feel hurt by the slight, as his troops were not the only Mamluks being brushed aside by the new ruler. As is the way of the Ayybuids, Turanshah has already begun replacing his father's Mamluks with those from his own smaller force.

Whether they believe it or not, all of al-Salih's Royal Mamluks have begun the slow descent into the lower status of qaranis, men ousted from noble standing. While some hoped the sheer number of al-Salih's Mamluks—one thousand plus—would somehow preserve their favored status, this has not been the case so far.

In just over two moons, Turanshah has managed to alienate virtually all of his father's senior amirs, those in both the Jamdariyya and the Bahri having been relieved of key posts. The Grand Master of the Armour, the Grand Chamberlain, the Grand Major Domo, the Grand Treasurer—all of the top positions, which took an entire career of blood and misery to earn—were taken from them in an instant and spread to Turanshah's cronies.

Even the lesser stations—the Cup Holders, the Masters of the Robe, the Shoe Bearers—are filled by the new sultan's Mamluks. Cenk reckons even the lower ranks will not be spared—that possibly when even the bachelors of the Bahri return to their island citadel, they may find themselves ousted from their barracks and forced to live in town.

One of the most distressing rumors is that Turanshah plans to renege on his promise made during his return trip for Hisn Kayfa to promote Aqtay, the high-flying Amir of One Hundred in the Bahri, who traveled there to fetch Turnashah after his father's death. If the rumor proves true, Aqtay would be livid. Perhaps more insultingly, the queen, Sharat al-Durr, al-Salih's widow, was forced to hand over not only the state treasure but her personal jewelry to the new sultan, whom she had once known as a sniffling child.

Cenk begins to wonder if he could tolerate serving close to the boy sultan, even if given the opportunity. Al-Salih had been a sultan and a warrior, as well. He was a serious man, and despite the distrustful actions of his Ayyubid kin, he loved and believed in his Mamluks. A man who seized his opportunities in life when they became available.

Cenk sees none of these qualities in Turanshah. Opposite from his father and also from his dead brother, who would have been fit to lead the realm, Turanshah is rarely seen to bend a leg in prayer. Instead, he is too often distracted by the drunken civilians he brought with him from the Jazira. Matters of the army seem trivial to him. Cenk reckons Turanshah is neither a man of the book nor of the sword—just a childish puppet, his strings manipulated by his own greedy Mamluks. None of this bodes well for a stable sultanate.

Cenk has never paid much attention to the politics and power positioning among the senior amirs, nor to the leadership above them. He just carried out his duty. It was easier that way. Yet, now more than ever, he realizes that al-Salih had been not only the empire's unifying force but also that of the regiments. He worries that since their patron's death, a wedge has been driven in among the dead sultan's Royal Mamluks. A slow unraveling. The corps now filters into two factions: the Bahri under Amir Aqtay and the Salihi under Amir Aybeg.

He sighs. "The drama. Politics," he mutters.

Cenk's smaller unit, the Jamdariyya, is caught in between, with no inherent loyalty to either side. He and the others in al-Salih's personal guard must eventually decide on their own which way to turn. Having never appreciated Amir Aqtay's soft ways during their shared time in the training ranks at Hisn Kayfa, Cenk feels himself gravitating toward Aybeg, despite the man's lofty ambitions. Especially after today. If Cenk's guards have a future in the regiment, it may well be as Muizziyya Mamluks— Muizz Aybeg's personal Mamluks.

As for Cenk, maybe extraction from the entire situation is wisest. Hang up his sword, bow, and quiver. Perhaps move to a small villa on the coast or a cozy flat on the edge of Cairo. He smiles, thinking of it. But soon, his grin is wiped clean as he frets on his stream of funds. Turanshah's need to pay his own Mamluks may cause Cenk to have his income-producing iqta taken from him and given to another. Likely.

Enough. What does he control? Little. With the sun dipping, he lights two candles and grabs the rusty sword from the table. He eases himself onto the bench. Sharpening the swords: this is what he still controls, what he should concentrate on. Let him handle the small, mindless tasks and let the others worry over the bigger matters of civil affairs. He grins.

Three knocks on his tent frame—the signal that the visitor

is a man from the Jamdariyya, one of Cenk's guards. The ceaseless interruptions are reason alone to retire.

"Enter," Cenk says.

A flustered guard steps in from the dark, locking his body. "Amir ... Cenk, I ... I ... "

Cenk looks up with a grandfatherly smile on his face. He laughs. "Come now, faris, spit it out."

The usually self-assured guard looks at him with an uncharacteristic expression of panic, a slight paleness already filling his face.

Cenk narrows his brow. "At ease. What is it?"

"Amir Cenk, I just heard something ... that I feel you must know."

Cenk lays the sword on his table. He motions with his hand. "Sit."

The guard places his long-handled ax in the rack and pushes aside his sword, as he sits on the offered stool. He looks behind him and then leans close to Cenk, and whispers. "Just moments ago, while walking the perimeter, past the sultan's fort ..."

The man brings his bottom lip up and takes a deep breath of air, as if to work up his courage. He shakes his head. "I heard the sultan talking to himself. He sounded drunk ... I could hear him swing his sword. I could hear what I thought were the tops of candles landing on the deck. He was muttering the names of our amirs. This stroke for him, this stroke for another. This is how he would deal with each."

Cenk leans back on his stool and looks upward. In time, he moves forward, placing his elbows in front of the guard. "Are you completely certain it was he who spoke—Turanshah?"

"Yes, my Amir. I don't think anyone else was in the room."

"And the sword strokes. Could they have been something else? Anything?"

The guard shakes his head. "He once struck the candle holder. I heard the clang."

Cenk nods. He straightens himself on the stool. "If a single word you utter is a lie, I'll personally cut your tongue out." He appraises the youth, his eyes boring into the guard's. Cenk is experienced in catching young men in falsehoods fabricated to avoid suffering. He sees no signs of treachery from this guard, not one speck of guilt in his spoken words.

"And I'd wish it so." The guard says, never losing eye contact, seemingly relieved to have the burden of the words off his chest. "By Allah, my Amir. Regrettably, what I've said is true."

Cenk leans back, rolls his shoulders forward, tilts his head backward in thought. He groans and folds his hands atop the table. "Which names did the sultan mention when he was slaying candles?"

"Amirs Aybeg, Baybars, and Aqtay."

Cenk looks at him blankly. Ehh. By Allah, the boy sultan wishes to kill the best of his father's amirs.

CHAPTER

20

Leander
Fariskur
May 2, 1250

A hoot of laughter wakes him. Leander struggles to one elbow to orient himself. Bright light floods through the rolled-up sides of the tent. Half of the men about him nap; others chat from their cots. Some men stitch torn tunics, sharpen lance heads, or repair armor while sharing words. He turns over to his back.

The slower pace of the new routine has set in. After early morning training, all have retreated to their tents to keep the hot sun off their necks during the heat of the day. Amirs Duyal and Sedat have not objected, the pair spending the bulk of their time trying to fill the gaps in the amirate's unserviceable and missing gear, this campaign having taken its toll on the men's kits.

Leaders have resorted to scrounging and occasionally begging, the chore of providing for units of the Bahri made difficult by a supply system directed to give priority to the new sultan's own, rather than to his deceased father's Mamluks. Amir Aqtay asked to receive his kiswa—the biannual grant to cover clothes and replacement gear—early, but his request was rejected.

Leander yawns. None of it is good. Inactivity has never served armies well. After nearly four moons of fighting the Crusaders, the Mamluks surely need some rest and recovery, but instead have been sitting in the camp at Fariskur for nearly a whole month. The men are becoming lethargic. Gossip spreads like fog across the sluggish camp.

It is whispered among the tents that Turanshah does not attack Damietta because it will harm the desired truce that he is negotiating with the King of France. Nobody sees the new sultan leave his wooden fort, except to share the odd meal with his own men. Rumors swirl that Turanshah's personal Mamluks urge the treaty for no other reason than to quickly end the sultan's need for the Bahri; with the Crusader threat removed, Turanshah would be less dependent on his father's men, making the transition in power easier.

Word is that Louis will pay one million gold besants to purchase both his freedom and that of the ten thousand of his captured countrymen quartered in Mansura. Leander and his mates feel this is good—maybe some of that coin could be used to get the men some new boots.

Binny tosses a freshly repaired arm guard to a mate. "I know. The Franj said when the king was planning this campaign, even the Bishop of Paris pleaded with Louis to stay home and not leave their citizens with all the enemies of France surrounding them there."

"But Louis didn't care," Slap says. "He was too keen to empty his purse in Cairo killing Muslims, damned be the dangers at home."

"There's some truth in that," Leander says, his words distorted by another yawn. He rolls to his side and pulls a tunic under his armpit. For some reason, he feels duty-bound to filter the realities out from the lies and exaggerations in the secondhand stories passed to Slap and Binny from Mamluks returning from guard duty in Mansura. Those bored sentries spent weeks pulling fragments of information from the loose lips of Crusader prisoners at the detention area last moon.

"I believe it. Their king couldn't be any less a religious fanatic than those swine in the Templars," another Mamluk says.

"Yeah, but I meant truth about the enemies encircling France," Leander says, stretching, swinging his legs over the side of his cot. He runs his fingers through his matted hair, rests his elbows on knees.

They look at him, waiting for the former Franj to enlighten them.

"Those Crusaders blabbing at the prison camp were right. King Louis would've been wiser to preserve the health of his forces for a potential fight at home."

"Against the King of England?" Binny asks.

"Yeah, King Henry III still wants those western provinces in France that once belonged to his father. Just eight years ago, Louis had to fight the English in Poitou to crush that rebellion. That shit is far from over," Leander says.

Some nod, having heard of the conflict.

Leander continues. "Plus, there's danger for France with Emperor Frederick ..."

"The Roman?" a Mamluks asks.

"Right. Pope Innocent was no help in soothing the quarrel between the emperor and King Louis. Hell, the pope himself is no friend of Louis'. And on the way here, King Louis' men stoked up the old hate with the people of Avignon in their southlands. Those folks aren't fond of being called 'traitors and heretics', with the Cathar Crusade only twenty years past."

Empty stares from most of them. A man tips back to his tunic pillow. Too many names; Leander figures he is beginning to lose them. "Louis is surrounded by foes. For a lot of reasons, the French King should've just stayed home, that's all."

Slap stretches, cracking his knuckles over his head. "Just proves he's mad. Only a crazy man would leave his kingdom with that many enemies on his doorstep to go overseas and kill strangers and take another's land, all in the name of avenging Jesus."

"They said even Louis' mother cried when she found out the king had taken up the cross, even more so once her other three sons 'crossed themselves' right afterward," Binny says.

"Yep, and what was it both the mother queen and bishop tried to convince Louis to apply to the pope for? A ... dispension?" Slap asks.

"I think that would be a dispensation, my brother," Leander says.

Slap shrugs his shoulders.

Binny sits down. "I heard the same. They wanted to get the king out of his crusading pledge. They tried to convince him that his vow to his God was made while still foggy-headed on his deathbed back in France. Louis promised that if spared from his illness, he'd come over and slay Muslims."

Slap snarls. "He must've been loopy. If the king happened to hear a voice in his ear that day, I'm betting that it wasn't his Lord's, but the devil's. Should've listened to his mother, instead."

"Yep, mother would have kept her boy out of trouble. Sounded to me like Louis might have pretty well been a mother's boy—kind of like you, Slap," Binny says.

All four laugh. Some late chuckles from several of the adjacent cots, those lying with eyes closed but not sleeping.

Slap shakes his head and twists his face, scrunching the scarred mutilations across his cheeks and brow. "I don't know. My mother kicked me to the hills to fling arrows at the Mongol raiders. Your mammy taught her little favorite to read and write under the comfort of Kipchak felt, while my lowly ass was in the rain and snow pushing sheep. Who's the momma's boy?"

More laughter, spreading in volume across the row of cots.

"Right, right," Binny says, pretending to respect the well-played response. "Like you were the only one acquainted with sheep. Where am I now, brothers, even with my good mother's teachings? In the same smelly tent as you goons, after being put to the slave block years ago—thanks be to Allah—no different than you all. Would my mother allow that for one she considered her dearest?"

"Like us, she probably just got tired of listening to your shit, wishing she had never taught you to speak, much less read. Trade the prick off," Slap says.

A few sleep-drunk men giggle.

Leander's mind stays on the king. "It's always the same. Hindsight. If Louis had made it all the way to Cairo, the French would've hailed him. With our boot heels on their throats and his army spoilt, of course, some will now call their king a fool."

"Shit, most of our boots are in shreds and too long stowed under our cots." A Mamluk lowers his voice. "If we don't get off our asses and hit the Franj soon, their damn king may be hailed yet."

"Yeah, for all we know more Franj ships will come over the horizon. More men, more supplies. And we'll be back to where we were a year ago," Binny says.

Slap groans.

The high shriek of a woman pierces the air. Binny chuckles and shakes his head, assuming a man from another unit is playing a boredom-hatched joke on a mate. Another scream, this one sounding genuine.

The Mamluks look at each other. Some shrug their shoulders and roll over in their racks. Others pull on their boots with no sense of urgency and peek outside the walls of the tent.

"Oh, by Allah," a Mamluk gasps.

They pile out of the tent.

Sultan Turanshah sobs on the run from the dining tent of his amirs, making for his bedchamber tower, staggering across the chalky ground. He holds his left arm, his hand cleaved between the fingers, his yellow robe soaked in blood at the sleeve.

A labored thump in Leander's chest. An assassin hired from among the Persians. Somehow the Crusaders employed one to kill the sultan in their last-ditch effort at creating chaos among their Egyptian enemy, or to buy them more time. "Arm yourselves! There must be an assassin in camp!" Leander says.

Men turn back toward the tent, but then they stop in their tracks, mouths agape at what they see.

Amir Baybars springs across the scrubland after the sultan, a sword clutched in his hand. Turanshah looks back desperately at his pursuer. He reaches his tower's doors safely, shouldering them open and slamming them quickly behind him.

Leander, unsure of what will happen next, follows some of the others back into the tent. He goes to his rack, wriggles on his chain mail, and cinches the sword belt about his waist.

"What the hell's going on?" Slap asks, fumbling for his gear.

"I have no idea," Leander says, securing his buckle.

He and the others clamber out of the tent, unsheathing swords as they exit.

Through gaps in the half-constructed veranda, Leander stares in disbelief as the sultan climbs the last of his stairs, weeping, still cradling his injured arm. Al-Salih's son then disappears from view. Baybars clamps his sword under his armpit and yanks on the thick-metaled door handle.

Blood rises into Leander's temples. A lightheadedness sets in.

"What do we do?" Slap asks Binny.

The typically poised one stares with a look of worry on his brow. "Uh, right now, nothing. But we best be ready—for anything."

Soon, almost thirty Bahri Mamluks approach the tower, amirs and troopers both, some still pulling jawshans over their chests and plopping helmets on their heads. More trickle in, falling in behind Amir Aqtay.

Aqtay points to a few men, and several squads surround the bottom of the tower. A dozen or so of Turanshah's personal

Mamluks cluster into a loose perimeter away from the structure, outnumbered and apparently unwilling to defend their patron.

Leander mutters. "By Allah, this isn't the action of Baybars alone. The senior Amirs?"

Aqtay orders silence and then beckons the sultan. "Come down, Turanshah, and meet your fate!"

More Mamluks filter in, some nocking arrows. Leander sees the cold determination in Aqtay, witnessed before only in battle.

No response from the sultan's fortification.

"Come down and face your father's men with half the courage of the man who bred you!" Aqtay shouts. Amir Aybeg struts up and stands beside him.

"The Salihi also consent to this?" Binny asks.

Duyal arrives, out of breath. "Stay back! Stay back!" he says to those in his amirate. Without further orders, they fall into three files behind their squad leaders, away from the growing crowd.

Sedat elbows Duyal and points to an Amirate Leader from the Bahri, who rallies his men. Two troops in this outfit grab their kettle drums, one pulling felt-tipped mallets from his pack, the other poking his head under the thick leather strap and standing with the oak-framed war drum at his waist.

"Surround them," Duyal says, pointing.

Duyal's amirate forms a loose circle around the dozen Bahri, their swords still drawn.

A nervous smile forms on the Amirate Commander's face. "Amir Sedat and Amir Duyal. I never would've associated you two with such treachery."

"You'll find no Ayyubid blood on my men's blades," Duyal says calmly. "I suggest you have your men set down those drums and stow those mallets."

The opposing amir eyes Duyal's men as they surround his smaller force. He shakes his head. "One need not shed blood to be an accomplice to murder. Don't you see that our sultan is wounded, that men intend to kill him?"

Duyal nods. He remains calm. "I see it. If you pound those drums in alarm and bring the rest of the army here in a panic, you alone will have to live with the bloodshed that follows. Instead of one useless man dying, you'll bring the end to many good men needed to protect the empire. You wish to be the cause of that?"

The Amirate Commander cinches his mouth. He snarls and again assesses the disposition of the men encircling his mates.

No one speaks for an uncomfortable moment. Inside and outside the perimeter, white-knuckled Mamluks clench the ivory-handled damascene steel in their fists.

The Mamluk seems to grasp that either action—to fight or to sound the drums—is akin to suicide. His disposition lightens. "You seem the one willing to spill Bahri blood," he says to Duyal. "You're the one willing to bring punishment on all here once this is finished," he says, looking at the deployed swords. The Mamluk signals for his men to lower their drums.

Duyal nods. "If punishment comes to your men and mine, then we'll be in fine company. The best of the Bahri and Salihi, and two Amirs of One Hundred, look to be far more tangled than you and I."

All eyes return to the tower.

A pair of Mamluks apply torches to the base of the wooden stronghold. Flames race up the blue fabric that shrouds the place. The dry wood beneath the cotton wrap begins to crackle. Flares ride the wind, creeping up the fir-planked sides, curling upon the second floor of the fortress, consuming the new beams recently erected.

Amid the rising pops and snaps, Leander's head spins. He cannot believe Ayyubid royalty bleeds at this moment from a wound made from Mamluk steel; he cannot fathom that he was but one drum beat away from a fight with fellow Bahri. And before him now, the leaders of both regiments are trying to smoke out the rightful Sultan of Egypt. Or torch him. It appears they care not which.

The wind shifts, sending thick smoke across the cluster of men. Leander lowers his chin and closes his eyes as cinders peck his cheeks. He inhales the thinning smoke, seeing it split into twin puffs as he exhales through his nose. He licks a hint of charcoal from his lips.

The tower becomes a giant pillar of fire; the growl from the inferno dominates the camp. Aqtay and his Mamluks move back from the heat.

The tower doors burst open. Men ready their bows. Four half-dressed concubines pour out, coughing, silk pulled across their pretty faces. Behind them are three of Turanshah's compatriots, some of the sultan's civilian fools brought with him from Hisn Kayfa. These men stagger with their hands spread to their sides, tears streaming from their smoke-filled eyes, their heads pivoting left and right to the Mamluks around them. One robed man, with his vision obscured, bumps into a Mamluk near Aybeg. The Mamluk throws a shoulder, knocking the man down.

Out comes the sultan, exiting not like a royal, or a warrior, or even as a composed prisoner resigned to his fate, but instead fleeing like a wounded animal flushed from his hole. He runs through a small gap in the cluster of Mamluks and heads for the river in a sloppy, heavy-footed run, at times leaning, weaving his way to the water.

"Mine!" Baybars yells, the brute obviously wishing to take full responsibility, or at least finish the job he started.

With sword in hand, the long-legged Baybars lopes effortlessly after the stumbling sultan, like a wolf after a wounded doe. The pack follows. Baybars catches the sultan by the leg as Turanshah attempts to dive into the Nile and swim across. Strong as a bear, Baybars pulls the slight-built noble toward him, raises his steel and chops diagonally across the sultan's head. Not a word from the Mamluks gathered.

Baybars then grasps the dead royal by his robe and lifts the man with one arm to look into the weak one's eyes, each now peering monstrously in opposite directions with the head cleaved nearly in two. Satisfied that his work is finished, he flings the lifeless body into the Nile's current.

The Bahri and Salihi remain standing in an awkward silence, watching as the knee-deep water slowly carries the carcass downstream, the blood of Saladin forming a red-hazed halo around the man before being diluted into obscurity.

Baybars washes the gore from his blade with giant thumbs, inspects it without looking up or behind him. He clamps the weapon into his armpit and then proceeds to clean the crimson splatters from his forearm as would a man nonchalantly working through his morning routine. He cups the water and splashes it on his face, pulling the excess from his beard. He straightens, taking in the sky for a moment, before wading to the shoreline, expressionless. Not a drop of blood is visible on his tunic or trousers, the summer wool clinging to his muscles.

The throng of Mamluks parts as he strolls through them, his beefy hand again clutching his sword. Baybars halts. He turns to face them, water still dripping from his dirty-blond beard.

Leander tightens his grip on his weapon, unsure of what happens next, unsure of who stands before them: fiend or divinity, villain or a mythical prince, who has just slain the forbidden dragon.

Baybars roars to the onlookers. "'Tis nothing but God's will. The sword stroke which split the head of the imposter was not that from the hand of a murderer or disloyal subject, but from Allah himself. The great one culling the inferior brood of our good father, al-Salih. We all know it to be so."

Baybars looks into the faces of his fellow Mamluks—men who likely helped plan this attack, men who opposed it, and those completely surprised by it. He again speaks with a convincing tone that keeps the attention of even those senior to him. "We pledged our loyalty to one man, al-Salih Ayyub. The disgraceful son of our patron is now what he deserves to be—food for the eels."

He searches the faces of those nearest him, returning the sword to his scabbard. Finally, he turns. With eyes to the ground—and with no apparent fear of arrow, sword or lance—he heads back to his tent as one who has just completed a morning chore.

Some men turn back to the water, the sultan now a speck on the surface of the great river, drifting slowly seaward, slipping gently into oblivion. Most stand with their swords at their sides, mouths agape.

In time, the soldiers begin to stow their weapons. Mamluks shamble back to their tents in silence.

"What now?" Binny asks, turning to Leander with the look of a lost youth.

Leander only returns the stare for a moment before fixing his gaze upon the wide blue water. For generations, the Mamluks here always had royal blood to follow, an Ayyubid prince or sultan to lead the way. The only royal in Cairo now floats down the Nile, face first. Leander wonders how this void can ever be filled.

"I fear that's up to Allah," Leander says.

CHAPTER
21

Leander
Damietta
June 12, 1250

"Oooh!" Jacinta giggles as she scampers up the sandy incline, avoiding the wave's splash. Atop the dune, she looks both ways down the beach. Seeing no one, she removes the niqab from her face. She turns, smiling at Leander with the amused look of a young girl. He grins, having never seen her entire face before. She is as beautiful as he expected. Her teeth appear white as pearls; her smile is pleasing, disarming. He watches the child in her features diminish and the lovely woman return to her face. He does not tire of looking at her in either form—her clear, brown eyes and her dark hair tangled by the wind about her ears and lips.

Another wave crashes, sending a tumbling plume of mist into the air. A gust catches the spray, sending it over them. He takes in a deep breath of salty air, feels the comfort in it. He knows his peacefulness is born not only of the sunshine and the sand between his toes—it is mostly because of her. While he has had little experience with women, this one seems special; she has a soothing way about her that he has never experienced before.

Contrast. A mate of his in France used to profoundly state at the right times, "The greatest luxury in the world is contrast." His friend had learned the line from his father, and it fits at this moment of sublime placidity, coming after what felt like unending moons of war and intrigue.

For the past year it has been nothing but conflict and the emotions accompanying their struggle against the French invaders: the disappointment in the fall of Damietta last June, the sorrow over good friends lost and maimed, the apprehension over how he would perform in combat, the constant worry for his comrades, the joy in victory at Mansura and the saving of Cairo, the sadness in the passing of his patron, and the upheaval in the regiments since the slaying of Turanshah. The moons of this past year have limped by slowly, like years. No wonder the veteran Mamluks have the wrinkles of civilian men ten years their senior.

While Leander took no part in the translation work needed to finalize the treaty with the King of France, his current command did pull him away from his amirate in Fariskur to take part in the weighing of Louis' gold, the two hundred thousand pounds required to buy his men's freedom. A few weeks ago, Leander was ordered to help set up the scales and move the loads, keeping secret his knowledge of the French language so he might detect any deceit on the French side during the weighing.

A pair of terns fly just above the water, hovering in the wind, only a subtle movement of wings keeping them stationary above the slick of ocean current beneath their ivory breasts. One swoops slowly, dropping his black head to pluck a tiny scrap of food from the flowing surface. He then dips a wing, banks, and returns effortlessly to his mate. Leander is jealous of the ease and simplicity of their lives. He wonders if he would trade their shorter existence of little anxiety for the longer life of up and downs faced by most humans.

He steps behind Jacinta and takes the place closer to the sea, so that she can walk the harder-packed sand and not fight the waves. In front of them is nothing but sand, sea, and bent grasses swaying in the breeze. A pelican dives in the backwash between waves. Cormorants overhead fly to more fishable water.

"You have a way of asking many questions, but offering little of yourself," Leander says.

She smiles. "Well, I've never known a man from France. There's much to learn."

"You had told me that your father knew some of the amirs and that he'd gotten you the job in the infirmary. How does your father know them?"

"He oversees many of the holding ponds and canals on the east bank, where the wheat and barley are grown. As you know, the routing of the water is important, so my father must deal often with both the land owners and growers. Of course, the amirs in both regiments own some of this land."

Leander nods, recalling his conversations with a few of the grubby workers on the canal repair crews. "Water is liquid gold in Egypt," one of the thick-armed men had said.

And it is so. While a rich layer of silt is deposited annually on the land beside the Nile during the summer flooding season, once the water recedes, farmers must irrigate their fields with river water from reservoirs, or from the Nile itself. As Egypt receives very little rainfall, this undertaking of routing and storing as much floodwater as possible is critical, and trusted to some of the brightest minds in Egypt.

This water—stored in ponds and moved via a web of ditches—is not only a complicated but also a very political business. Men in charge of maintaining the infrastructure are highly valued in the delta. The consistent flow of floodwater through the farm lands keeps the wheat fields producing and the silver flowing in Cairo. If improperly managed, there is not enough water to last the entire growing season from October to February.

"So, how is it that a lovely twenty-year-old daughter of a rich man isn't already married off? How is it that she wishes instead to empty bed pans and change bloody dressings and watch men die?"

Her lips tighten. "It was time to do my part. Contribute. By Allah, the invaders were on our shore."

Leander nods.

"I had to do something. I found they wouldn't let a woman join the ranks of the Bahri," she says with raised eyebrows.

He smiles, shakes his head, dodges a crashing wave, and inadvertently presses his shoulder against hers. She giggles. He scrunches his brow. "Seems there'd be a more pleasant way to serve. A less disheartening place to work."

"True. And you're right—compared to most, my father does have some silver. But I was a cook before. It's not as if I've lived a life of privilege. I love food, cooking, spices."

"Maybe you should've cooked for the army."

She grins. "Maybe. But when our people's land, our way of live is threatened, we all must engage in some of the horridness in the mission at hand. Do a job that others would not. But I don't need to explain this sort of thing to you."

He smiles. "No, you don't. I mean, I don't know much about the wealthy family part, but I understand miserable jobs."

They both laugh.

"With the Crusaders gone, will you continue to work at the infirmary?" he asks.

"Yes, but not as much. It sounds as if they'll only need me to fill in when they are short, until all of the men are healed. I feel good that I helped when I was needed most."

"And well you should feel good."

"You, too, should feel good. Because of you and your mates, the Crusaders have left our shores. The aggressors and their king are gone. Because of the lions. The lions of Islam." She grins.

Leander shakes his head.

"What?" She interlaces her fingers with his.

He feels a warmth inside at just feeling her skin, but then is overcome with a sadness.

"Nothing."

"Really?"

He sighs. "The future of our corps, the future of Egypt. All is not well."

"But the enemy—they're gone. There's been so little to rejoice in. We have this now. Egypt has bought some time to heal and let the leadership settle out."

"Yes, but I worry about the Bahri, worry about what has happened, worry over the way our victory was won, worry about who will lead going forward."

"Maybe you worry too much. The Franj have left. Isn't that the most important thing?" She looks up into his eyes.

"Mostly. But what remains of the victors ... and their souls?"

"Souls?"

He sighs. "Yeah, souls. You see, when in the tibaq as youths, the instructors pounded the core traits of the Salihiyyah into our heads—not just forcing memorization but evaluating our conduct there on those principles. Magnanimity, courage, loyalty. These were the values the Mu'allim stressed, those which defined our regiments, the ethics from which we could never stray. I fear we've drifted from our standards, our honor. I fear the consequences that may result."

She looks up at him again, her eyes urging him to continue.

"*Yücelik*—magnanimity. The quality of being noble in mind, high-souled and dutiful to our God. Where was this trait when we slaughtered thousands of sick Frenchmen on the Nile shore? What would Saladin have said? What would he have done?"

She raises a lip. "Killed them. He would've killed them as you did. Your duty was—is—to slay the enemies of Islam. Aren't you obligated to show benevolence toward those who embrace God, not those who come to disgrace and occupy the holy places?"

He looks down, flips a shell with his toe. "Yes. But it's not that simple. The Bahri are also taught to fight virtuously. I feel we've broken our code."

"Saladin likely would've seen magnanimity for the Bahri in the same light as the Third Pillar of Islam—helping the needy.

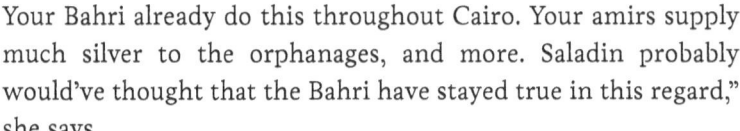

Your Bahri already do this throughout Cairo. Your amirs supply much silver to the orphanages, and more. Saladin probably would've thought that the Bahri have stayed true in this regard," she says.

"Maybe. But what of courage—*cesaret*—recognizing the fear of danger or criticism, but proceeding in the face of it with calmness and firmness? What courage does it take to slaughter ill soldiers or unarmed men who are guilty of nothing but holding firm to their faith? What courage does it take to slaughter our own sultan—blood of our patron—a woeful man with no training?"

"Life is rarely tidy," she says, a rare grimace setting on her face, a fork in her brow.

He turns to her and sees that the child is back in her face, this time wearing a look of despair. A wave crashes against his calf.

She tucks some of her windblown hair behind her ear. "I have no words for Turanshah's slaying. But with the Franj … a soldier destroys the enemy when he is told to do so and in the place where he finds the foe and in whatever condition the enemy may be."

She looks up to the sky, as a puff of cloud blocks the sun. "I have no place lecturing war to a man who has lived it, but why not rejoice in the easy kills—those that removed the enemy without harming your friends? I've spent months doing nothing but treating Egyptian wounds from Crusader swords and lances. And you're losing sleep that your regiment killed the Franj with less than the acceptable amount of honor?"

He looks out to the vast skyline. "Yes."

Her smile is a bit jaded. "Sorry. I don't mean to be brutish. But if you must be a truth-seeker, take solace that it took some courage to kill the infidels in a way less honorable than your values dictated." She rubs his back. "For me, I'm happy to know so many Franj are dead. Dead Frenchmen cannot kill Egyptian soldiers and take our people's land. I'm happy the aggressors are gone."

He nods and reflects. "Fair enough. Maybe the most concerning to me is *Sadakât*—loyalty, the quality of faithfulness to Allah, Egypt, and the Corps."

"You and your men could not have been more loyal. To each other. To Egypt. You saved her. Generations will look back on the regiments as gifts from God. Your conduct will be seen as reflecting glory not only onto the Egyptians, but onto Allah himself. Saviors of Islam."

"But what of our loyalty to the Corps? Was killing al-Salih's surviving male heir the way we showed loyalty to our patron?" Tears fill his eyes. "His other son was murdered by enemy. Yet we, his prized ones, killed his descendant, the one he chose to lead the sultanate. It was not our choice to make."

"You didn't kill Turanshah."

"But I and the others allowed it."

They say nothing for a long while. The sun sinks into a layer of dark gray above the horizon. As they walk, he thinks back to the last moon, reflecting on his conversation with the old Crusader at the scales, just before the king and the remnants of his army were freed and departed for Acre.

The King of France sat on a bench, a pair of guards on either side of him, watching as the last of his gold was loaded onto Muslim carts. So strange, Leander thought, to see a king nearly alone. Just another man. He looked wretched, almost silly, still dressed in the black samite robe provided him by Turanshah, a garment trimmed with beaver and squirrel fur with gold tassels hanging from his collar and waist.

Leander felt pity for the king and approached him. Some local children had given Leander an earthenware jar of milk; he decided to offer it to the king. Louis saw him coming and raised his hand to release his guards. Leander bowed. In the king's tongue, Leander offered the milk to Louis. The king had heavy bags under his eyes and his face was still gaunt from the sickness that had ravaged him and his lords. He stared at Leander. "How is it you speak my language so well?"

"I once lived in France."

The king pushed away the jar. "Get him away from me. I have no more to say to him." He turned, arrogantly lifting his chin, as if just then remembering his superiority—a royal prisoner somehow recovering his imperial dignity.

Leander grinned, nodded, unsurprised at the response. He picked up the jar and walked away.

Another Frenchman, a lord close to the king, approached Leander. "I overheard your exchange," he said. "How is that you're with the Saracens?"

"I came just before La Forbie and served under Walter of Brienne. I went over to the Mamluks."

"The Count of Brienne, of course." He sighed, rubbing his gray-stubbled beard. "We lost Erard of Brienne at Mansura."

"I heard—and his brother, too. I knew both while I was a page there. My father served their father."

The lord raised his eyebrows and shook his head. "Oh, how this world can shrink right down."

"Yes."

A troubled look fell upon the lord. He looked up with eyes revealing compassion. "Surely you know that if you die here, serving the infidels, you'll go to hell. As gracious as our Lord is, he'll have no mercy on a former Christian."

Leander heaved a sigh. "I often wonder if the Gods the Christians and Muslims worship—the two Gods who bring both sides to such brutality—will not, in the end, be the same Lord."

The Frank looks at him, confounded.

Leander continued. "Perhaps on the day of judgment, when each man's sins are exposed, those who best followed the law of God—for the spirit of the edicts are similar in both books—will be the ones gifted with a life in heaven. Perhaps those whose actions strayed from the word of the good books shall be the ones cursed to hell."

The Frank looked at him, a grin slowly taking over his face.

"Seems you've thought some on this topic. Perhaps trying to rationalize your way to heaven? Trouble is, there's only one true God, only one true set of laws, and you've rejected both."

"Maybe," Leander said. "Or, if Allah is the only God, possibly you have done this, not I. But I suppose neither of us will know until that final day comes."

The lord looked down, and spoke. "Methinks we'll never reach common ground on the topic of God. But perhaps you could enlighten me on the topic of man, as you're obviously not a stupid one. So, how is it you could switch sides? How is it you could leave the civility of French life and join these barbarians?"

"French civility." Leander mulls the phrase and nods. "Is this the redeeming quality that fueled the king's invasion, that motivated the slaughter? And 'barbarians'? If not for the medicine provided by we 'barbarians', thousands more of you would be under ground, your spirits having already met your God—or, maybe, reckoned with mine."

The French lord smiled.

Leander smiled back. "Barbarians would have slain you weeks ago and not allowed your release. Civility, you say? I'll tell you this, until the events of recent days, which have upturned the Egyptian cart, there was far more honor and accord in the Egyptian forces than in those of the Franks."

"You think? See our most royal there?" The Crusader pointed to his king. "Things have been much graver here for us than for you. But we have not slain him. You've beaten us down on this Crusade, yet in the process, these Saracens, these mongrels from the steppe, murdered their own sultan. You'll tell me this is the action of an honorable people?"

Leander looked about him. He chuckled. "Your king probably wishes himself dead, as surely his heart is broken, abandoned as he has been by so many of his men, none bothering to ensure his safety on ship but departing for France without him. Leaving their king to wait alone for his surviving brother. Your lecture on French civility and allegiances does not hold up well, sir."

The lord's smile left.

Leander, too, bristled. "Then again, I wouldn't expect you to understand. The men of the Bahri ... you see, they were loyal to one man, al-Salih Ayyub. For decades, you could find no fighting force on this earth more devoted to their leader. His son, Turanshah, was a stranger to them—to us—and not half the warrior of his father. Turanshah spurned his father's forces. His death is just the nature of things."

The Crusader looked at him almost sadly. "Frightening, the way they've indoctrinated you. The nature of things? The murder of their lawful ruler, the one chosen by their patron? I suppose this is natural for the Mamluks?"

The Crusader shook his head. "Even if your argument were valid, one doesn't have to look far to see the treachery in the Saracen ways. Is this what was agreed to in the treaty?" He nods to the simmering pits in the distance, the charred remains of pigs destroyed by the Egyptians smoldering alongside those of Crusader bodies, the fire ignited by the chopped pieces of Crusader siege engines that the sultan promised to preserve.

"Know thy enemy, my Lord," Leander said sarcastically. "Could you expect the Mamluks to keep true to an agreement crafted by Turanshah—a man they despised? An agreement in which they had no say, following a year of war which they alone won through their own blood and sweat with not a finger raised by al-Salih's soft-handed son?"

Leander spit. "And could you expect any Muslim to safeguard filthy pigs for a beaten enemy, or keep secure the siege engines that could someday be used against him once again? Or protect the Franj you left behind, those wracked with fever, sickness that could spread to the entire Egyptian army as well? There isn't enough medicine to treat the scourge that runs through your ranks."

The Crusader had heard enough. "You have a clever answer for all of your army's misdeeds."

Leander chuckled. "Oh, if we only operated with the cooperation and moral discipline of the holy warriors from the west. Even your queen was abandoned by her subjects—your *land's most noble lady having to bribe her vassals with gold and food so they wouldn't depart Damietta before the king was released. You couldn't get three units of the king's Crusaders to agree about putting out a fire, even if the flames were on the beard of Louis himself."*

The lord walked away.

Leander digs a shell from the sand with his toe and with his right hand, slowly rubs Jacinta's back. "Sorry for concentrating on just the tragedy of it all. As if you haven't seen enough misfortune firsthand. As if all war forever hasn't always been terrible," he says.

She smiles. "It's all right. I, too, worry about what happens from here to Egypt."

"Between us, my friend," he turns and looks into her eyes. "I fear for Egypt. I worry that the entire force of Mamluks is coming apart at the seams. For the first time ever, I question if I may have made the wrong decision in joining them." He bites his lip.

She stares, baffled.

He stoops, picks up a fistful of sand and pours it into the other. "The Bahri—as a Frank, I watched them for moons like a jealous man watches another's pretty wife. They and the other Mamluk regiments were unified by al-Salih. Fused together as the Salihiyya and purified by Islam and their dedication to its core values. I had to have her. I yearned to become one of them."

He wipes his hands clean of the remaining grains on his palms. "Sure, there was always healthy competition between the Bahri and al-Salih's other Royal Mamluks, but now the regiments are starting to look too much like the Franj I left—disjointed, struggling with their leadership, every man maneuvering for his place, absorbed with his landholdings and how the rest of the realm views him."

She tightens her grip on his hand. "Who do you think will lead the sultanate?"

"I'm not sure, but we'll know soon, for the amirs are meeting as we speak. For stability of the empire, I would think they'll consider a prince with some Ayyubid blood running through him."

She nods.

"Al-Nasir Yusuf of Damascus—he'll be scheming, sensing that he now has an opening to total rule. Our amirs will have to act quickly. They may even choose Shajarat al-Durr, al-Salih's wife."

Jacinta squints. "Really? A woman attempting to be the first in Islam to rule in her own name, in these conditions?" She looks to the dark horizon, uneasily. "What about al-Kamil's grandchild, al Musa?"

"Too young, not even in his teens. The amirs would know that by electing the young one, they would invite his murder, as well."

Leander groans. "Al Durr is the closest one left to al-Salih himself. That is powerful. But I wonder, too, who they will elect as *atabak*, leader of the army. I'm not sure the most senior among us, the most able, will step in and lead."

"Why not?"

"Well, the best of them is dead. Fakhr al-Din, killed in Mansura. Jamal al-Din Muhsin of the old guard, the Jamdariyya, can think only of retirement. The vicegerent, Husam al-Din, wants nothing to do with the sultanate, according to rumor. Perhaps, as a Kurd, he figures holding the position among this lot of disordered Kipchaks could get him a sword across his gourd like Turanshah."

"So, who does that leave?"

"Two more Kurds are next in seniority, but I doubt they'll bite, either. Only the most senior, the most aggressive of the mid-levels—the Amirs of One Hundred—would be willing to take the chance under these circumstances."

"Which do you prefer?"

He looks at her sideways. "I trust our Amir of One Hundred,

Aqtay." He shrugs. "How could I not support a fellow Bahri? Plus, I haven't seen enough of the others to know them fully capable or not, especially those working from the other house."

"Hmm..." She tugs on his hand, slowing their pace.

He turns to face her. "Not that it matters. I'm just a mounted crossbowman. We usually don't play much of a role in formulating successions."

She smiles, the wind blowing hair across her brown face, revealing tiredness in her eyes. "At the infirmary back in February, when I said my father forbid me to see you anymore ..." Her eyes meet his. "I didn't mean to upset you. I ... I no longer worry about what my father thinks, no longer worry about ..."

He pulls her close, a craving inside him wanting love and anything resembling normalcy. Harmony. She exudes this. He leans and kisses her forehead. She looks up again with that child-like face, unassuming, innocent.

A tenderness seeps through his virgin heart. He thinks that she may feel the same. He lowers his arms around her waist. "You always seem to make things better."

Her smile fades and he thinks he sees a hint of tears in her eyes. "I wish to always be that for you," she says, burying her head into his shoulder, nuzzling as would a puppy. She reaches up to hug his shoulders tightly.

He holds her, setting his bearded chin atop her head.

The pair of terns revisit, effortlessly hanging in the wind above a patch of nervous water, dipping their elegant heads to snatch bits of baitfish floating to the top. Beneath the quivering surface, he pictures the unseen—a school of jacks driving the smaller fish into a ball, their fellow predators then slashing through the darkened mass of flesh, tearing the innocents below to pieces.

"I dread what the sultanate will look like in the coming year. Selfishly, I worry where they'll send me and for how long. I may not be able to see you for moons," he says.

"I know. It'll be all right."

They walk farther. In the distance, he sees a bloated corpse rolling in the surf. Not wishing for Jacinta to have to see death this day, he stops.

"You look a little tired. Maybe we should turn back now," he says.

CHAPTER

22

Cenk
Cairo Citadel
June 27, 1250

Cenk lumbers down the slippery stairs, bracing himself against the seeping block wall. "Watch your step, old biddy," he says to himself wearily, wincing from the pain in his knees with every step. He turns down the corridor. Muted sunlight from the hippodrome casts a fuzzy glow upon the dark-stained rock, becoming gradually brighter with each step he takes toward their training arena. He exits the passage, emerging into the U-shaped viewing area. He shades his eyes, the daylight accentuating his headache.

His sleep has been sparse the last two moons. The recurring nightmares of his past, which had left him for years, have unexplainably returned. As was the case more than a decade ago, he now dreads bedtime. It is not good.

His wife has grown timid, likely anxious that her husband will start drinking again. He is worried, too.

Maybe this is the price he pays for his new position with Amir Aybeg; this is what happens when stress and responsibility are heaped upon an old man. He must not let it take him down the wrong road. He must not take even one sip of wine to free himself of the strain.

Fourteen years ago, his nightmares were of the attack to the south, down in Aleppo, where he lost his first patron, Amir Turkmani. At that time, his amirate had patrolled for many moons, tasked with protecting the goods coming in and out of Hisn Kayfa, as the Khwarazmians had been hitting the caravans in the tight sections of the trade route. On that fateful day, his mates were tired and the weather cold. Turkmani's amirate stumbled upon an enemy unit twice the Mamluks' size.

> With his back to the blowing sleet, Cenk sat amongst the protection of a jagged rock, cradling Turkmani in his trembling hands, Cenk's horse tugging the lead wrapped about his leg. Turkmani smiled, "If only they could all be like you, my son."
>
> Cenk's patron spoke again, but this time his words were garbled. Cenk leaned closer, so as to hear over the beat of hooves and the shouting.
>
> But then he felt no breath on his neck. He lowered the head of his master to his knee and looked squarely at the ashen gray falling upon his patron's face. Amid the flying arrows, he glanced skyward and whispered, "No, no. What have we done?"
>
> He looked down. His master's blood dribbled across the dark hair on his forearms, saturating his yellow trousers with puddles of wet scarlet. Tears.
>
> Their unit's lack of awareness and inability to put arrows on the enemy at the critical moment had caused Turkmani's death. While the arrows in his master's body came not from Mamluk bows, they had still killed their patron.
>
> There, consecrated by his master's blood, Cenk made a promise. "My father, oh, my father, I will make this right. I will cleanse the weak from our ranks." Though the life had left Turkmani's eyes, Cenk knew his master heard him, if not in this life's form, then in the one drifting above him.

The events of that day were repeated in Cenk's dreams each night for years—stumbling into the Khwarazmians at the waterhole, the battle, his Amirate Commander's death, his promise to Turkmani. Eventually, the nightmares changed. For many moons, instead of surviving the battle, he awoke gasping for air, his throat slashed by a sword, or trying unsuccessfully to pull an oversized arrow from the chest of his patron.

Cenk thought he was past all of it. But recently, the bad dream altered again. Now, it usually starts near Aleppo with his old unit on horseback, and ends each time in the same new place.

"You've served long enough. You have a family and only so many more years to enjoy them. Resign. By Allah, relish what you have left," Turkmani says from behind a table, his smile pleading, his palms outstretched, almost cradling the pair of arrows lodged in his chest, crimson oozing from the wounds.

Cenk's eyes bounce about their cramped cell, mildew covering the walls, a bar-divided block of light bisecting the stone between them. He looks up to his patron. "Yes, my Amir, I know, I know. But the realm has become muddied. My services are needed more than ever. I've been promoted to a position higher than I could ever have imagined. I'll work it for just a few more moons. It'll be fine, my father."

Turkmani sighs, lowers his head, his elbows coming to a rest on the tabletop, blood from his thighs now dribbling into puddles beneath his chair. "Ehh." He looks up sadly to meet Cenk's eyes. "But the work you do from this elevated post—how well does it mesh with that promise you made to me in Aleppo, my son? The promise ..."

Cenk looks across vacantly.

Turkmani smiles and looks down at his chest and the arrows protruding from his legs. "You remember what happened when just some weak infiltrated our ranks. By Allah, what is to happen when the weak lead the entire empire?" He then laughs heartily, tears streaming into his thick beard, the nocks from the buried arrows ticking the tabletop in time with his guffaws.

The weak now includes Amir Aqtay from the Bahri. Turkmani speaks to Cenk from above. He *must* mean Aqtay. It has to be.

From high amid the bench seating, Cenk looks down. A squad of men has just finished their sword work. A giant among them hollers some parting instruction. His men respond immediately, some grabbing rags to wipe down blades, others picking up the short shovels to scrape clay from stout-legged tables.

Cenk's timing is good, the schedule is accurate.

The lumbering Mamluk below looks down the length of his blade for some defect before clomping to the exit.

Cenk whistles twice. The Ox looks up. Cenk waves him over, and the big man adjusts his course, works his way up the two tiers of stairs. Sidestepping toward Cenk down the aisle, Ox gives him a hesitant smile, their infrequent encounters now only slightly less awkward than they were when Cenk was Ox's Mu'allim, or Furusiyya Instructor, some fourteen years ago.

Back then, Cenk had initially made Ox his guidon, the novice leader of his first training tulb. Yet as the training progressed and finessed skills with the bow and lance became more important than the brute strength needed to wield the sword, Ox faltered. Cenk demoted him to squad leader.

Later, Ox had proven himself hopeless on the bow at long distances and Cenk tried hard to get the big man ousted from the citadel. Then again, in those days, Cenk attempted to boot all of them out at one time or another, convinced that nearly all the novices were pathetic and unworthy of the title.

"How's Amir Cenk this fine day?"

"Good. Sit down."

Ox lays his sword on the wooden bench and sits facing him.

"Let's skip the niceties. I have an opportunity for you," Cenk says.

Ox raises his eyebrows.

"As you've probably heard, I'm serving as a temporary

advisor for Amir Aybeg. He's pulled several of us to help him with fleshing out his forces, with making some troop and billeting decisions."

Ox grins. "Yes, fortunate for him to have some wise counsel."

Cenk scowls. "Right. Not exactly the role I expected to be filling at this stage." His mind wanders fleetingly to when he will soon walk away from it all, to Inci and the boat ride on which he has yet to take her.

Ox nods.

"So, my slot with the guard is going to be opening up. It would be an advancement for you. More men. Some iqta to come, maybe a decent chunk of land," Cenk says, furrowing his brow and meeting the big man's beady eyes.

Ox slides his leg over the bench to squarely face Cenk. "You're serious."

"Yeah."

"What about my men, my squad?"

"They could be moved over with you."

Cenk watches the ogre process his proposition. He wonders how much brain is actually within a skull that must be twice as thick as that of most soldiers'. Cenk guesses that if smashed open, Ox's gray matter would be about the size of that of his namesake's. A look of despair sets the giant's face.

"What? You've a problem with a promotion? An aversion to income-producing land?" Cenk asks.

Ox stares past him at the empty seats in the distance, pinching his nose in thought.

Inside Cenk chuckles at the calculating Ox. The giant is still but a dog on the steppe. Chuck him a piece of meat and the goon would be distracted from any task. Maybe like a raven, drawn to any shiny piece of metal. No, not a raven. Not smart enough to be a raven.

Ox looks up with the obliviousness of the novice he was a decade ago. "I appreciate you thinking of me." He looks Cenk in the eyes. "But I don't think Aybeg cares much for me. I've been passed over twice, now. And what's left of my brothers—Duyal, Singer, and the few others—are with Aqtay in the Bahri. Amid the shuffle, I was hoping to land there."

Ox's brow softens; his eyes now implore his old instructor. "I don't have many years left in these legs either, my Amir. If you have any pull at the top, across the river is where I'd really wish to spend the end of my career."

Cenk raises his lip. Smoldering cinders that have long been at rest in his depths, long dampened since their shared days at the tibaq, begin to flicker in Cenk. Gusts of anger puff away at the ash, revealing red sparks of annoyance down under. These begin to pulse with life.

Embers of rage flash inside him. A fire now ablaze in his stomach, the vapors spreading up through Cenk's lungs. "Are you rejecting my most gracious proposal? Do you know how many desire my old post, Ox?"

Cenk leans closer. "Since when could you see past promotion and riches? Since when was loyalty to your old brothers such a priority of yours?" Cenk raises his eyebrows in mock enlightenment. "Oh, wait! I can remember a day about twelve years ago, back at the citadel in Hisn Kayfa, right after manumission, when devotion was very, very important to you and your dear old friend, Demir, Allah rest his soul."

> Demir pulled the stopper from the vial banded about his arm and dumped the contents into the spout of the top pot, his back to the crowded dining room, his sleeve mostly covering his work. He replaced the cork, picked up the teapots, and headed back to his assigned table.
>
> Cenk straightened and rose in his chair. Unbelievable. They couldn't be. His novices wouldn't be so clever. He eyed Ox.
>
> The oaf scanned the dining room, taking in the space full of red-jacketed amirs at their tables, drinking their post-meal tea and talking quietly among themselves. And then Ox's eyes went large when meeting Cenk's—the loner at the crowded table, the

only man in the room not absorbed in discussion.

Cenk smiled, raised his black eyebrows and extended his chin, impressed with his former novices' ploy and their execution. He leaned forward, shifted his gaze back to Demir, as the ape-armed boy filled the head eunuch's cup.

By Allah, look at that. The biggest of his goons aren't useless after all. They will kill that ball-less prick, Safir. Good boys. He leaned back, nodded slowly, his dark eyes squinted, assessing. He grinned as Ox's knees went wobbly, the recent graduate now realizing that his former Mu'allim was on to them.

Demir strode to the galley, eyes locked forward, eager to dump the pot before another amir signaled him for a top off. Planned. The two had it all planned. Cenk watched the lad until out of sight, his forehead rumpled in calculation.

Later, mid-meeting, Safir rose from his chair, placed his hand on Aqtay's shoulder, bent uncomfortably to his senior's ear, and then quickly rushed out the door in pain, the blood draining out of his face.

With elbows resting on the table, his index finger bisecting his nostrils in thought, Cenk rested his eyes upon Ox. Let the ogre squirm. Let the Ox know that he is caught, that forever his old nemesis will have leverage over him.

Cenk looks over his shoulder and then about the stands. "Surely you remember that day, my comrade. Surely you remember that nasty potion you dumped in the poor eunuch's tea all those years ago, don't you? Surely you didn't forget that revenge you took for the wrong done to one of your fellows, vengeance realized for Safir nailing the innocent novice, Ichami, to the cross?"

Ox's face goes a ghastly white.

Cenk leans back. "Did you think I forgot? Even today, oh, what a mess it would make if word of that story got out. Especially to Aqtay. Yes, he was quite fond of that ball-less one, Safir." He shakes his head in bogus pity.

Ox's lips tighten and his shoulders slump.

Cenk smiles, pictures a wriggling marmot caught in a snare back in his native Bashkir country. He has Ox. "Fortunate for Demir that he's already six feet down. But his cunning accomplice in the poisoning—what a shame it would be for old Ox to spend the last of his days in the dungeon or more likely to lose his head at the chop block. Even in these disorderly times, the command doesn't tolerate a murder within the ranks, even one from so many years past."

A single bead of sweat dribbles down Ox's forehead.

Cenk moves closer to him. "So, what I'm getting at is, this proposition I make is not really an offer, but maybe more of a courteous order. You understand?"

Ox nods his head resignedly. "Why me? Why would Aybeg possibly want me now when he passed me over twice?"

Cenk shrugs his shoulders casually. "Situations change. The ranks are flipping. It's not just about you. Amir Aybeg is looking for a handful of men in key positions who are completely committed to him. That's not so unusual, now, is it? Surely, you've proven your capacity for loyalty, eh?"

Ox looks away.

Cenk leans forward, a scowl settling upon his face. "For a promotion and a respectable fief, certainly you could find a way in your heart to return Aybeg's graciousness with some newfound allegiance, couldn't you?"

Ox sighs. "Yes, my Amir. I suppose so."

CHAPTER

23

Leander
Cairo
July 18, 1250

early five hundred men stand with hands locked behind backs, wearing the dress summer uniform of the Bahri, a phalanx of white and gold atop Mokattam Hill, elegant in both their attire and formation on the western assembly area of Saladin's Citadel, Qal'at al-Jabal, Fortress of the Mountain. Leander glances at a unit adjacent to his own, his eyes moving from their turbaned heads down their stunning white coats to the Ayyubid yellow of their trousers—not a blemish upon them. He squirms at seeing their feet, white and bare and covered in dust.

He wonders what is more unusual—that they stand bootless, or *where* they stand bootless, outside the house of their rival regiment, the Salihi. The Bahri admire Saladin, who fortified the structure some seven decades past, yet they refer to the massive shelter of the rival regiment as "the old house on the hill." The new sultan "requested" that both regiments, in a show of forced solidarity, begin their procession from where the founder of the Ayyubid dynasty had once resided.

For Leander, Saladin's Qal'at al-Jabal is a fortress at which to marvel. Even with the Fatimids thoroughly defeated, Saladin wisely saw merit in not only the high ground at Mokattam, but also in the urgings of his advisors to greatly improve the existing citadel. The story goes that many of the blocks needed for the project were pulled from the smaller pyramids in Giza. Using labor from his army plus that from the captured Crusaders, Saladin reinforced old walls and raised those that still surround both Cairo and Fustat, the old capital to the south.

Having visited this fortress only once as a guest many years ago, Leander appreciates the fresh view of Cairo from this elevation, with the entire town stretching before him. The sun dances off Elephant's Pond to his front and also farther west along the Nile, where a scattering of sailboats dot the river, tacking in the lazy breeze. Bisecting the river just south is the landmass of *al-Rawda*, where the Bahri's Island Citadel sits, white and prominent among the palms.

Farther to their south is *Gebel Yashkur*, or the Hill of Thanksgiving, the place Noah's ark was said to have rested, once the great flood receded. The Mosque of Ibn Tulun now dominates the hill. Today, Egyptians pack the exterior spiraled staircase of its minaret and line the rails three-deep at both of the two-tiered structures near the top—the locals wishing to better see the spectacle to their east and north. On the southwest horizon, the pyramids rise from the stark desert like enchanted mountain peaks.

In the lowlands between the mosque and citadel lie the endless mud-bricked houses of the poor, some of them containing the odd row of tan blocks—these of higher quality, taken long ago from the rubble of Tulun's original city, which flourished four centuries past. Atop the flat roofs of these humble structures, their inhabitants also watch the hundreds of white-coated Mamluks depart the fortification and snake their way up the main road. In the distant north, the lead amirates of the Salihi already disappear between the twin minarets of the southern gate, entrance to the city proper.

As Leander stares across the river at al-Salih's palace within the Bahri's Island Citadel, a familiar sadness sweeps over him. His former patron had gone to such expense and effort to sequester his most valuable men, to protect them from the impurities and trickery of the world. Now, like an overprotected daughter running wild and confused once free of her father's control, so have al-Salih's Mamluks conducted themselves since their patron's death. Al-Salih's prized force has not only killed the sultan's own son, but become befuddled in deciding who should lead them next.

Leander remains dumbfounded. Not even the ever-confident and aggressive Aybeg could have dreamed that he would be sultan only seven moons after the death of al-Salih. Such an idea seemed preposterous, but Sultan Aybeg was elected by both his peers and rivals. And perhaps only a man as outrageous as Aybeg would take the throne in these tumultuous times.

Aybeg rose to power primarily because nothing went as planned by the Mamluk Amirs who clumsily orchestrated the succession. Just two days after the Sultan Turanshah's murder, the amirs gathered in the sultan's charred pavilion in Fariskur—the place where the Mamluks had smoked out al-Salih's son—determined to not leave the place until Turanshah's replacement was agreed upon. Succession in Egypt had been often bloody, but simple, for generations: a brother or son of the deceased ruler usually maneuvered his way into the Cairo palace, or if the preceding sultan picked an heir in advance, the chosen man simply slid into power seamlessly. There was no easy route for the Mamluks. They were upon uncharted waters and determined that votes cast by their amirs should decide the next sultan.

As Leander expected, al-Salih's widow, Sharjarat al-Durr, won the show of hands as successor; she would become the sultana. To reinforce the impression of Ayyubid legitimacy, especially since she had been a mere slave before her marriage, she took the throne name of *walidat Khalil*, "the mother of Khali," evoking memories of her late son, fathered by al-Salih.

The supreme military command was offered to the Kurd, Husam al-Din, but the old man refused it, as did two other senior Kurds. The Mamluk amirs in Fariskur nervously worked their way through the senior ranks, and contender after contender withdrew his name from consideration. Most took the opportunity to retire from the service altogether to avoid living with the constant worry of another assassin's blade. Forced to drop their search down into the mid-ranking amirs, the Royal Mamluks eventually settled on the ambitious Turk, Amir 'Izz al-Din Aybeg al-Turkmani al-Salihi. Amir Aybeg became the atabak, their commander.

With the key positions of sultana and atabak filled, al-Durr and her advisors sent an envoy to Damascus, the principality second only to Cairo in significance for the empire. The sultana demanded Damascus's continued allegiance. The vicegerent in Damascus, Jamal al Din, and his sizeable army would be made to submit to the new regime in Cairo.

Bahri units deployed to Damascus from Cairo were predictably willing to comply, but the bulk of the Muslim forces in the Damascus citadel—principally the Kurkish Qaymariyya— refused. The two commanders in the Qaymariyya could not stomach the thought of Mamluk sovereignty in Egypt.

The great Saladin was a fellow Kurd and his succeeding Ayyubid ancestors had ruled the realm for generations. Damascus had always been an unenthusiastic subject of the power center in Egypt, its complicity for years resting on a series of wobbly compacts made between vacillating brothers and cousins. These alliances were largely binding due to the Ayyubid blood running through the veins of Cairo's enduring leadership. And now Turanshah's killers —men of mostly Kipchak blood who had chosen to serve under a slave woman—wished the Qaymariyya and its pure-blooded governance to bow down? No. The vicegerent in Damascus also refused to succumb.

With both commanders of the Qaymariyya and the vicegerent in Damascus united, this combined opposition to Cairo's rule called upon the Ayyubid prince in Aleppo, al-Nasir Yusuf, al-Salih's former subject, to control Damascus. Al-Nasir went quickly to Damascus, and the Qaymariyya literally left the gates open for the prince's forces to enter. All in the Syrian city surrendered to al-Nasir's army without a fight. Damascus now had a powerful prince and a rightful Ayyubid in charge.

Leander worries for the scattering of Bahri brothers that remain in Damascus. These men were left hung out to dry by Cairo: arrested, shackled, separated from each other, imprisoned at outlying castles and their fiefs taken from them by al-Nasir and distributed amongst his new allies, the Kurkish Qaymariyya.

Leander figures none of this resulting turmoil would have surprised his former patron, al-Salih. Ayyubid loyalties were as fluid as the water levels in the Nile; al-Salih's kin knew an opportunity to shun centralized rule when they saw it. The Syrian anti-Egyptian alliance was born, with al-Nasir at the head. Damascus' justification for shirking Cairo's rule—a revolt against the rule of a woman and revenge against murderers of the reigning bloodline.

The Mamluk amirs received no better response from the caliph in Baghdad than they did from Damascus. When the caliph, Mustasim—the most relevant religious voice in the empire—heard the results of the Mamluk election, he wrote a short note to Cairo, stating his position as the leader of Islam: "Perhaps you have forgotten that the Prophet said, 'Unhappy is the nation governed by a woman.' If Egypt has no men, I will send you one."

Anxious to head off anti-Egyptian sentiment and render groundless the criticisms from both the Syrian Ayyubids and the caliph, the Mamluk leadership elected as sultan the atabak, Aybeg, removing al-Durr. No leader in the empire is fooled. Aybeg is merely filling the role as figurehead, while the queen al-Durr still holds the real power. "Spray of Pearls" continues to handle the affairs of the state and signs declarations autonomously.

The entire situation puts Leander and most Bahri on edge. In just over four moons, Cairo went from defeating the crusading enemy and relative calm to a kingdom tottering on crisis. Any Kurdish amir or high-ranking civil official that even smelled of disaffection toward Aybeg was chucked into prison by the Muizziyya, Aybeg's personal guard.

Leander feels some sympathy for him, since Aybeg may be ignorant of the fact that he is disposable goods, his promotion merely an expedient measure while the strongest leaders decide who will take charge in earnest. Nevertheless, the amirs swore an oath of allegiance to him, and Aybeg was hastily married to the queen, al-Durr. Of course, this is no marriage of love, but rather another of Cairo's measures to prop up the illusion of the Mamluk sultanate's validity.

Leander wonders if Aybeg will prove a greater embarrassment to the amirs than the woman they just removed. The men in both Mamluk houses do not consider Aybeg a pure Salihi, since he was a sayfiyah all those years after his initial patron died in battle. In the eyes of Mamluks who had al-Salih as their only patron, Aybeg is little more than a barely accepted stepchild in the Salihi family, a stray urchin of the amir class.

Jacinta's words two moons past echo in Leander's head: "Life is rarely tidy."

Amir Duyal signals. Their column of threes begins the descent toward the main road, Amir Aqtay at the head of the entire Bahri regiment. Leander stubs his toe on a rock in the road, wincing as he hobbles on the sore foot. Others curse quietly as they cross the sharp stones.

"Papa Frank, you probably haven't walked shoeless since your mother had you in nappies," Binny whispers.

"Damn near," Leander says.

"Well, Amir Aybeg will see this as a strong signal of your loyalty and subservience, then," Binny says.

Leander rolls his eyes. "That would be *Sultan* Aybeg. And I prefer to show my 'subservience' from atop my horse, or if walking, with my boots on."

Some laughter from those around him.

Traditionally, when consenting to a new ruler, all units in the army proceed humbly in parade, barefooted, as would common slaves. The ceremony is purely symbolic, the military displaying its willingness to serve the succeeding sultan. Of course, only their bare feet link the Bahri to the peasant class as the Mamluks walk tall in flawless white with the ivory-handles of their swords protruding from scabbards.

They pass the old Christian cemetery where Moses had a conversation with God and where Abraham slew his sacrifice. Then to where Ibn Tulun in the 9th century divided the original town into special *katais*, or districts, for each segment of the population: the servants, the blacks, the soldiers, the guards, the Greeks.

As the Mamluk amirates peel north, more locals filter along both sides of them. They crowd the walkways and stand atop empty carts and any raised structure along the route. Not often are they given the opportunity to see both giant stone houses emptied of their warrior contents and thousands of Egypt's best men strolling the streets in their brilliant uniforms. The army's regiments proceed in order of their status. Falling in behind the Royal Mamluks come the Halqa, then the Egyptian infantry.

Leander wonders if the locals sense a fight brewing today between the Bahri and Salihi. Surely the people have heard enough rumors and can smell the turmoil between the two regiments of Royal Mamluks. Perhaps the citizens turn out so as to not miss the brawl. Maybe they come to see if this display of killers really will submit to the newly elected sultan.

Duyal's amirate approaches the southern gate, *Bab Zuwaylah*, *Bab* meaning "door" and *Zuwayla* being the tribe of Berber warriors from the western desert who once guarded this gate. Oatmeal-colored blocks reach heavenward on either side of the giant, arched gateway. The huge door has been swung open to them.

From spikes atop the eastern tower, six severed heads of recently convicted thieves greet the Mamluks. Some of the criminals' skulls stare with white-glazed eyes. Others have been there longer, their eyes sunken into hollow sockets, tufts of dark hair matted to skin gone hard as leather. Two recent heads hang from strapping, the strip fed through nasal cavities and out their twisted mouths. Clumps of flies inhabit the blackened cavities and pulsate upon the decaying flesh.

Entering the high-towered confines of the gate, Amir Duyal places his hand on his scabbard, his eyes scanning the crowd lining the street left and right. His men behind him do the same, their heads swiveling, checking overhead for any threat from atop the minarets or the parapets that line the lower, rounded towers.

A grief takes Leander as he looks up to the only empty space atop the wall, the platform where al-Salih routinely watched the beginning of the *Hajj*, the annual pilgrimage to Mecca. Out of respect for their former sultan, today no citizen stands within five paces of the spot.

The columns of Mamluks tramp through the neighborhoods of the Mamluk amirs, fine houses lined with gates painted in personal coats of arms—one bearing a cup, another an inkwell, another a long-necked Arabian—the emblems depicting each amir's role in the empire. Mamluk wives and their children on the walkways point to the various units of men passing, trying to spot their husbands and fathers, as they pass in formation. A fair-skinned Kipchak rests her one-year-old upon her hip. She speaks to the blonde-haired child and points to one man in a passing amirate, yet the toddler seems unable to distinguish his father from the multitude of tan-faced men wearing identical white and yellow.

The street vendors' racks have been cleared and boys stand atop them. The crowd thickens. The smell of cumin and coriander from the windows sift in and out of the multitudes. Leander senses the feeling of a mandatory festival.

The Mamluks stroll through the Greek quarter, Egyptian citizens observing them with vacant faces. Amid the crowds, the aroma of toasted nuts and cinnamon and garlic waft, cherished foods consumed on special occasions to sweeten the coarse bread of daily life.

"The locals act as if this is another funeral for a sultan, not a welcome ceremony for their new one," Binny says quietly.

"Maybe they know plenty of funerals will be coming because of us and this new leader," Leander says.

Cheers erupt two blocks north, the main column approaching the place from which Aybeg watches. Ahead, Binny and Leander can see the ceremonial *ghashiya*, a fancy saddle cover, being passed from one commander to another Amir of Forty.

"Ah. Our new sultan doesn't just want to witness his bootless subjects demonstrate their obedience by cutting up our feet on these streets. He wishes to see each Amirate Commander show his deference by fondling the imperial ghashiya," Binny mutters.

"Appears that way," Leander says with a chuckle.

The ghashiya is a traditional emblem of royalty and a special insignia for the Egyptians, with designated "stirrup holders" usually carrying it before their sultans during parades and feasts. Yet today, Aybeg wishes to not have the ghashiya precede him, but stations himself to personally observe the amirs from both regiments submit to him publicly, via passing the saddle cover from commander to commander.

The amir to their front lifts the leathern saddle cover over his head, the embroidered gold fabric about it marked with jewels and dangling tassels. He presents the ghashiya to the left and right for all onlookers to see—the symbol of the new sultanate at street level.

The golden covering slowly makes its way back from the amirate in front of them, as Duyal's Mamluks ease forward, closer to Aybeg's raised stand. An amir to their front raises the gilded cover, not giving it up until he has turned toward the new sultan.

Near the sultan, a roar rises from the crowd, its throbbing din stinging Leander's ears. Most makers of this clamor praise with expressionless faces, like poorly trained actors imitating joy or a populace wishing their false enthusiasm will bring stability to Egypt's volatile situation.

Aybeg replies with a nod, as if accustomed to such esteem, the untried noble looking strange out of his Mamluk uniform, adorned in the elegant robe of a sovereign, golden staff at his side.

A lull in the commotion, as the ghashiya is again handed off.

Leander flashes a sideways glance to Binny and rolls his eyes.

Binny half-smiles. "These folks hail as if a formation of archers stands behind them in *encouragement*," he says.

"Or, like they already have coin in pocket in agreement for doing so," Leander says.

Leander scans the crowd, his eyes stopping on one man. While those either side of him cheer, this man claps his hands slowly, his lower lip quivering as he watches the saddle cover being passed to Amir Duyal. Tears begin to stream down the local's cheeks, a pitiful look of sorrow fills his face.

Leander is pained by the disparity he sees among the citizenry. Just five moons past, the town folk had praised the Mamluks for stopping the Crusaders in Mansura. Women sobbed jubilantly in the streets, throwing their arms around the soldiers. Men praised with hands over their heads.

Look at them now. Look at this man. Tears shed for al-Salih, still? Maybe. The population had loved their patron, the old sultan bringing wealth and steadiness to Cairo. Tears of sadness for the death of the son, Turanshah? Not likely. Tears of exultation for the new sultan Aybeg? Even more doubtful.

The common people love these rough Mamluks, yet simultaneously hate them, as well. Coin from hefty Mamluk purses helps feed the local economy. Love. Full of testosterone, Mamluks were forever trying to seduce local daughters. Hate. Possessing unquestionable battle skills, Mamluks are the region's best deterrent against attack and Cario's most capable defender. Love. Mamluks killed a legitimate sultan and propped up one of their own in his place. Hate?

In the faces of the citizenry, Leander sees more fear than admiration. There had always been an Ayyubid to guide and restrain the elite slave armies across the Middle East. Clearly these citizens of Cairo wonder now what will happen when the ruffians actually rule. Yet, given Egypt's threats from every direction—Damascus, the remaining Crusader strongholds on the Eastern Mediterranean, and whichever other Ayyubid princes now conspire—perhaps some figure the Mamluks are just what Cairo needs right now. Maybe.

Tears stream down the face of the man whom Leander watches, the local looking down so none will notice. When he finally looks up with red face and swollen eyes, their eyes meet. The Egyptian wipes his face and shouts a tribute lost in the ruckus, as Duyal hands the ghashiya to another amir, the gold ornaments clanking against his Amirate Commander's forearms. From the corner of his eye, the man nervously watches to see if the Frank still stares.

CHAPTER

24

Ox

Cairo Citadel

November 18, 1250

Departing the stairwell at the top of the eastern wall, Ox looks for his trio of men on watch. The northern man is at his post, but the center tower and south tower men chat, their backs to the center parapet. One of them sees Ox and locks his body. The other follows.

"Could I offer you ladies a cool drink?" Ox asks, walking up to them. "At ease."

"He just called me over to answer a question," the senior troop says.

"Bullshit. Any of it can wait until after your watch," Ox says, taking a step closer. "There's no excuse for leaving your post and having your eyes anywhere but on that damned horizon," Ox says, pointing eastward.

"Yes, my Amir," his Mamluks reply in unison.

"Especially on this wall. Al-Nasir's already proven twice he'd come as far as Gaza. You think the prick wouldn't come all the way here with his entire army next time, not just his vanguard?"

"Yes, my Amir," the older Mamluk replies.

"You think it couldn't happen on your watch?" Ox asks, poking his finger into the senior's chest.

"No, my Amir."

"If I ever see you two anywhere other than where you're supposed to be again, it's your ass. If it'd been anyone else but me this time, you'd already be on your way to the chop room. You know that, right?" He says, scowling at both men.

"Yes, my Amir."

"With your eyeballs gouged from your heads, you'd never again have the boredom of watch duty." He turns to the oldest of them. "Get back to the south tower."

The guard locks his body.

"Go," Ox says.

The man sprints back to his post, while the other turns back to his duty.

Ox struts back to the stairway, shaking his head. "By Allah. At their age, we'd never have considered leaving our station." He catches himself sounding like the old man he is turning into.

The eastern threat he lectured on was not exaggerated. Just three moons past, al-Nasir Yusuf of Aleppo and Damascus displayed just how irritated he was with the recent affairs in Cairo. Seeing himself as the only legitimate Ayyubid heir to the dynasty, al-Nasir sent a large vanguard west toward Gaza, looking for a scrap.

In response, Sultan Aybeg sent a Salihi detachment eastward from Cairo. This Mamluk unit located, engaged with, and later broke contact with the Syrian enemy. But then, the Salihi amir in charge did the inconceivable. Instead of returning home, he led his men south and east past the Dead Sea to the fortress in Karak, declaring his unit for the prince of Karak and Shawbak—al-Salih's nephew, al-Mugith, whom they saw as the rightful Ayyubid ruler of Egypt. Aybeg now has fewer elite cavalrymen at his disposal.

Ox shakes his head. Egyptian Mamluks offering themselves to the enemy. As far as Ox knew, this outfit's split from the Salihi was unprecedented conduct within Egypt's Mamluk corps. Ox figures there will be more of it to come.

The devil, al-Nasir. Emboldened by his modest success and smelling dissention among what were once al-Salih's Mamluks, al-Nasir kept his advanced guard near Gaza. Last moon, Sultan Aybeg tasked his rival, the Bahri's leader, Amir Aqtay, to run al-Nasir's thugs off, likely hoping that Aqtay would be killed in the fighting. One less internal foe. Unfortunately for Aybeg, Aqtay did not die in the process. Fortunately for the empire, Aqtay did send al-Nasir's forces spurring away from their camp in Gaza.

This gained Aqtay increased prestige amongst his men and the civilians in Cairo. Heartened by his victory, Aqtay—along with Amir Baybars, the slayer of Turanshah—demanded another election and voted al-Malik al-Ashraf Musa, one of the grandsons of the former Sultan al-Kamil, as sultan.

The stakes and tension in Cairo are heightened. The Bahri changed their minds and no longer recognize Aybeg as sultan; their pledge of obedience to him is now void. The Bahri's justification is that six-year-old al-Malik, nephew of al-Salih, is the legitimate Ayybuid heir to the sultanate.

Ox chuckles. All this talk of Ayyubid legitimacy. Enough of it! The only legitimate sovereign that mattered—or will ever matter—was al-Salih. Their former sultan was the only man who could ever hold unwavering Mamluk loyalty. After his death, it is no surprise that his former patron's elite splinter.

If only the great man could have lived forever. With al-Salih's absence, Ox feels the only constancy that endures for thousands of Mamluks is that of the Khushdash, the solidarity among brothers in common servitude and manumission, the tie of those who shared years of training and the same theoretical release from slavery. Certainly, there is still love of God and mother Egypt, but aside from their comrades, what else do these men really have?

The problem is there are too many strains of the Khushdash throughout the Royal Mamluks. Within the same families of comradeships—men who earned the title of Mamluk together and became blood brothers at graduation—infighting was inevitable without al-Salih to smooth their differences. Brothers will always brawl. When personal rivalries developed between warriors within the same Khushdash and opposing factions formed, comrades often owed faithfulness to each side and could, therefore, pass from one group to the other without difficulty. So, even two rival Khushdashiya were by their nature, very fluid. With blood brothers from the tibaq now split between the Salihi and Bahri, the web of allegiances is made even more complicated.

Will the power of the Khushdash be enough to keep the warriors from each other's throats, especially if they now reside in opposing regiments? Or will these same chains of nobility, those invisible yet binding links between brothers, lead to an internal war?

Ambition, greed, power. These things have a way of rusting the ironclad bonds formed between men as adolescents. While none from the Bahri, Jamdariyya, or the general ranks of the Salihi will admit it, loyalties are situational and fluctuating during these uncertain times. What seems silently agreeable to all is that no Mamluk will again charge into battle and risk his life and fortune for any leader sitting atop Egypt. This they did for al-Salih alone.

Ox looks up to the bright sky, smiles, and takes in the fresh air. He had no regrets serving al-Salih those dozen years. But from now on, he will put himself at risk only if he sees some reward tied to it. Reward meaning increased status or coin in his pocket.

"You earned it. Look at the less deserving about you who have grown rich. Long overdue for you," he mumbles to himself.

As promised, Ox kept his old squad and runs the guard once commanded by Cenk. After four moons, Ox has not yet been promoted above the rank of Amir of Ten and does not yet wear the purse of an Amir of Forty, but he has command, in essence. He is a trusted insider. He has Cenk's assurance that Ox's promotion will happen soon, and with it will come a pay increase and some land, an iqta. His standard is being raised. Finally, some luck coming his way.

Maybe just in time. Ox will take his cut before he is so old that he serves no tactical purpose in the army. He is a realist; he knows he is what the Grand Treasurer might call "depreciating goods," a rotting fish that is beginning to smell on the vendor's cart. Now is his time.

Although Ox would prefer to join what's left of his old mates in the Bahri, for now he follows Aybeg. Hell, what choice does Ox really have? Cenk has him firmly by the balls. Despite the six-year-old "sultan" elected by the Bahri, Aybeg is still the man whose face is pressed into Cairo's coinage. Aybeg is the one leading the entire army, and that is where the real power lies.

Ox enters a stone-arched passage and descends a stairway narrower than the last. The thick smell of mold and rusted water. He turns left down a dark corridor to where another pair of his Salihi are on watch. At a passage intersection, he nearly bumps into a troop.

"Sorry, my Amir. I've been looking for you."

"What is it?" Ox asks.

"Al-Durr asks for you."

Ox squints. "What?"

"She sends for you, my Amir."

He tries to conceal his fear. "The queen asks for me, personally? Are you sure?"

"Yes, my Amir."

"All right, all right. Carry on."

The Mamluk scurries off.

"What now?" Ox groans. He curses himself for his reluctant feeling of contentment and wonders if he remains jinxed. He leans against a tan-blocked corner, thinking long on what she could possibly want of him. He has spoken with her only once, three moons past, while on an escort. He had felt the conversation uncomfortable, one that he could not end soon enough. His pits dampen, a tightness constricts his chest. "Ugh! It's probably nothing. Just get it over with."

Reaching the queen's chamber, Ox stops before the two guards at her door. "The queen asks of me."

The pair look as if they expect him. One knocks on the door. A heavy latch clanks on the other side. A slight-built eunuch cracks it open and looks over the guard's shoulder to Ox. The dark-haired Greek opens the heavy door and extends a hand.

"Ball-less prick," Ox mutters to himself, stepping past him.

Ox takes one step in and sees the braids of black hair hanging down the back of the queen, nearly touching her shapely buttocks. She wears a cream-colored gown that brushes her toes, yet her arms and upper back are uncovered. He cannot help but stare at her olive skin. So clear and pleasing. He puts his eyes to the blocks on the opposite wall above her head and locks his heels. She is gorgeous. No wonder al-Salih chose her among the many when she was only a common slave.

The queen turns from looking at her view outside. "That isn't necessary," she says to Ox, nodding for the guards and eunuch to leave and shut the door.

Expecting the worst and feeling the need to remain formal, Ox places his hands in the small of his back, the crook of his thumb jammed against his opposite palm, his legs rigid and shoulder-width apart.

She looks at him with amusement. "Neither is that. Relax," she says, lifting her chin.

Awkwardly, he lowers his arms and stands with his giant-knuckled hands at his sides, as would an ape.

Three women without veils enter the room, pushing aside a fringed curtain. Silk dresses cover only one shoulder, lavish fabric draping seductively over their curvaceous figures to the floor. Beautiful hair falls sensually over their breasts; dark eyes blink long lashes.

Ox turns his head away. He executes a left face, so as not to disrespect them.

Girls of the harem. As Islamic royals had done for centuries, al-Salih kept a collection of concubines for many years. Compared to his Ayyubid kin, the old sultan's harem was small. Al-Salih, probably following the example of his great uncle, Saladin the Great, wished to avoid any display of luxury and consumption. Aybeg must have inherited, or simply taken, all of his patron's women.

Ox keeps his eyes locked on the far wall. His thoughts drift to the handful of Mamluks in the regiment who must squat to pee like women, their penises having been hacked off after being caught attempting to plow one of the harem's gorgeous slaves. And to the former guard he saw led out of the citadel six years past with bandages wrapped about his head, his eyes carved out after twice being caught by the eunuchs peeping into the bath of al-Salih's *Ikbal*, his select group of favorite concubines.

He will not be one these mutilated men. There are less dangerous women to have in town. He has resumed the position of attention without realizing it.

Al-Durr snickers. "A shame. I find these girls beautiful, but apparently, you do not share my view."

Sweat dribbles from his pits. He realizes that he is not breathing. "Breathe," he tells himself.

"Just look at them—it's fine. Face away much longer and they'll soon begin to doubt themselves. You don't want that, do you?" she asks.

Most of the army figured that al-Durr still ran the empire and was the person making the decisions, despite Aybeg's position. She had a reputation for handling details well. But given her increased responsibility since al-Salih's death, Ox is surprised that the capable woman never delegated her duties as *Valide Sultan*, or "Queen Mother" of the harem—the one setting the rules, choosing the sexual partners, and schooling the women to mingle with visiting emissaries and wealthy merchants.

The harem is not just an assemblage of pretty faces; many of its members are educated, skilled, and shrewd. Their screening and instruction in languages and foreign affairs results in a high failure rate amid prospective women slaves, similar to that experienced by the novices in the citadel's tibaq.

Once vetted and trained, harem members comprise a cadre of sharp, attractive women able to not only speak intelligently on current affairs, but also bump a visiting dignitary toward the sultan's position on issues. The women are given a salary depending on their rank and how well they perform their various missions, no different than the soldiers. How much they get paid is a mystery to Ox.

Ox tries to calm down and face the queen, her eyes dark and free of bags beneath, her skin unwrinkled, despite the burdens she shoulders. She nods toward the women.

He cannot bring himself to let his eyes ravage their bodies. He saw some of the concubines years ago, though they were always veiled when the sultan traveled with them, one going to this prince for that favor or to that dignitary as a gift. They were protected by soldiers, as if they were trunks full of silver pieces.

Some of these women, once their formal education was complete, were manumitted and even married to dignitaries in the empire. Such was the case with al-Durr. There was stature to be achieved by women skilled in the harem's workings.

Never before had Ox seen these women without veils or cloaks, uncovered. Yet here before him are three lovelies. Incredible. A panic comes over him. Why would the queen bring him here? Was he soon to be punished for his drinking and misconduct after the battle in Mansura? Was the queen teasing him before imparting a harsh punishment—forcing him to drool over the prettiest lasses in the empire, before lopping off his head or, worse yet, his penis? He tries to hide his labored breathing.

"Pick one," the queen says.

He does not understand and hesitates. "Don't say something stupid," he thinks.

"Forgive my ignorance, my queen, but I don't understand your request."

"Of course, you don't understand. It's hard to know which one you'd like to take if you don't look at them."

The three women giggle softly. His mind swirls. There is no way. Mamluks are not allowed to seduce the sultan's concubines. Apprehension turns into dismay. He feels slickness between his sweating fingers. Why would she let him do this? His tongue feels as if tied in knots. What feels like moments pass. "My Queen, respectfully, why would you offer one to me, a common soldier?"

She smiles, certainly anticipating the question. "Common soldier? A soon-to-be Amir of Forty is not a common soldier."

Ox tries to read her intent.

"I'm not offering them to many. To just a few of the men whom I believe have promise. Things are not stable, as you know. A queen likes to know that the men in her guard have her back. Some favors passed help ensure devotion. You can understand this. You'd likely do the same if in my position, yes?"

Only the most faithful were chosen as personal guards to royalty. He cannot remember a single story of one of al-Salih's guards ravishing a concubine. Ever. Perhaps some of the guards were given this privilege, yet were sworn to secrecy. This is possible, but surely word of such would have slipped from a drunken guard's mouth one time. Or maybe all has changed since al-Salih's death because of the instability in Cairo and beyond. Yes, perhaps the rules have changed.

He lies. "Maybe so. But my fidelity need not be bought, my Queen. By coin or flesh. Regardless, I'm humbled by your offer."

She smiles. "One needs ... allies up and down the ranks. This makes sense to you, doesn't it?

"Yes, my Queen."

"Go ahead now and pick one," she says, with a hint of impatience in her voice.

He turns, his eyes for the first time feasting on the women.

Looking each up and down, he feels the heat in his flanks. This is a dream. This cannot be real.

The woman farthest left meets his gaze. She smiles shyly, then looks away. Olive skin and a slender ass. The woman to the far right runs her fingers through her hair.

He is drawn to the rounded breasts of the girl in the middle. Seeing where his eyes go, she looks at him briefly, unable to hide a glare, perhaps disgusted that she may have to lie with a lowly Amir of Ten when accustomed to lying with the sultan, or at least with important guests and rich men. He catches her subtle sigh. He wants all three. He mustn't get an erection in front of the queen. He mustn't waste the queen's time. Quickly, decide. Quickly.

A yearning grows in his belly. This middle one thinks she is better than he. Thinks he is not worthy of her. He will pick her and show her what a man is. "This one, please, my Queen," he says pointing to the middle girl.

The chosen girl shows no emotion and is probably trained to act so. Or, perhaps she knew he would pick her all along, as seductive looking as she is. She remains, while the others saunter away through the curtain through which they had entered.

"Take him to your chamber," the queen says.

"Yes, my Queen," the girl replies respectfully. Without looking at him, she takes his offered arm and leads him away.

He turns to the queen. "Thank you, my Queen."

She nods and turns back to her view outside.

Again he feels his loins begin to tingle, more deeply.

Finally, he will collect what he deserves. Finally, those in the highest positions realize his value. Finally, he is away from Isa, his useless Amir of Forty. Finally, he is attached to a new sultan, a man of ambition who sees his worth. Ox is now part of the Muizziyya, Aybeg's personal guard. Maybe he read Aybeg wrong. Maybe Aybeg had plans for him all along. Maybe he has no need for Aqtay and the Bahri after all.

As he strolls with the woman on his arm, the distress that once filled him is replaced by excitement. He could get used to this. Women. Beautiful women. And one day soon, riches to go along with them.

Out of the queen's view, he looks down at the woman's chest. Mmm. Access to those women only touched by the inner circle, those exclusive ladies, taken by the royal family and distinguished emissaries. About time the higher-ups started treating him like a man of distinction.

CHAPTER

25

Leander
Cairo
February 20, 1251

The Mamluks steer him down the road by lance point, the old man's head down, his hands tied behind his back. A waning crescent above him in mustard yellow cracks a sideways smirk, a passing dark cloud fully revealing its ominous sneer. Those soldiers not carrying swords or maces extend torches out and behind them. The flames do little to brighten the area where they walk, yet illume the group to the rest of Cairo. Aside from the watchmen's slipper lamps, the city is dark.

Their prisoner is al-Salih Ismail, great uncle of their former patron, al-Salih Ayub. Ismail mutters something to himself; maybe he prays to the heavens, his eyes trained upward. Surrounding the old Kurd are a dozen men, mostly senior amirs from the Bahri, Salihi and even the Jamdariyya, most of them old companions from the earliest Khushdash. These are men who trained together as adolescents upon the hill at Saladin's citadel under a young al-Salih, who, acting as vicegerent, purchased these men as lads with the rest of his original one thousand while his sultan father was away in 1228.

Leander feels a tug on his cloak. It is Duyal, lightly pulling him forward, trying to snap Leander out of his sleep-deprived stupor. Leander nods, pats his commander's arm in apology, and quickens his step.

His tiredness is understandable. Following his watch duty and after he was settled in his rack, he was rousted by his replacement, the man shaking him, his exclamations almost frantic. Compelled to hastily dress, Leander ran from the River Island Citadel across the northern bridge to the canal, meeting those here who had called for him.

His purpose on this stroll is to recognize any of the Kurdish that may occasionally slip from Ismail's lips. The disheveled man is known to struggle with his Turkish and his thick Kurdish dialect is foreign to most of the amirs present.

Ismail stumbles and regains his footing. He takes another prod from a mace head, meant to center him again between the flanking Mamluks. Firelight dances upon the wrinkled Kurd and the mob that surrounds him, conjuring a timeless scene of the condemned, of ancient clerics pushing forward one affected by the evil eye or a discovered witch who needed to be made into ashes.

Leander shudders and pulls his cloak higher upon his neck. Breathing in the fumes from the torches, Leander recalls passages from the Quran describing the *jinn*, the evil eye. Rascals created from a smokeless, scorching fire, possessed by evil. Demons able to communicate with both people and objects and likewise be acted upon by each. Men concealed from their senses, lurking at night, and causing the common folk to wear jewelry and fashion door knockers in the image of the "Hand of Fatima", the daughter of Muhammad, to keep away those cursed with the "evil eye."

To the Mamluks of al-Salih, Ismail is entirely evil. For their former patron, al-Salih, and his sultan father before him, al-Kamil, Ismail represents the most devious from Saladin's blood.

Surely, he will go down as the ultimate Ayyubid conniver, as no other man had been a greater obstacle to al-Salih's taking and maintaining the sultanate. Never did the relentless bastard quit, Ismail's resolve only hardening once al-Salih's slave sons came to power.

Tonight, the Mamluks leave sleeping the other Syrian Princes allied against Cairo, those now captured and locked in the citadel's dungeon: al-Nasir Yusuf's elderly father, now Prince of Aleppo; the Prince of Tall Bashir, and Nursat al-Din, one of the last living sons of Saladin. Ismail will not be gifted such leniency.

Ismail's capture was pure luck or perhaps Providence. After Turnashah's murder, al-Nasir of Damascus wasted no time in tearing apart al-Salih's carefully assembled structure of provincial government. One-by-one, al-Nasir assembled his Ayyubid allies from the other Syrian principalities until only Hama and Karak remained unaligned with him.

With his vanguard recently run out of Gaza by Amir Aqtay, al-Nasir decided his time to take Cairo had come. There was enough dissention in Egypt's ranks to bring a full Syrian army straight to the city. So, during the middle of Ramadan last month, he gathered his allies and advanced to Egypt, headlong into the utter strangeness that would later be called by the locals the "Battle of al-Abbasa."

Al-Nasir had smelled fear on the green sultan, Aybeg. The Mamluk-turned-royal released two of Ismail's sons from prison, bestowing them robes of honor prior to their departure. Aybeg also lied about a nonexistent alliance with the Prince of Karak. Both of these actions aimed at breaking apart pieces of the Syrian alliance against Aybeg. Al-Nasir did not flinch. The Syrian army was poised for attack, only a two-day march southwest of al-Salihiyya, the doorstep to Cairo.

At dawn on February 3rd, al-Nasir's allied forces, under Shams al-Din Lu'lu, swooped down on the Egyptian lines, scattering the huge force in every direction. For Duyal's Amirate Three, there was no battle, just running. The Syrians pursued. Cut off from their fellow cavalrymen and outnumbered by the enemy, many Bahri spurred back to the Island Citadel, fearing all was lost but the defense of their fortress.

Duyal's amirate managed to stay together with another two hundred and fifty Mamluks under Amir Aqtay, yet their comrades and even their ghilman with the Mamluks' camels and donkeys were nowhere to be found. With so many of the enemy between them and Cairo, Aqtay rested his force at a waterhole, eventually deciding that the fortress of al-Shaubak, just south of the Dead Sea, was their logical sanctuary.

Six horsemen approached.

"Would you like me to ride out and meet them?" Duyal asked his mentor.

Amir Aqtay did not answer, waiting until he recognized their armor. "No, they're ours."

He grabbed the red-lioned pennant from his guidon and rode up the bank of the hollow that concealed them, signaling for the riders to come in front of the thick palms.

The riders approached at the canter, Leander squirming when seeing their lead man was the sultan himself.

"Where are you going?" Aybeg asked, his giant bay shaking its head from the bit digging deep.

"Al-Shaubak," Aqtay said.

Aybeg scowled. "And abandon your sultan and the rest of the army?"

"On this day, the sultan no longer has an army to lead. It would take you a week to round them up. Those of your infantry are still running. Even our Turkmen took flight," Aqtay said.

Aybeg nervously thumbed the pommel of his sword. "So, you'll go to al-Shaubak and put your allegiance there?"

"No. I will take these—the bravest of my men, those who did not shy from their duty this day—to the fortress there, temporarily. As the good sultan knows, we must live in order to fight. Valuable Mamluks tossed against an overwhelming force

and made dead will not be very effective in protecting Egypt another day."

"There may not be another day. The Ayyubids may well be at our east gate now. We ... "

Aqtay pointed to his front, motioned for Aybeg and his six to join him on the opposite side of the slope.

From below, Leander saw only the yellow tops of the Ayyubid banners and knew that Aqtay and Aybeg had seen the composition of the forces from atop.

"They are few—I saw the pennants of both the Nasiriyya and Aziziyya. Al-Nasir must be with them. We must attack. It's our only chance," Aybeg said.

Aqtay nodded, signaling his seven amirate commanders forward. With a hasty disposition of the forces settled, they stretched across the width of the dune, shoulder-to-shoulder in two ranks.

The red-lioned pennant snapped erect. Hooves scrabbled up the rocky bank and the Mamluks came online, shouting obscenities at the foe. Surprised at the force bearing down on him, al-Nasir fled eastward with some of his own Nasiriyya Mamluks. Yet the Aziziyya—the personal Mamluks of al-Nasir's departed father—did not follow.

Witnessing what was likely another unforgiveable example of cowardice from their patron's son, the Aziziyya peeled off, reined in, and formed a tight perimeter, lances stowed, palms forward in submission.

When the Bahri were upon them, the Aziziyya's leader minced no words. "Like yourselves, we'll not follow the weakling son of our patron, would rather die fighting with you—if not fellows of our same banner, then at least men of our same Kipchak blood."

Aybeg gladly took them in, placing the Aziziyya at the front of his formation.

Meanwhile, the main body of Syrian troops had been waiting just outside of Cairo, with the royal pavilion already raised in joyous anticipation of their Syrian sultan arriving from his place in the rear. Al-Nasir would be the new Sultan of Egypt. He would lead them victoriously on the final push into the city. But when hearing that their noble had fled the battlefield and that his commander-in-chief, Shams al-Din, had been executed by Aybeg upon capture, the Syrian allies became skittish.

Learning the next day that the Egyptians also held several other Syrian princes, al-Nasir's allies did the unthinkable: they broke down their camp and headed east. Even knowing the Egyptian Army was scattered and unable to effectively defend their capital, they turned back to Damascus and their other principalities.

Some of the oldest Mamluks characterized the whole sequence of events as beyond bizarre. Leander and his mates figured that only the hand of Allah spared Cairo that day. Their God had given them a second chance. With the Egyptians' execution in battle falling short, Allah's will alone turned yet another enemy away from their great city.

A deep voice whimpers behind him. Uneasy, Leander continues walking, his eyes ahead. Another Mamluk sobs, as they near al-Salih's burial place. Then a yowl and the sound of slicing flesh. Leander turns with his sword bared.

A Mamluk with dagger in hand gashes himself across the shoulders and arms, his tunic already cut to ribbons. Blood oozes down his muscular arms. He roars through clenched teeth, his bearded jaw twisted. Another man does the same, ripping off his shirt, releasing a primeval scream into the frosty air.

Ismail gawks at the scene, his mouth open, his lips trembling. A pop to the back of his head returns his eyes to the fore. Leander stows his sword and tries to conceal his agitation. He recalls fellow adolescents years ago at the tibaq describing self-mutilations that took place on the steppe by heartbroken men aback ponies, riding circles around the grave of a respected warrior or strong ruler.

Round and round, the nomadic fighters would push their stout-bodied ponies until the warriors' trousers were soaked with sweat from their beasts' flanks and until the ponies' hooves dug a muddy ring around their esteemed. Men lacerated themselves in a show of reverence for the fallen, releasing the unbearable grief inside them. A muddy and bloody tribute shed for the lifeless.

Their old ways now reappear, revealing that the tribalism in these men was not completely beaten out of them while teenagers at the tibaq. Their ancestral essence, pushed into the recesses of the Mamluk psyche for decades, resurfaces like a sloth of hibernating bears angrily emerging from their dark caves.

Tonight, Leander senses the most primal spirit of the Kipchak creeping into the very front of these Mamluks' minds. He wonders if they wish to feel not only agony, in the hopes of healing their own hearts, but also to relieve decades of pain suffered by al-Salih, hurt by his scheming kin, epitomized by this disloyal uncle of his, the man now pushed before them.

Leander shivers, his coat too thin to keep out the evening cold. The gaggle leaves the road and walks through the stone gate of the Qarafa Cemetery, the blazes casting wavy light upon the smooth blocks and the metal-pronged gate which is always kept open. Approaching their departed patron's mausoleum, more men cry and others fight to keep their composure. Their torches shed light on the tomb's inscription that they have read dozens of times.

Several take a knee at the smooth rock monument and cover their mouths, their heads quaking. Teardrops speckle the tan steps. The sight is surreal: hardened men, some the most senior in the regiments, exposing the tear-strewn faces of boys, as overcome by emotion today as they were on the day of the sultan's funeral.

"Look, Father, look! We've brought your enemy here. Tonight, we bring you justice," a Mamluk says, his swordtip between Ismail's shoulder blades.

While Ismail may not understand every word these Mamluk speak, he seems to comprehend their tone. A gloom falls upon his crinkled face. Ismail already visited his nephew's gravesite.

He was dragged to this place only a few days prior, when he was taken prisoner with the other Syrian Princes after the battle. Leander wonders if the man has the capacity to regret the endless lists of ploys and lies and double crosses that he had leveled at his nephew. Doubtful.

Ismail drops to his knees to pray, but the Mamluks kick at him.

"Up, up! To your feet! Your last words will not be to our God, but to us, those sons of al-Salih, whom you wished to slay."

With his arms covering his head, Ismail fights to regain his legs. The man still wears the dusted trousers and tunic of his battle dress. He turns to Aybeg and begins to ramble nervously in Kurdish.

Leander walks forward, comprehending only half of what the man says.

Aybeg glares at Leander. "What does the swindler say?"

"He said something about some of our brothers having already come over to the Syrian side and so can we. And he warns us what al-Nasir will do to them, our comrades, if we harm him now."

Aybeg scowls. "A trickster till his last breath. Tell him that we don't care what happens to any traitors. Al-Nasir can do to them as we have planned for him now."

Leander does so, the words pouring out in an acceptable fluency.

Ismail's face grows pale under the crackling firelight. Again, he speaks, this time more desperately.

Leander turns to the group. "He says, uh ... free him now and he'll give us more silver than our camels can carry. Says ... al-Nasir will come back with an even larger army. Let him go and he'll convince the Prince of Damascus to change his mind."

The Mamluks look to one another and laugh, their dark chortles born by a collective joy that all present are not fooled by the supreme deceiver. A blissful hoot that at least the spirit of their old patron will be able to witness the worst of his foes finally punished.

Aybeg takes a step toward Ismail, and then turns to Leander. "Tell him that he'll not talk his way out this time. One too many times, he betrayed our father. And even after al-Salih's death, he came with the others to steal Cairo from us."

Unable to control himself, Aqtay lunges himself at the old Kurd, the force of impact knocking Ismail to his back. "Enough talk!" He slams Ismail's head against the ground, his fingers laced about the man's neck.

Ismail struggles, jerking his head side-to-side. In time, he gurgles, his face reddening.

A pat on Aqtay's back. The Bahri's commander grudgingly releases his stranglehold with a simultaneous spit into Ismail's face.

The Ayyubid gasps for air and recovers, his chest heaving. His throat half-mangled, he blurts out undecipherable words. These are cut short by the strong hands of the oldest Mamluk among them, who now straddles Ismail's chest. The old Kipchak squeezes, his chin jutting out in satisfaction, his tears dripping on Ismail's face. The others around him yowl, an unsettling, communal cry. In moments, the elder Mamluk rises with no prompting, refusing to be greedy.

One of the shirtless amirs takes his place, his bloodied hands slicking up Ismail's throat. His wet triceps glimmer in the soft moonlight. "You'll die, wicked one. You die tonight!" The Mamluk screams.

This man is bumped aside by the knee of Aybeg. Seeing the sultan above him, the Mamluk crawls out of the way, like a chastened pup. He spins to sit, his ass only an arm's reach from the gasping Ismail. He insists on an intimate view of the finale.

Having partially regained his breathing, the defiant Kurd begins to blubber in heavy gasps. With crimson stripes encircling his mauled neck, he wheezes one of the few Turkish words he has bothered to learn, "Mercy ... have mercy."

With this, Aybeg buries his knee into the prince's chest. He locks his thumbs on either side of Ismail's windpipe and applies gradual pressure. A giant owl with it wings spread wide, entrapping its prey, its talons clenching, squeezing. Aybeg lowers himself, until he is almost nose-to-nose with the Kurd. Again, the uncle burbles. A thin huff of air.

Sensing the end, the semi-circle of men amplifies its shrieks, a peculiar mix of hilarity and wailing. A pack of Mamluk hyenas without a true alpha in charge. Just lethal jaws and sharp teeth, seasoned beasts primed to destroy. Leander snugs the collar of his coat.

Around him are the strongest, most disciplined warriors he will ever meet. Many of them are clever and even highly intelligent, by any measure. Yet today, they are men with the emotional aptitude of boys. In their weathered faces, he sees clearly the former lads of the steppe, as distraught and dysfunctional at the long-ago death of their patron as most must have been at the loss by Mongol bow of their birth fathers so many years past.

Oddly, Leander realizes for the first time that in front of him are unbeatable men. Only they are capable of destroying the newly-born Mamluk Sultanate they have formed.

A crunch of cartilage. The Kurd's chest no longer rises. Aybeg rears back and punches Ismail in his lifeless face. The Kurd stares into the starlit sky, the torchlight flickering across the man's glossy eyes.

Suddenly the pack goes quiet. Just the crackle of flame. All eyes on the dead Kurd.

For an uncomfortable moment, Leander worries for his life. He knows not how this episode ends. Afraid to look anywhere else, he too gapes at the dead Ismail, hoping more eyes on the great uncle will mean fewer eyes on him, the only among them who is not a Kipchak, the only one who does not share the blood of their tribe, much less their Khushdash.

Aybeg stands. He looks over each shoulder at the Salihi, Bahri and Jamdariyya around him, too many brothers from the earliest Khushdash turned adversaries. He sighs, then glances to al-Salih's mausoleum and finally up to the sliver of moon. He steps over the corpse and forces his way through those standing around it, Aybeg being the first of the hyenas seeming to realize that the purpose behind the rivals' short-lived merging has ended.

CHAPTER

26

Cenk
Ashmoon, Egypt
June 7, 1252

Aybeg waves his open palm across the flooded plain. "A stranger to the delta would have no idea what a beautiful site this is, eh?"

"Yes, my Sultan," Cenk says, observing the flat of glimmering water, the expanse looking like a deep lake from the old country except for the odd stalks from last year's harvest which stick up like missed whiskers.

"In another four moons, this water will be gone, leaving this flood plain blessed with soil dark as night, much better than the ground at your old fief. In no time, the barley will pop. Over there, just north of that rise, is the start of your land," Aybeg says, pointing in the distance.

"My Sultan, I can't thank you enough. Your generosity is..."

"Horseshit. We must look out for one another. It's that simple," Aybeg says.

Cenk shakes his head, blinks away the forming tears. Once al-Salih died, Cenk thought he would lose the iqta granted him by his patron. Instead, he now has four times the land—prime fields that will produce six times the crops of his previous plot. With the subsequent coin collected, he will be able to fund his retirement. He just has to hold on for a year, maybe two, before the land is likely snatched from him and given to another more deserving and more valuable to the sultan—or worse, given to the next sultan's own cadre. It is possible.

The changes in the realm. All of it happened so fast, once Turanshah was killed. Immediately, Jamal al-Din Muhsin—Cenk's commander of the Jamdariyya—retired, the turmoil in the citadel reason enough for the old man to step down from a long career of soldiering. Cenk decided to do the same. He gave notice of his intent to retire, pleased to be done with the temporary advisory role that he had been filling. But Aybeg would hear none of it.

Once becoming sultan, Aybeg had clung tighter to Cenk and a few others from his Khushdash, those from his past whom he wished would become his inner circle. Aybeg envisioned Cenk a member of his "advisory council," a position free of the daily burden of leading troops, so that his mind would be uncluttered and able to provide sound guidance.

> "I'm honored, truly, but I promised my wife and daughter that I would retire. Plus, I don't know that I have much more to offer at this age. I'm but a simple troop leader, not a high-level counselor," Cenk said, when offered the post.
>
> Aybeg had anticipated his concern. "You're exactly what I need. A man with horse sense."

Even as Cenk waivered, Aybeg pulled Cenk's men into the royal guard under the command of Ox. Their pay was doubled. Cenk was baffled for days, then skeptical. How could any sultan desire a lowly Bashkir hunter from the Ural Mountains to be his advisor, a man better suited to be sent back to the tibaq to train novices than to an upper echelon staff? He figured in the end it came down to trust, only trust. In these turbulent times, Aybeg simply needed men in whom he could confide. Feeling obligated, Cenk took the post.

Cenk takes in the expanse of his new land. Once again, he feels he is defying the odds, landing another position that was seemingly out of his reach. Luck has followed him since the day he stepped upon the slave block. Having dark skin, he was fated to become a common slave like most of the other teenagers gathered from the far north. Yet his first patron, Amir Turkmani, had rescued him from this life of misery, purchased him, and pulled him into the Mamluk ranks.

After Turkmani's tragic death, by God's grace, al-Salih granted him the opportunity to attend his rigorous school to become a Furusiyya Instructor. Cenk graduated from the arduous course, becoming the only *Bashkir* in memory to be given the responsibility of instructing young novices—an honor not only to himself, but also to his former people.

And now, with the end of his soldiering in sight, he is raised to a role many tiers above his old rank, to a position of which most men only dream. Of course, Cenk does not consider the appointment to be risk-free, as the division between the two factions in al-Salih's Mamluks has eroded into a chasm. Men walk the dark corridors of both citadels with their palms resting on the pommels of their swords. Most of those in the River Island Regiment would prefer Aybeg dead.

Aybeg seems to read Cenk's mind. "Aqtay and Baybars. My friend, I worry that their successes on the battlefield keep eating away at our base."

Cenk nods, contemplating the situation, while absently watching a gray heron hunt the flood plain. The sultan is right. Instead of turning his rivals into casualties as planned, Aybeg's decision to send Aqtay eastward only increased his rival's prestige. The Bahri's victories two autumns past at Gaza against al-Nasir's vanguard and their commander's survival that same winter at al-Ababasa gained Aqtay favor within the Bahri ranks and among the populace. Aqtay's understudy, Baybars, had proven himself worthy by his recent conduct in Upper Egypt, putting down a separate Arab uprising which had compromised the water routes vital to Egyptian trade.

Cenk calls to mind Aybeg's reception for the Arab chiefs who traveled to discuss terms with the sultan—the Arabs' throats slit as soon as they dismounted and the taxes on their people doubled. Cenk reminds himself that the man at his side can be ruthless. Maybe given Egypt's dire conditions, Aybeg is almost driven to such harsh conduct. While honor and compassion might find their ways into the enemy reception under al-Salih and even earlier Ayyubid Sultans—and maybe even under Mohammed himself—this is not so with Aybeg.

Cenk spurns the softness in his thoughts. One must take callous steps at times to save an empire and to save one's place in it. He turns to the sultan. "I've been thinking on this matter a good bit. Thinking what al-Salih might have done, if he were in our position."

"And?" Aybeg crinkles his brow in interest.

"Al-Salih would've acted like a spider."

"He'd what?"

"With their relatives forever plotting behind their backs, both al-Salih and his father were adept at neutralizing one enemy and tangling him in a web so that they could concentrate on addressing the most urgent foe."

Aybeg squints and raises his chin in deliberation.

"I think for us now, God is our web and you have already spun half the trap." Cenk smiles.

"I don't follow."

"We take the proclamation you made last fall and carry it to the next level."

"You mean my decree stating Egypt belonged to the caliph in Baghdad and that I was merely ruling the land as his governor?"

"Yes. I think we consider sending an emissary to al-Musta'sim, imploring the caliph to make a peace between you and al-Nasir. For the good of Islam."

Aybeg cringes. "Why encourage a truce with the Syrian alliance, when we just humiliated al-Nasir in al-Abbasa?"

"I think we need the caliph to make an accord precisely because we humiliated al-Nasir. The time for truces is after victories, not after defeats."

Aybeg, too, watches the solitary heron lift his thin legs high and gently place them back into the shallow water without stirring a ripple. Stealth. An astute animal sneaking up on its prey. Aybeg turns to Cenk with a grin. "You *have* been thinking, my friend."

"We need to entangle al-Nasir. And soon. Think about it. We just sent him, the great-grandson of Saladin, scampering back to Damascus, while his forces had Cairo in their grasp. His army was just waiting to be led through our gates. All of the princes loyal to al-Nasir and those almost nine thousand soldiers throughout Syria now wonder if their prince is a coward. Yet the reality for us remains sobering—at al-Abbasa, we hardly impacted the strength of al-Nasir's forces."

"Yes, but they also know that al-Nasir's commander, Shams al-Din, is dead, the one man possessing the courage to attack us en masse. With him gone, why would we seek a settlement?" Aybeg asks.

"Because Shams' death is not enough to completely ensnare the Syrian alliance. Another man will step up. We, the spider, remain vulnerable."

Aybeg frowns.

"Al-Nasir knows his flaws exposed to all," Cenk continues. "What is more troubling than an unconfident man, a deficient man with something to prove—especially with a big army at his disposal? A big army that he knows will only be available for a finite period of time."

Aybeg nods slowly. "Yes. And the caliph in Baghdad. All he wants is the land of Islam docile. He'd be foolish enough to take up the task." Aybeg purses his lip. "Let the man closest to God be the one to set terms binding al-Nasir. Ultimately, ours is God's work. God's will."

Cenk watches the heron with eyes half closed, still analyzing. "And, this way al-Nasir still preserves at least part of his honor. His faintheartedness and indecision, which come so naturally to him, would now be justified by an edict from God. Sure, the caliph will preserve al-Nasir's current territories." Cenk chuckles. "Yet, what do we care of the terms? The truce will only last until we have the situation in Egypt under control."

Aybeg pats Cenk on the back. "Then the spider circles around to pull the bumbling al-Nasir back under our control."

"Put the mace to the scoundrel's head. But at a time of our choosing. Not now, as the meddling Franj King would want, stoking war between Muslims so that he may weasel more land in Palestine for the Kingdom of Jerusalem."

Aybeg nods.

Cenk looks him in the eye. "And with any treaty made, Mamluk legitimacy takes a firmer foothold. In the end, the spider can only apply his fangs to one enemy at a time. What spider on the hunt wants to keep looking over his eastern shoulder and wondering if every dust cloud on the horizon is yet another great enemy? The wise one, our old patron, would want to first concentrate on the enemy closest to its nest."

"Aqtay."

"Aqtay ... Let the spider neaten his nest before venturing out."

The heron crouches, then springs upward, flapping heavy wings up and up to better hunting grounds. Cenk watches it climb until it is out of sight. He thinks back to his time training novices in Hisn Kayfa, and of how many times he was called up the winding stairs to Aqtay's office in the citadel and forced to listen to the amir's drivel on how Cenk was culling too many of the weak novices from his ranks in the tibaq.

Aqtay stopped, closed his eyes, and then smiled at Cenk, seeming to regain his own composure, or perhaps deciding on a different tack. His elbows went back to his desk.

"You've been selected from many to be the dragon, yet are also tasked as the primary artisan, the one who will shape the raw clay into fine pottery. You must be not only the slave driver, but also the older brother to these novices. We must build up and train this regiment, not decimate its training ranks."

Cenk sat up straighter on the edge of the chair, opposite his commander. Cenk refused to let his commander's reasoning penetrate his head, the Mu'allim envisioning the feeble words pinging off him, like arrows from his shield.

Aqtay balled his fingers into a tight fist and raised his top lip. "Our prince has too many dinars, too much planned for these novices, to have them all become moat fillers. At your unit's current failure rate, you'll have no novices to train in two years. Do you understand me, Mu'allim?"

Cenk fumes, just as he did fifteen years past, thinking of Aqtay, the man turned soft by his prolonged interaction with that black-skinned eunuch, Safir. Cenk struggles to hide his disgust and levies a calm upon himself. Aqtay was the wrong leader for the tibaq back then; his leadership of the entire empire now would be disastrous. Al-Nasir, the Crusaders, and even the Mongols on the eastern edge of the empire are all watching mother Egypt. Aqtay must be blocked.

Aybeg smiles. "You see now why I wouldn't let you retire with the others? Your judgments are essential here. An old hunter, a guard, a Mu'allim of the tibaq. I knew you had the mindset made to protect Egypt and our rule."

He looks over Cenk's shoulder and points. "Good, here they come."

Two riders on Arabians approach.

"So, on this meeting. You'll remember al-Salih and Fakhr al-Din had his spies among the Franj, some of them quick-witted women, disguised amid the whores in the Crusader camp?" Aybeg says.

Cenk nods.

"Well, they also had a few snoops in the beer houses, a few in the eateries, others sprinkled about both citadels. Even with the Crusaders under heel, we left some in place, especially now with the widening split in the Mamluk houses. I wish for you to start becoming familiar with some of them and their work."

Cenk raises a lip. "Why women? Aren't you worried these infiltrators will somehow grow attached to the men they snoop on and possibly start rooting their targets?"

"All the better. Empty sacks lead to loose lips. But don't be shortsighted on this, Cenk. I could bore you for hours on why women spies work. And it has nothing to do with favors for sex. They're better at playing a role. Any role. They're superior to men when it comes to stifling their own selves in order to attain the goal. They listen better, can read people better than men. They're women."

Cenk rolls his eyes, grins at the sultan. He is not convinced. "Yes, my Sultan. But I'd rather deal with a man."

"Perhaps. But given who's proven themselves the most effective in this trade, given who gets the information we need, I'd most often take the woman. And, we lose less of them."

Cenk scrunches his brow. "Hmm."

"As you say, they always have the alibi. When caught with a man in a place they shouldn't be, one naturally assumes an affair. I'm telling you, women ... when they're good at this work, they're very good. You'll be meeting such today."

Cenk grimaces.

"Plus, this girl, from what her father says, has little interest in men. She's refused the marriages he has proposed to her. She seeks no man on her own. She's all business."

"Since when do fathers give their daughters the choice in marriage?"

Aybeg laughs. "She's been valuable. Al-Salih once told me that this one is capable of much more than her current function. Much more."

Cenk raises his eyebrows. "What kind of father would let his daughter engage in this kind of work in the first place?"

Aybeg turns from him. Cenk regrets the comment.

Qutuz, Aybeg's vicegerent, dismounts. "Good afternoon, Sultan," he says respectfully, nodding afterward to Cenk. He helps the young lady from her horse.

Aybeg stands with hands behind his back. "I see you have brought one of the most productive of your entourage with you."

Qutuz smiles. "Indeed."

Aybeg smiles at the woman. "Greetings. I chose this meeting place not just so we would be unseen, but also so that you would remember to needle your father. Maybe just a reminder so he doesn't forget about us land barons on the northeast when the flood waters recede. He'll keep our irrigation channels full again this year, right?

The dark-haired woman frowns. "You'd know better than I. I haven't seen my father in many moons—I'm too busy in the infirmaries, patching up the gore you and your amirs have caused for most of the last three years."

Cenk scowls. "Hold your tongue, woman. You do know that you address the Sultan of Egypt."

She steps up to him. "Why yes, I do."

Cenk glares. "I suggest you address him respectfully, or I'll have your rudely flapping lips removed by dagger, before you're separated from your head."

Qutuz pats Cenk on the shoulder, while exchanging grins with Aybeg. "It's all right, Cenk. I can see the sultan has not yet informed you of the unusual relationship he shares with this woman. Fakhr al-Din insisted from the start that she be absolutely direct with him. And al-Salih, too, found her candor amusing."

Aybeg chuckles. "Given her usefulness, I asked her to not change her ways." He turns to Cenk. "I want them to gather facts, but also want to hear their true feelings, not the babble of what they think an important man wants to hear."

The woman still eyes Cenk. "And as far as losing my head—I suppose such comes with the trade. But in this line of work, usually the ax falls on the head of the liars, or those who get caught by the foe. I don't intend to be either. My Sultan, may I please meet this man?"

"Of course, forgive my insolence," Aybeg says. "Cenk, please meet Jacinta."

CHAPTER

27

Leander
The Island Citadel, Cairo
December 24, 1252

Leander props his crossbow against the backside of the parapet and gazes into the windless evening, a faint pink cast upon the bronzed mountains opposite, reflecting dully across the river. He yawns, his evening shift on watch almost complete.

Two Bahri cross the northern bridge, the echo from their hoof clops sounding against the stone face of the citadel. One has a pair of chickens lashed to his cantle, the dust-covered birds flopping on either side of his giant bay's hindquarters. The other has his saddlebags hastily stuffed, a corner of purple silk hanging out from under its flap.

Once off the bridge, their voices reach his tower, barely perceptible.

"Like the twiggy-armed weasel was going to do anything. Shit, he didn't once look me in the face. Once he saw the yellow turban, it was straight to his coin pouch," the first Mamluk slurs.

Where the path widens, the second rider comes up beside him. "We're both fools. We left untouched that thing most valuable. Tell me you didn't see his daughter? Some time alone with me and she'd still be hollering in pleasure."

The first Bahri belches. "Oh, she'd've have hollered—out of fright of your gnarled mug or from your yak-shit breath."

Both laugh hysterically, bent over on the swell of their saddles. Still chuckling, they slow their horses to a walk as they approach the east gate. Leander leans over the edge of the wall. The guards swing out the giant wooden doors, swallowing the drunks into the bowels of the river island fortress.

Leander laments. As it goes with most criminal activity, the regiment's crimes started as petty acts—men snatching a loaf of bread to make up for reduced rations, hungry lads stealing the odd goat. As the weeks passed, however, the offenses grew more brazen. Now kidnapping for ransom, sacking a home or even breaking into bathhouses to rape women does not raise an eyebrow.

The Bahri amirs do not encourage such behavior, but neither do they stop it, turning a blind eye from mischief and unspeakable offenses. Who in town is bold enough to stop them, anyhow? Leander wonders if the amirs wish the populace to see that its new sultan is unable to keep order. Perhaps Cairo will raise its voice for another leader.

Much of the pillaging is purely a result of the Bahri's pay cut. Although their *jamakiy*, or base salaries, remain unchanged, every other form of payment to the troops has been slashed: their lahm, or meat ration; their *aliq*, or fodder ration for their animals, and even the *kiswa*, or biannual pay to cover their gear and uniforms.

The reason behind the pay decrease is simple. Most of the coin which supports these payments is derived from the amirs' iqta and now huge chunks of those fiefs once held by the Bahri are gone. They were initially taken from the amirs and doled out to Turanshah's Mamluks after al-Salih's death. They were subsequently seized by Aybeg for his Mamluks across the Nile and the prime lands given to the senior amirs. Adding salt to the wound, neither Turanshah nor Aybeg paid the *nafaq*, or silver, traditionally given on the eve of a campaign or on the ascension of a new sultan.

The end result: after almost three years of on-and-off fighting and scant resupply, the Bahri are not looking their usual elite selves. With less money in their pockets, gear is left in disrepair and missing weapons and kit are not replaced. In Duyal's Amirate Three, several men wear jawshans with rotted silk cords, others have holes in their cuirass, shoulder plates hanging loose and armor twisted out of shape from being stowed wet. Some in the regiment see themselves having little choice but to steal, rationalizing that their actions are a self-imposed tax on the community they protect.

Leander and those in his amirate have restrained themselves, knowing the conduct wrong and not wishing to dishonor Duyal. The Bahri's recent conduct is not the way of Saladin and not the way of al-Salih. It is not the way of Allah. Such criminals do not act like the band of exclusive brothers he left the Crusaders for—they now veer too far from the Mamluk creed he learned just a few years ago. Perhaps the hushed whispers from Cairo's citizens are true—only the heavy hand of Ayyubid royalty kept the Mamluks from being no more than a roving horde for past decades.

Then again, none of this happened when Amir Aqtay was here to keep control. Now, their Amir of One Hundred is away. To keep his primary competition far from their Fortress of the Mountain, Sultan Aybeg pushed the ever-popular Aqtay and nearly half his cadre of Bahri—plus some in the Jamdariyya—to the bastion in Alexandria, nearly a four-day's ride north of Cairo.

Of course, Aqtay did not go out of obligation to the sultan's wishes, as the Bahri do not even recognize Aybeg as sultan. Aqtay likely figured this important assignment was just the fulfillment of the promise made to him by Turanshah, when the amir escorted the young sultan south from Hisn Kayfa after his patron's death. Aqtay was simply collecting on that old vow from a real sultan.

At his assignment in Alexandria, the mid-grade amir acts as if he, too, is a ruler, sealing messages to other princes in the region as if the coastal fort is a separate empire. Aqtay has even gone so far as to marry a princess of Ayyubid blood, daughter to the prince of Hama. Rumor is that after the marriage to al-Muzaffar's daughter, Aqtay demanded from Aybeg permission to reside in the sultan's citadel, in accordance with his status. Bold.

Leander wonders if Aqtay loves the girl or if his move was pure manipulation. Love. Hopefully his commander married for love of the woman.

> Leander and Jacinta strolled the marketplace, through the smoke from roasting meat, past a steaming kettle of bram rice, a woman tending the tiny fire beneath it. They continued, Jacinta pointing to the little girl making tahini, the traditional sesame paste, with her mother. "As my mom did with me," she said, with a squeeze of his hand.
>
> He pulled her off the road a few steps into an alley. Now, he thought, as perhaps there would never be another chance. She looked up at him with her dark eyes, glassy from the flicker of the globe lights swaying near them. He held her face in both hands and kissed her lips. She smiled, her eyes becoming slits, as they did when she was happy. She took in a breath to speak, but then seemed to hold it in.
>
> He grinned, caressing the back of her head. He gave her one last peck on the forehead, leaving his nose buried in her sweet, perfumed hair. Forever. He wished he could stand right here forever. He took her hand and pulled her back onto the cobbled road, Jacinta looking up at him, beaming.

Twinkles of bouncing light on the mainland catch his attention. He smiles. A small group of Christians toting candles, likely on the way home from friends' homes after breaking their month-long Advent fast with a large meal. By Allah, it is almost Christmas. Tonight, the few Christians in town will start their twelve-day celebration of the birth of his old God, Jesus Christ.

The clusters of light become lost behind the hills and buildings, the flickers extinguishing one by one. A wave of sadness falls over him. He reminiscences on breaking the fast back in France—boar's head, cheese, fresh bread, venison, partridges, geese, ale, and wine. Good cheer. His father grinning as carts rumbled into the square, their splintered beds mounded with food, gifts from Lord Erard for the entire hamlet of Ramerupt.

Those twelve days of Christmas celebrations in France were peaceful times, an opportunity for quiet prayer and reflection. Christmas Day was festive, but less so than the Epiphany on January 6, celebrating the historic visit from the three wise men.

Leander thinks of his family, picturing himself and Jacinta with them, surrounded by neighbors, a fire crackling ... Silly thoughts. Impossible thoughts. He is distraught at the irony: that as the Christians on the opposite bank close their fast of repentance, his fellow Muslim brothers in the Bahri are the ones doing a majority of the sinning. He is embarrassed by their actions. This is not who they are.

He rubs a blemish from his crossbow. The old elm stock is recently varnished, the composite staves of horn, wood, glue, and sinew remain in fine shape. Another sweep of depression flows through him as he lingers on memories of the old country, his obsession with the crossbow there and the joy he had developing his skills with the weapon.

As a page in France, he knew every corner of Lord Erard's vast lands. In rabid anticipation of his fall and winter hunts, Leander prepared in the summers and early fall, saving his sparse coin to purchase bolts from the artillator, and after his daily chores were done, crisscrossing the estate for sign of deer and fox. When the air finally became crisp, every evening he would charge afield with crossbow in hand, the stalk for game being his sole release from the drudgery of endless duties and study.

After any success, he would sneak from the castle at night to where he had hidden the dressed animals and hump back to his father's house with the carcass on his back to hang a red stag or roe deer in his father's cellar. By the time winter fell, fox fur lined his father's hats and mittens and coat, as well as those of his friends and neighbors.

A door across the river opens, sending familiar notes across the silent flow of river. Stringed instruments and voices singing, adding flavor to his reflections on Ramerupt. The door bumps shut, ceasing both the flow of musings and the Christmas song emitting from the cheerful home.

The crack of bamboo-on-bamboo behind him takes the place of the music. He walks to the opposite end of the rounded turret and peers over the side into the hippodrome, their training arena. Struggling to make out the men in the dark, he picks out Amir Baybars speaking with another leader. They watch four of his troopers spar with lances, the men likely forced into after-hours training by their skilled amir.

Steps from the bottom of the stairwell. A scuff closer. He strolls back to his station, again resting his hands on the smooth rock of the parapet. A pair of Mamluks emerge from the vestibule. Seeing his amir, he locks his body.

"At ease. Tranquil on the eastern wall?" Duyal asks with a grin.

"Yes, my Amir. Sadly, the only real threat to Cairo has been from those in our own ranks," Leander says.

"More Bahri pillagers?" Binny asks woefully.

Leander nods to his friend.

Binny groans. "Not good."

Duyal shakes his head. "But predictable. Hard for an Amir of Forty to meet his contract when his fief is half what it was—if he's lucky."

Leander affirms. Regardless of the requirement laid out in the feudal charters, most amirs gave out roughly half of their fief's income to the troops. These days, many amirs go above their obligations, giving away two-thirds of their reduced income, or even more. And it is still not enough to keep their men fed and equipped.

"I worry what will happen when Amir Aqtay hears of it. Half the Bahri may be in chains," Binny says.

"I worry if the other amirs continue to allow the looting, if we'll be able to win the population back," Leander says.

Duyal glowers. The pop of lance shafts breaks them from their individual thoughts.

"Only you and Amir Baybars have kept us in the hippodrome and out of town, out of trouble," Leander says.

"No surprise there," Binny says.

"My Amir, was Amir Baybars from your same Kipchak tower?" Leander asks.

"No. Why do you ask?"

"In Mansura, he told us that he knew your older brother, said that he'd learned from Amir Gozde, while still on the steppe. I just figured that you all must've known each other as boys."

Duyal grins. "As a young Mamluk in Hisn Kayfa, my brother had been on one of al-Salih's missions north on the Kipchak steppe to put eyes on the Mongols. Gozde's team was attacked, some of them killed, scattered. Badly wounded, my brother stumbled upon Baybars, while still a Kipchak lad, plus his aunt and uncle. Their tower took Gozde in, nursed his wounds."

"Really?"

"My brother came down with the fever, nearly died. Baybars' people saved him. And once healthy, Gozde took to training with weapons to regain his strength before his return journey to the Jazira. The young Baybars, of course, took to my brother, who worked with him, set him on the path of the Mamluk. Years later, Baybars found himself on the trading block and after his stint with Amir Bunduqdari, al-Salih eventually bought him."

"My Amir, I'm surprised that tale isn't better known. I suppose the rest is legend—your brother. Three ribbons of valor," Binny says.

"And Baybars not saying much, but never forgetting his first mentor," Leander says.

Duyal grimaces. "Unfortunately, legends often require their subjects to be dead men. They buried Gozde with four ribbons of valor. My brother was the best—man and warrior and brother. Gone too early."

"No wonder Amir Baybars is so fond of you," Binny says.

Duyal shakes his head. "If he's fond of me, it's only because of Gozde."

"No brownnosing, my Amir, but I'd bet Baybars sees the brothers sharing a few of the same strengths," Leander says.

Duyal looks down. "I don't know about that."

Binny and Leander trade smiles.

From atop the northern minaret, the muezzin sings his ghostlike cry. A muffled call to prayer commences across the river—a muted version further south on high. The chanting blends in the still air, resonating off the towering block walls.

The trio remove their belts, lay their weapons against the wall, and face Mecca, kneeling to pray on the hard stone floor.

CHAPTER

28

Cenk
Infirmary, Cairo
September 27, 1253

"Sultan, please," Cenk says, extending his arm to allow Aybeg to enter the storeroom first. Cenk looks down the corridor in both directions and then eyes the lead guard. "Knock four times when she arrives."

"Yes, my Amir," the bull-necked Mamluk replies.

Cenk enters the cramped space, closing the door behind him. The smell of clean bedding. Shelving on three sides, tight bundles of dressing and bandages stacked in rows. Qutuz rises as Aybeg enters, knocking his knees on the makeshift table in front of him. Four small stools surround the crate.

"Sit, sit," Aybeg says. The men scooch up to the box, looking like adults prepared for children's tea. Aybeg nods to Qutuz, his second-in-command.

"Sorry on the arrangement here," Qutuz says. "She'll be on break soon, knows to meet us here. Conforming to her schedule, moving our meeting spots will help keep her from being noticed,"

Aybeg nods. "Yes, yes ... So, we've enough room for them. You agree?"

"Yes. We can make some barracks space in the east wing."

Cenk strokes his gray-flecked beard, crosses his arms over his chest.

Aybeg straightens. "I know that look. What are your thoughts, Cenk?"

"If the Nasiriyya were willing to abandon their patron, their own father, at al-Abbasa when al-Nasir needed them most, how is it that we can trust these Mamluks now?" Cenk leans forward.

"Is it their fault that al-Nasir's a coward—that they abandoned a man who wouldn't even stay and fight beside them?" Qutuz asks.

Cenk snarls. "Yes, it is. You'll get no argument from me on al-Nasir's faintheartedness, but they betrayed the man who took them in as boys and fed them, trained them, gave them their weapons, the best mounts—their lives. Vile is their conduct. And we wish to not only ally with these men, but also bring them into our own house?"

Aybeg leans back against the wall, pinches his chin in thought.

"Are we any different than they are?" Qutuz asks. "Not only do most of us share the same original homeland—didn't we just kill our own sultan for the same reason they left theirs? Weren't we also unwilling to serve a man unworthy of our dedication?"

Cenk bristles. "You know full well that it's not the same. We faithfully served our only patron for decades, until his parting breath. We had no obligation to al-Salih's useless son. The Nasiriyya—they betray their original father. It's unforgiveable."

Aybeg nods, stroking his beard. The sultan begins, looking squarely at Qutuz. "Remember my friend, Cenk and I are both sayfiyah—orphans of the regiment. We know the pitiful mindset of the fatherless men forced to search for a new purpose, a new patron." He teases his beard, finishing with his hand in a fist.

"It's hard for us to fathom—these men, deserting their father, regardless of the situation. It's concerning."

A crease forms in Qutuz's brow. He addresses Aybeg, "Respectfully, at some point it comes right down to numbers. A third of our forces are now loyal to the Prince of Karak. We don't have enough cavalrymen to counter the Bahri and those traitors in the Jamdariyya. By bringing both the Nasiriyya and the Aziziyya into the citadel, al-Nasir's men will see we truly accept them as comrades."

Qutuz lowers his voice. "Again, with due reverence, both of al-Nasir's units may as well be sayfiyah themselves, and we all know that given a second life in a new regiment, men in this position can be eager to show their loyalty, their lethality in battle." He looks at Cenk and then back to Aybeg. "Often, a Mamluk needing to prove himself ends up doing just that."

Cenk feels the heat rising up from his core. Bullshit. Patches of white and red appear upon his neck. Catching himself rubbing fretfully on the stub of his finger, he places one hand in the other in a sham gesture of serenity. "My friend, I understand our predicament, yet letting the wolves into the lamb pen does not feel like the right option. Ally with the Nasiriyya if we must, but to bring them in...and the Aziziyya."

The sultan meets his eyes.

Cenk raises his lip in disgust, thinking of the Aziziyya, the Mamluks of al-Nasir's father. The Aziziyya have even less to lose. Treachery and angling for position will be their chosen course. "It feels more prudent to put the Aziziyya to the sword, rather than open our gates to them. We ... "

Four knocks on the flimsy door. Cenk closes his eyes, belches up an acidic brine, and wonders if this job will kill him before he can quit it and retire.

"Enter," Aybeg says.

Jacinta squeezes in sideways, her light blue smock smeared with a brown crust, her dark hair tied above her collar. "Good afternoon, gentlemen." She stops in front of the open stool and looks to Aybeg.

"Sit, please," Aybeg says.

She settles and places her hands upon her thighs. She glances quickly above to the supplies, her eyes drawn to the stacks that are not perfectly arranged, those columns of white near tumbling. She avoids making eye contact with any but Aybeg, perhaps never forgetting Cenk's coldness at their first meeting more than a year past, her bad first impression. And another unpleasant meeting after that.

Cenk glares at her. Fucking moles, who can trust them? Part-time actors and full-time deceivers—a necessary evil, he supposes.

"All right, you know the situation," Aybeg says, shifting to face Jacinta. "Our plan to push Aqtay and half his Bahri to Alexandria hasn't worked out as hoped. Dividing them didn't weaken their stance. Instead, our move has practically done the opposite and emboldened each half."

Aybeg raises his thick eyebrows, his eyes bouncing quickly to each of the group. "Without Aqtay's presence, the Bahri left on the island have done nothing but stir the merchants and civilians into a lather. Soon the traders will use Cairo's insecurity as reason to skip their tax payments. We can't have that silver in jeopardy."

Qutuz nods emphatically.

Aybeg leans forward. "A confrontation with the Bahri is coming." He turns to Jacinta. "We've been meeting with most of our agents in the field individually. To prep the field, I wish to see if we can pluck some of the best of Aqtay's men."

She stares at him, expressionless.

Aybeg shrugs his shoulders. "Bring over the disenchanted and those men of prospect. And for those who cannot be bought or persuaded otherwise ... " He looks at the blue fabric across Jacinta's small breasts and unashamedly to the only skin showing at her ankles. "Then eliminate those River Island amirs most valuable."

The men nod in agreement.

"If they continue to loot, then I'm thinking in town and on the drunk would be the place and time to take some of them out," Qutuz says.

"Do we try playing nice first?" Aybeg turns back towards Jacinta. "From your contacts, which do you see as men who could be swayed by silver—amirs, of course?"

She scrunches her eyebrows in thought. "Possibly Bedri ... or maybe even Taavi, yet their morale may improve once Aqtay builds up his treasury in Alexandria, this making them less desirable targets. And we'd have to be confident in them accepting the offers. Once we propose this, I'd be revealed. Perhaps my work for you done."

"Done?" Aybeg chuckles, looks to Qutuz. "Oh, you're too valuable to slide out of your duty now. Now is when we need our strongest players to rise." He looks over to Cenk, who scowls at the woman.

Jacinta remains straight-faced.

Aybeg turns to the others. "But her point is valid. If it comes to wet work, this would need to be coordinated, done nearly simultaneously, as once on to us, the game would be up."

"Done the same night, the same hour," Qutuz says.

Cenk feels another bite in his stomach, thinks of his wife, Fidan, and her words when he was offered this post.

> *"It doesn't feel right. Too dangerous, things are not stable,"* she said, her eyes flooded with imminent tears.
>
> Cenk laughed, rubbed her on the back. *"Dangerous? My love, on the field is where the danger is. I'll be merely flapping my lips, always behind the stone walls. My pay quadrupled, no troops to care for."*
>
> She looked away.
>
> *"After this, I'm done—and we'll have a purse-full of coin that we'll use to forget about this old life."*

When she looked up again, tears crept across her red cheeks. She fed the cooking fire, sticking out those pouty lips that always melted his heart.

"Come now. By Allah, what could be safer?" he asked, pulling her in, kissing her cheek, the taste of salt lingering on his lips. "Only for a year or two."

Already it has been three. From the start, it has been endless maneuvering. Now, they scheme about assassinations within the Mamluk ranks. A mess. And he is mired, knee-deep in it. Fidan was right. He should have retired when he had the chance. Yet, he had ironically stayed on because of her and Inci, figuring he owed them for what he had put them through for so many years.

But this new position has been harder on them, not easier, with long days, too many away from home. Still, Aybeg's offer was too good to refuse. "Just long enough for the fief to bring in one, maybe two seasons of crops. With that silver, our worries will be over," he had told Fidan.

A screech from Qutuz's stool as he turns to face Jacinta. "So, we could track the best of the Bahri amirs. Take our shots at those prospects. We wouldn't get them all, but we'd get some of them."

The room stays silent for a time.

"Amirs would be a priority. But should we also look at those of value in the ranks? Like what about the Franj who speaks all of the languages?" Aybeg asks.

Cenk turns to Jacinta, her face growing a bit pale. "Leander," he says, watching as her fingers clutch the seam of her smock under the table.

Qutuz frowns. "He's been very useful to them, as he was to the Franks before. Is there any way he'd come over to us?"

"He's a Frank—he's already proven himself willing to switch sides," Aybeg says, disgusted.

"I doubt it. He's devoted to a fault," Jacinta says, her hands now folded upon her lap.

"Hmmph," Cenk groans.

"No surprise, considering his boss," Qutuz says.

"Amir Duyal?" Aybeg asks.

Cenk nods, smiles. "He was one of mine at the tibaq."

"You're of the same Khushdash?" Jacinta asks hopefully.

The three men laugh.

"See this gray, woman?" Cenk runs his fingers through his groomed beard. "I was Duyal's instructor many years back. He was in my first tulb back in Hisn Kayfa. If this Leander is anything like Duyal, he'll be impenetrable. But I doubt the Bahri have a better translator."

Aybeg shrugs. "If he's important, let's at least snatch him in town and toss him in the dungeon. If he'll not come over to us, let's at least keep him out of our opponent's hands."

"Prisoners cost silver, silver we need to refit this army," Cenk says.

"Perhaps I should've made you a treasurer instead of an advisor of strategy," Aybeg says grinning.

Qutuz opens his palm. "Then let's just kill him."

Cenk looks to the girl. He tries to read her eyes and what he can see behind her veiled face. Her left hand goes back to the hem in her garment.

"This idea bother you, Jacinta?" Cenk asks, brows drawn tight, his eyes going from her hand to her face.

"Yeah, it does. He's probably my best contact. For what he lacks in willingness to join the Salihi, he makes up for in his cooperation to talk. He's smart." She sits back. "He seems to have a better sense of what is going on in the Bahri than most of those senior to him."

Cenk leans closer to her. "You haven't gone sweet on him now, have you?"

All eyes fall upon her.

She huffs, rolls her eyes. "Of course not. Who likes the idea of their best source being killed off?" She raises her upper lip at Cenk.

Cenk leans back, crosses his arms. "Is that all there is to it?"

She shifts to face him. "That's all and it's plenty. I have many moons into developing this contact. You'd get a little testy, too, if others proposed to dispatch your hard work." Her bottom lip quivers subtly. She tightens it. "Plus, the agreement my father had with al-Salih was for me to be an informant, not an assassin."

Cenk smiles. He distrusts her even more. "Don't worry, I don't see you capable of killing him. You're not the right person for that assignment."

Her eyes burn into Cenk's.

He refuses to be the one to look away. "But maybe you're right—I guess we don't have to kill your sweet boyfriend."

Her face goes calm, a fake grin crosses her lips. "Boyfriend. Oh, my father surely would be pleased for me to bring home a Crusader, wouldn't he? Please."

Cenk tilts his head. She deflects, thinking herself coy, he thinks. He shrugs his shoulders, holding them up for effect.

She goes calm. "I can still pull more from Leander in a day than what we might get from my others in three moons. What word will we get from him, once he's in the dungeon, or dead?"

"Seems to me that we've already pulled what information we'll get from him," Qutuz says. "His value now is not in word, but words. His translating skills. Along with the best of the Bahri amirs, let's just kill him."

Cenk smiles. "She's close to him, it's obvious. I've found the best way to attract flies is to take a shit. Our mole here," he nods toward Jacinta, "is a very fine turd, perfect to attract this translator man of hers."

Aybeg scowls.

She remains unflustered. "My Sultan, with all due respect. You made clear to me after al-Salih's death that my business with you was to continue collecting intelligence from my existing sources, and to alert you of those in both regiments who were a threat to you. I'm telling you, this man is not a threat. I would prefer not to be involved with this kind of bloodwork. This is not the duty al-Salih designed for me."

Aybeg scooches forward on his stool, his knees bumping the table, jamming the plank into her legs. "You listen closely. I don't care about the original agreement between al-Salih and your father. Your job was and still is to serve the Sultan of Egypt. That's me!"

Cenk's eyes burrow into her. Her body language is still composed, but her slender fingers are back at her smock.

Aybeg spreads his legs and props his elbows on his knees. "The fate of Cairo is in my hands, and I must do whatever I see fit to save her. Much of it is unpleasant. Much of it I don't enjoy. All of us are dealing in distastefulness. You, too, as a servant to this realm, must do your share."

She stares at him vacantly.

"Our father, our patron, Allah rest his soul, is underground. So is your past function in serving al-Salih. These are not games we play here. If you and your father and your mother wish to stay above ground, then I suggest *you* quickly embrace your expanded responsibilities. Do you understand me, young lady?"

"Yes, my Sultan."

Aybeg grunts. "So, enough of the disruptions. Enough of the insults. Progress. Let us make our plans. Allah has assigned us the most critical of tasks and placed us here to work together in preserving our Mother Egypt. There's much to be done."

CHAPTER

29

Leander
Cairo
November, 29, 1253

They step inside, Leander ducking to keep from hitting his head on the door frame. His eyes flit from wall to wall, taking in the place. Flickers from lanterns flutter from above. A low, warm light blankets the tables. The smell of oil, fried falafel, a hint of fish beginning to bake, maybe mullet. Two vertical posts that radiate horizontal supports anchor the room, terminating in an arched lattice of thatched cane above. The faint sound of a whisk applied to a bowl in the kitchen.

A woman in a straight-fitting dress sets down a stack of plates and approaches. Seeming to recognize Jacinta, she flashes a nervous smile, opens her palm to the table closest, takes only a quick peek at Leander, and snugs her worn cloak further up around her neck.

Leander pulls the chair out for Jacinta, lifting it over the thin Persian rug which appears recently swept. He sits facing the door. Looking about the tables, he notices two other couples.

They do not acknowledge his and Jacinta's presence. Another family, likely a merchant's, dine quietly.

Jacinta takes a sip of water from her cup and leans across the table. "Our family used to come here. The Fattah is excellent."

Leander smiles and reaches across to set his hand on hers. Their time together the past two and a half years has been sparse, their separate duties taking them in opposite directions and often pulling at least one of them out of Cairo. They have made an effort to see each other whenever possible—often every moon, sometimes only once every three moons.

"You'll head north to see your father next week?" Leander asks.

"Yes, just for a few days."

He nods.

The woman comes to their table with her hands folded politely across her abdomen.

"I think we'll both have the Fattah, please," he says.

She bows and turns back to the kitchen.

Jacinta smiles, then looks away, her smile fading more quickly than usual. She looks about the room at the people at the other table pretending not to watch them. She kicks him hard under the table as she pushes back her chair. He looks at her quizzically, finding it strange that she does not apologize. Then he reckons that she must have thought she kicked the table leg while moving to stand.

"I shouldn't have drunk so much from that spring. Will you excuse me for a moment?" She asks. She rises and heads for the door, closing it slowly behind her.

A soft laugh from a table across the room. A clinking of silver on ceramic. From the kitchen, a man carries a tray resting on his palm and shoulder, the plates on it covered in linen, a piece of flatbread protruding. He passes. The lingering smell of lentils. Leander's stomach grumbles.

Another server makes a line for their table. Their first course. The server squats, reaching to rest the tray on the table's edge. The man's tunic sleeve slides up, exposing momentarily the curled tail and segmented body of a scorpion tattooed on his forearm.

Leander grins, recalling a similar tattoo on the wrinkled arm of a wool-cloaked Dervish he met several years back. The old man enlightened Leander on the origin of the Dervishes' whirling dance, explaining how the twirling part of their Sama ceremony is performed as a means to enter the door of enlightenment.

Legend has it that the dance originated with the winding of wool. The tale is of the tradesman at his stool: the artisan's left hand pulling a strand of wool from the bale, whirling the wool into a thicker strand to his right hand, the right hand winding the wool around a large spindle in continuous motion, all the while chanting "la illaha illallah." The artisan was forced to be present in the moment because any irregular movement would break the string, requiring him to stop and tie a knot.

To the Sufi, this story was life. This was awareness. The highest plane.

Awareness. The scorpion. Leander's mind flashes to the Bedouins he saw cutting the zilla plant, heating its thorns in the fire and pricking the skin to create the image of that animal on their arms and backs. Then the dead Bedu near Mansura, a damaged broadsword left stuck through his bare chest, impaling the big scorpion etched on his skin. "They think those scorpion tattoos protect them from evil. Didn't work for this one," Sedat had said with a smirk.

Evil. The scorpion. Awareness.

A lurch. A glint from under the tray. Leander's hand already on the grip of his boot-stowed dagger. He backslashes the tattooed arm. A scream and the Bedu's thin blade falls silently to the rug. A crash of plates and silver. The man doubles over, holding his gashed forearm. A second and third Bedouin charge out from the kitchen, one with a butcher knife. Not enough time to make the door.

Jacinta! Where is she? Having already eyed the shutters, Leander sprints five steps and launches himself through the low window. A smash, splinters. Pain in his shoulder. He rolls to his feet. Jacinta. He looks both ways down the alley and sees no one. She must be still squatting, or heard the commotion and has hidden. She will be safe for now. She will realize there is trouble and stay away.

A bang as the door slams open against the block wall.

They follow. Run. Now.

He sprints toward the mouth of the alley. A look behind. The smallest of the Bedu pulls away from a slower one. Leander turns the corner, arms pumping. Maybe only one set of steps behind him now. Why is he running? He could kill this armed man easily, even without a weapon. No. Run anyway, the others may be trailing. If they want him dead, there may be even more of them, who knows where.

Past the shuttered shops and empty vendor carts and stalls picked clean.

He turns a corner, slipping, regaining his footing. Past the slanted timbers mounted into the mud walls, past the stalls with roofs of stretched cloth. Past the empty tables, where the scents of old fish and spoiled fruit are pumped into his lungs and quickly exhaled. Past the cooking pots turned upside down to dry. Past the empty hooks, which in the morning will hold blankets of every color and design, whether he survives tonight or not.

He ducks into an alley and hides behind a barrel. No footsteps. Leaning back against a smooth-blocked wall, he fights to control his breathing. With chin protruding and lungs burning, he forces deep, slow breaths. Quiet. Complete silence. Your life depends on it.

He listens. Boot stomps, heavier, slower than before. They clomp nearer and then past the entrance and further down the street. He reaches down to his own leathers to check his dagger.

In time, he rises and peeps around the corner. Nobody. Clear the other way. It was the Salihi. Those amirs on the hill. Has it come to this?

Jacinta. He must go back for her. They would kill her just for being with him. No, go to the island—grab Slap, Binny. Fuck this place up. No. No time for that. Think. Think. He must go back now and find her, in case she does not know and goes back into the restaurant. He pulls his dagger. Be prepared to fight in the restaurant.

In his head, he hears Amir Duyal's warning in formation. "I don't recommend going out into town alone anymore."

He grits his teeth. His gut tells him to get back to the island and stay away from the restaurant.

He sprints toward it anyhow, back east, circling in from the other direction. His eyes dart left and right as he passes the side streets. He leaves the stone walkway and stays to a dirt path, where his boots will be quietest. Nearing the restaurant, he slows to a walk, catches his breath. Voices. He stops. An argument.

He sneaks along a wall and slides under a vendor's stall, quietly pulling some canvas atop him. The smell of cumin and cilantro.

"Amateurs?! Maybe if you'd followed the plan and stayed at the table to distract him, we'd have been able to do our job." One of the Bedouin.

"You couldn't even wait a bit to piss?" Another of the men.

"Plan? You didn't ... " She breaks into tears. Jacinta.

Leander rocks his head back against the stone wall, digging his skull into the edge of the rock.

"Right—cry! We had one chance and blew it. You go back to Qutuz and sob your version of our failure," the Bedu says.

"I'm gone," the other says. "Soon the Bahri will be hunting us both down, now until forever."

Two sets of footsteps depart, the padding of their soles soon becoming inaudible.

Leander closes his eyes and buries the handle of his dagger under his lower jaw. He leans on it until he feels the intended dull pain. "Fool. You should've known," he murmurs to himself.

He stays there with his head between his knees. When the area has been quiet for nearly an hour, he crawls from under the slanted table and takes a looping route back to the citadel, an emptiness filling him. Naiveté. The restaurant, the entire staff must have been planted. The infirmary. Her sweet smile. Their talks. All of it horseshit, all of it a setup. All of it planned so that he would get close to her. All so she could pull intelligence from him.

Fool. He never had a chance with her. Her rich father. Like her class of Egyptian would ever allow a union between them. He had been stupid. He knew better. Dreaming. That face, those eyes, her words—all of it had fooled him.

He must have proven himself no longer useful to her. Why him? Why so much trouble to take out just a lowly Bahri trooper? What of value had he really told her?

But why did she not stay to help finish him off? Why was she crying? Willing to be an accomplice, willing to drag him along for years, yet not able to stomach watching the final deed? Maybe.

He grinds his teeth. Horseshit. She knew her business— never had any interest in him. He cuffs himself across the head. And again. Tears well in his eyes. A fool. Even now, almost skewered, just a fool.

CHAPTER

30

Leander
Bazaar, Cairo
December 10, 1253

"So how long will it take you to make a new one?" Leander asks the grubby-aproned man.

The smith slides a slab of wootz steel into the coals and then steps away from his scorching fire. With hands on hips, he studies the fractured lance head on his blackened table and then at the stack of work to his right—a heap of oblong yoke clevises, pole rings, and bent door hinges—some laid on scabbed shelves, other lying in disorder on the dusty ground. He rubs a filthy sleeve across his sweating face, raises his eyebrows, "Ah, six, seven days."

"All right. And same price as before, right?"

"Yes, same price."

"And don't forget the puppy engravings," Binny says. "You remember my friend likes the little puppies. On both faces of the lance head."

The smith turns to Leander, a confused look on his face.

Leander looks down and chuckles. "Haven't you learned to ignore him?"

The smith scrunches his brow.

Leander sighs, tilts his head towards Binny, and speaks to the smith in his native tongue. "He's full of shit."

The beefy-armed smith smiles and nods, pulling his long tongs from the worn peg on the wall.

Binny grins. "If you're going to offend me, at least keep it in Turkish so I can defend myself."

Leander shakes his head and then winks to the smith. "Until later, my friend," Leander says.

They stoop under his cinder-burned awning and step into the street.

He squints, peering through the dust at the bright street bustling with traders and shoppers. He freezes, his heart seeming to skip a beat. There, across the street. Her shining dark hair and sad eyes. She waits for them.

Binny sees her, too. "Ah, there she is, the girl of your dreams. One day the mother of the Baby Frank."

"Let's get out of here," Leander says, feigning nonchalance.

Binny looks at him sideways.

She walks up to them. "Please, can we speak?" she says to Binny, her eyes pleading for him to leave.

Leander casually looks up and down the street and then behind him.

"Sure," Binny says. He flashes Leander a coy smile. "I'll see you at dinner."

They watch the lanky man stroll away. Leander moves to the side of the road, where he places his back to a stucco wall. She follows him. He checks her for obvious bulges in her clothes, looks around for anything out of the ordinary, and then sets his eyes on what shows of her veiled face, a profound sorrow coming over him. He places his hand on the pommel of his sword. "You come alone—should I inspect the area for throat slitters?" Leander asks.

She meets his gaze, her eyes water, and a tear follows the seam of her nose.

"Is this part of your instruction?" he asks. "Did Aybeg teach you this at his school for assassins—tears as a way back into your prey?"

"Stop it. I know what I did was unforgiveable. But you don't understand the truth of it. It's complicated."

"No, it's simple. Very simple," he growls, constraining himself to keep his voice down, his eyes darting about the place.

"I was forced into it, trapped. I tried at every step to prevent it, but could not. Why else would I come alone right now?"

"You think I could trust anything you say now?"

"Yes."

"Please. Save your words." He continues to look about him. He expands his search to the slanted roof across from them and then down to street level, to the buyers who paw through the contents on the carts, the women who fondle the fresh goods, and those who carefully scoop the spices from wooden bins.

Sensing nobody behaving strangely, he stares at the smooth skin on her face, the puffiness about her eyes looking so out of place. Again, a wave of gloom moves through him. "Why do you come here?"

"Because I love you," she says, her eyes begging.

"Love. Hiring out those Bedu goons to slay me—that's the way you show love?"

"I hired no one. Listen to me. It was your patron himself who hired *me*—al-Salih."

A fire ignites in his belly. Leander scowls. "Don't soil his name with more of your lies."

She wipes her tears and looks both ways before meeting his eyes. "Please, listen. Al-Salih asked me only to listen to the men's talk in the infirmary—to let him know which I thought were most faithful, which were deserving of more reward. I felt it a way to do more for Egypt than simply binding her soldiers' wounds. My father suggested this arrangement."

Leander looks at her, unbelieving.

"It's true. I loved al-Salih as you did. He was like my grandfather. We'd chat over tea. I looked after him some when he was sick. Our private talks were of nothing more than who I detected were the best of his dutiful. I had nothing but good words about you. Your patron died knowing that you were among his finest."

A tear comes to Leander's eye. "Don't. Don't speak of my father. Don't distract, to lessen the evil in your deed."

"All I did was try to spare you." She pauses and takes a deeper breath. "Aybeg. When Aybeg came, things changed. I tried to leave. He wouldn't let me. He was obsessed with information on those disloyal to him. I tell you truthfully, he wouldn't let me quit, kept drawing me deeper into his ploys. I feared what he'd do to me if I resigned. I feared what he'd do to my family if I left town. I didn't want to go to that restaurant."

"Very noble. So, you'd have me and others killed to keep you and your family safe?" he asks.

"No." She surveys both sides of the street. She lowers her voice, the tears returning to her eyes. "Of course not. They assured me in the end that they would only apprehend you—that there'd be no weapons. That you wouldn't be hurt."

Leander shakes his head. "Right. No weapons. And the Bahri are famous for surrendering to unarmed cooks."

His eyes go back to the rooftops, places where a crossbowman might deploy. "How could you possibly think that I wouldn't kill you right here? It's not like I have to worry about the command chucking me in the hole."

"Because you love me, too."

He looks away. She is right and knows it. He is stupid, a perfect subject for the skilled infiltrator—no smarter than a thick-skulled boy with two bandaged hands who would again touch the red-hot coals.

He becomes disgusted with himself. She knows his every weakness. "If you're worried that I've alerted the command, fear not, I've told them only of your Bedouin friends. Not you. Your spy cover is still solid. You can continue pretending to be a nurse."

"I *am* a nurse and never wanted what Aybeg would have me be."

"Uh-huh. If you're here to protect yourself and are troubled that my mates will be stepping out of shadows with swords to spill your guts, you needn't be. For some stupid reason, I haven't told them, either."

She looks at him, unaffected. No sign of relief at his words. Only grief on her face, deep, like that of a widow at her husband's funeral.

"You think that I'd be here if I didn't half wish that to happen? I came only to say that I love you. As long as the Salihi leave my folks alone, I care very little now what happens to me."

He searches her face for a sign of deception, but can find none. He does not know what to make of her or her visit and is baffled as to why he feels sorry for her. A disgust inside him again rises—not with her, but with himself. Somehow, he believes her. Dumb! He is simply dumb. He won't let it happen.

"Well, I have to leave."

"All right." She looks down and then up with that child face.

No. He will not let that look work. He again studies those around him, looking for the odd man in any attire who could be concealing a weapon. His eyes flit from flat roof to flat roof. Without turning back, he steps off in the opposite direction that he took on the way in and takes a different, wider path home. He walks in the middle of the road, keenly attentive, his fingers flat against his scabbard, trying to ignore the ache that expands in his heart.

CHAPTER

31

Ox
Citadel, Cairo
January 8, 1254

Ox shakes his cupped paws, grinning, the chunk of bone clunking inside the giant cavern made of his palms and callused fingers. He looks up to Allah and then across to his remaining competitor at the table.

"You know, I threw this same bone as a child on the steppe— can't remember a time I lost with it."

Chuckles from five other guards standing about them, those already eliminated from the game, chums from Aybeg's personal bodyguard of Mamluks, the Muizziyya.

"I'm dead serious," he says.

"Yes, my Amir. I don't doubt that," the Mamluk grumbles.

Ox raises his eyebrows playfully, while sweat droplets brew upon the forehead of his final opponent.

Ox whispers to the rattling ankle joint. "Old camel side, just bring Ox home." He lowers his hands, feigns a release, and then brings his lips back to his knuckles. "Old camel, step on the goat, step on the back of that unlucky goat."

Half-hearted laughter fills the room and a sigh of frustration escapes from his young challenger at the table.

He lets loose the old relic, its faces covered in hairline cracks like a broken eggshell. It tumbles across the wooden slab, between the stacks of dinars littering Ox's side of the table. All eyes now on the yellowed bone, it settles with the thick side down, the signature hump of bone upward, the camel side. The goat side of the bone, bearing a single cavity, faces the loser in an almost taunting fashion.

A roar of hilarity from the men at the ogre's unfailing good luck. "Ox!"

The Mamluk across from him buries his head between crossed arms.

Ox shrugs and pretends to yawn, as if expecting this outcome all along. His challenger sits back, shaking his head in disbelief, as he watches half of his month's pay being pulled away in one swoop of the large man's hands.

Ox holds up the bone, admiring its smooth surface and rounded edges polished from the oil of hundreds of hands over the years. "By Allah, I told you only fools agree to compete when she's involved. Magic." He brings it to his thick lips and kisses it while simultaneously stuffing the dinars into his open pouch.

He grabs the shoulder of the youth, who now has his head in his hands. "You're just off the tit, my little brother. Worry not—you still have many years to make those dinars back. You should feel good about passing your share on to an old, grizzled member of the flock."

Three taps on stone from the toe of the door guard's pike. Two men lift the table, placing it back to its regular position. Mamluks stash their bones in pockets and pretend to be preparing their gear. Ox secures the flap on his pouch.

Amir Qutuz, the sultan's second-in-command, passes through the doorway. The vicegerent appears flawless, with chiseled facial features, a meticulously trimmed beard, and battle kit that would pass any inspection, from the shine on his red-lioned helmet to the edging on the soles of his boots.

"On your feet!" Eight Mamluks snap to attention.

Qutuz takes in the room. "Carry on. He'll be here soon. It's time to make the final preparations."

The men snatch shields from the rack along the wall and snug sword belts around waists.

Ox cinches the last buckle on his arm guard, looking down at the sulking Mamluk. "No pouting. I'll soon give you another chance to lose more."

"Yes, my Amir," the young Mamluk moans.

Ox's detachment assembles about the senior amir. Qutuz brushes a fleck of lint from a Mamluk's coat and gives the others a final look. "We've been over it three times. Any final questions about anything related to the reception?"

The men look at one another with stone faces, their eyes finally resting on Qutuz's.

His fiery eyes burrow into each them. "Be sharp," Qutuz says. He looks to Ox. "Go over them over once more and then down to the courtyard."

"Yes, my Amir," Ox says.

His men form a single rank and Ox makes his way through each, mindlessly checking gear that he already knows is ready. He inspects for any strains in their chain mail hauberks, any loose or damaged scales on the cuirasses, allowing his mind to wander.

He wonders if any duty will satisfy him. Maybe he is just too long at this trade. He's been promoted, even assigned a small fief in the north. His pay has been nearly doubled. His men are some of the best in the citadel. This is what he wanted. Yet he has become a little bored with the formal guard duty.

In some ways, he prefers the rough and tumble life of cavalry, where formal appearances and stuffy formations are swapped for execution on the battlefield. He should not complain. Certainly, no Mamluk dreads any duty more than these parades, heavy on the ceremony and the unnecessary primping of uniforms— standard when placed in close proximity to the sultan, such as today.

"Let's go. To your places—I'll meet you down there."

Ox walks the corridor and then up the boot-scuffed stairs leading to the parapets. Out the hatch. A blast of blinding sunshine against the white walls. The cloudless sky above. He passes his crossbowmen at their stations, past the archers in theirs. Reaching the western wall, he looks over the ledge, down the hill.

Amir Aqtay's formation of Bahri wind their way up the road, several hundred men on Arabians of gray and chestnut and black, the red-lioned pennant of their former master heading the dual columns, banners with red numbers on yellow delineating each amirate behind it.

Through rising dust, the sunlight flashes from the tack at the horses' mouths along the line and glints upon the tops of helmets, the only part of the Bahri headgear not wrapped in the signature yellow turban of their regiment. Even from a distance, Ox admires their red coats and the swirling pattern on their yellow trousers.

"You have to admit, they're a sight to behold," Ox says turning to a guard.

"They are, my Amir. I'm surprised Amir Aqtay even responded to our sultan's polite invitation."

"What civil man wouldn't appreciate the chance for two leaders to meet face-to-face and settle their differences?" Ox says, flippantly.

"Aqtay comes mostly to survey his new quarters."

Ox laughs. "I reckon so."

Ox, and likely most of the Muizziyya, are bewildered at Aqtay's audacity. First, his royal marriage to the beautiful daughter of al-Malik al Muzaffar, the Ayyubid Lord of Hama. With a princess of Saladin's blood in his castle and his racked-up battlefield victories, Aqtay is itching to be relieved of his assignment in Alexandria and take residence in the citadel, appropriate to his new status in life. Ox figures it is not so much a desire for regal treatment but rather an angle for Aqtay to place himself back within the eyes and ears of Aybeg's own Mamluks, where the opposing regiment can see who Aqtay thinks should really be leading the realm.

Closer now, the thumps of hoof reaching up the wall. Now able to make out their unit flags, Ox sees that the amirates are a mix from Alexandria and those Aqtay ordered to stay put at the River Island Citadel. Spread throughout each amirate are men whose company he shared when he first arrived at the Hisn Kayfa citadel back in 1236—men he slept, ate, fought, and bled alongside. Sadly, the bond of the old Salihiyya in its entirety seems to have died with their old master.

Amir Aqtay halts his columns at the bottom of the hill. Four commanders ride to the front of the formation, where they apparently confer with the Bahri's leader. One leader returns to his command in the formation, while the other three continue speaking with Aqtay.

"Amir Aqtay. You went to the trouble of dragging them all here. Come on in," Ox says.

"We didn't spend a week prepping our uniforms and gear for you to turn around now," the guard adds.

Finally, Aqtay breaks off the talks. He and another amir put their horses to the trot, the pair nearly bouncing in unison as they head uphill toward the citadel's western gate, while the remainder of the force stays in place.

"Very well," Ox says, turning to leave.

"Good day, Amir."

"Yes, it is."

Ox returns to the courtyard, joining three of his Mamluks in a side corridor.

The clops of hoof on dirt shift to clacks on stone as the pair of Bahri wind their way through the high-walled passage to the courtyard. Four guards pull open the metal-banded doors and both riders enter the wide space without breaking pace.

On cue, the musicians commence. Standing rigid with their timbal drums about their necks, they strike with open hands, alternately hitting the center of the drum head with the meat of their palms to produce the deep bass and then rapping the outer hoop to create higher-pitched sounds.

More Turks join in, their different-sized drums creating a formal beat, the instruments' calf skin stretched in varied tensions to produce a variety of tones, their complementary rhythms pulsing against the stone walls. The four-holed *chalil*, or pipe flutes, chime in, their cheery notes fluttering an array of pitches and intensities, producing a most agreeable atmosphere.

Ox chuckles. Music of this magnitude is not meant for an Amir of One Hundred. Such is warranted only when the sultan himself returns to his citadel. Aqtay halts, absorbing the scene. The square-jawed man smiles. He and the other amir dismount. Ghilman sweep in to take their horses. The doors behind them squeak slowly closed, followed by the unnoticed thump of the wood bar on the opposite side.

Sultan Aybeg, alongside his queen, rises to his feet. On this signal, the *chatzozerah*, or Middle Eastern trumpets, blare, adding an imperial sound to the mix, their volume purposely meant to be heard by the Bahri troopers down the hill. Attired also in his dress uniform, Aybeg, too, grins.

His commanders lock the bodies of their Mamluk formations, turning to face the Bahri with their polished swords at the present. Aqtay takes a step upon the wide swath of raked ground leading to the sultan and his queen, a gap made for him between the opposing Mamluk formations, his fellow amir by his side. A second step. A third.

Aybeg loses his grin and raises his right hand only slightly away from his side. The biggest of the kettledrums launch, men pounding their felt-tipped beaters in a militarized fashion upon the trio of leather heads surrounding them. The rich sound drowns out the other instruments, save the ear-splitting horns.

The hollow thumping of the kettledrums resounds, growing subtly in tempo and volume, until soon the heavy beat is hammering off the sheer walls, shuddering the ground beneath them. Fiercer now, the music goes belligerent, crashing into the lines of presented troops, booming and echoing against the bulwarks. A reckless thunder in the courtyard ricochets about the walls.

Aqtay drops his smile and narrows his eyebrows as he turns to the man beside him, the two still striding in step toward the new sultan. Just before the pair reach the entrance to the two-columned procession, Aybeg raises his left hand.

A swarm of arrows whiz in from above, men just now exposing themselves from behind the short walls of both parapets. From both directions, arrows fly in a crisscrossing squall of willow and maple and feather. Steel heads punch their way through the chain mail of the two amirs, the two men staggering.

The drums cease and the trumpets sound—the signal for Ox's team. The giant one glances around the column concealing them. From across the courtyard, four Mamluks from his reactionary force charge the surprised Bahri. Fueled on adrenaline, Aqtay and his mate meet the attacking men with drawn swords, ignoring the buried shafts which jut from their shoulders, backs, and legs at every angle.

Again, the pound of drums, louder now, muffling the clank of steel, heightening the dance of death playing out on the packed dirt between the Mamluk files.

Ox steps out from behind the partition. Seeing the Bahri engaged with his other men, he turns to his three Mamluks. "Now!"

They sprint toward the clash, the desperate Bahri now back-to-back, fighting off the first four Muizziyya. Already, the gold in Aqtay's trousers blotches with pocks of saturated red.

Ox digs hard and is the first to reach Aqtay while the amir is engaged with two others. In stride, Ox takes a massive diagonal stroke just above Aqtay's neckguard, the power of his strike nearly cutting the man in half and the two Salihi battling him spin away at the last moment. The other three faris move to Aqtay's companion, yet the blond-haired man is already done.

The eight men step back to the cheers of men in ranks. Aybeg raises both hands, causing the kettledrums to cease and the other musicians to again resume their more royal tune. Ox, too, raises his arms in triumph amid the trumpets' elegance, the horns masking the hails.

The sultan strolls down the human passage. Midway, he pulls his sword. The music hushes. Ox stares at the dead Mamluks, his heart thumping, the blood coursing through his chest in steady thumps, as that of the would-be sultan drains into the sand.

A tickle on Ox's fingertips. A slipperiness between his fingers on his left hand. He looks down at his arm. A sliced flap of mail hangs loose above his arm guard; blood oozes from his cuff. He had no idea that he had been cut. He forms up his men in front of the twisted corpses. Facing the approaching sultan, he salutes.

The music ends clumsily, as Aybeg reaches Ox's men. The sultan nods to them. Absently, he mutters, "At ease." Aybeg then kicks the helmet from Aqtay's head and winds the amir's blond hair around his hand twice. In one motion, he lifts Aqtay's hacked torso from the ground and comes across the man's neck with a mighty sword stroke. He rises with the skull gushing, Aqtay's lips still contorted from his struggle.

Aybeg rotates his wrist, giving a nonchalant glance at his enemy for the last time. He returns his bloody sword to its scabbard and calmly strides to the stairs of the western wall, the head trickling a line of crimson in the dirt, the cranium carried with the normality of a child lugging a killed hare by its ears to his mother's pot. Reaching the top stair of the parapet, he turns and raises the severed dome with a scowl, rotating the grizzled head for his entire regiment below to see.

His men roar, a blast of deep voices resounding against the thick stone walls.

Aybeg walks to the parapet, faces the Bahri outside the walls, and again lifts Aqtay's mug high overhead, the blood of his nemesis blending into the red sleeves of Aybeg's dress uniform. He crouches, lowers the head below his knees, and heaves it off the tower at the Bahri Mamluks below with a primordial shout. Again, a howl from his troops in the courtyard.

For a time, Aybeg watches the Bahri's reaction, his hands locked behind his back in satisfaction. Nodding, the sultan then raises his hand. A holler of commands and his men below move back against opposite walls.

Then, from the guts of the citadel, a reverberation, followed in an instant by the rumbling of hooves. A variety of browns and grays rush past them, the Arabians shrouded in scarlet and gold, their heads shielded in hard-leathered armor.

Pennants of Aybeg's Muizziyya flutter past, as well as those of the Nasiriyya and the Aziziyya—the men of al-Nasir of Syria who ditched their master and are now embraced by Aybeg, Mamluks yearning to prove their worth to their sultan. They rein in, slowing their horses before entering the bottle-necked corridor. Across the stone floor, the wild assemblage clap and skid their way through the corridor before spewing out the gate like a fountain toward Aqtay's men.

Qutuz joins Aybeg atop the wall, the pair watching in contentment as their forces give chase.

The din of hooves and clanging of tack gradually subside. Ox turns and dismisses his men. The stomped bodies of the Bahri amirs reappear as the dust settles, Aqtay's beheaded corpse pounded nearly flat by the Arabians' hooves.

Ox glances absently at his own wound. He takes a few deep breaths to encourage a draining of the adrenaline from his body. With his blood-greased hand still shaking, he struggles to center his sword tip into the scabbard. He jams it in, a clump of hair and tissue wadding atop the locket and across the quillion of his sword. He pulls up his arm guard to put pressure on the slash.

Mamluks have taken to the stairs and up to the high walls. He steps off to join them, his first two steps wobbly. En route, men pat his back as they pass him, yet he does not lift his eyes to acknowledge them. He trudges upward, his thighs burning as if he had walked all night, his purse jingling from the coins just won. He finds an open space on the parapet and peers over.

A vast haze of sullied powder to the south, where it appears most of the riders went. To his front, the chase of horsemen westward as dozens of Bahri make for the northern bridge and their stone refuge on the island. He rubs together his sticky fingers, the blood of a fellow Salihiyya Amir literally upon his hands. He has seen enough.

He turns from the chaos, walks down the stairs, and uses the wall as a crutch for his unsteady legs. With the clinking of coin marking his descent, a heaviness fills his heart, becoming weightier with each step he takes.

He halts, deliberating as to why. He has accomplished his mission; each of his men survived. If the sultan had any doubts about Ox before, they are surely gone now. Cenk said Aybeg wanted men "completely committed to him." Ox proved this today.

Men brush past him on the stairs. A wave of sadness comes over him. A shade of guilt. What will become of his old mates—Duyal and Singer and the rest? He thinks of them now. Old comrades. Decade-long friendships and long-time citadel training mates now forever pulled in opposing directions.

A profound regret seeps into him. The Bahri. His gut had told him that with the last of his brothers was where he wanted to be. This will never happen, now—and his own sword has been a direct cause of it.

Aqtay. Dead. Aqtay—one of the first Mamluk amirs that Ox and Duyal had ever seen back in the summer of 1236, upon first reaching the citadel in Hisn Kayfa.

The Kipchak youth sat mutely on the rows of benches, taking in the foreign squiggles of Arabic etched high into the blocked walls, trading glares with the other teenage strangers who had also passed the screening and were allowed to begin their training in the tibaq.

"On your feet!" the eunuch boomed, upon hearing the echo of boot heel on stone in the corridor from his station at the entrance.

Out of the darkness, a tall man burst through the passage and into the light, striding with a firm purpose, each step radiating an energy that practically illuminated every limestone rock he passed. His thick shoulders and v-shaped torso bulged, the muscles refusing to be hidden by his chain mail armor and covering tunic, his belt drawing attention to the slenderness of his waist and stoutness of his legs.

"Where do they find these guys?" Duyal asked.

"The same places they found us," Ox said.

The amir's jaw looked tight and unyielding, like the white blocks which magically lock together the arch he walked under. His eyes were somehow soft, and his complexion perfectly clear. He was handsome and seemed to hold back a grin. Ox could not quite place the aura that surrounded the man.

Safir, the black eunuch, smiled broadly at his boss's arrival. The strapping man halted in front of his new recruits.

"Kipchaks, be seated. My name is Amir Aqtay. I'm an Amir of Mamluks, in the service of al-Salih Ayyub, governor of Hisn Kayfa. I'm the commander of the training regiment. The prince has purchased each of you, and my sole mission here is make you into his warriors."

Raising his eyebrows, Ox grinned. He looked over to Duyal, whose jaw still hung open in awe.

Aqtay, dead by Ox's own sword. Money, women, prestige. Cenk, the queen, Aybeg. Ox had allowed it to happen; they had played him. Tears well in his eyes. Was he so shallow that he could be this easily manipulated by these desirous things?

Then, a shudder, as he pictures the face of his former patron and imagines the look he would receive from al-Salih, if his father were before him now. Aqtay, one of al-Salih's favorites, headless and trodden by hoof.

More Mamluks sweep past the wide-shouldered man on the narrow stairway, yet he hardly notices. His thoughts return to Duyal, his friend vastly outnumbered and scrabbling to get his men out of the snare. Duyal, his old mate from the days on the slave galley, now galloping for his and his brothers' lives.

Ox tries to blink a tear from his eye. Unnerved, he continues down the stairs, placing his bloodstained hand over his purse to quiet the clink of silver.

CHAPTER
32

Leander
Citadel, Cairo
January 8, 1254

"**B**y Allah," Leander says, looking up to the top of the parapet.

Their eyes follow his to the nearest tower. The sultan, Aybeg, in the red coat of the Salihi, hoists the Bahri commander's head above his own.

"The fuckers," Slap groans.

Aybeg hurls the severed head, sending it spinning in the air. Reaching its apex, the grisly dome seems to float for an instant, Aqtay's blond hair spreading like the beams from some fleeting sun—the man's final glow, an innocent expression on his face. From on high, the skull begins its descent, plummeting down the slope of the hill, its locks wrapping about the stub of his severed spine, covering their commander's eyes, as if Allah wished to mercifully spare Aqtay from witnessing the known outcome.

The Bahri sit their horses, dumbfounded, entranced by the surreal scene. The head dropping, dropping. Thirty paces from them, it lands with an unglorified thud, coming apart like a melon upon the rocky soil. A splattering of white and gray and red tumbles down the hill in chunks.

"Go, we go!" Amir Duyal yells, pointing back the way they came.

Dazed, Leander turns his mount and follows at the canter, the shock of it still sinking in. Near the base of the hill, horses bunch at a narrowing stretch in the road, no man wanting to push his Arabian into the bigger rocks and rough terrain off-path.

"Fourth Squad. Where the hell's Fourth Squad?" Duyal asks.

"Way up, way up," Sedat says. "Pushed in front of Baybar's unit."

Duyal grimaces, looking to the west, where nearly two hundred men spur for the northern bridge leading to their citadel, the farthest string of galloping riders already lost among the thick dome palms riverside. To their front, Amir Baybars looks back once more, unruffled, his sad eyes back up the hill to the bits of bone and gray matter that were his former commander.

He and Duyal had warned Aqtay not to go inside, knew that Aybeg and his Muizziyya could not be trusted, that their invitation was likely a ploy. Baybars' eyes widen.

"Look!" a Mamluk from behind them shouts.

All eyes return to the citadel on the hill. A dozen Arabians have already exited the gate, including Aybeg's Muizziyya, with the pennants of al-Nasir of Syria's men—the Nasiriyya and Aziziyya—flooding out behind them.

"Allah help us," Leander mumbles.

Still looking rearward, Baybars points left, guiding his unit south toward the cemetery road, the curved one eventually intersecting with the track bearing northeast into the arid region. At the cemetery road intersection, Duyal slows and steers his mount off the path and on to the rough rocks. His remaining three squads do likewise, as riders behind them push hastily past.

Some amirates follow Baybars down the southern road while others head back west to the River Island Citadel. Those men likely do not wish to test their Arabians against Aybeg's fresh horses, as some of the Bahri's mounts remain fatigued from their four-day journey from Alexandria.

Amirs scream orders, yet units become disorganized. Formations break apart, all the while a haze of dust slowly thickens about them.

Shouts become lost in the thundering hooves. Duyal looks to their stone house across the river, his amirate's estranged squad of ten now out of view, and then to the shifting brown cloud showing Baybar's way, its tail rising and curling eastward.

"This way!" Duyal says, crossing the rough ground to the southern path.

"My Amir, we don't have Fourth Squad! Fourth Squad!" a squad leader yells.

"Move! Move!" Duyal says, his eyes up the hill to the distant Muizziyya.

Some of the men do not hear Duyal's order, or outright ignore the command, pulling their mounts westward, perhaps not wishing to abandon their mates in the separated squad. Leander squints through the darkening veil until gradually he sees nothing, a lethargic fog of grime roiling about him.

Leander blocks out the din while the dirt fills his nostrils. He closes his eyes, an eerie silence filling his head. He sits oddly alone amid the mayhem, indecision gripping him. He licks his lips, the taste of chalk lingering, a burn in his lungs, hooves clattering atop the rugged stone as the horses try to regain their footing. A man coughs only a few feet away; another blows snot.

With the intersection now a screen of hanging dust, each man is able to decide his fate within his own private compartment of choking powder. Idle mares grow fretful in the murk, snorting, clinking their tack as they shake obstinate heads. In the distance, the unsettling beat of Arabians drumming the paths both south and westward, warning Leander of what must be determined.

What shall he do? He could make it to the safety of the island citadel, where plenty of the Bahri will be. From there, they could reorganize, but would there be war with the Muizziyya? And in preserving his own safety there for the short term, how could he live with himself in disobeying an order and ditching Duyal and the rest of his amirate?

Or will he go east with Baybars, Duyal, and the others into the brutal Sinai—as surely that is their aim? He pats his saddlebags. Two, maybe three, days of food in them. He checks the stoppers on each of his water flasks. His horse is fresh enough to make the run eastward, but to where, or whom? And with the Bahri split, how long could his brothers left on the island survive without the support of the entire regiment—especially if Aybeg laid siege to it? And what of Fourth Squad? A lump builds in his gut.

He grits his teeth. Decide. Just decide. You must decide.

He pulls Luna's head to the south and puts his horse to the walk, plodding forward almost blindly in the hazy murk. Hearing the three-beat canter of two horses coming up, he moves aside. Let them go. He will not break his horse's leg. He eases her back on the path. Up the hill behind him, the pound of a hundred horses—the Muizziyya—forced also to the walk by a lack of visibility.

Into the open, a waft of breeze kisses his cheek, stronger now, pushing the ashen blanket of soot across the path. The lay of the road and a gaggle of riders emerge. Go now. To the gallop.

He turns. No Muizziyya are on his trail—those men are still stuck in the dust. Soon, he catches some of the other Bahri. Together, they cover the distance quickly, past the mausoleums and tilted tombstones, past the stretch of ancient sycamores shading the worn track.

Leaving the last clump of trees, they finally bump into the tail end of main body, men slowing to the pace of the riders in front, those taking the "Y" in the road that heads east out of Cairo. Another glance behind. More Bahri stragglers, and farther back, a curtain of gray surely divulging a quickened pursuit by the Muizziyya and their allies.

What of Slap and Binny? He scans the backs of fellow riders, yet cannot pick them out. He hopes his mates are far to his front with Duyal and not those whom Aybeg's Mamluks close upon. He hopes his friends did not make for their citadel.

In twin files, they stay on the Via Maris—"the way of the sea," what the Mamluks call the "Great Trunk Road"—that ancient trade route heading northeast to the south shore of the Mediterranean.

In time, they put some distance between themselves and the Muizziyya, more and more of the Bahri trickling in, adding length to the columns of silent riders. These men do not search for brothers in their units, but rather stay in the order they arrive, perhaps out of a desire for some semblance of discipline among the turmoil.

To Leander's front, a Mamluk they call Singer rides beside Duyal. It appears this newly-promoted amir was separated from his entire Amirate of Forty and now rides alongside his old friend. Singer, a leader now without troops.

They ride into the afternoon. The formation is rejuvenated when ordered to the harness-jingling, three-beat gait of the canter and put into a state of half-slumber when required to back off to the mind-dulling pace of the walk. The amirs are systematic in their wish to put some distance between them and their pursuers without exhausting the horses.

Leander pats Luna on the neck as they slow to the walk. The formation settles to the squeak of leather on saddle frame, the jumbled chink of jointed bits. A tiredness sets in as the last of the adrenalin clears from his body. The rhythmic beat of hoof on beaten path and steady rock in saddle combine to make his eyelids heavy.

They ride between rolling fields of barley and wheat sown last month—young plants covering the flats and subtle hills in a fresh carpet of two-tone green on some of the immense plots owned by the fleeing amirs. Surely, they wonder if these fiefs will still be theirs when they return. If they return.

Baybars halts at a roadside canal, posting security elements to their front, rear, and flanks. Leander takes stock of the men: thirty-one from Duyal's Amirate Three, forty-two from Baybars' Amirate Seven and a remaining eighty-odd men from three or four other amirates separated during the confusion.

In silence, the men water their horses and fill flasks, sensible for the parched country on which they bear down. Canisters tipped up, they chug water, their eyes still drawn westward for any sign of the trailing foe. Leander, too, gulps the remaining water in his jugs and then refills them. Having drunk all that his stomach will allow, he clops his way up the column, looking for Slap and Binny.

Men cluster under any leaf of shade, many lying in the shadows beneath their horses. A thick powder coats the armor and weapons of the faris; soot fills the lines in their faces. The proud scarlet and gold of the Bahri is obscured in the drab taupe of the land, the dust masking even the colors of their beasts and their covers. Blond and red beards are coated a dull beige, each hair layered thick like ice on tree branches after a freezing rain. No man brushes this natural camouflage from himself or his mount, knowing that they remain the hunted.

Clay. Slabs of clay. Once again, he and his comrades have become no different than the blocks of riverside soil wrestled to the training tables by the ghilman, the mud wenches of the tibaq. Featureless blocks made ready for their sword training.

Of course, those many years past they had been molded, like clay, by their instructors—their bloodlines, education, personalities, peculiarities, prior accomplishments all having become irrelevant long ago, screamed and stomped and kicked out of them by the black-belted instructors. Back then, they were forged into one exact form of desired being, their body shapes and unacceptable thoughts pounded and sculpted and hardened into a more solid piece of scarlet clay.

But now, they seem to have taken on their more original form of mud. Back to that of the riverbank, bland and beaten and exposed to whatever the elements would make of them. Together, they comprise the clay of fellow prisoners, chained and bound together as one, judged for execution, united by a sentence of death, void of any recognizable shape—not clay crafted usefully into a plate or cup but just that of the ground to be pushed by the giant river, scorched by the glaring sun, and eroded by heavy rains.

Leander notices a thick-backed torso of brown rocking purposefully in the saddle. Beside it, the lanky frame of Binny. Tears come to his eyes. "Thank you, Allah," he says, closing on them. "By Allah, am I glad to see you two."

Binny smiles, a dark grit set in the gaps between his teeth. "See, Slap, I told you if he didn't defect to the Franj in Mansura, he wasn't going over to the Muizziyya this day."

Slap turns and grins, his pink gums contrasting with his dirt-covered face. "By Allah, the Papa Frank lives!"

Leander chuckles, reaches out and grasps the outstretched arms of his friends. He cannot remember being happier to see them. "Seems that Baybars has not had time to inspect his new followers, somehow allowing even you two laggards to ride with him."

They smile, their faces quickly returning to the grave expressions shared by the others.

"Never thought I'd see a day like this," Slap says.

"Like a bad dream," Binny says, picking the crust from the corner of his eye.

Slap's sway in the saddle grows wider. "Al-Salih's Mamluks slaughtering their own. Aqtay dead. Inside Saladin's own house— the very soldiers of al-Salih's enemy, the Nasiriyya. Our patron would be sickened by Aybeg, sickened by his sons."

"True," Leander says.

If their master could have imagined a worst case after his death, this would be it: his son Turanshah murdered by those most loyal to him, the principalities of Aleppo and Damascus ruled independently by his rival, al-Nasir, and now factions of al-Salih's prized force on the run, the rift between his once-unified Salihiyya sealed in blood.

The columns advance slowly without signal. Men remount.

Leander falls in behind his friends. More men join the column, having caught up during its stop. They take up the rear.

Soon the road empties into a vast plain. Ahead is nothing but the sandy flats of the desert, shouldered on either side by rugged mountains and wispy dunes. On the horizon, a backdrop of ominous black hovers over the blond landscape.

Amir Baybars leads the way into known country with their futures very much unknown. A bronze shroud skirts the expanse, where behind him two hundred-odd men follow the course of a wadi, their entrance into the scorching tan of the arid region.

Squad leaders direct their men to shed their armor and stow helmets. The troops lean forward, peeling off their scaled jawshans and chain mail hauberks from their backs, folding and stowing the heavy shirts in a manner allowing them to quickly redress if need be. They retie their turbans on the move, sparing material for extra wraps under their chins and around their necks and face. Men fortunate enough to have captured chameleons at the last stop now pull these creatures from pockets and place them inside the bowl of their turbans, the lizards agreeable with catching the tormenting flies landing on the riders' heads.

Silently, they push across the stony plains, leaving no tracks, their heads down and eyes half-closed to keep out the buzzing flies and blinding flashes glinting from the sand-polished hooves to their front.

They climb between towers of wind-swept dunes, the heat baking them, the horses laboring in the softer sand while the long-tongued chameleons snatch insects from the air. More Mamluks dribble in, adding length to the snaking columns.

Two pair of white ears crest an adjacent hill, erect and

cupped like a deer's. A peek over the top. Dark eyes, snouts pointed like the foxes from his homeland. Jackals, curious as to the strangers entering their territory, yet innately cautious, their slight chests and long legs still hidden by the dune. Two vultures circle high above, floating upon the currents, lazily following the riders. A distant yipping from the jackals, a signal to mates that the danger has passed. For them.

The riders push deeper into the desert, up through a section of mountain country, at times plowing through thick patches of menthol-scented samwa and beside groves of nabug trees, their fruit just starting to appear. They cross the remnants of a pillaged caravan, leather bags rotted and emptied. Three camels lie face down, their hulking, withered hides sucked between bleached ribs, their skin darkened as if charred by fire.

Leander takes to breathing only through his nose, both man and beast knowing they must conserve the moisture in their systems. Descending into a washboard of dunes, Baybars orders his unit to halt. He calls up his leaders, who confer. Word is passed down to the squad level.

Leander takes the last swig from his flask, his eyes searching eastward. Nothing but the pale expanse of the barren lands and juts of darker stone in the far distance. To the south, a shimmering sea of sand with hazy waves of heat wiggling clear to the skyline. A dark ribbon in the sky grows and skulks toward them, harboring far-off branches of silent lightning that surges streaks of stringy yellow into the vast blue-black.

Sedat rides over. "Binny, I'll drop back with your team as the rear guard to collect friendlies that straggle in, and see if we're still being trailed. Amir Duyal and the other two squads will stay up with Amir Baybars."

Binny nods.

Sedat leans on the wooden frame of his saddle, squinting what seems an assessment of the morale of his men. His eyes stay on Leander. "The Franj aren't looking so bad an outfit now, eh, Papa Frank?" Sedat says, only half-sarcastically.

All in his squad look at him.

"The Franj are beaten men. It's not ideal for us, but if forced to simmer in a shit pot, it may as well be with you bastards," Leander says, believing his own words.

Binny grins.

"Let's go," Sedat says.

They stomp off opposite the main body, Binny leading the team at a walk westward through the high ground they just passed, the sun still two fists off the horizon. Leander yawns, the stress of the day catching up to him. He attempts to swallow the parchedness out of his throat, but his saliva has gone dry. They head north toward a mountain which will afford them a view of the country westward.

Sedat's comment lingers. How would have things been if Leander had just stayed with the Franks, if he had survived LaForbie those years past and then Damietta and Mansura? Likely, he would have now been up in Acre near the king, waiting to go home to his family's little house in France.

There, he likely would have been promoted and gone back to Brienne's castle, where maybe they would have made him a crossbow instructor or urged him to upgrade his standing by pursuing a place in the chevaliers engage, the esteemed knights. Back to France, where there were still enemies, but none on his heels as they are here.

Foes. He has never felt more surrounded by them—the Crusaders to the north, Aybeg's Muizziyya and their allies behind them, al-Nasir of Damascus still brooding to the east, likely itching for revenge—and even farther east, the Mongols, whom he has heard contemplate a move southwest toward the rich cities of the Mediterranean. And for all he knows, maybe even the devil.

He looks at his brothers. Despite their fatigue, they ride high in the saddle, the slits in their turbans revealing puffy, sand-encrusted eyes that scan all directions. Their horses drag their hooves, some occasionally stumbling, through the shingle.

What could be filling his brothers' heads right now? For some, this escape undoubtedly takes them back to their childhoods, to another time when they fled for their lives as adolescents, remnants of their Kipchak towers—their tribes— fleeing the relentless Mongols. Surely Slap is thinking such.

All in the ranks must ponder the long trek to the Black Sea as boys, the captured ones on forced journey, all things known in their lives changed forever. Back then, they trod with Mongol bows trained at their backs, behind them their gers trampled, their towers' herds butchered or driven away. At best, they were forever separated from their families on the steppe. At worst, they had just buried their siblings and parents.

Today, only the type of hinterland they traverse is different from that youthful memory. The scenario is all too similar. Their leader murdered. Their wives, friends, homes, and fiefs back in Cairo are either dead, gone, or in grave risk of being lost. These early wounds as teenagers—healed through years of pride in Mamluk cohesion, love of brothers, and steadfast obligation to their father-figure, al-Salih, and their commander, Aqtay—have been violently reopened, their worlds again turned upside down.

Reaching the reverse slope of the big hill, they ease their horses through some scrub, hoping to break their outline as they glance over the crest.

In the distance, a haze mushrooms on the western skyline, then drifts crossways in the wind. Closer to them, breaching a knob of dune, a dab of yellow. A flutter—Aybeg's banner. His vanguard. Leander and the others slowly back their horses.

"By Allah, they still give chase," Binny says.

A spit of rain taps the back of Leander's hands, his only exposed skin. The breeze picks up. He looks skyward. The band of black engulfs the sun, begins to swathe the blue above them.

"Let's get back," Sedat says, falling in behind Binny's men.

They turn their horses eastward and put them to the gallop on a new route to better intercept the main body's progress, the rain now pecking their cheeks. Back over the hills and across a sandy wadi they ride, past pillars of dark rock rising from the earth, some looking like mounds of bubbling wax half-melted from the scorching sun. Ahead, jagged rock hems in both sides of the craggy path, its stacked layers cracking and crumbling.

Before entering the canyon, Leander glances over his shoulder. Sedat has dropped back, the man off his horse.

"Keep going, I'm going back for him," Leander says to Slap, pointing.

"Quickly," Binny says.

Leander finds Sedat standing with his horse's head resting on his shoulder. The animal groans, his right front hoof held off the ground, the leg hanging half-crookedly, swollen at the animal's forelimb, just above the knee.

Sedat looks up with tears in his eyes. He shakes his head.

"It's terrible, but we must go. We must go." Leander hops off his mount, securing his reins to a shrub. He begins to unbuckle Sedat's saddlebags and stowed weapons.

"We have to leave her. If they cross our tracks, they'll be on us soon."

Sedat nods. "Nine years, she's been with me."

"I know. Baybars has a few remounts." Leander flings Sedat's saddlebags across the front of his saddle while Sedat removes the last of his armor.

"Lead my horse forward a little and I'll finish the work here. I know you don't want her to suffer," Leander says solemnly.

Sedat frowns and the two men trade positions, Leander immediately caressing the animal's forelock.

Still petting her, he pulls the dagger from his boot, hiding his action under her girth. "I'm sorry, girl. So, sorry." Raindrops plop atop his head, water dribbles down his back. A turn to confirm Sedat is out of view. He slides his hand down to the horse's chin, grasps it tightly, and with his other, brings the dagger deeply across the horse's throat latch. The horse rears. Leander pushes her away and runs without looking back, hastily wiping the dagger on his sleeve.

He finds Sedat securing the last of his things to the saddle. Leander mounts. Reaching down, he grasps his Amirate Leader's forearm and pulls the man upon the croup of the horse. As he does so, the clouds release their load, the rain pelting them, soaking quickly through their coats and tunics.

"Thanks for coming back. If you hadn't, I ... " Sedat looks woeful, his coat shrouded in a layer of fine mud, streaks of the same coursing down his hollow cheeks and into his beard.

"Of course. There is no other way," Leander says.

CHAPTER
33

Leander
Western Sinai
January 11, 1254

Leander rides slumped over his reins, his grip loose, his torso pitching forward on each of Luna's front hoof strikes. His lips are cracked, matching the splits at nearly all of his fingertips. Through the dense fog, he stares at the back of the rider before him, the soiled scarlet and gold of his regiment.

The last few days blur together in his mind.

Their winter wools had dried quickly, the sun scorching them after a day and a half of rain. The muddy coating on their uniforms had then fractured and peeled off in hunks as they rode, taking him back to his favorite mountain stream in France. There, such empty husks rode the surface film of the river alongside molted mayflies, reborn and bouncing atop the current, drying their new wings after they emerged from the stone bottom, the bugs launched for the first time, their old life underwater over, their new life in the air just beginning. New life. Flying away from all they knew.

But the sunshine was short lived and a dense fog crept in

behind the rain, blanketing the desertscape for the past two days. They have fled northeastward on the Great Trunk Road for four days now. They rode through the first night, shivering in the cold rain. They spent the second night on the east bank of the narrow salt channel, which empties the Red Sea and Great Bitter Lake into the Mediterranean. Baybars had insisted on putting the canal to their backs as a line of defense against the pursuing Muizziyya and the Nasiriyya, even though the relentless showers had washed away the Bahri's tracks and the ensuing fog had at times limited their vision to the distance of the riders beside them.

With every flask empty, the men spread their oilcloths upon the ground, sucking in the collected rainwater until so tired they collapsed, pulling the covers atop them. They slept huddled in twos and threes in a useless attempt to get warm.

They awoke to word from their scouts that the Muizziyya and Nasiriyya had turned back to Cairo, likely unwilling to split their own forces to regain the Bahri's trail. That morning, four horses were dead and another three animals refused to get up, those Arabians having not properly recovered from their long ride from Alexandria prior to starting this unplanned exodus.

All seven horses were butchered, stripped into thin slabs of meat, and draped over the blood-reddened rumps and shoulders of every living mount to dry—fly-covered ribbons hanging like soggy battle streamers along the flanks of their Arabians. When they reached a camp of Bedu horse traders, Baybars depleted his purse in buying remounts for the seven men plus Sedat, and promised a dear sum in the future for the three camels he acquired.

Knowing that there were no reliable waterholes all the way to the base of the Bardawil Pennisula—and being familiar with the supply stashes, due to his time fighting in Gaza—Baybars made for Aqtay's water cache. Once finding the leather cases, hidden in caves, the Bahri filled their flasks and dumped some upon rock depressions, makeshift troughs for their thirsty horses.

They strapped the last six water bags to the camels and tacked these slower movers onto the rear of the formation. Yet once they reached the softer sand of the Sinai country, the horses were little faster than the camels.

Luna snorts, breaking Leander's spell of indolence set by the weary drag and clomp of hooves on sand.

The windless sky dims, filled with minute particles of moisture hanging thick and lifeless. The damp smell of horse and reek of filthy men wafts through the formation. He wipes his hand across a sleeve dotted with specks of water and licks his palm. He reaches down and shakes his empty flask, absurdly hoping that new water will somehow appear in it.

The dual columns continue mindlessly. Baybars following the hoof-pounded trade route, his flank, rear, and front security—elements normally stretched out to the limits of visibility for miles—now being close enough to touch, for fear of becoming disoriented in the mist.

The rider to his front jerks to a halt. Luna bumps her head into the thigh of his horse. The men around him dismount, most hanging on to the pommel and cantle of their saddles with each hand and lowering themselves gingerly to the sand. Cringing, Leander removes each boot from its stirrup, allowing his sore knees to slowly straighten. For the last two days, since arriving to the looser sand, Baybars has ordered the men to rotate riding and leading their horses, not wishing to further stress fatigued animals.

The tread of men and beasts. The hoof clops from camels and horses intermix with the tired boot scuffs of the men. Yelps on the sand, merge with the multi-pitched clanks of tack. Beside their own prints, he makes out the rounded edges of tracks from other men who had done the same, old evidence from other sapped riders next to their beasts, traders who were pushing eastward for coin and a known destination. Perhaps only Baybars knows where these Bahri go. And what does he have to offer in trade? Nothing but spent soldiers, so sick already of killing and being killed.

He buries his face in Luna's sodden mane and rubs her forehead. "Good girl," he says.

They walk in silence, darkness beginning to overtake the gray fog. No ribbing, no small talk. Not a scrap of laughter in either column, just each man and his animal quietly enduring their own misery. He knows the Bahri in their entirety are suffering when the chatter ceases completely.

His boots begin to feel as heavy as a pair of anvils. The tendon along the back of his left foot burns with each step. He fights off the cramps in his hamstrings and tries to think of better times, of peaceful things.

Jacinta's clear face leaches in to his mind. The crash of waves on the beach. A stolen kiss. Her hair in the wind. He feels a stab in his chest as his heart recollects what his brain forgets— that the one who had brought him tranquility and something to look forward to for so long had ultimately betrayed him. He knows he is a fool for still loving her. Regardless of her effort at reconciliation, he could never again trust her.

He stayed mute on her involvement during that night they had tried to kill him, had only told the command that it was the Bedu. Despite her treachery, he could not stomach the thought of her being pursued by the Bahri's own spies. Perhaps his silence is just the continuation of his own ignorance, his own weakness showing through.

Al-Salih's Mamluks had been trained in the tibaq to know the way of the infiltrators, lectured to by the eunuchs about traitorous Mamluks who committed their deceit because of their love of clever women. Then, when learning that their lovers had been moles, these duped Mamluks still believed the women spies would wait for them and marry them if the command spared the guilty their executions. "A talented woman spy is shrewder than a wolf and twice as ruinous—steer clear of the women in town who pretend to idolize you, who cannot hear enough of your work," the leather-faced eunuch had said. Skilled women. Jacinta had been one them. She had tricked him utterly and stolen his heart in the process.

In the back of his mind, he wonders if her words at the bazaar were true. Maybe, but doubtful. She was too smart to make any mistakes, too savvy to become emotionally attached. Expert moles do the trapping, they do not blunder into traps themselves. He is still a fool. Like the deceived Mamluks in the eunuchs' stories, he still believes that she really did love him and that she still loves him.

He grins cynically, further splitting the dried fissures on his lips. Look where you are, jester! Regardless of her true feelings and even if she loved you, you are destined to become nothing but a dwindling memory to her. A close call averted.

What does it matter? Who knows if he will ever see Cairo again, much less Jacinta's face. He scolds himself for the self-pity he feels. Many men in these columns have it worse—wives and young ones left fatherless and vulnerable to Aybeg's wickedness in Cairo.

Selfish. He should have informed the command, especially after learning of the other two assassination attempts on Bahri amirs that same night. Would knowledge of the coming attack have kept Aqtay from going into Aybeg's house? Probably not. Their leader had grown overconfident since his victories on the field and marriage to the princess. Did Aqtay really think Aybeg would someway *share* the sultanate with him?

He notices some lameness in Luna's gait. He pinches the skin on her neck above the point of the shoulder. He pulls out, twists it slightly and then releases. The skin forms a tent, staying longer than it should before flattening out. His horse needs water—now.

Just as last night, no long shadows fall upon the crags and wide valleys here. No brilliantly colored sky will buoy their spirits. There is only a darkening of the mist until they can see nothing. He looks forward to stopping for the night, yet worries if they will be able to find a waterhole in this weather.

They tread into the dark, a bone-chilling breeze blowing across them depositing dribbles of water on his cheek. He licks the moisture from his lips. Steadily now and stronger, the vapor pushes through the formation, as if they walk in the clouds. He sneers at the incongruity—that they walk through an infertile hell that feels at this moment like the misty access to heaven. To complete the illusion, he looks up to God. Above them, the cloud begins to thin. To the east, a faint orange light parts the murk just above the horizon.

"By Allah," a man ahead murmurs, as moonlight spreads to the north, divulging the westward base of the Bardawil Peninsula and the thin arm of water that marks the westward shore of Lake Bardawil.

Soon, a brilliant glow of auburn punches through the haze. After nearly four days of fog and rain, the scene takes his breath. Some men chatter. There is a laugh from mid-formation. An injection of tempered optimism sweeps through the ranks, the men knowing that nearby is the first of the waterholes in the area.

The clouds break in earnest, casting ginger sparkles upon the lake's saline waters. The sight is simply beautiful. A waning moon, three quarters full, wispy clouds passing its face on occasion. It illuminates a sky mostly clear of cloud and below it, the scrub-speckled hills on either side.

Baybars orders their security elements pushed out in every direction. They mount their horses. Now visible to the others, most of the Mamluks straighten their posture in the saddle as the radiance from the rising moon intensifies into a golden yellow. They ride.

A man from the forward security team rides back at the canter. The formation halts. He excitedly reports to Baybars. Down the line, the men pass that the tops of many date palms were spotted and that the forward security element were conducting a reconnaissance of the area. Date palms mean water. They have found the oasis. Leander trades a half-smile with Binny, neither man willing to smile fully to widen the cracks in their lips.

The columns drop into a basin. Baybars and the other Mamluks eye the habag mixed in with the short grass in the bottom, the horsemint growing thicker as they move east. A gurgle of water chugs from the base of a rock; a small pool trails a thin stream into the desert. From the brush, an old camel is roused to its feet. The men are quickly upon it, their ropes cast around its neck and feet.

Baybars halts the column, exchanges a few words with his leaders and then signals for all the men to gather about him. A solemn grin takes his face, as he takes in the condition and mood of those around him.

"We'll send a small vanguard west, just to confirm the Muizziyya have turned back, that they do not circle around. We'll set out security, camp here, and then continue on tomorrow."

Leander eyes the hollow. The gully is large enough to conceal the horses, the rock outcroppings surrounding them appear sufficient to muffle their noise. There is a circular plateau, flat ground, where the horses can be hobbled and the men can sleep. Baybars' words resonate, Leander unsure if they are made acoustically pure by the rock encircling them, or if it is simply the nature of the man's voice and the confidence it conveys.

Baybars grins. "No long faces, my brothers. Feel no shame in our fleeing, for was not Islam's first refugee, our Prophet Mohammad, forced to leave Mecca and take refuge in Medina? In this instance, we follow his lead. Recall the Prophet when you shut your eyes this night and remember what he later rose to accomplish. We may have lost Aqtay, but by evading now, we live to fight another day. We live to right this wrong."

Many Bahri nod. Some reflect with crumpled brows.

The men turn to, removing saddles and flopping soaked horse blankets over shrubs and rocks to dry in the wind. Men shamble on stiff legs, collecting deadwood from under acacia trees, which occupy the bottom. The found camel is slaughtered and skinned, its blood poured into a gut bag. With limited wood about them, in the way of the Kipchak, several men make a hide bag from the camel's skin, filling it with water and chunks of meat from the creature. From one communal fire, they heat rocks until glowing hot, toss them in the bag, and seal it to steam and boil the meal.

Teams of men lead horses to the waterhole, one squad at a time. Men drop to their knees and gulp the water, some nearly nose-to-nose with their mares. One of Baybars' men walks over to a group of twenty Mamluks who have been separated from their units. He finds the wounded man he seeks and dresses the gash across the stranger's arm.

Leander pulls the wooden stake and hobble from his saddlebag. He holds the leather strap at its end, drops the stake, and lets it spin until all the cord unwinds from it. He drives it into the hard ground at an angle with a rock and secures the leather-tied cinch on his horse's right front and rear pasterns, below the fetlocks. Removing his saddle and blanket, he then rubs Luna's back and loin to increase circulation.

The other men also tend to their horses, picking rocks from their hooves and paying particular attention to those Arabians who hang their heads and flatten their ears. Three Mamluks gather about a beast, which now stands uncomfortably, shifting its weight nearly continuously. With most of the animals too tired to eat, men take the last of their grain from bags and roll it into little balls, moistened with a few drops of water from the spring. They feed their animals by hand, stroking the horses' necks.

Duyal signals that it is their turn at the water. They limp to the pool. Leander splashes water on his face, cups his hands and drinks. The first gulp enters his parched throat painfully. Again and again, he drinks. He feels the liquid's immediate effects—his body soaking up the moisture like a sponge, clearing his head and energizing him. He fills his flasks.

Soon, bloody-handed men move between the groups of men, distributing perfectly-cooked camel meat. Smiles and words of gratitude among them. Several Mamluks pick the plume-shaped leaves from the horsemint plants and move around the camp, offering handfuls for men to use to flavor their tea. Without being ordered to do so, men dump their rations into a community pile. Squad leaders redistribute dried meat and the remaining bits of fire wood. Tiny cook fires begin to flicker.

By unit, they spread out their blankets and oilcloths. Leander looks up at the clear sky, the stars dimmed by the bright moon.

"How quickly things can change in one day, my friend," Binny says.

"In one moment," Slap says, rocking slowly.

"Yeah."

"But what will become of us?" Slap asks, sitting cross-legged on his blanket, the smoke from their tiny fire feathering a fine screen across him.

"Hard to say yet," Binny says, chewing on a hunk of gristly meat.

Slap pulls their pot from the fire. "If the bastards would chase us halfway to Gaza, what would the Muizziyya have done to Fourth Squad and the rest of the Bahri, who rode to the island?"

Leander shakes his head. "That's the worry."

"What of all the families left behind?" Binny asks.

The three men sit wordlessly, staring at their little flame and the single pot beginning to steam.

Baybars' four-man rearguard returns in the twilight. Their leader goes straight to Baybars, while the other three reach down to unbuckle the straps beneath their horses' bellies. With this action, all eyes go back to their fires, the men knowing that the scouts will report confirmation of Aybeg's disengagement.

One by one, the fires about them fizzle out until only the moon lights the camp. The wind drops off, yet what is left carries cold through them. Slaps widens his rocking. The hobbled mares hop to feed on tufts of thick grass, testing the length of their ropes.

"Feels like we're starting over," Binny says. "Nothing will be the same again."

"Old units, old rivalries, iqtas, monthly pay—none of it matters now," Slaps says.

"Likely so," Binny says, taking a sip of tea and then handing the wooden cup to Leander.

"At least most, maybe all in our amirate are still alive ... and if we had to be attached to another unit in the regiment, I'm not sure we could've done much better by choice," Leander says.

Binny and Slap nod, watching the silhouettes of Baybars' men, who whisper about the fading coals of their fires, some tipping over to sleep.

The breeze picks up. Leander pulls the damp blanket around his shoulder and takes a sip of tea, the mint in it reinvigorating him, the smell of his horse on the blanket bringing him solace.

CHAPTER

34

Leander
Gaza
February 12, 1254

They crest the slope, one-hundred-and-seventy-six men shifting from echelon to line formation. Behind them on his giant gray, Baybars calmly adjusts the position of his units with short blasts from his horn. Back and forth, he rides his horse at an elegant trot, his unit commanders mirroring his orders.

Once they are fully on line, Baybars sounds a long single blow, its solitary note falling heavily across the barren desert. His Mamluks steer their long-legged horses downhill with muscular legs, men in the center increasing their dispersion, fanning a spread in the formation across the base of the hill, the men's bows up and at the ready, fists of arrows precisely staged in both draw and bow hands.

Two short blasts from the horn.

Zip, zip, zip.

Arrows fly in an almost constant succession, filling the air with a flurry of projectiles and the hollow thud of steel penetrating the down-range hide targets of goat skins stuffed with vegetation that were crudely staked across the berm. The archers slow their horses to the walk, inching down the hillside. Now, only the whiff of arrows, the clicks of arrow shaft on bow rest and the twang of hide strings fill the air.

Leander concentrates on the fingers of Duyal's chum, Singer. These move in coordinated perfection, flicking arrows from the palm of his draw hand to the bowstring, shooting arrows as fast as he nocks them. Leander figures this man must have been a fine musician in his Kipchak tower, the ivory ring on his thumb twanging at the bow with the same speed and dexterity as the best pluckers of the stringed *baglama*. With his right hand now empty, Singer begins flipping up arrows with his left thumb, the projectiles already staged, fletching down, in his bow hand.

When out, he calmly reaches into his saddle quiver and stages another double fist of arrows on the move, while his mates continue shooting. His horse responds with no apparent command by hand or leg, or at least none discernible to the eye—the Arabian so in tune with his rider. With at least a third of the archers shooting in this method at any one time, the burst of shafts descending from the hillside seems a continuous sheet of arrows, nearly all of them finding their mark.

Leander looks at the Bedouin beside him, the dark-faced man covered in the sheepskin wraps of his people. The man gawks, shaking his head, glad not to be on the receiving end of the Mamluks' shower shooting. He and the several tents of his fellow Bedu here appear as ragged priests, some of the wool in their robes still tinted a subtle violet from the curing agent used by their women. Each of the grimy turbans wrapped about their heads has two wraps of cloth passing beneath their long, black beards.

In defilade, nearly sixty of these men sit their camels. The Bedu's credo is that no man can die, other than on his assigned day. For this reason, they refuse armor and carry into battle only their swords and long spears. Yet today, they appear tired, some of them maybe bored, not accustomed to the repetitive training required by this band of Mamluks that is a term of their new alliance.

Upon reaching Gaza last moon, Baybars quickly wooed the Bedouin into his camp. Termed a goum, these tents of Bedu are linked by blood and marriage. While these people follow the law of Ali, Mohammed's uncle, as do the Assassins in Persia, Baybars cares not. He has made enough of an impression on them to warrant a meeting soon with the sheikh of their larger tribe.

Being one of the few Mamluks able to decipher their dialect of Arabic, Leander is assigned as their unofficial liaison of sorts. Early in their relationship, Leander acted as an interpreter between Baybars and the Bedu elders in forming their loose partnership. Since then, Leander has helped negotiate trades for their goats and even a few horses to fill gaps in the Mamluk ranks. In the evenings, Leander enjoys his conversations with them.

He finds this strain of Bedu to be as cordial to guests as they are hostile to foes. One would have good reason to shudder at the sight of their long spears, but if a traveler touched their tent pole, the Bedouin were compelled to accommodate this traveler and his animals for several days without compensation. Leander understands that even opposing tribes are known to meet and, with great hospitality, share meals and stories of their most remarkable horses. The Arabians are so valuable to the Bedu that many spend their lives in the same covered living quarters as their human owners.

Naturally, these wanderers consider horses a gift from Allah. To mix any foreign blood with pure Arabian strains is considered incomprehensible. Leander figures this Mamluk-Bedu alliance has, as its base, an unspoken commonality. The Bedu live similarly to the way most Mamluks did when they were mere Kipchak youth—as nomads, bound to their horses, migrating throughout the year, following water and vegetation for their herds of camels, sheep, horses, and goats.

Baybars again raises his horn.

"Be ready, be ready!" Leander says. Three Bedu echo his communication down the line.

Three long blasts bellow through the valley. The barrage of arrows ends as quickly as it started. A Mamluk amir among the nomads lowers his lance, the red-lioned pennant of al-Salih at its tip.

"Now! Now!" Leander hollers.

The Bedu drop the tips of their long lances. They scream, some of their camels roaring in response. The Bedu move up the incline and then shamble down the gentle slope toward the flat valley below. The camels grudgingly transition from the lurching gait of their walk—both left legs forward, both right legs forward—up to a jerky gallop.

To steer the beasts, the Bedu tug on their halters, the thick leather running under the camels' throats and around their noses, and connecting to rope around the backs of the animals' ears. Some men push the camels with opposite legs to steer the half-cooperative grunters. Leander drops behind the formation.

Accustomed to Mamluk camels being used mostly as cargo movers and transportation for troops on long treks across the desert to save their horses' legs, Leander is still not used to the scene of camels in the erratic charge. He would find the scene almost amusing, if not for the Bedu's reputation for violence and success on raids using both revered Arabians and these modest camels.

The Bedu begin to bunch up in the center.

"Spread out!" A Mamluk amir among them yells in broken Arabic.

The men lean forward on their blanketed saddles, two forked pieces of wood lashed together between dual slats with a thin leather pad underneath. They assault through the objective of arrow-riddled targets spread below.

A single, long blow from the Muslim horn ends the flanking movement exercise.

Baybars and his archers approach the target area at the trot. At first glance, and perhaps according to Bahri standards, the Mamluks appear shoddy. Yet, in just one moon since the death of Aqtay, each man has found a way to make his assortment of gear and weapons serviceable—a significant challenge, considering the almost continuous combat over the past five years and the last two sultans' refusals to provide the Bahris new gear or the silver for its repair.

Hence, those riders without the bamboo lances of the Mamluk carry the spear of the Bedu with several feet cut off the base. Men with damaged armor wear neatly mended jawshans patched with strips of leather cut from camel hide and fire-hardened sections of leather filling in the vacant spaces of missing metal scales. Some men's scabbards encase new swords. Several even lug the clumsy blades of the Franj. They make do.

Upon finishing their journey across the Sinai last month, Baybars offered his services to al-Nasir, prince of Damascus, the longtime nemesis of Cairo. Al-Nasir was apparently delighted, since his army was undermanned. Most of his own Mamluks, the Nasiriyya and those of his father, the Aziziyya, had gone over to Aybeg moons ago.

Within days of Baybars' proposal, al-Nasir sent a goodwill detachment to Gaza, the envoy carrying food, fodder, weapons, and bags of silver as welcoming gifts, which Baybars has used to support and equip his growing force. Perhaps as one might treat a yet untrusted pack of vicious guard dogs, al-Nasir throws the Bahri enough scrapings from his plate to keep them near his house, but stops short of asking them to nestle up at the foot of his bed.

The men form a half circle around their leader. Baybars backs his horse to better see each man. He eyes his amirs. "We're getting there! Those on the left flank, where did we fall short?"

"We were too long in getting our dispersion, once we topped the hill," an amir sheepishly responds.

Baybars, enthused, "Right, but better! The quicker we achieve the correct spread in line, the better the shock effect, the quicker the enemy is unnerved by our cloud of arrows raining down upon them. The faster we go home and recover our mother Cairo."

"Err!" the Mamluks grunt.

The guilty amir tightens his lips and nods in agreement, disappointed in himself yet clearly determined to not again repeat his unit's mistake.

Baybars turns his gray. "And in the middle, at times, our rate of fire lacked. We need to overwhelm. The faster we weaken them, the sooner they run."

The Mamluks about him soak in their leader's words with intense eyes, their brows furrowed in concentration. All seem to feed on the genuine motivation Baybars consistently displays. Leander is impressed with these men, each Faris having every reason to lack morale and question his future. Yet in these circumstances, they work tirelessly, their sole motivation being a refusal to let down their new commander.

"All right, a break. Some water. A feed! Tonight, we work on the night ambush," Baybars says, grinning.

The men make their way to the spring, some stopping to pull ticks from the crotches of their uncomfortable horses, a few of the mares lifting a leg to make the task easier for their Mamluk. Leander seeks the shade of a sprawling acacia tree to wait for the others to finish filling their jugs. He dismounts. Binny and Slap follow.

Into camp rides a pair of Baybars' hunters. They are smiling. One Mamluk has a jackal and each have a handful of hares adorning their saddles. They are rewarded for good performance by being granted permission to augment the unit's meat supply. They are given a day to scour the scrubland adjacent to Bedu flocks or comb the rolling hills with bows ready, listening for the jackals' howls at dawn and dusk. Once located, the lanky predators are called in by the hunters with only a squeak from their lips or a piece of grass secured between their tongues and roofs of the mouths, squealing the sound of a wounded rabbit or mimicking a goat in distress.

Slap looks over to the amir who is still brooding from his unit's conduct in the exercise. "None wish to make a mistake around here."

Binny chuckles. "You wouldn't want to make a habit of it. If Amir Baybars was willing to slay a Sultan of Egypt, he probably wouldn't think twice about putting a blade between the ribs of any underachieving scoundrel among us, eh?"

Leander chuckles. "I'd be more afraid of his mind than his blade, if I were you."

Slap says, "Oh, he's plenty smart. I just hope those of us not in his original unit don't get forgotten here."

"Huh?" Leander grunts. "You smelling favoritism? If anything, he's been harder on his original forty. No man's been singled out here in the last moon, as long as he was doing his job."

"I suppose," Slap says.

"And those amirs who've been relieved—didn't they deserve it? Didn't he simply replace those lacking enthusiasm or skill with other men more keen?" Leander asks.

"Seems you're growing fond of our self-appointed leader. Your time with him and the Bedu has allowed you two to grow close?" Binny asks with a smirk.

Slap chuckles. "Binny, remember that the 'Bunduq' in 'Baybars al-Bunduqdari' is Arabic for crossbow—Baybars' first patron was an expert in crossbows. So, you know the source of our chief's soft spot for Leander."

Binny smiles. "Those crossbows, those twin girls of his—saving his ass again, putting him in the sweet spot."

"Right, right," Leander says. "You say Baybars is self-appointed? I see no other man stepping up. And my time with him and the Bedu has allowed me to see his discipline and evenhandedness—made me realize we're lucky."

Binny and Slap share a grin and look at him amusedly.

Leander tightens his lips. "You've seen it. Baybars' only focus has been in getting this mob organized. He's combined the best of our old units' tactics, weighed our shortages, prioritized what's needed most, and traded or bought what he could. And not one of al-Nasir's coins has found its way into his own pocket, or been spent on his own kit, or squandered on his own amirate."

Binny raises his eyebrows, nods.

Slap looks away, begins rocking in place.

"He's right. And nobody keeps you here, old woman," Binny says to Slap.

Slap scowls.

"You could bugger off and find one of those bands gone rogue—join those Bahri-turned-highwaymen along the Jordan. Pillage the caravans," Binny says in jest.

"Shut up," Slaps says, his sways growing wider.

"Or, from what those stragglers just in said, you could link with the Bahri who fled to al-Mughith Umar in Karak, or those who went to the Seljuk Sultan of Rum," Binny says.

"I'm not going anywhere," Slaps says.

"It's probably no fluke that more Bahri have trickled into this camp than have snuck away at night," Leander says.

"Hmm. Looks to me like some in this little army are fixing to sneak away right now—in the broad daylight," Slaps says.

They turn.

Pairs of Bedouin women roll up their "Damascus hides," the camel skin covers of their shelters. Theirs are the same style of hooch that Baybars' Mamluks have slept under for more than a moon. The women unlash the bent hoops from their poles, packing them in giant bags attached to their camels' sides.

The women, dressed much like the men, wear sheepskin cloaks that nearly reach their ankles, their thin brown arms protruding through half sleeves. They work quietly, sharing short nips of conversation amid the soft ticks of staves being stowed into carriers.

"If you wish to know the Bedu's intent, just watch their women," Binny says.

"Pushed too hard today. By morning, there'll be nothing but their camel prints in the sand," Slap says.

"All this training—it's not their way," Binny says.

Leander nods. "Nope."

"Baybars'll be pissed," Slap says.

Leander smiles. "I don't know. He probably figures the Bedu will be back and he'll have them—and likely more—when he needs them." He looks to the waterhole.

The last of the Bahri fill their water jugs, chatting. Dirt-covered men sit in groups of three and four in the scant shade, eating dried meat pulled from their saddle bags. Under the shade of a larger tree, a swelling bunch gathers as two small cages are placed near a larger one, the fighting cage.

Leander feels eyes upon him. Baybars. Their leader lifts his chin towards the Bedu camp. Leander cocks his head, purses his lips, and raises his palms. Baybars nods and winks. A grin parts his lips.

"By Allah, you're right. He's not worried," Binny says.

Leander smiles. "It's been strange here. Our fiefs, our uniforms, our weapons, our friends—all left behind and vulnerable in Cairo. Our mates—scattered, imprisoned, some dead. And same with our brothers' families. Our stone house? Maybe Aybeg's catapults are launching missiles at it right now. And the woman I loved ... " He shakes his head, looking down.

"And our best path at success now looks to be bearing arms against some of the very brothers we trained and fought beside for years," Binny says.

Leander nods. "Yet here, in the quiet desert, where all we do is toil, it seems we put aside the past, stow the bad. Here, in the now, I'm oddly happy, almost relaxed. Even with our allies looking to depart, maybe for good, I worry little. How can this be?" Leander asks.

Slap's rocking shallows.

Binny grins. "Heh, nothing but war and disorder in mother Cairo for years. Here in the barren lands, even with so much uncertainty, there's more stability, not less. We make progress toward one common aim, away from the things that add worry to one's life—coin, scheming, promotion, assignments," Binny says.

"Women, beer," Leander says.

They laugh.

"Right, no worries here, except just the little things, like who is over the next hill—bandits, Crusaders, Aybeg's hunters, the Mongols," Slaps says.

"Nothing's perfect, my friend," Leander says.

A roar from those at the shade tree as the scorpion and tarantula are dumped from their coops and into the big fighting cage.

Binny turns back to his friends. "I'm serious. With no Cairo, there are no shops, no whores, no lax population to distract us. No choices to make. Nothing here but the unit and each other; nothing to think about except getting better. There's a relief in that."

"There's a purity in that," Leander says.

"Ehh. And there's some regret in that. I'd kill a man to be in Cairo tonight, sitting at a table, burdened with some of those difficult choices. Would it be a plate of *Hamam Mahshi* or maybe two stuffed pigeons? Mmm." Slap's rocking becomes reminiscent.

They chuckle.

"I don't know—even the roasted goat tastes better out here at sunset," Binny says.

Leander pulls out a strip of dried meat, tears off a piece, and tosses the rest to Slap. They watch the Bedu women secure the flaps on their bags, some of them now tending to their cooking fires. In the shade, Baybars now chats with a Bedu elder, his hand on the man's shoulder, nodding. The Bedu walks away, turning to crack a brown-toothed grin at Baybars' parting comment. Their commander saunters back to his men.

"Look at Baybars. It's like he was made for this, as if he were meant to be right here, right now," Leander says, analyzing the man. "Somehow, I feel the same, as if I were destined to be here."

Binny and Slap exchange glances.

"Seriously, Baybars knows this little army is his—that his allies may come and go, but the core of his tribe is what's most important," Leander says.

Slaps turns to him. "Tribe?"

"Tribe," Leander says.

Binny faces his mate. "Come on, Slap. You see it. We're no different now than our fathers before us and theirs before them. We're nothing but warriors back in the old country, trying to regroup after a setback and the loss of our tower's khan."

Binny grabs the offered meat, rips off a chunk with his teeth, and chucks the last of it back to Leander. "We may be rehearsing Furusiyya tactics on Arabians, but right now we're more Kipchak than Mamluk, my friend. Even Leander can see we've come full circle."

Leander smiles, watches Slap's reaction. "Yeah, Slap, somehow even the dopey Frank can sense it. Somehow, even though we've lost everything, old Papa Frank has a feeling that things will sort out."

They look at Leander, waiting for him to continue, yet he shrugs his shoulders and looks down.

"That's because the blood of a tribesman runs through you, too," Binny says, grinning. "You're only a few generations removed from those Gaulish warriors who roamed the lands of the Franj. The age-old lessons learned from your kin are as firmly ingrained in your heart as they are in Slap's and mine. All of us instinctively know when the boat is beginning to right itself, when the tribe is gaining strength. Know when things have gotten on course."

Leander nods.

"One beauty with the Kipchaks. A bad leader of them is like a cup of rotten mare's milk, eh, Slap? The tower can stomach a few sips, but if they drink the whole cup, eventually they'll puke," Binny says.

Slap nods. Their eyes all settle back to the waterhole. Baybars sits amid his amirs. He chews, listening intently to a story being told. He then throws his head back in laughter. Jovially, he hoots, his mouth open, his head turning from side-to-side, reveling in the chortles from the others.

"If calm falls over you and some of the others, it's because what's happening is natural. The strongest of us has taken the reins. Any better man here could've challenged Baybars. That didn't happen, that isn't going to happen and we all know it," Binny says.

"And look what's back in Cairo. An amir-turned-sultan, propped up artificially. What do you think is going to happen there with Aybeg?" Leander asks.

"The revolt against his authority in Upper Egypt may gain backbone if Amir al-Afram's Bahri join in. And if Baybars can wear down al-Nasir, showing the weakling the necessity in taking back Egypt for God, then Aybeg will have hell trying to fight a war on two fronts," Binny says.

"No matter the circumstances that surround him, Aybeg's like a field dressing stuck into a stab wound. Like a blood-soaked compress, he'll soon be flung aside, once his purpose is served," Leander says.

Slap nods, his sway now slow and comfortable.

Leander tips his flask, savoring the last of his warm water as it coats his dry throat. "I've been thinking a bit on this. Remember the story of Genghis Khan—his low point? The Mongol flight from Ong Khan's warriors? Genghis' stay at Lake Baljuna, the horse that miraculously wandered into camp?"

Slap and Binny nod.

"I think often of its similarities with what happened to us last moon," Leander says, his eyes narrowed in thought. "Genghis was lured away from his homeland to witness the marriage of his son to the Kereyid Khan's daughter. Yet the meeting was a trap and the Kereyid fell on Genghis no differently than Aybeg's Muizziyya fell upon Aqtay and us. Treachery.

"But Genghis and his small group escaped and they came upon the lake and the horse wandered in—like we found the water hole that fourth night and the camel drinking there," Leander says, his eyes meeting Binny's.

Binny nods. "Hmm. And even days before that. It was as if Allah was there. Allah sent rain during the dry season to wash out our tracks, then created the fog to hide our evasion. Without these, the Muizziyya would've continued to follow, might've caught us. And then when our foes were gone, He blew the haze away to reveal that waterhole, to nourish His faithful. We all felt it that night—it felt ordained, blessed."

Goosebumps rise on Leander's arms. A tingle up his spine ends with a shudder. Slap stops rocking.

Leander leans toward them. "That meal of horse meat saved Genghis and his men. And that camel fed us all—like some communal meal, heaven-sent, binding us together. Another gift from Allah. God looking after His cadre of refugees, hungry and spent."

His friends reflect, the setting sun casting a golden hue across the sandbanks and darkened ridge.

Binny eyes the distant rock faces. "And from that hiding spot on Lake Baljuna, Genghis sent word of his planned counterattack to his followers scattered on the steppe."

"I remember. His forces reunited and the rest is legend," Slap says.

"So, you're thinking Baybars is our Genghis?" Binny asks, eyeing Leander.

Leander raises his eyebrows. "I'm just saying the similarities in the stories are remarkable." Again, that quiver up his spine, departing out his fingertips.

"We just don't know how the revenge will play out on our end. Genghis had thousands of warriors; we're less than two hundred," Slap says.

"For now," Leander says. "I don't wish to overstate, but since that modest camel meal, I feel a new Khushdash, a new brotherhood, growing among these men. Not one formed the traditional Mamluk way, by following the strict process of the Furusiyya. Not a camaraderie developed through doctrine, taking years to build trust among novices. But a fusion of men and units, accomplished through one violent, unexpected act—Aqtay's murder last moon—like the eruption of some volcano."

His eyes bounce back and forth between his friends. "More and more men, more lava flowing here to Gaza. And Baybars taking his shovel and scooping them all up, placing us in his cauldron, where he burns off the impurities of our bad habits and jealousies between men and amirates. A rebirth for us, similar to what I experienced not far from here at La Forbie those ten years past." Leander looks them in the eyes, wondering if he is losing them, if they will hurl a barb at his comparisons. They do not.

Leander looks to the horizon of mounded dunes and endless sand. A warm light now throws shadows against the rock faces. "Baybars stoking the fire, boiling off the rock, pouring out the hot metal, folding the slag, pounding us back into shape, into forms better than the original metal we were. Hammering, whetting blades into his vision of what we should be. Something more than unified and well-trained, something unbeatable. Into the true Lions of Islam."

A roar erupts from those men gathered about the big crate. One of the caged fighters has emerged victorious.

ACKNOWLEDGMENTS

Thanks to Linda for enduring my hermit-like behavior and tolerating this off-duty obsession.

Semper Fi to my publisher, Mike Sager. He is a rare bird in this business, providing his old colleagues and new friends with a pleasant place to publish their works, free from the red tape and hands of those who would alter an artist's work. Thanks for personally answering the questions and attacking the tedious administrative tasks inherent in this game. You are the same mensch (a caring, ethical human being) that your father was.

Thank you, John Pahl. A line-editing trooper.

Much gratitude to Pamela Hill Nettleton, who kindly and tactfully guided me into thrashing much of the weakness and confusion from my writing. Her editing contributions to this book are too lengthy to list.

Thanks to "C.D." Dahlquist, a thoughtful, diligent woman with the keenest of proofing eyes.

Cheers to my friend, Dave Murphy, for his continual support, marketing knowledge, and concern on all things writing and beyond.

A nod to my Marine brother, Steve Rose, for his early read and encouragement.

Kudos to the talented artist, Siori Kitajima, for her excellent work on the cover and interior design; also to Chernysheva Viktoria Sergeevna for bringing Leander to life on the front cover. Same to Jenifer Thomas for creating the beautiful maps.

To Mike Franzak—always present in the adjacent fighting hole—"Wolverines!!"

ABOUT THE AUTHOR

Brad Graft is a businessman who runs a national chain with his partners. A former U.S. Marine officer, he helped develop a military program that assists wounded servicemen and families of the fallen. He continues to steer fundraising for charities serving this cause. An avid fly fisherman and hunter, for decades he has pursued gamefish and predators in remote places around the world. Also a history buff, his research on the *Brotherhood of the Mamluks* series took him to the Middle and Far East, where he studied Medieval-era routes and fortresses and trekked the Mongolian steppe on horseback, learning the ways of native hunters and nomadic herders.

ABOUT THE PUBLISHER

The Sager Group was founded in 1984. In 2012 it was chartered as a multimedia content brand, with the intent of empowering those who create art— an umbrella beneath which makers can pursue, and profit from, their craft directly, without gatekeepers. TSG publishes books; ministers to artists and provides modest grants; designs logos, products and packaging, and produces documentary, feature, and commercial films. By harnessing the means of production, The Sager Group helps artists help themselves. To read more from The Sager Group, please visit www.TheSagerGroup.net

MORE FROM
THE SAGER GROUP

Chains of Nobility: Brotherhood of the Mamluks, by Brad Graft

The Living and the Dead, by Brian Mockenhaupt

Three Days in Gettysburg, by Brian Mockenhaupt

Vetville: True Stories of the U.S. Marines at War and at Home, by Mike Sager

For more information, please see www.TheSagerGroup.Net

www.ingramcontent.com/pod-product-compliance
Lightning Source LLC
Chambersburg PA
CBHW032136190626
46814CB00005BA/1720